Boen overcame his initial paralyzing shock and bellowed an ancient war cry. His massive broadsword gleamed in the firelight, wicked and destructive. The Vengeance Knight charged at the enemy, knowing he lacked the strength required to kill them. His muscles strained against his will, threatening to revolt in the primal need to be set free. He was a caged animal remembering the scent of the fresh kill. Forgotten strength flowed to every end of his large body. The split second between when he attacked to making contact with the Gnaal whispered doom for them all.

Beast and man collided in raw fury. Flesh was cut. Their combined roars wailed a mournful song. Boen struck rapidly with three successive blows at the Gnaal's midsection. Without any definable body parts other than the head and arms, it was difficult to find any weaknesses. Boen continued to attack while the Gnaal reeled backwards without striking back. The Gaimosian got the idea that he was being toyed with and leapt back into a defensive crouch. The Gnaal attacked immediately.

Each footstep was like thunder. Leaves and burned embers popped up around the Gnaal. Elongated fangs sliced down from its upper lips. Boen witnessed the sheer intensity in his enemy's eyes the moment they collided. He braced himself for the impact but it wasn't enough. They crashed to the jungle floor and began raining blows on each other. Strong as he was, Boen knew it was only a matter of time before the Gnaal wore him down and killed him.

EMPIRE OF BONES

BOOK IV OF THE NORTHERN CRUSADE

Christian Warren Freed

Copyright © 2020 by Christian Warren Freed

Excerpt from *The Madness of Gods and Kings* 2021 Christian Warren Freed
Cover design by Melissa Andres
Cover copyright 2021 by Warfighter Books
Author Photograph by Anicie Freed

Warfighter Books
Holly Springs, North Carolina 27540
https://www.christianwfreed.com

Second Edition: August 2021

Library of Congress Cataloging-in-Publication Data
Name: Freed, Christian Warren, 1973- author.
Title: Empire of Bones/ Christian Warren Freed
Description: Second Edition | Holly Springs, NC: Warfighter Books, 2021. Identifiers: LCCN 2021912787 | ISBN 9781736804445 (trade paperback) Subjects: Epic fantasy | Military fantasy | Paranormal

Printed in the United States of America

10 9 8 7 6 5 4 3 2 1

Law of the Heretic
Immortality Shattered Book I

'If you're looking for a fun and exciting fantasy adventure, spend a few hours in the Free Lands with the Law of the Heretic.'

Where Have All the Elves Gone?

'Sometimes funny and other times a little dark, Where Have The Elves Gone? brings something fresh and new to fantasy mysteries. Whether you want to curl up with a mystery or read more about elves this book has something for everyone. Spend a few hours solving a mystery with a human and a couple of dwarves - you'll be glad you did.'

Other Books by Christian Warren Freed

The Northern Crusade
Hammers in the Wind
Tides of Blood and Steel
A Whisper After Midnight
Empire of Bones
The Madness of Gods and Kings
Even Gods Must Fall

The Histories of Malweir
Armies of the Silver Mage
The Dragon Hunters
Beyond the Edge of Dawn

Fractured Universe
Dreams of Winter
The Madman on the Rocks
Anguish Once Possessed
Through Darkness Besieged
Under Tattered Banners*

Where Have All the Elves Gone?
Tomorrow's Demise: The Extinction Campaign
Tomorrow's Demise: Salvation
Coward's Truth*
The Lazarus Men
Repercussions: A Lazarus Men Agenda*

A Long Way From Home+

Immortality Shattered
Law of the Heretic
The Bitter War of Always
Land of Wicked Shadows
Storm Upon the Dawn

<u>**War Priests of Andrak Saga**</u>
The Children of Never

SO, You Want to Write a Book? +
SO, You Wrote a Book. Now What? +

*Forthcoming   + Nonfiction

For Mom and Dad.

ONE

A Cold Winter Night

Ingrid crouched in the knee-deep snow under the walls of Chadra Keep. Her breath came out in thin plumes. Her cheeks were bright red, nearly frozen from prolonged exposure. Soot smeared her face. Her blond hair was pent up under a heavy cloak. Her lithe body was hidden beneath thick, dark clothes. The short sword in her gloved hands felt cumbersome, almost alien. Blue eyes as sharp as ice glanced up towards the battlements where iron-helmed guards patrolled the frozen winter night.

Sunrise was still hours away, giving her plenty of time to accomplish her purpose. Twenty of her best were lined up behind. They comprised the heart of the new insurrection. Ingrid stole the position, to be sure, through ferocity and her desire for revenge for her husband's death. Using the plague for cover, Ingrid used her influence to gather fighters loyal to her ideations and deposed the former ruling council.

All her desires and actions led her to this point. Only days ago Lord Harnin, in a fit of madness, had Lord Argis executed atop the very walls of Chadra Keep. He personally flung the severed head down into the massed crowds of spectators, laughing insanely to the winds. While Argis was certainly no paragon of virtue, it was he that allowed the prince of Rogscroft entrance into the Keep to rescue his love. Argis maintained the pretense of being faithful to the decaying monarchy while secretly joining the rebellion. Captured during a massive purge, Argis was dragged away in chains and held captive until his death.

Ingrid saw this event as the catalyst for igniting the flames of rebellion across the entire kingdom. She intended on making him a martyr for the cause. His death, hopefully, would spur the sluggish population into action and they'd be able to finally overthrow Harnin One Eye and King Badron. Argis' murder inspired Ingrid. The one thing *her* rebellion lacked was passion. She aimed to change that this very night. All she needed was his body.

Dreams of a free Delranan were too distant for Ingrid to focus on. She still had a, thus far, mediocre rebellion to orchestrate. Many friends already lay deep in the dirt, something she blamed on improper leadership. Argis was strong, but he'd been too concerned with trying to keep from being discovered to be effective. Still, his death was precisely what the rebels needed.

"Quickly, take your team and get the body. The guards won't be back for seven minutes," she ordered quietly to Orlek, her second in command.

The dark-haired Orlek nodded and gestured for his team to follow. Ingrid waited as the scene played out much too slowly. She was nervous beyond belief. A life of violence was almost alien to her. That didn't prevent her from stepping up and taking control of the defunct rebellion. The people of Delranan needed strong leadership if they were going to find their way out of the growing darkness and she was the only likely candidate. Heart pounding in her chest, Ingrid watched her fighters sneak to the base of the walls.

She knew this was the trickiest part. One of her middle agents managed to bribe Harnin's guards so they'd turn a blind eye to the recovery. Ingrid was no fool. She recognized that those guards could have easily taken the money and still intended on turning the rebels in. No one could be trusted in these troubled times. Of course, she fully intended on exploiting the recovery for her own aims, more than likely signing a death warrant for the greedy guards. She didn't think that was her problem. The only thing that mattered was recovering Argis' body and letting the kingdom know that Harnin wasn't invincible. He could be broken.

Orlek's team disappeared behind a series of small mounds comprised mostly of trash and offal. Chadra Keep had fallen far since the night Badron's son was assassinated. Ingrid paused in thought. If only she could find Princess Maleela, the entire kingdom would rally to her cause. Justice would return and life would improve. Only no one had seen the princess for months. Ingrid bore a worried suspicion that she was already dead, despite Badron's cause to go to war with neighboring Rogscroft.

Nervous minutes passed without any sign of Orlek. Ingrid wanted to follow, to take part in the task herself if only to relieve the rising tension of uncertainty building in her chest. Any number of things could have gone wrong, death being the least. She was suspicious, though not always. Once, before her husband was taken, she'd been overly trusting and of a good nature. The war changed her in ways she had yet to understand. Survival dictated many of her actions. Survival and the overwhelming need for revenge.

Finally, after what felt like hours, Orlek and his rebels came scrambling back. Ingrid flashed a wry grin upon seeing the body wrapped in old blankets being carried on their shoulders. The sudden stomp of boots striking cold stone broke the silence. She froze. Torchlight reflected off the top of the walls. The guards had returned too soon. Orlek was still twenty meters away and without the benefit of cover. He'd be spotted. She envisioned mounted guards pouring from the gates to surround them all. The rebellion would die and she'd be blamed.

Cursing her decision not to bring archers along, Ingrid tried to crouch deeper into the shadows. Orlek would be discovered at any moment and she was powerless to prevent it. She briefly considered fleeing while the window of opportunity was open but thought better of it. Any cowardice would travel faster than the recovery of Lord Argis. Doomed with either choice, Ingrid hoped for the best.

The guards were speaking loud, suggesting they weren't onto her scheme. Hope flickered. Ingrid was no fool. Her enemy was sly, cunning enough to burn the entire city of Chadra to the ground if necessary. Their select indiscretion atop the Keep's walls might only be a ruse. Desperately, she clutched the hilt of her tiny dagger. It was the only comfort she could think of until the moment passed.

Orlek's team halted abruptly and huddled to the ground. Ingrid cursed under her breath. A stiff wind sliced across the open field, slipping beneath the frayed fabric of her collar and down her back. Chills racked her body. Her teeth chattered noisily, so loud she was sure to be caught. She closed her eyes and waited for the worst. Gruff words were exchanged between the guards, followed closely by the torrential sound of water striking the ground.

Ingrid's eyes flew open in time to see buckets of waste splash against the rocks and snow-covered ground. The torchlight weakened and faded altogether. Then tension had passed. Ingrid could breathe easy again. It only took Orlek a moment to get his team up and moving again. They dashed the final few meters and kept running back to the cover of the houses. Ingrid and the remaining ten rebels picked up and followed.

"It was foolish to put yourself at risk like that, Ingrid," Orlek scolded. The slightly older man stood with his arms folded across his chest. His perpetual scowl seemed harsher in the low candlelight.

Anger flashed in Ingrid's eyes. "We must all risk much if there's to be any hope for the future, Orlek. What would you have me do?"

"Be a leader. Use your head, not your heart."

She balled her fists. "And be like those fools I replaced? They sat hidden in the dark and expected everyone to die for them. Look where they led us. We were at the brink of ruin."

"They did what they thought was right," Orlek replied. "True leaders can't be expected to get their hands dirty without proper cause. Inaella was a good woman. I knew her before all this. She led the rebellion in the best way she knew how."

"She let us grow stagnant to the point we became ineffective," Ingrid countered angrily. "How many of your friends were killed?"

Orlek stayed silent. The truth was too awful to admit aloud. He'd joined in the beginning when everyone was bright and optimistic. They didn't think about death back then. He scowled. Back then. It was only a handful of months ago when the rebellion started. He'd been there when Argis and Joefke led the raid on the arms locker at the docks. He'd lost friends at every turn and kept fighting. His prowess on the battlefield led him to numerous promotions but it wasn't until Ingrid usurped the rebellion from the former council that he attained his higher position. Now it was his job to keep her grounded and the war going in a logical direction. She didn't make it easy.

He slowly licked his lips before answering, "Ingrid, we have all lost ones dear to us. It's not about their deaths; it's about how we measure their lives. Each person in the rebellion died so that Delranan can be free again. Our enemy has over five thousand regular army troops and access to near unlimited weapons stockpiles. We fight and scrape for every used arrow or nicked sword. The process must be slow and orderly until the time comes when we can finally spread across the kingdom. That time is not yet."

"You advocate sitting with our hands tied while the enemy gets stronger? Inaella tried that and look where it led us. We stood on the precipice of ruin."

"The plague destroyed our ranks, not Inaella's inactivity," Orlek countered. "You don't honestly expect me to believe we accomplished nothing during those first few months?"

"We didn't accomplish enough," she replied. Her words were slow, measured.

He shook his head in disagreement. "This argument is pointless. We need to focus on the future, not the past."

She paused, lips pursed as if ready to continue her argument. Instead, she relented, "Agreed. Our mission tonight was highly successful. I congratulate you, Orlek."

"I don't need thanks, give it to the others. I did what was asked of me," he replied modestly.

Her opinion of him rose slightly. "Our next task is to spread the word that we have recovered Lord Argis' body from our enemies. He should be revered as a hero to the cause. Spread rumors. I want him martyred for his deeds. The rebellion needs to use his murder as a rallying point."

"We are still weak from the plague. Half of Chadra was quarantined and burned down. The Wolfsreik no longer comes down to patrol but the population is decimated. Nearly one in three died."

She closed her eyes briefly, knowing all too well the high cost the unexpected disease bore away. Ingrid was surprised there were still enough fighters left to carry on. "Turn that around. Two in three survived. What you said is true. Our enemy holds every advantage except one. He lacks the desire to be free. Harnin One Eye is a twisted monster, Orlek, but we can beat him. By only using hopeful messages and through the sheer determination of the people's fighting spirit."

"You ask much from a broken people," he said.

"No more than what I ask of myself."

"What are you really fighting for? You're no soldier. My guess is you've not done a hard day's work in your life," Orlek said, hoping to learn more about the woman he'd tied his fate to.

Ingrid fixed him with a withering glare. Until now she had kept all details of her previous life secret, fearing they'd undo her if anyone found out. Trust did not come easily. She'd been betrayed by those closest to her in the past and had surrounded herself with hardened killers. Anything to put the past behind her. She decided it was time to include Orlek into her darkened vision of the world.

"You're right. I was considered a lady of society. I wore the finest clothes, went to the balls held up on the hill and had enough money I didn't need to work hard. I cooked and kept track of our finances. We weren't wealthy but managed to live comfortably."

Orlek's suspicions confirmed, he said, "There's no shame in that. Plenty of good people used to live like that. I never had it that good. Sounds like you had a good life. What changed?"

"My husband was taken in the middle of the night on charges of treason and executed in the middle of the street by soldiers he had known for years," she answered tightly.

It was a sad tale played out a hundred times over since Harnin assumed control of Delranan. He waited patiently, suspecting there was more to the tale.

Ingrid debated telling him everything. Some secrets hurt too much to expose. It was her need to have him totally on her side that won through, however, forcing her to tell him her darkest secrets. "My husband was an officer in the Wolfsreik."

For once, Orlek didn't know what to say.

TWO

The Betrayed

"What do you mean missing? Didn't I instruct that site to be monitored closely at all times?" Harnin asked, seething with hatred. The one-eyed usurper of Delranan slammed a fist into the aged wooden table in Badron's former council chamber. His skin had taken on a grayish tinge. His good eye was sunken and ringed in black. Heavy, dark robes concealed his dramatic weight loss. He was little more than a walking skeleton, hardly befitting the title of king.

Jarrik felt his face flush crimson. "It was being guarded. Someone gave orders to have the guards shifted. The confusion left enough time for the rebels to sneak up and steal Argis' body."

"Someone? Aren't you supposed to be in command of the guards, Lord Jarrik?"

Jarrik swallowed hard.

Across the table, Skaning saw an opportunity to exploit his position. "Lord Harnin, I've had teams sweeping the Keep and surrounding grounds for the traitors. We'll know who it was that betrayed you before nightfall."

Torchlight flickered subtly, reminding them of time when strife or chaos weren't prevalent in their frozen northern kingdom. The large circular chamber was mostly empty, making it appear hollow. Half of the chairs hadn't been filled since before King Badron took the bulk of the Wolfsreik and went to war with neighboring Rogscroft at the end of autumn. Cold, stone walls mocked the three lords, echoing their words to pointless levels.

Jarrik shot him a violent glare.

Harnin broke out in a fit of snide laughter, surprising them both. "Ever you seek to prove your value to me at the expense of another's mistake, eh Skaning? I think I should have removed you long ago, because you've certainly done nothing usable since winter began."

"I've given this kingdom, and you, everything! My soldiers have secured countless enemy positions and stores, right up until the plague struck."

Harnin leveled his gaze and said, "Your soldiers have, but not you. You've kept yourself warm at my fires, eaten my food, drank my wine, and slept with my women but you've not gone out to the wolves and hunted. You show poor quality for a lord of Delranan."

Skaning opened and closed his mouth quickly.

Harnin turned back to Jarrik. "I want the commander of the watch brought to me immediately. If I find any wrongdoing on his part he will be executed. From this moment every guard's loyalty is in question. Trust none. This castle is no longer secure. I had thought the rebellion was finished, but they seem resilient. Perhaps your purge of Chadra wasn't so successful after all, Lord Jarrik."

Entrusted with eradicating the rebellion during the time of weakness, Jarrik sent routine patrols into the main city and the docks with the standing order to kill on sight. They'd killed dozens. Under normal circumstances the number would have been inordinately small, but the plague practically devastated the capital city. He felt dread growing in his stomach. Harnin would surely turn mediocre numbers into dismal mismanagement. The image of the executioner's axe dropping on his neck chilled his blood.

"Our patrols executed their tasks to standard, I assure you. The city was in disarray thanks to the effects of the plague. I wasn't willing to risk the lives of my soldiers just to…"

"To carry out the will of your ruler?" Harnin snapped bitterly. "If my own captains lack the willingness to fulfill their tasks what need have I for them?"

Rebuked, he struggled to cover his inaction. "We will redouble our efforts. The rebels must have been considerably weakened. Rooting them out shouldn't pose a problem."

"See that it doesn't. I have no need of incompetent minions," Harnin said, his voice deceptively calm. "Bring me the captain of the watch."

A pair of guards dragged the captain of the watch's body away by the ankles, careful not to get blood smears on Harnin's carpets. His death was deemed necessary, even if there was no evidence linking him to the theft. Harnin needed an example. The guard captain was dead the moment Harnin summoned him. It was just a matter of how. Harnin was no stranger to violence. He'd been a warrior in one fashion or another for most of his fifty-odd years. Various battles and campaigns led him to the man he was today. Or, rather, *would* have been if not for the dark, Cimmerian influences of the Dae'shan.

Wiping the needle-like dagger clean, Harnin sat behind the grand desk that had belonged to the kings of Delranan for centuries. Wolf heads were carved on each of the four corners. Ever had the kings been protected by the might of the Wolfsreik. It was only fitting that their desk bore the likeness of those fierce, proud warriors. Twin braziers on either side of the desk provided light and warmth.

Harnin steepled his hands in front of his face and slowly closed his eyes. So much had happened in just a few quick months he often found it difficult to accept. He knew in his heart that this was not the vision he once harbored for his beloved kingdom. Delranan was supposed to grow under his control. To develop into one of the major kingdoms in Malweir, a northern rival for central Averon. He imagined being proclaimed high king and having lesser lords and nobles make pilgrimages to honor him. None of that seemed likely now.

Delranan was plunged into despair. The people, what remained, were petrified to leave their homes in the day, much less the night. Under the guidance of the Dae'shan, Harnin took his beloved kingdom deeper and deeper into abject misery. The sad part was he found perverse pleasure in it. Harnin One Eye was not the ruler he should have been, and he had little qualms with it.

He'd served as Badron's right hand for decades, always carrying out the dirty work behind the scenes. His intimate knowledge of the king's dealings gave him leverage and undeniable power. Taking control once Badron had gone off on his ill-advised campaign was all too easy. He'd rounded up those still loyal to the king and had them executed before anyone knew what was happening. The council of lords added weight to his actions, giving him blanket control without the worry of stealing power for themselves. Still, Harnin trusted no one.

Consolidating power was proving problematic. The main army was gone, leaving a five-thousand-man reserve he called up and deployed across the kingdom. One fifth remained in Chadra for security and in the event an outside threat presented itself. Normally the threat of the Wolfsreik being turned loose kept neighboring kingdoms from having ideations of conquest but with Badron and the army trapped on the eastern side of the Murdes Mountains, the kingdom was wide open for invasion.

Winter had been brutal thus far, leaving him with the false impression that he had time to enact his plans. Only they weren't his plans. They were the Dae'shan's. Pelthit Re clearly had designs for Delranan and wasn't inclined to include Harnin. One Eye recognized the fact he was a puppet ruler but couldn't find a way out. Not without giving away everything he'd struggled to earn. Trapped, he took a deep breath and exhaled slowly.

The room chilled suddenly.

"You seem troubled, One Eye."

Harnin's eye snapped open, no longer surprised with how easily the ethereal Dae'shan came and went as they pleased. He still hadn't discovered how they simply folded darkness around them and vanished. Until he did, there wasn't any way to combat them.

"Perhaps I disturb you," Pelthit Re hissed from under his cowl.

The Dae'shan hovered a half a foot off the ground. Six feet tall, he was slender and swathed in dark robes of heavy gray. His hands were folded within his robes, leaving no sign of physical form. Darkness surrounded the Dae'shan. Arrogance pulsed off him, disturbing Harnin more than the Dae'shan could know.

"No, your council is always welcome," Harnin replied tersely.

Pelthit Re studied his puppet with cold, unfeeling eyes. He'd lived for centuries. Always in the shadows of the greater Amar Kit'han, the lesser Dae'shan had once been a virtuous Man. They were the neutral representatives of the old gods, but when the gods of light went away the Dae'shan fell into corruption. They swore allegiance to the dark gods and worked tirelessly to open the gateways between worlds so their new masters could return to lay claim to all.

"I sense a great deal of turmoil within you," Pelthit Re said.

Harnin lowered his hands and scoffed. "There is much concerning me lately. I can manage my own kingdom."

"A kingdom you have neither earned nor won. You wouldn't be in that chair if not for my assistance. Remember your place, One Eye."

"My place is the lord of Delranan!" he snapped. "I am the power in this kingdom. My will is law. Not yours. You remain in the shadows while others go forth to fight and die in my name. Delranan belongs to me."

Pelthit Re cocked his head. "Perhaps you need to be reminded of your station."

Waves of power, shimmering in the air like heat on a summer day, lashed out at Harnin. It struck with enough force to blow him back against the wall. Pain shot down his legs as the back of his head hit cold rock. Harnin groaned and rolled to his hands and knees. Coughing blood, he struggled to rise. The Dae'shan struck again, forcing him back to his belly. And again, slamming his body against the wall. Only when Harnin stopped trying to rise did Pelthit Re stop his assault.

"I warned you," the Dae'shan accused. "Do not trifle with my power. I am an agent of the dark gods. Mere mortals can't harm me. I am disappointed in your lack of judgment, One Eye. I gave you this kingdom in the hopes that you would prepare it for a glorious age. Instead you let these pathetic rebels sink you into ruin. Perhaps I should take your head like poor Lord Argis."

Harnin coughed, spitting a wad of blood and phlegm. "I can handle my own affairs. Argis was their figurehead. His death was a great blow to their cause."

"Was it? You couldn't prevent his body from being stolen, nor did you extinguish the rebellion at its weakest."

"I have already addressed Jarrik's incompetence," Harnin said in a useless gesture of self-defense. The Dae'shan would know the truth of it. "He'll either succeed or find himself under the axe. Delranan is mine."

"Your inability to control your own lords is hardly my concern. Will you be prepared when Bahr, brother of Badron, returns with his niece?"

Harnin frowned. "Why should they return? I burned his ship, his estate. I took everything he had in Delranan. He has nothing."

Pelthit hissed laughter. "He doesn't seek to reclaim any past glory, fool. No, his intentions are far more wicked than even you might imagine. Bahr seeks the Blud Hamr, an impossible weapon from a forgotten era. Should he find it, and return alive, he will remove everything you have done or hold dear, Harnin One Eye. It appears you cannot escape that family."

Hatred blossomed in Harnin's heart. First Badron and now his brother. He cursed that family. "Can't you stop him?"

Pelthit Re remained silent, fearing any answer would only give away their ineffectiveness at stopping the king's brother. Until Amar Kit'han found a way to neutralize the wizard and last descendant of the order of Mages, Anienam Keiss, there was no stopping Bahr from retrieving the Hamr.

Harnin picked up on the hesitance and tried to laugh, stopping quickly when his ribs hurt too badly. "You can't, can you? Otherwise you wouldn't be putting so much pressure on me. Your precious Dae'shan are just as weak as we mortals."

"I wonder if I have made a mistake in choosing you," Pelthit Re accused.

Shock widened his eyes. All his dreams and possibilities for advancement came crashing down. No matter how weak the Dae'shan might appear, he knew he was no match for even one of the demons. "I can fix this. I swear. Delranan will be strong once again."

"See that it is. The alternative will not be…pleasant."

Darkness swirled, coalescing around the Dae'shan. The room grew frigid right before the nightmare disappeared. Harnin One Eye lay in misery, alone. Pain lingered throughout his entire body. Smoke puffed up from his hair. He felt abused, both physically and mentally. He was not up to the unique challenge the Dae'shan presented. His only hope was to force the rebellion into making a mistake so drastic Pelthit Re didn't need to return with threats. Compounding his problems was the nasty rumor that the Wolfsreik was trying to find a way back across the mountains. He frowned, knowing there wasn't anything to be done about that. He needed to focus on ending the rebellion and fortifying his defenses for when the king returned.

Harnin groaned as he picked himself up and, using the wall for support, ambled over to the double window overlooking the town of Chadra and the eastern plains that led to the steps of the Murdes Mountains. Somewhere out there, Bahr and Maleela headed towards a weapon of unimaginable power that could not only destroy Harnin's fragile hold on Delranan, but the fate of the world as well. Scowling, he regretted not putting either to death when he had the chance.

Grumbling at being pulled away from the warmth of his fire, Sergeant Refle secured his sword and went to the small metal door built within the main gates of Chadra Keep. It was well beyond midnight and freezing. A fresh storm had blown down off the Northern Ocean and was attacking Delranan with impossible strength. Snow drifts piled high in the courtyards. Refle could only imagine how bad conditions were in the nearly ruined city. Not that he cared. The rebels could freeze or starve to death in his eyes. They were a pox on Delranan and needed to be cleansed. The pounding increased.

"Mind yourself! I'm coming," he roared through the massive red beard covering his lower face. Ice crystals had formed in the hairs, giving him a wild appearance. Even with gloves on he was loath to touch the freezing sword hilt. "If you've got weapons put them on the ground and have your hands raised. I won't hesitate to run you through, just for getting me out in this damnable cold!"

He fumbled with the deadbolt and triple locks before setting his hands on the heavy iron locking bar. It took a bit of strength to pull it free but the door swung easily open after. He drew his sword and waited for the visitor to make himself known. Refle tensed as the figure emerged from the night. Not himself, but herself! He briefly considered lowering his sword but had learned that females were just as dangerous as everyone else in these times. He had no intentions of dying for anyone tonight.

"State your business," he ordered.

"I am here to see Lord Harnin," she replied.

Refle drew back, taken off guard by the bold request. No one in their right mind wanted to see Harnin. "Who are you? Show your face."

She slid a few steps forward until she was cast in the glow of the fire and slowly removed her snow-colored hood. Refle gasped. Her face was pockmarked and shallow. Her eyes seemed much too large for her face and she bore scars from the plague. Her hair, once raven black and luxurious, was stringy and missing in places.

"My name is Inaella. I was once a leader of the rebellion. I wish to join Lord Harnin."

Refle swore under his breath.

THREE

The Voyage South

The Fern River begins on the northern coast of Malweir and flows all the way down through the jungles of Brodein and into the Bay of Cuerlon, covering some three thousand leagues. Moving at a swift pace, the river barge was making nearly one hundred leagues a day. Bahr and the others watched as they left the frozen northern kingdoms and headed towards the fringes of the Jebel Desert on their right. The river men warned of desert pirates but Bahr was convinced the river men were the greatest threat. The very looks in their eyes warned that they were going to make a play for everything the moment Bahr let his guard down.

Pushing sixty, Bahr had made a living on the water, though in a far different capacity. His ship, the *Dragon's Bane*, was the stuff of legend. Or had been until Harnin turned on him and burned it to the ground. His gaze hardened at the memory of seeing the flames rise high about the surrounding dock buildings and warehouses. Targeting the self-exiled son made no strategic sense. Bahr, the older son, abdicated all rights of the throne to Badron and took off to raid and explore the northern coast of Malweir. The thought of being trapped by cagey politicians and endless hours of meetings left him feeling uneasy. His one true love was the water. There was an inescapable freedom to be had with the wind on his face and sea spray on his hands.

His adventurous lifestyle provided him great wealth and standing among the noble houses. Several approached him to perform odd jobs they didn't want traced back. He became as famous as he was feared. Bahr often thought that was the underlying cause of dissent between Badron and him. One rose to notoriety while the other became mired in politics. Life was fine for the longest, until the day his niece Maleela was born. Badron's wife died in childbirth, leaving the distraught king hating his daughter. It was an animosity that carried on to this day. Bahr stood up for the hapless girl, causing a rift between brothers. The rift gradually turned to hate and Bahr seldom returned to his birthright after.

Badron tolerated his absent brother while turning a blind eye to his piratical actions. Harnin, ever in the shadow of greatness, hungered to see Bahr removed permanently, viewing the lesser son as another obstacle. Looking back, it all made sense now. Bahr realized Harnin was a troubled soul with the strong need to take what wasn't his. The One Eye was the source of a great many problems and a thorn in Bahr's side. Removing him would go a long way in reestablishing relations with his brother.

"I can't recall the last time you didn't wear a troubled look."

Bahr grinned wryly at Boen's comment. A son of the long vanquished kingdom of Gaimos, Boen was the definition of a Vengeance Knight. The name was ancient, stemming from the need to reclaim their fallen kingdom. They were the best warriors in Malweir and the most dangerous. He and Bahr had been friends for many decades.

"I can't recall the last time I didn't need to," Bahr replied.

Boen grunted and nodded. His gaze swept out to the sand dunes pushing right up to the riverbanks. "I've never liked the desert. Too arid and boring for my tastes. Give me the forest and a host of enemies to prove myself against."

"Haven't you had enough enemies for a while? I was sure those Dwarves were going to be the death of us," Bahr said. Thoughts of their participation in the Dwarf civil war were still fresh in his mind, even days later.

Boen turned to him. "The Dwarves are capable fighters, but they're not Gaimosian. Give me a company of Knights and I'll sweep our enemies from the face of the world. Still, those Dwarves provided a damned good fight."

"That they did," Bahr replied. The horrors of the Dwarf civil war surpassed anything he had ever seen. He'd never imagined gunpowder weapons, much less cannons capable of such wanton destruction. Everything else paled in comparison. It was only a matter of time before that weapon knowledge spread across the various kingdoms of Malweir. Warfare would grow more violent, deadlier. He prayed he wasn't alive to see that happen.

"When do you think it will happen?" Boen asked, shifting the conversation.

"Hard to say. I don't think they're going to wait too much longer. The desert isn't a good place. It's too open. There's no natural cover other than these dunes," Bahr replied. "My guess is they'll strike once we get closer to rocky ground."

"The Graven Forest lies to the east not much further down the river. There are plenty of places for ambush."

Bahr nodded absently. They hadn't had a moment of respite since fleeing from Chadra in the middle of the night. The Dae'shan sent Harpies after them. They'd fought bandits and Delrananian guards. He was feeling every bit of his six decades. There was no end in sight. Anienam Keiss, the wizard, insisted that they needed to rush to reach the mythical city of Trennaron to recover the Blud Hamr. A lifetime on the open seas left him without much of a sense of urgency. It went against his grain to rush into anything, even something so dire as the salvation of the world.

Boen folded his massive arms across his chest and spit into the river. "We should take care of it before they can ambush us."

Bahr sighed. It was the same argument they'd been having since before leaving the Dwarves. The river men were bandits and it was unspoken knowledge that they aimed to rob Bahr and the others the instant they felt their guard was down. Reluctant to kill without good reason, Bahr felt his options steadily shrinking.

"We'd give ourselves away," he said quietly. "Whoever they have waiting downriver will be expecting some kind of message."

"That's only a problem if we let it become one. Let me take Ironfoot and finish this. I'm tired of looking over my shoulder for no reason." Boen had that familiar glint in his eye that Bahr had come to dread. Years of friendship left him too close to a great many truths.

"Can you do it quietly?"

Boen grinned. He knew the old Sea Wolf would give in. "Quietly enough. It'll be finished in a few seconds."

"Leave one alive, just in case we need to deal with their friends later," Bahr instructed.

"One is a very good number," Boen replied. "Fitting for a Gaimosian. I'll go get the Dwarf. You keep the others out of it."

"Are you sure you don't need Dorl or Nothol?"

He shook his head. "They'll just get in my way."

Bahr started planning ahead. They were still days away from the jungle and the mythical city of Trennaron, if it even existed. Bahr had his doubts. He trusted his friends, though Anienam Keiss remained an enigma. The last surviving son of the ancient order of Mages continually steered them in the right direction despite having secret designs of his own. The Sea Wolf knew he wasn't being told everything and, for one used to being in command of his own destiny, chafed at the restriction. He decided it was time for the old fool to come clean. Before anyone else died.

"Fine. Make it quick. I'm going to have a little chat with our wizard," Bahr said.

Boen left without another word. A true professional, he was one of the best at what he did. Hundreds had died at his hands. He was a mercenary, assassin, and sword for hire. Kings and queens sought the remnants of vanquished Gaimos for all their dirty work. He didn't mind. Kingdomless, Gaimosians roamed the world in search of that one quest that would give their lives definition. None of that mattered to Bahr. Should Boen fail, or even one of the river men escape, it would mean the end of their quest. A quest he still wasn't sure was going to end well.

Nerves growing, Bahr made his way to the back of the barge to confront Anienam. He found the wizard expecting him. "Are you ever surprised?"

Anienam shrugged and popped a piece of old bread in his mouth. "Rarely, though normal people tend to do strange things unexpectedly. What troubles you, Bahr?"

He pursed his lips, struggling to decide how to say what he felt. "Honestly, you do."

Anienam flashed that devious smile he'd done a thousand times already. "I can't say as that I'm surprised, perhaps only that it's taken this long. Speak your mind, Bahr."

"Now isn't the time," Bahr cautioned.

Anienam swallowed. "Boen is going to do it?"

Bahr scowled. He hated how the wizard knew things without being told. "Can you conjure a spell to keep them from shouting out?"

"If you wish," the wizard replied. "Though I hardly see how that will help."

"It will keep them from alerting any lookouts they have on the shore."

"Bahr, the river men are pirates. Men you know how to deal with. Killing this bunch will only delay the inevitable, not stop it."

"How long before we reach Trennaron?" He hated feeling rushed but time was against them. They had less than one hundred days before the hour when the dark gods would make their next attempt at entering Malweir. That felt like a long time, but Bahr was no fool. They'd lost countless days already and still had to make the return trip to Delranan. He doubted they'd be able to do it in time.

Bahr cursed his luck. The dark gods were akin to myths. He wasn't sure they existed at all, despite Anienam's assurances. According to legend the dark gods were banished countless millennia ago but, like all evil, managed to find a way to return. Once every thousand years the planes of existence aligned perfectly, creating a bridge back to

Malweir. This singularity led to the corruption of the crystal of Tol Shere and the subversion of the Dae'shan, not to mention a thousand other calamities plaguing Malweir's history.

Once every thousand years and it happens to fall during my lifetime. What a charmed life I live. It got worse. There were only three places in all Malweir where the dark gods could come back. Two had previously been destroyed, leaving only Arlevon Gale in the remote regions of Delranan. Bahr's kingdom had become the battleground for the fate of the world and he didn't like it. He didn't know, but hundreds had already died in both Delranan and neighboring Rogscroft.

"Three, perhaps five days," Anienam replied. "Getting to the jungle will be easy, through it another matter. We are fortunate to have Rekka with us. She is from Teng and quite capable."

Rekka Jel was an incredible asset, one Bahr was more than happy to have in his favor. Her skills with a sword were almost a match for Boen. She didn't speak much and had only recently taken a passionate liking for Dorl Theed. The relationship threatened to cause havoc between the members of his band, but he wasn't worried about Rekka. She was as cold as deep winter. Dorl, however, was a ball emotion Bahr didn't want to deal with.

"How can we be sure this Hamr still exists?" Bahr asked. He had a thousand unanswered questions, each of which capable of altering the future. "We're trusting an ancient text that no one remembers."

"Much of the future is already built in the past. We are just wanderers through this great story, Bahr. The tools to defeat the dark gods were created thousands of years ago with the knowledge that there would be a finale. We are living in that time. The final battle is looming on the horizon and we are the key players. Everything else is merely part of the great show."

"Great show? How many lives are going to be lost because of this game?" Bahr demanded, his voice rising before he realized it. A few heads turned their way. "My kingdom is the battleground between good and evil. Will there be anything left?"

"One cannot say. All I know is that at the end of these hundred days either good or evil will triumph," the wizard said with sadness in his voice. "I don't predict the future, Bahr. The risk is too great."

Not hearing what he needed, Bahr grunted and stormed off.

Boen yawned and slid the thin rope from his sleeve, pulling it tight. The Dwarf captain, Ironfoot, was already on the opposite side of the barge doing the same. Boen's best chance was to strike quickly and tear through his enemy like a late summer storm. He casually walked up behind the nearest river man. Most men would feel their hearts race, their palms sweat, and their mouth go dry. Boen was Gaimosian. He did this for a living. It was as easy as breathing. His one concern stemmed from having to do it in the middle of the day. The river men insisted the river was too dangerous to traverse in the night and put to shore at the end of each day.

The river man glanced over his shoulder and nodded gruffly to the bigger Boen. Smiling fiercely, the Gaimosian threw the rope around the pirate's neck and twisted sharply. A sharp crack broke the man's neck. Boen dropped him and hurried to the next. He only had a few moments before the others got wind of what was going on. Speed was his asset. He launched himself at the next, crushing the man's throat with a strong punch. Gagging, the body dropped into the river. Boen snarled but there was nothing he could do about it. The river man leader drew his curved saber and barked orders in his native language. Boen threw down his rope and drew his mighty broadsword. The weapon was easily three times as heavy as the saber and twice as thick.

Boen gestured for the man to make his move. Doubt flickered in his eyes, giving the Gaimosian the time he needed to attack. Unsure, the river man tried to throw up his saber in defense. It was already too late. Boen raised his sword and brought it crashing down on the swarthy man. There was so much force his saber sliced deeply into the man's chest and shoulder. The river man screamed even as Boen brought the pommel around and punched a strong blow in his face.

A second man, hidden behind crates of supplies, leapt onto Boen's back, punching and biting anywhere he found vulnerable. The Gaimosian left the crippled captain and managed to snatch his attacker by the collar, dragging him up and over his back. The man landed on top of his captain, face down. Boen stabbed down. His sword pierced both men and lodged in the deck. Knowing it would take too long to reclaim the weapon, Boen drew a dagger and spun to search for new targets.

There were ten river men in all, leaving six more somewhere on the barge. Ironfoot's job was to storm the wheelhouse and take out the bridge crew. Boen got the heavy work by design. He stalked his way down the deck. The barge was massive for a river boat. Nearly fifty feet long and twenty-five wide, it was large enough to fit their wagon, a Giant, and all the horses while still having both crew and passenger cabins. Bahr and the others were within the passenger cabin, leaving the Gaimosian free range of the deck.

The others were valuable fighters but he meant what he told Bahr. They would only get in his way. He needed the room and ability to maneuver without worrying about friendly fire or people bumping into him. Gaimosians worked best alone. A river man lying atop a stack of crates took a swing for his head. Boen ducked and stabbed up, catching the man in the throat. Blood sprayed down on Boen's head as he twisted the blade and ripped it free. The man died without a sound. Boen kept moving.

He came across a pair of bodies gruesomely savaged. They lay at awkward angles and had been hacked, inexpertly, to death. Boen frowned. The Dwarf was more zealous when it came to fighting than he was. Seven dead, three to go. He knew the rest would be in or around the wheelhouse. Boen took the short flight of stairs leading up to the bridge and stepped over a corpse hanging down the first three steps. He'd died where he tried to escape. Inside Boen found another body shoved into a corner. The last, which he presumed was the captain, stood with hands tied behind his head and a dirty rag shoved in his mouth.

Ironfoot turned from his view out the bridge window and nodded briskly. "They didn't put up much of a fight."

Boen noticed the specks of blood staining the Dwarf's sleeves and knuckles. He'd been expecting more and knew he must look like a complete mess compared to the general cleanliness of his comrade. "The ship is secure. That the captain?"

"As near as I can tell he is," Ironfoot replied. The Dwarf combed his thick fingers through his rust-colored beard and spit. "He's not very compliant."

"Would you be?" Boen asked. "Keep us in the middle of the river. I'll get Bahr. We're not stopping tonight."

The river captain glowered at Boen.

Once the bodies were dumped overboard and most of the blood washed off so as not to upset the horses, Bahr followed Boen back to the wheelhouse. He glanced at the captain before gesturing for his gag to be removed.

"You bastards! I'll see your throats slit from ea…"

Ironfoot backhanded the captain across the mouth. A tooth fell out as the river captain grimaced. "Enough talk."

Bahr ignored the Dwarf, instead crouching down to eye level with their captive. "Where is the ambush set up?"

The river captain spit at him. "Ambush? You're the murderers! You killed my crew. Good men. I'll see you hung from the walls of Paedwyn for this."

Boen laughed hard.

Bahr leaned in closer. "What you fail to realize is that you're expendable. We don't need a captain because I am one. Now, tell me where your friends set up their ambush and we might let you live."

The river man, wild-eyed, looked from Bahr to Boen before exhaling heavily and hanging his head. He knew he was dead either way.

FOUR

A Long Night

Bahr piloted the barge down the Fern River well after night fell. They placed Ironfoot on the bow since he and the Giant Groge had the best night vision. Groge stood in front of the wheelhouse, his massive height allowing him to look into the bridge without bending down. The river captain remained tied and under guard. Only the gentle sounds of water lapping against the aged wooden hulls marked their passing.

"I still don't agree with how you handled this situation," Anienam admitted once they were alone.

Bahr shook his head. He was tired, frustrated, and more than a little anxious to be done with this task. Anienam's doubts only pushed him closer to snapping. "Like it or not it's already finished. The river men are pirates and it was only a matter of time before they turned us over to their friends, like you pointed out. We took the best path available."

"Killing should never be the best path," the wizard scolded. "We both know what that leads to, Bahr. There will be time enough for dying in the days ahead."

"What would you have me do? Let them all go or just sit idle while they rob and kill us?" Bahr asked. "I've dealt with these types before and it never ends well. Boen saved our lives, yours included, by taking control of this barge."

"Perhaps," was all he said.

The water continued pushing the barge south. Bahr, not feeling like talking, watched the river for signs of submerged rocks or rapids. He may have been a captain but his skill and trade were on the open sea, not the narrow confines of an unfamiliar river. His instincts warned him to scan the shoreline for signs of the enemy, but the river demanded his full attention. The true danger lay in uncertainty. Like most of the others, he'd never traveled this far south.

Bahr smoothly turned the wheel controlling the rudder, straightening the barge with the center of the river. It felt good to be standing at the helm again. Disturbingly, his legs seemed to have forgotten the feel of the water. He frowned. It had been far too long. His thoughts gradually turned back to the river captain. The swarthy man was rightfully incensed at being captured and forced to watch the bodies of his crew unceremoniously dumped into the river, but what he'd planned for Bahr and the others was far more diabolical.

The ambush spot was still a few hours away, at least according to their prisoner. At the southern fringes of the Jebel Desert was a great bend, causing a bottleneck. The river men had been using it for years to conduct their raids. While the captain insisted there would be no more than a score of his people waiting, Bahr expected far more. Wordlessly, he piloted the barge south.

Dorl Theed finished checking his quiver and stretched. "I don't care for this."

His longtime friend and partner on many quests, Nothol Coll, rolled his eyes. They'd been sell swords for nearly a decade and had gotten into more trouble than most people did their entire lives. That was fine with both, but this latest quest was grinding them down. Worse, Dorl was growing increasingly more focused on his love for Rekka Jel. Nothol knew that any slip of concentration might end with their deaths. He needed his friend to keep his mind clear.

"You complain too much," he chided. "Bahr has gotten us this far. Trust him to get us the rest of the way."

Dorl snorted. "The way to where? We've been attacked nonstop since fleeing Chadra. Sooner or later our luck will run out."

"Keep talking like that and it'll be sooner. You've changed."

"What do you mean by that?"

Nothol sighed. "I mean you used to be the fearless one. You never hesitated to jump into desperate situations. Now you've got a woman in your life I'm starting to think you handed her your balls."

"Mind your tongue, Nothol," Dorl bristled. "I'm still dangerous enough to cut your tongue out."

Nothol laughed in his face and checked the string of his bow. "Now you're delusional. You and I both know I'm better at swords, bows, and any other weapon you can think of. Stop trying to show off for your girlfriend."

Rekka sat atop the wheelhouse overhearing their conversation. Her soft, almond-shaped eyes lit up as they fell on Dorl. Amusement danced across her face. She felt no jealousy or anger off Nothol Coll. Instead, their relationship sparked melancholy. She'd never had such strong ties of friendship and was envious of them. Her sword sharp and sitting in her lap, she continued to listen while thinking of how the villagers of Teng were going to receive her return.

She'd been away for a very long time, more than five years. The dream masters trained her group to serve the gods of light. Never did they imagine the end battle for the world would occur in their lifetimes. Barely out of her teens, Rekka was sent to Trennaron to serve the last true Dae'shan, Artiss Gran. It was a great honor bestowed on the trainee with the highest scores and most prowess. Only one a generation received the detail. Rekka was honored. Her family would be heaped with pride until her dying days.

The Dae'shan continued to serve the gods of light, defending the castle of Trennaron from evil influences. Many great secrets were stored within the castle. Secrets some argued were best left forgotten. The Mages often traveled deep into the jungle to share knowledge and even store their most precious lore with the guardian. Artiss Gran was the gentlest of souls. His even thinking and mild demeanor left him at odds with his fellow Dae'shan. The rift grew between them until he decided to flee. Amar Kit'han, now a servant of the dark gods, never forgave him.

Rekka trained under Artiss for many years. Instead of weapons, she learned from books and maps. He entrusted her with a wealth of knowledge that few ever obtained. However good her life was, it was also cursed. She knew, as did Artiss, that the time was fast approaching when all her skills and dedication would be put to the test and she might have to give her life for the cause of the righteous. Dying didn't bother her. She came from dust and knew she must eventually return to it. Her life was solely dedicated to good. Developing emotions for Dorl left her exposed, suddenly uncertain.

Love was unlike any other emotion she'd ever felt. Her pride in serving Artiss had gone unmatched for nearly a decade before she happened upon Dorl Theed. The sometimes foppish sell sword had a charm and charisma that compelled her attention. He was a good man, even if he didn't know it himself. Rekka considered herself fortunate to have found a man she could confide in. She prayed their time together would be enough to fulfill their need for companionship. Both were lonely souls in need of more. She wasn't sure she could provide more. Her death at the end of this quest was almost a certainty, leaving her with the question: how does one give more than they have?

"Captain Bahr says to get ready. We're coming up on the spot," Skuld announced to each of them as he made his way from stern to bow. The young street thief was steadily growing into a man before their eyes. He'd snuck aboard the *Dragon's Bane* thinking to find treasures in the Murdes Mountains. What he got was much more.

Skuld was the definition of confused. He wanted to be a great warrior like Boen, wise like Bahr, and Anienam was convinced he'd make a fine wizard. He often grinned himself to sleep, thinking that his life had nowhere to go but up. Perhaps with a little time he might grow to be all three. He'd put on muscle since leaving Delranan to rescue the princess. His hair, already unkempt, now hung past his shoulders. His clothes were starting to fray and he generally smelled bad from the inability to take a bath but he didn't care. He was more alive than ever, even if he didn't know which direction to take his life. He paused when he found Princess Maleela listening to the twisted, broken Ionascu close to the bow.

"Princess, you must think of your people," Harnin's former spy cooed. "Delranan is dying and your family has lost power."

Her face brightened in the pale moonlight. "My family abandoned Delranan long before Harnin stole power, Ionascu. You were one of his puppets. You know more than anyone how foul his deeds have become."

He nodded too eagerly. "True. True, but there is always hope that he can be removed. Would you see your father back upon the throne or…yourself? Perhaps it is time for the kingdom to have a queen."

He smiled wickedly. Once a trusted spy for Harnin One Eye, Ionascu was betrayed and tortured until his body was broken. Harnin discarded him after the mission to rescue Maleela from Rogscroft. He dreamed of the day when he'd be able to exact his revenge on the One Eye, falling deeper into dementia as the days fled. The visions didn't come until their time in the Dwarven kingdom of Drimmen Delf. Nightmarish figures came to him in the cold night and whispered promises of power, and more. He quickly fell under their sway even while knowing they were the servants of great evil. They promised to restore his former glory. All he had to do was deliver Maleela to them.

"Why are you so interested? You didn't seem to mind working for my father and his band of thugs," she replied tersely. Yet despite her rough tone, he managed to plant the seeds of doubt and worse, the desire to be more than the limitations of herself.

He shrugged nonchalantly. "Harnin abandoned me and your father never cared. I am alone in the world, Princess.

All my men were murdered before your very eyes. What else can I do but try to change what is?"

"We have all made sacrifices, Ionascu. Don't try to make me believe yours is more than any other on this ship. Go back to your hiding and leave me be."

Properly scolded, the broken man snickered. "Delranan is going to need new leadership when this is said and done. Why not the daughter of the king?"

He took up his walking stick and hobbled off, whistling under his breath. Maleela let out the breath of anger she'd been holding and wiped her face with her palms. Men like Ionascu were part of a greater problem she hadn't come up with a solution for. Closing her eyes, Maleela tried to think of a time when her life wasn't so arduous. She couldn't. Badron blamed her for the death of his wife, her mother. The queen died giving life to Maleela, leaving a permanent scar on the relationship between father and daughter. She didn't know why, but her thoughts suddenly veered down the direction of Ionascu's urging. Questions sprang to life. Why couldn't she be queen? The ruler Delranan deserved. Ideations of grandeur sprinkled through her mind, making it hard to focus on the task at hand.

"Excuse me, Princess," Skuld interrupted. The look of concern on his face told her he had overheard much of Ionascu's conversation. "Captain Bahr says it's time to get ready."

She blinked rapidly, hoping to erase the devious thoughts in her mind. "Thank you, Skuld. Are we ready?"

"As far as I've been told. Those river men will never know what hit them," he beamed proudly. "Captain's got me up on the bow with Ironfoot."

Maleela thought that bit was too much and decidedly more dangerous than the youth was prepared to handle. She wasn't prepared to confront Bahr, her uncle, directly about something she was sure would be brushed off. Skuld had undergone numerous challenges and death defying acts since stowing away about the *Bane*. Who was she to debate that?

She laid a warming hand on his wrist. "Be safe, Skuld. We've come too far for any of us to get hurt now."

"It'll be all right. I promise." He gave her that youthful smile of his and marched off to take his position on the bow.

Skuld suddenly discovered self-doubt. He'd been so sure of himself right up until hearing Ionascu. The man made his skin crawl. He couldn't understand why Bahr kept him on. Useless, the former spy was their greatest liability. After hearing his conversation, Skuld was now convinced Ionascu served some nefarious purpose and Maleela was his target. He decided to look after her. The only trouble was in not letting her know.

"This is no place for a boy," Ironfoot said as Skuld approached.

The Dwarf warrior stood with his hands on the bow rail. He reveled in the wind kissing his face. Having spent most of his life underground, Ironfoot took in each new sight with delight. Iron torcs made his biceps bulge. A horned helm sat on a nearby crate. His battle axe and pair of black powder pistols were close by. He only wore his chainmail chest armor over a leather jerkin.

Skuld would have been taken aback a few months ago but he'd come to realize his companions were of iron spines. It was his duty to match them. "Captain Bahr sent me."

The Dwarf nodded. "I figured. Has the Giant spotted anything yet?"

Avoiding the obvious height reference, Skuld replied, "I don't know."

"I can't see a damned thing from here," Ironfoot said. "It's been long enough between battles. I figure it's time to get our hands dirty again."

Skuld flashed back to the bodies being dumped into the river. All his childhood dreams of becoming a mighty warrior died a little more with each new fight. He didn't see how anyone could come to disregard life so casually. Ironfoot glanced back at his sudden quietness and looked on the boy with understanding.

"This isn't an easy life, Skuld. We fight. We die. If we're fortunate we get to live a full life in between. Don't be so quick to judge. No one on this barge kills because they want to. Now be a lad and go see if the Giant has seen our opponents. I'd just as soon not get my head taken off while waiting to don my kit."

Glumly, Skuld nodded and headed back towards the bridge and Groge.

The barge scraped over a series of low rapids. Stone and wood colliding echoed over the gently rolling valleys on both sides of the river. Bahr cringed, the sound louder than thunder to his ears. Torchlight illuminated small areas on the surrounding hills.

"There are many figures moving in the night," Groge called back over his shoulder.

Bahr strained but couldn't make anything out. Small trees rose on both sides, preventing his line of sight from extending very far. Large boulders populated great portions of the shore, making the going more treacherous. His only option was to trust the young Giant until the enemy gave themselves away.

"How many can you see?"

Groge paused, silently counting. He turned and gave Bahr a dreadful look. "More than thirty."

"That means there must be at least fifty. They wouldn't all be in the open like that," Bahr grunted. His best ally was the current. The barge would only move as fast as the river let it, giving them too much time in the kill box. He looked at Anienam and said, "I don't suppose you have any spells that can speed us right along?"

"No," the wizard replied. "Our best option is to keep our heads down and hope for the best."

"I've never been the sort to rely on hope," Bahr told him. "Groge, when I give the word I want you to blow on that horn of yours."

"Yes, Captain," the Giant said.

Satisfied that there was nothing else he could do, Bahr piloted the barge into the ambush.

FIVE

Ambush

"They're not sure what's going on," Bahr said as the barge continued through the bend.

Anienam agreed. "They expected to have torches lit and their captain delivering us without our knowledge. Running dark was a good idea, Bahr."

"For the moment. It won't be long before they decide something's not right. We're nowhere near out of this yet."

As if on cue, a single arrow sped from the trees to strike the wheelhouse. Torches burst to life along the banks. The river men popped up, weapons in hand. Bahr grimaced tightly. All the river men he could see were armed with sword and bows. *That's a lot of arrows. Heads down might not be good enough.* "Groge, now!"

The Giant smith put the horn to his lips and gave a mighty blow. The sound was deep, thunderous. It swept across the hills and fields, trembling the very earth. Men dropped their weapons to cover their ears before the pressure burst their eardrums. Bahr shied away. Even behind Groge the sound was incredible. The Giant gave another blow, followed closely by another. A scattering of arrows sailed back in response.

Rekka Jel was the first to respond. Her aim was true. The dark shaft took the river man in the middle of the chest. He dropped into the water. Incoming fire from the shores picked up. Dozens of arrows now peppered the barge's hull. The battle began in earnest. Dorl and Rekka fired opportunistic shots, only doing so when they had clearly defined targets. Enemy fire increased as the bend grew tighter. Soon Bahr would have to be extraordinarily adept at maneuvering the barge or they'd run aground. Then the fun would really begin.

"This is nuts," Dorl snapped under his breath as he released another arrow.

Nothol, stationed a few meters away, agreed. "We've been in worse. Keep your trap shut and keep up your fire."

Dorl checked his quiver. He had less than twenty shots left. Not much considering the enemy had seemingly endless amounts of arrows to draw from. He privately wondered how much longer they were going to last before the decision was forced.

"Fire! They've got fire arrows!"

Dorl wasn't sure who shouted, but his heart sunk, just like the barge would if enough of those arrows took hold.

Bahr resisted the urge to kick the cackling river captain in the face. Instead he watched, helpless, as dozens of flaming arrows struck the barge. Maleela and Skuld raced to put the flames out. He knew it was only a matter of time before the inevitable happened and they'd be forced to abandon ship. Images of the *Dragon's Bane* burning taunted him. He vowed not to lose another boat, at least if he could help it.

"I told you! You'll never escape us," the river captain snarled, having slipped the gag down to his neck. Wild delight danced in his eyes. "I'll see to it you die last, Sea Wolf. You'll watch every one of your companions die painfully first."

"I thought I told you to gag him?" Bahr snapped at Anienam.

The wizard frowned, only now realizing what had happened. A handful of arrows struck the wheelhouse. Sparks and flame dripped onto the deck.

"Can't you do something? We're going to burn to the water soon!" Bahr shouted angrily. He was tired of being used.

Anienam pushed his heavy sleeves up to his elbows and narrowed his eyes to slits. His lips moved in ways that no words could form. The barge rocked as if being pulled from the water and gently set back down. Bahr felt his skin prickle. His hairs stood on end. Outside, Groge busily extinguished the flames with his massive slabs of calloused hands. They already appeared black in the semi dark.

The world darkened suddenly, so black Bahr couldn't see the wheel. Violent humming grew in his ears, turning into screeching whistles. Letting go of the wheel, he threw his hands up to cover his ears just as a blast of frigid wind rocked the barge. He was certain it was a cyclone, even though he'd only rarely heard of similar outbursts of nature on land. When he opened his eyes every torch and burning arrow had been extinguished, including the numerous fires he'd spotted on land. Anienam had saved them, for now.

Any relief he felt was short lived at the sound of multiple splashes. His face darkened. The river men were going to attempt to board and recapture the barge. He only had moments before they made the short swim to the hull. Bahr jotted to the door and shouted, "Prepare to repel boarders!"

The sound of swords being drawn answered him. Boen and Rekka took the port side while Nothol and Dorl, against his protests, went starboard. They worked too well as a pair to break up in the middle of a determined fight for survival. Ironfoot remained on the bow, ready to assist whichever side needed him more. That left Groge patrolling the aft, though Bahr somehow doubted anyone in their right mind going anywhere close to the Giant.

Wet hands stretched up to grasp the rails. A score of river men pulled their way onto the barge. Naked from the waste up, they were covered with tattoos and armed with cutlasses and daggers. None of them knew what they were getting into. Boen brought his sword down with a violent two-handed chop, cleaving the first river man's skull before he managed to get to his feet. The corpse fell back into the river as others climbed aboard. They bellowed curses and roared defiance at the people who'd killed their friends. The

Gaimosian stepped back and gestured for them to attack. They did.

He hacked. Slashed. A body crumbled under the tremendous force of Boen's blow. Hot blood washed across the deck. A horse whinnied from the bow. An arrow whipped past Boen's face, the feathers neatly cutting his right cheek. Snarling, Boen doubled his efforts. Bodies began to pile around him, enough that the river men in the back slunk off in search of softer targets. The Gaimosian sliced through his remaining enemies with little effort.

When it was over he stood hunched. Blood coated his chest and arms. His breath came in ragged gasps. He suddenly felt very old. Maleela's cries got his attention and he forced away any thoughts of weakness. The princess needed his help. Hefting his sword, he hurried towards the passenger cabin where he found a pair if river men trying to break in. Great chunks of door already lay on the deck. They hacked away with small boarding axes, eager to claim their prize. Boen never gave them the chance. He slashed the closest across the back, severing his spine. The river man died in silent agony. The second spun in time to see Boen's blade take his head off. Boen kicked the head away with disgust.

"Princess, are you all right?" he asked between labored breaths.

Relief in her voice, she replied, "Yes, thank you."

"Good. Keep this door barred until we come back for you," he instructed and took off before she could answer. Sounds of combat still raged from the bow.

Moving as fast as his old legs could go, Boen slipped past the wagon and horses to find Dorl finishing a river man with a blade plunged down through the chest. Nothol had another against the rail and was punching him in the side of the head as hard as he could. Rekka and Ironfoot had multiple bodies heaped around them. A quick scan told him the rest of the barge was secure.

The Dwarf wiped his axe clean. "A good fight. Are there any others?"

Boen shook his head. "I took care of the ones in the back. Still, we should check. I don't want to be surprised in the middle of the night."

Dwarf and Gaimosian swept the barge for any more river men. They found one half-buried under a stack of burlap sacks and crates, clearly waiting to slit their throats once the battle ended and everyone bedded down. Boen stepped aside to let Ironfoot finish him off. There wasn't any need for prisoners. They heard no further splashes. No announcements of the river men trying to repeat the failed tactic. Boen didn't think that meant the attack was over; merely the river men were going to be more cautious. They still had the numbers, though without the skill or tenacity. He directed Dorl and Nothol to begin dumping the bodies in the hopes that the sight would deter more attacks. Psychological warfare was almost as important as actual fighting and Boen aimed to take full advantage of the situation. Being trapped on a slow moving barge left him with little options and no place to hide or run to if things got too bad. He hated the feeling.

Passing Groge, he looked up and asked, "What do you see?"

"The others are holding back. I do not believe they expected such violence," the Giant answered. His tone was awkward, as if laden with sorrow.

Boen shrugged it off. He didn't have time to deal with emotions, not if they expected to survive the next few minutes. "I wouldn't be in a hurry to come at us again either. Too bad some people just don't learn."

He stomped up the irritatingly steep flight of steps to the wheelhouse and leaned heavily against the doorframe. Bahr glanced back at him. His eyes were raw, bloodshot. "Any casualties?"

"A few scratches, maybe some bruises," Boen replied. "I could use a drink."

"We all could. These river scum just don't know when they've been beat."

Boen shot a look at the bound captain. "What about this one? He doesn't serve any purpose now that we've sprung the ambush. I say we get rid of him now."

"He might still have some information we can use," Bahr cautioned. The idea of killing a defenseless man didn't sit well.

Boen recognized the defiance in the river man's eyes and knew there'd be no further information given. Especially not after witnessing so many of his people get cut down. "Keeping him around is a liability. They might keep coming if they know he's still here."

Bahr considered the possibility, reluctantly admitting he'd overlooked it in the heat of the moment. The last thing he wanted was a running fight with tribes of river men. There wasn't time, nor was he inclined to devote so much energy to such a trivial cause. They hadn't come down the river to fight. Trennaron awaited. His decision became painfully evident.

"Time to go," Bahr said and snatched the river captain by his collar.

The smaller man protested, desperately trying to kick free but Bahr was stronger and had the advantage of having his hands free. He dragged the captain out of the wheelhouse and down the short flight of stairs. Hate-filled eyes stared up at him, the silent curses almost making Bahr laugh.

"Any last words?" he asked.

Ironfoot ambled up, arms folded across his thickly muscled chest. "What's this?"

Bahr paused. "Old trash. Boen, care to do the honors?"

The Gaimosian grinned savagely and hefted the river man up over his head.

"Try to get him close to shore. We wouldn't want him to drown before his friends can get him out," Bahr suggested.

Boen frowned and tossed the captain out into the river. They were still in shallow enough water he wouldn't drown without a lot of bad luck. The barge had only gone about a hundred meters downriver before others splashed out to rescue him.

SIX

Revengeance

Winter continued to grow colder the later the season became. Weeks of heavy snows hampered even the bravest soul, with rare moments of sun and blue sky. Aurec, newly crowned king of Rogscroft, stood with his hands on his hips, head titled back to enjoy the kiss of sunlight on his chapped face. There were too few tranquil moments in his life of late and he meant to take full advantage when possible. He closed his eyes and daydreamed of a simpler time, one spent in the arms of his love, Maleela.

They fell in love purely by accident, but then again, what love is intentionally created? Both knew their fathers would never approve. Badron and Stelskor bore a hate going back decades for reasons Aurec's father never truly understood or accepted. So Aurec and Maleela were forced to live far apart, in entirely different worlds. Aurec struggled with this and finally came up with the idea of rescuing her from her father and building a life together where no one would bother them.

Life had other plans. The moment he broke into Chadra Keep and stole Maleela was the moment he set events in motion that could not be undone. Delranan and Rogscroft went to war under the false pretense of grief over the slaying of Badron's only heir. If only the people knew it was Badron's desire to conquer his neighbor, perhaps they might not have been so eager to call for blood. Badron immediately sent a small commando unit into Rogscroft to steal Maleela back even as he mobilized his vaunted army, the Wolfsreik. Aurec and Maleela's love would plunge both kingdoms into the misery of war.

Badron struck swiftly, bringing the full weight of his ten-thousand-man army to bear. They hammered the defenders until they besieged Rogscroft proper. The unexpected happened next. An army of Goblins from the Deadlands to the east marched into Rogscroft, apparently in league with Badron. None of Stelskor's advisors had any plausible solutions or reasons for the unethical alliance. Not that it mattered. The combined weight of armies broke the walls of Rogscroft and the city fell. King Stelskor was executed and put on display while Badron unleashed his armies on the countryside. Nothing less than total domination was acceptable.

Cities and villages fell under the crush of Goblins and Wolfsreik. Aurec did everything he could but it would never be enough. He reluctantly became the king of a nearly extinct kingdom. Until he was approached by members of the Wolfsreik staff, that is. General Rolnir was an honorable Man. One who didn't appreciate being used for murder. His hatred of the Goblins and the way Badron conducted the war led him to act in his best interests. Rolnir abandoned Badron to side with Aurec. Suddenly, Rogscroft stood a chance.

Aurec smiled appreciatively at the thought of the Goblin main body being crushed by the combined forces of the Wolfsreik and the Rogscroft defenders hidden in the secret village of Grunmarrow just days ago. The war had gone so poorly for him Aurec couldn't see any bright spots. He knew in his heart that Rogscroft was finished. It was only a matter of time. The impenetrable gloom crushing his spirit lifted when Rolnir suddenly switched sides. There was only so much evil one could take.

His thoughts shifted to the approaching task. The combined force was in the process of preparing to march on Rogscroft with the intent of taking back the city. Stelskor's murderers were going to pay for their audacity. Today was the dawn of a new campaign. One that would change the fate of his beloved kingdom, hopefully for the better. He grinned at the sound of boots crunching on fresh snow.

"Is it that time already?" he asked without looking back.

Venten came to a halt. The older man and advisor to the Aurec's father folded his hands over his lap. His gray hair hung down past his collar, reminding him how long it had been since he'd been properly groomed. "Yes, sire. The vanguard is prepared to deploy. General Rolnir requests your presence to begin."

Aurec turned slowly and looked on his old friend. They'd been together since Aurec was a child. There was no he trusted more than Venten. "Remember this day, old friend. Today is the day we take our kingdom back."

"A day that will be long remembered if we are successful." Ever the voice of caution, Venten didn't want to get his hopes up. Badron was a foul man with a clearly defined sense of bitterness, and Venten took Stelskor's death harder than Aurec and often blamed himself.

Aurec paused. "Of course. There is still much to do before our kingdom is free again, but I can feel the course of things changing, Venten. My father should be here to lead us, not me."

"This is not the time for doubt. Your father prepared you well, Aurec. There is no other I would see in command right now than you."

Thoughts of his father smiling down on him lightened Aurec's heart. He believed that the end of the dark times was near and that Rogscroft would be able to rebuild once the winter snows melted. He had to believe. Anything less was akin to surrender. So many had died because of one man's vanity. Badron was a cancer in need of excising. So much still needed to be done Aurec often felt overwhelmed. Life had been much simpler during the opening stages of the campaign when he led a small battalion worth of brave soldiers who sacrificed everything for the future of their kingdom. Now came the hour in which he could deliver vengeance for the bodies lying frozen, buried under the snow on forgotten fields. What bitter irony that he now marched with his former enemies.

"Thank you, Venten, for everything. You have been a friend and voice of reason when I needed it for many years. I am honored to have you by my side," Aurec said slowly.

Venten bowed curtly. "The honor is mine. You've grown to a fine man. I pray your reign over Rogscroft is long."

Enough said, the pair made their way to the head of the massive army. Aurec had never seen so many soldiers gathered in one place. Close to twenty thousand had answered the call and were ready to march on the capital. Most were men of the Wolfsreik. He marveled at their professionalism, even after all they'd been through to reach this point. A lesser army would have fractured and slunk away already. Each wore some sort of animal pelt draped over their dulled and dented chest armor. Their helms were lined with wool to keep their heads from freezing. Aurec was in awe of the sight. He secretly wished to have such strength at his command. No one would ever try to conquer his kingdom again.

Deciding not to waste time on dreams, the king of Rogscroft nodded to some of those he passed. Most of the Wolfsreik merely stared back, still unaware that he was the king of Rogscroft. When he finally made it to his men, he experienced different emotions. These were the heart of the kingdom: brave men all that had willingly sacrificed time with their families for the greater good of all. They wore whatever armor they could find. Some of it was taken from fallen Wolfsreik soldiers. Nothing about the five-thousand-man rabble so much as hinted at professionalism. They were the lesser army Aurec feared, but his pride was unequaled. They'd fought and bled for him, for Rogscroft. He owed them more than any man could provide. Most greeted him with cheers. They waved their weapons and chanted ancient battle cries. Their pride surpassed his.

Next was the enigmatic Pell Darga. The mountain folk were taciturn, often choosing to stay within their enclaves rather than dealing with lowlanders. Aurec had made friends with their leader, Cuul Ol, almost a year ago and their friendship blossomed into a strategic alliance. He never imagined the diminutive warriors had so much in the way of numbers. Far more primitive than his own people, the Pell stood roughly five feet tall and were lithe. Their dark brown skin blended perfectly with the caves and trees and they had the martial prowess of fearsome predators. He feared them nearly as much as he respected them. Their short spears had proven incredibly effective against the Goblin hordes. The tribal leaders nodded reverently to the newly crowned king. He expected nothing more.

General Rolnir stood in quiet conference with Cuul Ol at the head of the army while the command staff busied with final preparations nearby. The redheaded man was roughly fifteen years older than Aurec's twenty and every ounce the warrior. He'd been the commanding general of the Wolfsreik for seven years. Placing honor above loyalty, Rolnir steadily broke away from the depredations Badron concocted. He wasn't the same king he had been before the night his son was murdered. Rolnir suspected some outside influence over his king but couldn't prove anything. Regardless, he couldn't take anymore. The Goblins were the last straw. Every man had limitations. Rolnir reached his.

He turned and bowed formally. "Your Majesty, the army is prepared to move."

Aurec flushed, secretly hoping it was covered under his already near frost-burnt cheeks. "Excellent, General Rolnir. I must admit I am thoroughly impressed with the size of our force."

"I personally never thought to see such a sight," Rolnir confirmed. "Wolfsreik, Rogscroft, and Pell Darga working together. What's left of the Goblin army will fold under our approach. Your kingdom will be returned to you, though I cannot promise the condition in which I pass it off. Badron will not leave easily. I imagine anyone still living in the city will face reprisal."

"That is a difficult choice but one I feel needs to be made. Like it or not, I can't protect everyone from the enemy. All we can do as professionals is minimize the collateral damage amongst the civilian population." Aurec paused to think about where those words came from. A year ago he never would have talked like that.

Venten gave him a look of approval and mouthed, "You've grown up."

"What is your plan?" Aurec ignored him.

Rolnir clenched his hand repeatedly, trying to lessen the sudden cramp. "I'm pushing a scouting foray out. Two of yours are in charge, Mahn and Raste, I believe. Their mission is to get as close to the city as possible and report on enemy strength, troop movements, and emplacements. Once we have that intel we'll know exactly where to strike and how hard. Hopefully we can do this with minimal casualties."

"It was my understanding that we virtually destroyed the main Goblin army."

Rolnir nodded. "As far as I know we did, but we can't leave anything to chance. Badron is deranged. He'll stop at nothing to cement his power over both kingdoms. There could feasibly be a secondary force I don't have knowledge of."

Several of those gathered paused. The implications of his words struck deep. Underestimating the enemy was a cardinal sin for battlefield commanders. New questions sprang to life. What if Badron did have a second army? How strong? Where were they? Aurec's head swooned as visions of total annihilation arose. He may be king, but he was barely out of his teens. Young men shouldn't be forced to make such decisions.

When he spoke, it was slowly. "These are risks we must take. I don't see any way to avoid it. Is the main body to wait here until the scouts return?"

"No. Grunmarrow is at the base of the Murdes Mountains. Too far away for us to respond to any threats. I intend to march our army two days east and establish a field camp in the low hills just west of the city. We'll be able to get to Rogscroft in a day and still have the strength to fight upon arrival. Our biggest concern will be the supply trains keeping up."

"Speaking of which," Venten commented. "I don't happen to see any wagons."

"No. Commander Joach escorted them out before dawn. I don't need thousands of hungry soldiers waiting for no reason," Rolnir said with a smile.

"Won't they be at risk?" Aurec asked.

"I've used that same tactic against your men and others over the course of my career. It works and hastens the timeline considerably. It also boosts morale. Imagine how good it feels to have a hot meal waiting by the time you pull in from a full day's march. High morale makes better fighters, Aurec, and we need all the advantages we can get."

Cuul Ol, the Pell chieftain, slammed the butt of his short spear on the ice-crusted snow. "This is good. My warriors want to fight. Goblins don't belong here."

No one could have said it better. The Pell Darga clans distinguished themselves during what some now dubbed the Battle of Betrayal. Thousands of Goblins fell under Pell spears and daggers. Now that their blades had been drawn and blooded, the Pell wanted more. All pretense of peacefulness evaporated. Aurec feared for any army that became objects of their ire.

"Very well. General, you may deploy the army at your discretion," Aurec said, still smiling at Cuul's eagerness.

SEVEN

Badron's Madness

What remained of Rogscroft wasn't fit to be called a city. Grugnak's Goblins burned through most of the once proud buildings with ruthless abandon in retribution of their abysmal defeat at the hands of the Wolfsreik. Not even the promise of another fifty thousand Goblins en route was enough to cheer their commander. He authorized, without Badron's knowledge, the wholesale slaughter of the civilian population. What few Humans remained were hidden deep underground or fled under the cover of darkness.

Grugnak slowly took control of the city and the surrounding areas. The people suffered. Still he felt no better, took no solace from any measure of viciousness extracted. His army lay dead on the slopes of the Murdes Mountains, already buried under fresh snow. What little power he still held was laughable. Amar Kit'han promised a much larger force but they weren't Grugnak's. The relief force was a combination of remnants from the Deadlands and from faraway Gren to the east. Grugnak idly wondered how many Goblins were left in the dark, forgotten places of the world.

He marched with half a dozen guards to the former throne room of King Stelskor. The once pristine halls were now caked with muck. Several marble tiles were shattered. Piles of refuse choked the corners. Spiders came down to fill the ceilings with cobwebs. There was no glory left in Rogscroft. Grugnak intended to remake the kingdom in his own image. It started with wresting power away from Badron.

With most of the human forces abandoning the king in favor of the much liked General Rolnir, Badron stayed locked within the upper levels of the castle. He was fed and seen to. The only real reason Grugnak kept him alive was because he was the figurehead of the entire campaign in the north. No human would ever submit to the rule of Goblins, at least not willingly. Badron remained important for the foreseeable future.

"The king doesn't want visitors," snarled one of the guards outside the throne room. Larger and physically more powerful, the guard would prove problematic for the shorter Goblin.

"There is news from the east," Grugnak replied.

The guards exchanged cautious looks. Their dislike for the Goblins wore openly as they debated whether to admit Grugnak. Finally they relented. "Only you may enter. The others stay out here."

Unhappy with the decision, Grugnak resisted the urge to order his warriors to attack and humbly followed instructions. Fires dimly lit the expansive room but provided no warmth. Grugnak frowned. The room was always chill, much to his dislike. Badron preferred it cold and dark, often stopping in mid-conversation to confer with an invisible advisor. Today he sat upon the usurped throne with his hands in his head.

Badron was the younger of two sons and never intended to rule Delranan. His father had no choice when Bahr decided to abandon his responsibilities for frivolous adventure. Rumors abounded that he killed his father to gain the throne quicker. Badron never bothered giving any definitive answer. What did it matter? He was king and all bent knee to him. His rule was defined by jealousy. Stelskor was an adversary for many decades. Badron wanted everything Rogscroft had: the minerals, the natural resources, and the land. Delranan was too far to the west to be of importance in Malweir. He needed to conquer Rogscroft to build an empire to rival the rule of mighty Averon in the central south. It was only a matter of time before he invaded. Now, after years of plotting and planning, he sat upon Stelskor's throne and ruled the declining kingdom with iron.

"I did not summon you." Badron's voice was hollow, void of emotion or curiosity.

Grugnak choked back the spit filling his mouth. "I have news."

Slowly, the king of Delranan lifted his head. His eyes were red. Shadows clung to his face unnaturally, giving him a deathly appearance. "There is always news. Have you come to tell me of the approaching Goblin army?"

Grugnak paused, not expecting to be trumped. "How did you come by this? I only just found out."

Badron laughed wickedly. "Do not think to inflate your importance, Goblin. I know what your warriors whisper when they believe no one is listening. You will never be my equal. Never! I am a lord of men and no Goblin has claim to dominion. You are here only at my discretion, regardless of what you think."

"Fifty thousand Goblins say otherwise," Grugnak snapped. He briefly considered throttling the demented king but felt that same terrible presence lurking in the shadows. He wasn't strong enough to battle the Dae'shan. He began to wonder if they offered false promise.

"They'll never get here in time," Badron snorted.

"Time for what?"

The king waggled a finger. "Time to help save us. The traitor Rolnir and my Wolfsreik are preparing to march on the city. We don't have the numbers to stop them, much less delay. My scouts tell me there are close to twenty thousand enemy soldiers."

Grugnak balked, failing to comprehend where so many had come from. "How is this possible? You did not have so many soldiers."

"No. I didn't but Rolnir has joined forces with young King Aurec and those murderous people from the mountains. They will arrive at the city long before your relief force does."

The implications were terrifying for the Goblin commander. He'd obeyed Amar Kit'han's summons to leave their dreary stronghold in the Deadlands only to see most of his army destroyed, betrayed by the very men he'd been promised would help. Now those initial dreams lay in ruins and were potentially coming undone further with the enemy marching on him. Craven instincts urged him to take what few surviving Goblins he had left and flee back to the Deadlands. If they were caught here....

"Don't have the gall to stand and fight, eh?" Badron teased upon noticing the cagey look in Grugnak's eyes. "I don't blame you, but it won't do any good. Aurec is going to unleash the wolves against us. Ironic isn't it? Getting killed by my own army. The gods have a twisted sense of humor."

Grugnak didn't care about gods. He only wanted to live long enough to see his race rise above the prejudices and handicaps enforced by men, Elves, and Dwarves. For too long the Goblins struggled to survive. He knew their origins. That they'd been Dwarves once, before dark powers ensnared them. Time and endless devotion to their new gods twisted the colony until they became Goblins. To this day every Goblin longed for the time when he could live above ground and feel the sun's kiss. It was a foolish dream.

"What does the Dae'shan have to say?" the Goblin asked.

Darkness and shadow coalesced into the hovering, gaunt figure of Amar Kit'han directly behind the throne. Grugnak snarled while Badron didn't bother looking. The wraith-like Dae'shan was an ever present whisper in his mind's eye. Ice-colored eyes penetrated the gloom forever dominating his cowl. He radiated power, electricity dancing off his ethereal form. Amar Kit'han personified evil. Relentless, driven evil.

"You should be more careful when using my name, Goblin," he scolded with a raspy voice. "I am not as forgiving as others."

Badron winced, knowing there was nothing forgiving about the former man. "He merely wished council on these new developments. What does the mighty Dae'shan have to say?"

"Rolnir betraying you was inevitable. He is a man of great character. To do any less would be a permanent stain upon his soul. That he could coerce the bulk of his army to turn with him says a great deal. You chose wisely in making him general of your army."

"Wisely? He's gone over to the enemy and left me with bones!" Badron all but screamed.

Amar casually floated around the throne. "Bones? He's taken a great weight from you and left you open to new beginnings. The Wolfsreik was never the end, merely a means to your further evolution. They were bound to turn on you when they realized Rolnir didn't share your belief system. Proud men often fail to see the grander schemes of life."

"You forget to mention how they nearly wiped out the entire Goblin army in Rogscroft in the process," Badron countered.

"That was a…regrettable act," Amar said and paused in midsentence. Truthfully even he hadn't foreseen the ferocity of the combined army's attack on the Goblin army. Goblins were fighters, but not warriors. They lacked the training and discipline necessary to achieve the greatness of armies like the Wolfsreik. Losing them was unfortunate, but each death served to further his purpose. Time was running out and there was still much to do to prepare the gateway at Arlevon Gale for the return of the dark gods.

Grugnak roared. "My people destroyed for what? A madman's glory?"

"Now Grugnak, King Badron, or should I say, Emperor Badron, is hardly a madman. His quest to unite the kingdoms of Delranan and Rogscroft under a single banner was bound to endure massive casualties. An entire way of life needs to be subsumed for the greater enterprise to exist. Rogscroft has died so that Badron can make his dreams come to pass," Amar explained, knowing most of his rationale went beyond the Goblin's grasp. He marveled at the primitive culture. How had they endured for so long while the rest of the world passed them by? The probability of such was limited, making them a conundrum to his attuned senses.

The Dae'shan continued, "You are forgetting the one unifying truth of us all. We are here to bring enlightenment to another people. Goblins and men working together hasn't been seen on Malweir in our entire history. These are times of great honor. With that honor comes responsibility. Are either of you willing to sacrifice it all?"

Badron held out his palms. "Look around you, Amar, I already have. My army is gone. I sit on a throne of lies and my own kingdom has been usurped by the one I thought was my closest ally. You bring another army that proved useful for a while, but they too were stolen from my grasp. I am a powerless king. A haunted figurehead of something I still don't understand."

"Such is truth about many great leaders," Amar said politely.

Grugnak fumed with unbridled aggression. "I have nothing. My army is destroyed. The time has come for me to leave."

"Are you forgetting the new Goblin force even now marching from the Deadlands?" Amar taunted. "When was the last time you heard of such strength in Goblin numbers? Never. You have given them something they never dreamed of. They are suddenly important and awake. Kingdoms will tremble under their boots, Grugnak. Don't be so foolish as to dismiss this unlocked potential. Even if they don't follow your command."

The Goblin's eyes narrowed threateningly, even though he was no match for the impossible powers of the Dae'shan. Feeling helpless, Grugnak meekly stood by while the monster hovering before him continued to dissemble.

"It's not about who commands the sheep, but who stands atop the pedestal when the dust settles. Others have tried to accomplish what you are so close to. The Silver Mage nearly succeeded but was found wanting. The crystal of Tol Shere proved too much for his limited mind to comprehend.

It drove him mad and was regrettably lost when a small band of heroes were coerced to stand up to him."

"Why are you telling us this?" Badron asked. He failed to see how the abysmal performance of one was comparable to his long-term suffering.

"One cannot succeed alone," Amar answered too quickly for Badron's liking. "Therein lays the great failing of mankind. Your lack of vision hampers any ability to achieve true greatness. Would you cripple your campaign to control the north? To turn it into an empire rivaling mighty Averon to the south? All your life you've plotted, impatiently waiting for this day, and now you so willingly abandon it? This is one of the reasons I gave up my mortality. The acuity of your dreams is a waste of precious life spark."

"I did not ask you to bandy words of pettiness over my character, demon," Badron retorted. "I need counsel. All my advisors have abandoned me. Even fortune has turned her back, leaving me you."

Amar held up a hand, his bony fingers glowing in the faint light. "Mind your next words. Lesser men have suffered worse for such."

"You offer platitudes and fragmented wisdom but no clear path out of the darkness," Badron said with measured tones. "Where is the end? The way out of this building nightmare? I need answers, Amar Kit'han. Not mixed words meant to confuse."

"The toughest answers must be found from within. No outside influence is capable of enlightening you," Amar replied.

Badron lowered his head into his hands in defeat. "Then I have no choice but to abandon the city before Rolnir arrives."

"Minor defeats are to be expected along the way, king," Amar soothed. "Perhaps leaving Rogscroft is your best answer. The Goblin army will not arrive in time. In fact, I've given instructions for them to bypass this ruined city at all costs."

"You betray me, demon."

Lightning flashed, blinding them. Heat sizzled off the Dae'shan's black robes. "Enough! The Goblin relief force must arrive in Delranan intact. They will have a hard enough time crossing Dwarf lands. I don't need them wasting unnecessary lives here in what is sure to be a pointless conflict. Take what forces you have left and flee towards the mountains."

"The mountains? You are trying to get me killed," Badron accused. He no longer saw hope. The dawn would come and claim him, leaving his corpse to the wolves. "Even should we make it that far, the Pell Darga will fall upon us before we can begin the climb."

Grugnak snorted laughter. "You say Pell Darga are on their way here. Who remains in the mountains?"

"Precisely, Grugnak," Amar praised. "I have several agents that will assist your passage across the Murdes Mountains and further west into Delranan. Do not fear. You will be strong when the time comes to reclaim your lost crown."

"What of Rogscroft? I am a king of two crowns. I will not abandon what I have fought so hard to conquer."

"Nor should you, but there will come a time to focus your thoughts back on this frozen land. The time is fast approaching when the conflict will come to an end. Take heart, King, your hour of glory rises."

Shadows swirled, folding in on themselves as Amar Kit'han gathered darkness and vanished. Hour of glory? Badron saw only hardship and continued trial in the coming weeks. Winter was on the low side but there were still many weeks left of snow and ice. Worse, this winter proved to be fiercer than any in recent history. Badron felt as if the entire world was against him. Doubts rose. He'd always known Amar Kit'han had ulterior motives but no amount of studying had detected anything.

He felt helpless, like a prisoner on his own throne. Reluctantly, he made his decision. "It appears we are to be companions for a while longer, Goblin. Give the order. Abandon the city."

Grugnak growled low, his cheeks puffing out with disdain. "Not yet."

He whirled and stormed from the throne room. There was much to be done before his Goblins so willingly abandoned their hard-earned victory.

EIGHT

Storms

Bahr set down the chalk pencil and rubbed his tired eyes. He'd been straining at the course maps for hours, trying to decipher the river men code while determining their precise location. His only certainty was that they were still on the river heading south. Beyond that he was at a loss. The barge was uncharacteristically silent. Most of the others had fallen asleep after cleaning up after the battle. They'd gotten rid of the bodies and done their best to wash most of the blood and gore off, fearing the smell would torment the horses. It was fast pitched and over before anyone had a grasp of the flow. He feared the results would differ if not for Boen. The big Gaimosian was a monster with a blade: unstoppable and unkillable.

Heavy footsteps coming from behind brought a thin smile. "You don't ever sleep, do you?"

Boen handed him a green apple and shrugged. "There will be time enough for that once I'm in the ground."

Bahr grunted, taking a large bite from the tart fruit. Juice ran down his chin. His friend's pragmatic view on life was very base, often leaving him questioning his own belief system. "This is usually my favorite time of the day. When everyone is asleep and there's nothing but the wind in my hair and gentle sounds of water kissing the boat. It reminds me of simpler times."

"If we were all so fortunate," Boen commented. "The life of a Gaimosian is freedom. No kings to bend a knee to. No lands beholden us. We roam Malweir in search of meaning. There is no other liberty in the world quite like ours."

"Some would view that as a curse, my friend. No homes, no place to call yours at the end of the day," Bahr countered.

"The trappings of an easy life. Luxuries not needed," Boen countered. "When I lay my head down I am beholden to no one."

"So what is the point of living?"

Boen frowned, not expecting deep philosophical conversations at such a late hour. "To truly live. How many can say they experience all life has to offer? I'm not contending ours is the perfect life. Ever since the destruction of Gaimos my people have known only restlessness. We are denied the simplicity of having home or hearth. It is not a life I'd choose to live, to be honest, Bahr. I am getting old. I'm tired. My body aches from today's battle. There was a time when I would have shrugged it off and found a tavern. I fear my days are waning."

"We are both in the autumn of our lives, old friend," Bahr agreed glumly. He'd never expected to hear such confession from the proud man. "Gaimos was destroyed more than two thousand years ago. Why have your people never settled down and built a new kingdom?"

"There is a legend that says the spirits of our ancestors are imbued within each newborn. That way we learn our history, our heritage. Each Gaimosian knows the price paid for being the dominant military power in Malweir. All those kingdoms banding together just to wipe out our entire way of life. What a waste. We know there can be no revival of lost Gaimos. The world won't let us."

"I've never bothered thinking about it that way. I guess your lifestyle seemed so cavalier that I envied you," Bahr admitted with a rue grin. "The only thing missing is the rescued princess."

"What would I do with a wife?" Boen laughed. "I've had my share of loves over the last few decades, but the quest keeps me from settling. Women would only complicate matters. I don't need the distractions."

"You make it sound as if they're no fun to be around. I know this lady in Stouds that will change your mind," Bahr teased.

Boen gave him a mildly angered look. "Don't go putting words in my mouth. I like women just fine. I just don't have the time to take care of one proper-like. Besides, I don't see a wife in your cabin."

Bahr lowered his head slightly. He'd never been married, often blaming his brother for the lack of happiness he experienced. Their animosity kept him from his own kingdom more times than not. It was only recently Bahr realized he was using that excuse as a mask. Truth be told, he didn't know how to be a husband any more than he wanted to be king. Walking away from both seemed the easiest course in his life and he made those decisions without regret, until now. He tried to imagine what it would feel like to come home to a house filled with children's laughter and the smell of a freshly cooked meal on the table. It was naught more than a dream.

His life was on the water and a troubled marriage it had become. Everything he'd ever known or come to care about was steadily slipping through his fingers. His boat and estate burned. His crew dead. Only Maleela for family or at least family he still cared for. He was as close to being Gaimosian as possible.

Reluctantly, he admitted, "We are more alike than I care to think on, Boen. The only difference is where you were born to live this life, I chose it. I wonder what that makes me."

He shrugged. "It doesn't make you anything but a man. Don't try to change the world, Bahr. History seldom remembers the exploits of a single man."

"Try telling that to the wizard. He seems determined to either prove history wrong or make us all heroes in the end."

Boen's gaze tightened. "Heroes usually become such after they die."

The barge sailed on through the rest of the night and into a tepid dawn. Humidity rose well before the sun. Their clothes stuck to them and everyone had a generally miserable feeling. The biggest noticeable difference came from the massive amount of insects swarming the barge. Gnats and midges hovered in thick clouds, hungry for an easy meal. Mosquitoes with white bands on their legs constantly buzzed around their heads and hands. Every few moments the crisp report of a slap could be heard across the vessel.

"How in the world can anyone live like this?" Dorl grumbled as he tried not to scratch the latest series of bites on the back of his hand.

Rekka grinned sheepishly and handed him a small pouch containing a salve. "Rub this over the bites. It will help with the swelling and pain."

"What is it?" he asked, hesitant to accept something foreign.

"A salve made from various jungle plants. It lessens the misery long enough for your body to absorb the poison," she explained. She continued after noticing his queer look. "You are entering my world now. Forget all you know about the frozen north. The jungle is unlike anything you have ever experienced."

"That's not very comforting," he replied dryly. "I happen to like the snow."

Nothol glanced up from oiling his sword. His eyebrows peaked. "No you don't. You complain every day."

"Shut up, Nothol. I'm talking to her, not you," Dorl fumed. "Besides, I'm just trying to make a point. These bugs are killing me!"

Nothol chuckled and went back to his sword. Sometimes it wasn't worth arguing. Doral shook his head in distress and began applying the salve. It wasn't long before Rekka joined in on the joke.

"You haven't seen anything yet. There are spiders bigger than your hand, centipedes well over a foot long and can kill with a single sting, wasps and…"

"All right I get the point!" Dorl all but screeched. "There's bugs. Plenty of bugs."

"Want me to see if the wizard can fashion you some sort of special cape to keep you safe?" Nothol asked.

"Keep talking like that and you'll need one for yourself," Dorl fired back.

Sheathing his sword, Nothol rose and bowed at the waist. "You ladies enjoy your beauty regime. I'm heading up to the bridge."

Dorl's narrow eyes focused on his friend's back. He muttered under his breath, "Beauty regime. Say that again and I'll slice your lips off."

"He is joking," Rekka said, head cocked.

"I know, but he didn't need to say it." Most of his ire gone, Dorl frowned at the pungent odor coming from the salve. "Are you sure this is safe?"

"I don't understand. My people have used this for generations," Rekka replied. "I would not do anything to harm you."

"That was a joke, Rekka," he said, embarrassed for poking fun at her. The strange jungle lady had come to mean more to him than he ever imagined. Dorl wouldn't say it aloud, but he realized that he needed her. "It's a defense mechanism. I use humor to calm me down. Sometimes it works, sometimes not."

"You are a strange people to me, Dorl Theed. The jungle does not have much humor. There is no time for it. Too many things lurk in the shadows waiting to bite and sting," Rekka said and waited.

Dorl was about to open a pack of rations when he understood what she'd said. His head snapped up in time to see her crack a soft grin. "No humor huh?"

She held out her hands submissively. "I did not say I haven't learned it since leaving Teng. You should pay more attention to what I say instead of what you hear."

He smiled ruefully. *Perhaps I should at that. You are special, Rekka Jel. A very special woman.* Smiling, he went back to his breakfast. Another sting on his neck brought another slap.

Groge could not find sleep. He tossed and turned long into the late hours of the night. Tossed and turned right up until the first hints of dawn broke the horizon. Every time he closed his eyes his mind replayed horrific events. The crunching of bone as Ironfoot's axe split skulls. The way Boen's sword tore so effortlessly through a stomach. The smell of blood and viscera nauseated him. It was all he could do not to vomit over the side rails. He was a blacksmith, not a warrior. Until now he had only known peace. That the various lowlander races could entertain such violent deeds without thought troubled his soul. Perhaps Blekling had been correct. The true god did not shine his grace down upon these heathens.

Distracted, Groge finally gave up trying to sleep and sat up. Most of the blood and gore had been washed away but his large nostrils easily detected the lingering odors. Legends said that the Giants were once warlike but learned the error of their ways and fled to the highest mountaintops to study the teachings of their god. Peace and prosperity followed. They dedicated their lives to becoming better beings. All thoughts of violence were soon bred out of them. Groge grew up knowing nothing of warfare. His first true lesson made him want to return to Venheim.

"First time eh?" Ironfoot asked. The Dwarf was leaning back on a pile of crates close by. His thick, corded arms were folded across his chest. His eyes were closed.

Groge studied the Dwarf. They had many similar features, obviously coming from the same genetic pool. Whereas Groge was over ten feet tall, Ironfoot stood a few inches over four. One was bred for combat, the other for crafting tools and wondrous instruments.

"How do you do it?" he finally asked.

Ironfoot stifled a yawn. "I remember my first time. Puked my guts out so hard I was sure the surgeon needed to shove them back in! Ha! War is easy as soon as you learn the truth."

"The truth?" the Giant asked.

"Simple. Truth is every soldier is expendable. If we die, so be it. Nothing you or I do is going to change that. Once you figure that out for yourself the rest is easy," Ironfoot replied. "Still, it helps to think of your enemy as animals. After a while, all those faces turn up to haunt you night after night. That's the worst part."

"I don't understand, Ironfoot. Life should be treasured, not mutilated so wantonly." Groge scratched his cheek. The stubble was an unusual feeling. He'd always been clean-shaven when working in the forge with Joden. These last few days he had come to appreciate the ancient Giant forge master more and more. He wished he could hear Joden's wisdom now.

"I don't know how you Giants do things in Venheim, but life down here is hard, painful. You saw only a portion of what my people went through during the civil war. Do you think it's an easy thing, killing one's own people? I can assure you it's not. Be thankful you know true peace, for the rest of the world has never known the flavor."

Ironfoot fell silent, letting his words sink in. He hadn't meant to sound so severe, but there was no other way for the youth to learn quickly. Life on Malweir was filled with misery; there was often inconsolable suffering. The sooner Groge understood that, the easier his life would be. They didn't have time for extended learning cycles. With the jungle fast approaching and then the trek to Trennaron, this adventure was steadily picking up pace. Besides which, Ironfoot wasn't convinced the river men had abandoned their plans of revenge that easily. He hoped he was wrong. The world needed more innocence.

Groge stewed on this for a while longer. Never in his life had he imagined becoming entangled in such a web of violence that was practically second thought. The casual disregard for life was appalling on many levels, most of which he failed to comprehend. Groge knew some of the others looked to him as their greatest military asset without knowing a thing about him. The Giant wasn't sure if he was a pacifist or merely a concerned citizen of the world. He viewed life as the most precious gift their god bestowed upon the world. To treat it as anything less was almost sacrilegious.

Ironfoot cracked his eyes open and noticed his dilemma. "Don't think too hard on it, my young friend. If any of us had a clue what was going on we wouldn't be anywhere near here. Trust in Anienam. He is a venerable man. We are fortunate to have him with us."

"He is…enigmatic," Groge replied thoughtfully.

"Name one old timer that isn't," the Dwarf laughed and rolled back over to get some more sleep.

Groge reluctantly gave him that point and went off in search of Anienam Keiss. He had many internal conflicts spawning, irritating his rationale to great ends. Compounding his rising confusion was the fractured belief system. From what he gathered, the old gods were gone. Good gods left Malweir to its devices while the dark gods struggled to return. The very reason he had come down from the mountain peaks. He was the only one capable of handling the Blud Hamr. Each race also had its own gods. It was a confusing mixture of deities that mostly shared the same qualities. His head began to hurt from the hundreds of different scenarios and variants concerning gods. Couldn't these people see that having a singular deity was infinitely more satisfying and less confusing?

The Giants long ago abandoned their worship of multiple gods. Many found it distasteful; confusing and filled with obstacles. Questions rose after the gods of light abandoned Malweir. What god would willingly leave his subjects to the depredations of evil? The Giants cast their old gods over the side of the mountain and settled on a single entity worthy of worship. That the lowlander races continued their antiquated beliefs was an enigma to Groge.

He found Anienam sitting atop the wheelhouse, casually swinging his legs like a child on the banks of a great river. "Hello, Groge. How goes your morning?"

The Giant bowed reverently. "My mind is troubled, Anienam."

Smiling, the wizard nodded as if he already knew. "These are indeed troubling times but there is always hope lurking in the strangest places."

"More riddles?"

His shoulders rose slowly. "Keeps people on their toes. My father used to simply infuriate people with them. He probably would have gotten into a few fights if he weren't a powerful Mage."

"I fail to understand how you can joke in the middle of such serious times," Groge admonished, feeling guilty immediately after. "Anienam, what in Malweir is worth saving if people so casually throw life away? This does not sit well in my heart or mind."

The wizard sighed. He'd been expecting such concerns from more than one of the already beleaguered band of would-be heroes. Only now that it came, he wasn't sure how to answer. "Who can say why we kill one another? I don't have the answer you seek, Groge. This is the way life has played out in the countless generations since the gods of light left. I don't think this act should be viewed as entirely evil. Wicked beings roam Malweir and it falls upon the shoulders of the just to ensure they cannot build their brand of terror. We kill to stop evil from spreading. There is no glory or pride in being able to take a life, but it sometimes must be done."

"But why would the gods leave this world in such disarray? Did they abandon all life to the depredations of the foul?" Groge's massive slab of forehead scrunched in thought.

Anienam wished he had the answers. How many times over the years had he longed to be able to speak with the old gods, if only to learn the truth of their departure? Did they truly think Malweir could rule itself in their stead without conflict? "I like to think they left it for us to make a better place, even if that means cleansing the wicked."

"How can you justify taking a life, though? I was taught from an early age that all life is precious, put here for specific purpose. To have just one life snubbed without much thought or effort affects the balance."

Anienam viewed the Giant with much greater respect. The youth had insight and deep thinking patterns the wizard himself often lacked. He was a worthy addition to their band. "You view this debate from the wrong angle. Instead of disrupting the balance you should think of it as restoring the balance. Evil must be checked if we are to advance civilization. When I was a boy no one would ever have dreamed of gunpowder weapons like the Dwarves use. A lifetime brokers many changes. What will Malweir be like a hundred years after I'm gone? I will never know but it comforts me to think our actions today will affect the greater outcome."

"You think by killing, even someone evil, we can make Malweir a better world? I might be able to see that point of view if not for the willingness to degrade our morality by stooping to the same level as evil."

"Good and evil aren't as clearly defined as you want to believe," Anienam countered. "Often enough we find the lines blurred. Don't be so quick to judge others for their actions. You might find yourself in a similar situation before too long. Remember, only you have the ability to wield the Blud Hamr."

Groge fell silent. He'd come to the wizard to exorcise the storm brewing in his mind but was left with more questions. With much to ponder, he failed to notice Anienam stiffen suddenly. The wizard turned his head skyward, sniffing the building winds. Danger rode the wind. He immediately grew concerned and went to the wheelhouse.

"There's a storm coming," he announced upon throwing the door open.

Bahr looked back at him. "I see it. It doesn't look like much from here."

"No, this storm is unnatural, Bahr."

"What are you saying?" Bahr asked, his eyes narrowed with concern.

Anienam shook his head, as if still locked in doubt. "There is magical taint in the air. I fear we are being assaulted."

Bahr exhaled a deep breath and tried to decide his best course of action before the storm struck. He was steadily growing weary of this journey.

NINE

Shipwrecked

"Hold on to something!" Bahr shouted moments before the next wave slammed into the starboard side of the barge.

Walls of water poured over the barge. Lightning shredded the skies. Thunder exploded directly overhead, so low Bahr though the heavens were being destroyed. Several side boards had already been torn away, leaving the hull exposed to onrushing waters. Horses screamed above the storm. Most of the others were huddled in the relative security of the passenger cabin while nature destroyed the already fragile barge.

Anienam gripped the captain's chair for dear life. His robes were soaked. His white beard was plastered to his chest. He looked like a drowned animal. Red-streaked eyes desperately scanned the horizon for any sign of a break. He found none. The world conspired against them and it was all he could do to hold on before the waters rose to swallow them all.

"Can't you do anything?" Bahr shouted.

Anienam felt powerless. "This is no mere storm. It is beyond my power to counter!"

Disgruntled, Bahr spat onto the deck. "We're not going to last much longer. The ship is already breaking up."

"Perhaps it is time to run aground and abandon ship," Anienam suggested.

Reluctant as he was to admit it, Bahr found merit in the idea. They'd be able to better defend themselves against the battering storm on land. The risk of sinking would be gone. Lightning struck the prow of the barge. Wood and metal exploded. Bahr ducked as a large sliver of wood slammed into the front of the wheelhouse. Time was running out. He quickly decided, trusting it was the right one.

"I'm putting this thing to shore. Go below and get everyone ready to move."

Anienam released his death grip on the chair and staggered towards the door. "What of the wagon and supplies?"

"Get as much as we can and hope to salvage the rest. Move quickly or there'll be nothing left," Bahr said. *Including us.*

The wizard left Bahr alone. Not that there was much he could in the wheelhouse to begin with. Bahr was content with taking sole responsibility of the barge and their lives. It was fitting for a sea captain. Besides, the wizard proclaimed he couldn't counter the magic being used against them, making him rather mundane. This was a task Bahr needed total concentration for. He needed to be alone. He looked up just in time to see a massive oak tree slicing towards the barge like a massive spear and followed closely by a wall water. He barely had time to curse before they both hit.

Maleela groaned. She tried to move, to pull herself out from under the wreckage, but the pain was much too sharp. She fell back into the water and screwed her eyes shut. Unsure of what had happened, the princess no longer heard the horrific pounding in her head or felt the undulations tearing the barge apart. She wasn't moving and that was a good thing. The pain in her leg convinced her at least one bone was broken, perhaps more. A quick glance showed the water line barely went halfway up her prone figure. Random rays of sunlight poked down through the thinning cloud cover, lending the world a surreal effect.

"Is anyone there?" she called weakly. "Help."

A crow cawed from the unseen distance. She hadn't felt so alone since the night her uncle and his cohorts conspired to steal her away from Aurec and Rogscroft. Many hollow nights followed that point but none as hollow as lying in the wreckage of the barge, praying she wasn't the only survivor.

"Princess? Is that you?"

She felt hope. "Who is that?"

"It's Nothol Coll. Where are you?" he called back.

She looked around but nothing looked familiar. The barge was almost unrecognizable and there was a substantial amount of leaves floating around and more than a few branches. They had to be on land. "I'm not sure but it looks like I'm still inside the passenger cabin."

Silence followed. A long silence she felt was never going to end before Nothol answered, "Don't move. I think I can find you. The barge is pretty much a wreck. We're lucky to be alive."

"Don't worry, I'm not going anywhere. I think my leg might be broken," she said.

"Just hang on. I'll be there in a minute."

The confidence in his voice reassured her enough that her latent fears subsided. The prospect of being the lone survivor ended abruptly. She wasn't alone, though who knew how many of the others managed to make it to shore. Try as she could, Maleela remembered nothing of the impact or crash. Violent images of the storm assailed her thoughts.

"Maleela?" Nothol called again not much later.

She heard him rustling around not too far away. "Here! I'm half in the water by a stack of burlap sacks."

The overpowering stench of rotting fish tickled her nose, bringing her to the point of vomiting. Despite all the hardships endured over the last half of a year, she still wasn't accustomed to being around such rank living conditions. Royalty seldom was. A half-crushed box slide aside, revealing Nothol's haggard face. Covered with grime and dried blood, he still managed to smile sheepishly.

"I'll have you out just as soon as I can move some of this debris around. We took a nasty hit just before the crash," he explained. "That tree hit like one of those Dwarven cannons. Anienam said it was powerful magic that did it."

"I didn't think there were any other magic users in this part of Malweir," she remarked idly, not having anything else to do. The conversation eased her troubled mind. "Does he know who did this?"

"He's keeping it to himself if he does," Nothol answered. "Between you and me, I don't rightly trust him much. He keeps too many secrets."

"I agree, though no doubt many of them are for our own protection. He is the last descendant of the Mages. That can't be an easy burden to bear."

Nothol grunted. His cheeks puffed out and flushed crimson as he forced an enormous stack of crates out of the way. "Not my place to say. Bahr hired me to watch his back and that's just what I aim to do until this queer little quest is finished."

He squeezed into the narrow gap and knelt in front of her.

"Do you think it will ever be over?" she asked. Her voice was suddenly leaden, weary.

He paused. The question took him off guard. "I never gave it any thought. There's no point in worrying about things we can't control. Thinking about death gets us nowhere. All I need to do is pay attention to here, now. I figure the rest will take care of itself."

"You're pragmatic, Nothol Coll. I'm glad you're on our side," she said, and meant it. Too many nefarious individuals hampered life. Men like Nothol and Dorl Theed were rare. They weren't heroes or villains, but something in between. They often rose to the top during times of extreme duress. Maleela only felt safer in Aurec's arms. Briefly her thoughts strayed to her lost love. She had no idea if he even lived. Given the abuses distributed by her father to the people of Rogscroft, Maleela imagined the entire royal family was either imprisoned or dead. Badron would settle for nothing less. Enraged, she blinked away tears of frustration. She vowed to make her father pay for all the damage he had caused.

"Are you all right?" Nothol asked, suddenly worried. The look on her face was one he had never seen. Until now he didn't think she had the capacity for hatred.

Blinking rapidly to clear the tears, she offered a false smile. "Yes. Can you check my right leg? It hurts whenever I try to move it."

Nothol paused, unsure if her answer was genuine, before sticking his hands down into the brackish water. He fumbled blindly for there was too much flotsam to see beneath the surface. His fingers found her thigh and followed the bone downward. After a few seconds he looked up. "I don't feel any breaks but there is a nasty stick pinning you to the barge. I'm going to have to break it to free you."

"Do whatever you need to," was all she said.

He nodded and plunged both hands back in the water. Fresh jolts of pain lanced up her leg as he grabbed hold and started applying pressure. She felt the jagged edge puncture her skin and stifled back a cry. Maleela wanted, needed, to remain strong in front of the others. She was the rightful heir to the throne of Delranan and a noble born lady. Pain was for lesser people. The branch snapped with a loud crack and Nothol pulled the pieces free. She peered at it, shuddering at seeing the nearly three-inch-thick circumference. She could have easily lost a leg.

Nothol reached down and helped her up. "Lean on me, Maleela. Don't use the leg to support any weight for a while. Once we get to shore I'll clean the wound and dress it to prevent any infections. We're at the edge of the jungle. Who knows what sort of diseases and the like they have down here. Not even Rekka is sure of them all."

"Rekka still lives?" Maleela asked.

He nodded. "Yes. You were the last to be found. With the size of the debris field no one thought to look in the barge."

They slowly made their way out of the wreckage and waded through the knee-deep water to get to the shore. Maleela was greatly relieved to see a large fire burning and the horses, most of them, tethered to nearby trees. Stacks of supplies that had been salvaged before water could damage them irreparably stood high off to the side. She frowned at the loss of the wagon and most supplies. What little she knew of the jungle frightened her. She didn't see how they were going to survive long enough to reach Trennaron. Her gaze fell on broken Ionascu, and her stomach tightened. Oh, she wished the wicked little man had drowned. As if sensing her disdain, Ionascu sneered back. Secretly she wondered if Skuld had run to report her conversation with Ionascu. She hoped he hadn't, dealing with the broken man would be her deepest pleasure.

Bahr stormed over to her and took her in a great bear hug. "I thought you were lost!"

Despite the seriousness of their situation she couldn't help but giggle, for the act reminded her of times when she'd been a little girl. "Uncle, put me down! I'm all right."

He laughed and wept tears of joy for the first time in years. "I don't know what I'd do without you, Maleela. You are my only blood relative now."

"You should know it takes more than a little storm to kill one of us," she replied, though the dark implications of his words bothered her. She grew up knowing of the deep animosity between brothers but never imagined it would result with Bahr abandoning all bonds of blood and kin. *Father, what have you done?*

Bahr reluctantly set her down. "Let us hope so. Come, let's get you into some dry clothes and warmed up. The jungle is no place to walk around wet."

"We are truly here? The Jungles of Brodein?" she asked with wonder. After so many weeks and months of trials and constant hardship she didn't dare to dream they were so close to their destination.

"We are only on the fringes. The jungle is very big and very dangerous. We will need to be on our wits until I can guide us to Teng," Rekka said from near the fire.

Bahr looked up. "Teng? I thought we were going to Trennaron?"

"We will never make it as is. Perhaps if the storm hadn't wrecked us, but it is still very far. Much of our necessary supplies were lost to the water."

Maleela's heart sank right along with the barge. She didn't expect any of this to be easy, but after the intensity of their ordeals she figured they were due for a break. Any modicum of hope wasn't much to ask for. Instead the world continued to conspire against them. She doubted any of them were going to reach the mythical temple.

As if sensing her discomfort, Rekka offered a small smile. "Take heart, Princess. All is not lost. There are many hardships yet ahead, but we have strength I have seldom encountered. We will find our way through the dark. My people will help us when we arrive."

"She's right," Anienam added from beside the fire. The old wizard looked like a drowned dog, again forcing Maleela to wonder just how long ago they'd wrecked. "It's best to recover our strength here before pushing ahead. We should spend the night. Even with my magic and Rekka's expertise, the jungle is too dangerous to travel in the dark."

Bahr agreed. "I'll establish the guard roster. In the meantime I want this camp tidied up and made into a defensible position before nightfall. Whatever sent that storm after us is still out there. I don't want to run into it off guard. Let's get some food going. I don't know about the rest of you, but I'm starving."

They settled about their normal chores and prepared for an uneasy first night in the Jungles of Brodein. Bahr prayed they lasted the night.

Cold winds bit harshly across the snow-covered fields. Their haunting echo screamed down from the mountains reminding Amar Kit'han of troubling times. Once, when he'd been mortal, he became trapped in a massive snowstorm. Buried, he lay trapped for three days before managing to dig his way free. That first taste of frigid air burned his lungs. Centuries later it was a feeling he never forgot.

His ice-colored eyes stared at the others. "The storm proved only moderately successful. Our enemies have been run aground but are still a threat."

"It was your plan, Amar," Kodan Bak hissed from beneath his hood. "We should have sent more convincing measures."

"Gnaals are dangerous beasts. You know this. They kill indiscriminately."

"They were created by dark magic during the Mage War," Kodan insisted. "Their sole purpose is to serve our cause."

"They were created by Men, not the dark gods and certainly not by us," Amar reminded harshly. "We have no dominion over such creatures."

"I thought we served the dark gods," Kodan Bak attacked.

Pelthit Re glided back, careful to remain neutral in the event they came to blows. Ideations of stealing power entertained him for the time being.

Amar bristled with raw energy. "You dare question me?"

"Only your sense of purpose. Perhaps these mortals have eluded you for so long you no longer know how best to neutralize them?"

Rather than lashing out rashly, Amar folded his arms across his chest and decided to hear his subordinate out. The time was fast approaching when he would be able to remove the troublesome Bak without much effort, but not yet. Not until the dark gods returned to claim dominance over all life on Malweir. Surely they wouldn't begrudge him one minor act of retribution for all his years of dedicated service. "Explain yourself."

Kodan, thinking he had finally gained the upper hand, answered, "Gnaals are beings of pure dark magic. The Mages are gone, we helped see to that, but their creations still haunt Malweir. They answer to dark magic."

"Giving us control over them," Amar finished. The idea had merit and he was disappointed he hadn't thought of it himself. "This idea warrants attention. Find them, Kodan Bak. Enslave them to our purpose and send them after the princess and her fool wizard. I want that group dead long before they reach the jungle temple. Artiss Gran will not have his chance to execute his revenge."

"What of the Hags?" Pelthit Re asked. Ever the one to exercise caution, the lesser Dae'shan focused solely on his subjugation of Delranan and Harnin One Eye.

"Useless creatures," Kodan hissed sharply.

Amar held up a staying hand. "The Harpies still serve a purpose. Have them brought to me. I have a specific task they need to accomplish before their servitude ends."

"They have failed more times than not and only two remain," Kodan reminded them.

Harpies had been hunted to near extinction and what remained were sorry representations of what they had once been. Three had been contracted to harry and harass Bahr upon leaving Chadra. Instead of performing adequately, the Hags grew careless and made their play much too soon, or too late depending on the point of view. One of them had been mortally wounded, leaving the two survivors sulking in their mountain haunts. Kodan regarded them as useless in every aspect and couldn't figure out why Amar continued to keep them on a leash.

"Their assault on the wizard was unfortunate, but that doesn't negate their uses. Instruct the Gnaals to kill all but the princess."

"You mean to capture her again?" Kodan asked, the surprise in his voice was too evident for his liking and told Amar just how eager he was to forge a new destiny for the Dae'shan.

Amar fixed him with a deadly glare but said nothing. Let the fool stew in his anticipation.

TEN

Hunted

The night grew much darker than any they'd ever experienced in the north. Hundreds, thousands of insects chirped or hummed. Large predators with luminescent eyes watched them from the safety of the jungle. Occasional loud crashes sounded, making those few still awake cringe. All but Rekka and Anienam found the jungle alien. Even Boen, whose travels had taken him around the world and into almost every imaginable environment, felt displaced. His grip never left the hilt of his sword.

As soon as he dragged himself up out of the wreckage of the barge he gathered his weapons and patrolled the surrounding area. This was no place to leave anything to chance. Veteran of a hundred campaigns, the Gaimosian was finally back in his element. The freedom of moving alone and at speed thrilled him. He crept past fallen trees and blended with bushes. He froze when strange sounds reached his ears. His eyes, once dulled, were now sharp, watching everything with great interest. He was the warrior again.

Unbridled, Boen circled wide around the wreckage. He found one of the horses lying twisted with a large tree jutting from the ribcage. Grimacing at the horrible death suffered, Boen gave the mare a final pat on the neck before moving on. He fully expected to run into another party of river men anxious for revenge. Scum like that were little better than herd animals. He harbored no qualms about slaughtering them. Just like they deserved.

His turn at guard duty came and went but he couldn't find sleep. His nerves were wound too tightly. Boen snorted. He was always wound too tight. Men in his profession often were. Only the strongest became fully acknowledged Gaimosian warriors. Each was promised a lifetime of wandering, trying to find their niche in life. They held no titles other than Vengeance Knights. No homes. No lands to call their own. They were the children of the world and executed their special brand of justice on those found wanting. Boen discovered early on that he thoroughly enjoyed his life's calling. For him there could be no other way.

The call of a jungle cat followed closely by a strangled cry and silence forced his eyes open. Boen stared skyward, enjoying the stars one final time before they entered the thick, double canopy of the jungle. Heavy rustling drew his attention without raising his guard. Whatever had killed the animal was finished and unconcerned with this large of a group. Kill or be killed. It was the law of life. Boen gradually closed his eyes and let sleep claim him.

Dawn broke with unusual splendor. The dark clouds were gone, replaced by crystalline blue skies and only the faintest wisps of clouds. Boen yawned and stretched. His muscles were sore from sleeping on the hard ground again after so long. His neck felt pinched and his eyes were red, sore. He'd never felt more alive. Decades of life in the field trained him to endure moments like this. Fatigue often set in on the less experienced, the younger. He was beyond that. The soreness would pass and he'd be back to his normal self soon enough. All he needed was a few moments of solitude. Hungry, he decided to take his sword and run through a series of warm-up exercises and drills. There was only shame in being caught unprepared.

Dorl propped up on his elbows and watched Boen whirl through his drills. He'd never seen the like. The Gaimosian moved with such precision it hardly seemed real. Dorl thanked whatever god was listening that he didn't run afoul of any Gaimosians.

"He has much experience. You should know this already," Rekka chided from beneath the blanket next to him.

Dorl couldn't help but grin. They'd lain together long into the night, enjoying the feel of each other's arms.

They kissed for a while before sheer exhaustion set in. He enjoyed the intimacy they shared while secretly wondering if it was going to last when things went sour. Rekka was a capable warrior with more skills than he could ever hope to possess. That left him a liability. He couldn't decide whether she'd cut and run or stand by him to the bitter end.

"I've never seen him actually practice. I thought Gaimosians were born with the killer gene," he admitted.

"Perhaps they are but every weapon needs to be honed before it can be put to use. They are a proud people, from what little I know. He is a good man."

From what he gathered, Dorl seemed surrounded by good Men. That and a handful of good intentions wouldn't buy him a pint in the local tavern. "These aren't times for good men, Rekka. Malweir needs rough men who are ready to visit violence on others."

"That is a dour outlook," she replied. "It would serve you better to abandon it before we get too far into the jungle."

The jungle. He felt unrealized fear at the very thought. "What lies within?"

"Many things," she answered too quickly for his liking. "There is great beauty as well as mystery. Death and life are boon companions. It is the most dangerous environment I have ever been in."

"That doesn't help my confidence," he said flatly.

Rekka's hazel eyes shined in the morning sun. "Nor should it. The jungle can kill in a thousand different ways. Caution alone will not be enough to ensure our safe passage. Take heart though, my love, all is not bad. I grew up here. I can keep us alive long enough to accomplish our task."

Dorl wasn't entirely sure but had no other option but to trust in her abilities. She was their only link to the inside world of the jungle. He sighed and started to get up. "I hope this Hamr is worth it. I have a feeling we're about to have plenty more dumped on us before the end."

Rekka cocked her head, failing to understand what he meant by dumped. "Our enemies will not tire, Dorl.

Neither can we. This task goes well beyond your personal needs or mine. All Malweir stands in the balance. If we fail, the world will plunge into eternal darkness."

"You really believe that?" he asked.

"Yes. The guardian of Trennaron is very wise, ancient. He knows the dark times approaching have been heralded for centuries. As does Anienam, they are akin to each other."

The idea that another venerable magic user locked in his ivory tower for countless centuries contemplated the end of the world didn't sit well with him. Having Anienam around was maddening enough, he didn't relish the thought of being around two such beings. *No wonder the world banded together to end the Mage orders. They can't be trusted.*

"Everybody up and pack! We need to get moving before the sun gets too high," Bahr called from beside the stack of supplies. He and Nothol were already loading what they could on the horses. Some Groge put in his pack and hefted to his shoulders. The Giant had near infinite capacity to carry the heavy load.

Weary from a waterlogged night, the tiny band forged ahead into the jungle.

They kept moving until dusk, stopping only at Rekka's insistence. Going through the motions of a, by now, well-rehearsed exercise, they established camp and began the guard roster. The sun set without fanfare as the darkness swallowed the jungle. Insects and worse emerged from their daytime hiding spots. The jungle took on a completely different feel. It was claustrophobic, haunted.

Bahr didn't mind so much. He'd never been this far south but wasn't letting that stop him from enjoying this new world. Ever the explorer, Bahr studied the trees, insects, and what rare animals he found lurking through the thousand shades of green. Now older than he liked to admit, the dispossessed sea captain stifled a yawn. He seldom took later watches, knowing he was already past the point of exhaustion. Aside from Boen, he was the oldest of the group. Anienam didn't count, since no one rightly knew how old the wizard was and they didn't trust him to pull guard duty correctly anyway. *Let the young ones pull the middle shifts. I'm getting too old for games.* He smiled despite being beaten down and in need of a long vacation.

Bahr stiffened suddenly. His skin crawled with intense feelings of evil. Cold sweat poured from his flesh. He couldn't shake the feeling of being watched. A hand slid to his sword, subconsciously knowing it wouldn't be enough even if he managed to draw it in time. Almost frozen from fear, Bahr desperately scanned the area for signs of his assailant. Darkness leered back at him. The jungle was the darkest he'd ever seen, making it next to impossible to see more than a few meters into the murk. He was blind. Frightened.

Heavy footsteps announced the approach of a massive predator. The ground trembled with each fall. Leaves fell from branches. Stones cracked and shattered. Bats and nocturnal birds erupted from the treetops in waves. The cold feeling of dread continued to rise, as if the very world had grown diseased. Bahr felt bile rise in his throat. A pair of crimson eyes opened, staring directly into his soul. He cringed. Unable to look away or blink, the Sea Wolf watched as death stalked closer.

The flash of light blinded him. He roared in pain.

"Be gone from here!"

He didn't know who shouted or why. The dread slowly bled away. He could move again. Bahr drew his sword and staggered to his feet. Ragged spots peppered his vision, causing him to stumble and fall to his knees. Bracing himself, Bahr emptied his stomach onto the lush green undergrowth.

"Bahr, are you injured?"

He tried to look up only to discover he still couldn't see. "I'm blind."

"That is just a side effect of the magic. Your sight will return shortly."

"Anienam?"

"Yes. It's me. You're out of danger now," the wizard replied soothingly.

After suffering through a series of dry heaves, Bahr managed to ask, "What was that?"

"An evil from old times. It was a creation of the dark Mages and their lust for depredation. A Gnaal."

"Gnaal?"

"A demon of immense power," Anienam explained. "It has a singular purpose once loosed upon the target. I'm afraid we are being hunted."

Bahr's strength gave out and he slumped down. "Will it return tonight? I need to rouse the others. We can't…"

"Rest, Captain. I will see to the others. The Gnaal wasn't expecting to find a wizard so I doubt it will be back soon. There will be time in the morning to formulate a proper action. Now rest, I have work to do."

Bahr swooned as darkness claimed him.

"How do you keep from getting bit?" Nothol asked and frowned at the proud Dwarf captain pushing his way through the thick underbrush like a bull.

Ironfoot chuckled under his breath. "You clearly don't know much about Dwarves, lad. We've got so much iron in our blood these bugs would die upon biting us! If they could even pierce my skin. Tough as animal hide, it is!"

Jagged patches of sunlight managed to penetrate the increasingly thickening canopy at random, offering light in an otherwise gloomy atmosphere. Humidity levels rose with the sun until many of their group found it unbearable. The undergrowth grew so thick Bahr was forced to have them dismount and go on foot, furthering their misery. The deadly combination of blood-sucking insects and oppressive heat sparked thoughts of turning around less than a day into their journey.

No one spoke of Bahr's encounter with the Gnaal. Anienam worked quickly to establish more powerful wards afterwards and briefed them all at dawn. There wasn't anything for it, however, and the band was forced to push ahead. The Gnaal would be back once the sun relinquished its hold on the world. They would meet it then and could only push it to the back of their minds in the meantime. Brute strength wasn't of any use against the dark creature, leaving Anienam their one sole hope of defeating it.

Nothol slapped at his neck, again, pulling his hand away along with the blood-smeared remains of a dark black mosquito with white bands. He frowned. Rekka was normally taciturn when it came to speaking to the group but she had no qualms discussing the seemingly unending multitudes of diseases and illnesses caused by the bugs of her homeland. Nothol was certain he was going to contract one or more before they reached Trennaron. Sadly, they wouldn't have time to construct a proper funeral. He'd never be cremated, thus trapping his soul in the soft ground for eternity as bugs and creatures devoured his remains. The prospect didn't sit well.

"Rekka, isn't there something you can do about this? You're not getting bothered at all," Nothol begged. His skin had dozens of irritated spots filled with poison from insect bites.

The salve she'd made earlier was nearly gone and they would need to stop and forage through the jungle to find the proper ingredients. Time they didn't have. She looked at Dorl's best friend and slowly shook her head though it hurt her to do so. She and Dorl helped the others with what supplies she had while they lasted but they were dwindling fast. She briefly contemplated using the last of it now but that would only leave them sorely in need later, when they truly needed it. Teng was still days away, perhaps longer given the length of their column.

"I am sorry, Nothol Coll, but you know I cannot use the last of it without the ability to make more," she replied.

He frowned despite already knowing the answer. He just wished it were different. "Rekka, I don't like your jungle."

"I am sure the jungle feels the same about us," she said glibly. "We are invaders. The jungle will not adapt to us so we must learn to adapt to its ways. Too many outsiders come here without learning that lesson. You will see their skeletons along our path. Brodein is very dangerous and unforgiving."

Nothol reserved his opinion, not wanting to insult the swordswoman. He vowed to take his pound of flesh from Dorl once they were safely en route back to Delranan, provided they made it that far. A feat he was beginning to have serious doubts on. He pulled his sweat-soaked jerkin away and fanned it several times. Warm air was better than no air, though he doubted how much longer his body was going to be able to withstand such abuse. He could feel pounds dropping away with every bead of sweat. Making matters worse, Ironfoot trudged on without so much as batting at a fly. Nothol decided he didn't like the Dwarf either.

They reached a small stream and took a break. The pace was moderate, often slow due to unforeseen circumstances or natural barriers. Bahr saw no need to push them any further than necessary. Arriving at Teng missing members or wasted away did them little good. He needed everyone and their individual skills. Anienam's dire warning that their task was going to be much harder than anything they'd experienced thus far left him with an uneasy feeling rumbling around the pit of his stomach.

Ionascu dropped to his knees at the water's edge and plunged his face into the running water. He came up laughing madly and scooping handfuls of the cool liquid into his mouth.

"Don't drink the water," Rekka warned. "It is not purified. You will only get sick."

"Mind your business, jungle woman. I don't take orders from the likes of you," he spat back and continued to drink.

Bahr abandoned the idea of forcibly stopping him. Ionascu was of little consequence and, truthfully, more trouble than he was worth. Letting Ionascu get sick would be the least of his concerns. Bahr recognized that losing Ionascu to the jungle wouldn't be a bad thing, given his duplicitous nature and admitted affiliations with Harnin One Eye, but Anienam insisted the twisted man still had some part left to play in this great adventure. A quick sword thrust would negate any of that. It was all the sea captain could do to restrain himself.

He caught the look in Rekka's eyes and moved to stop her before she stole his glory. "Leave him be, Rekka. He is a bitter shell of what he was, too hardheaded to realize when someone is trying to look out for him. Let him get sick from the water. That's one less problem I need to worry about. The jungle can have his corpse."

She pursed her lips but remained silent. There was truth in Bahr's words. She'd seen it countless times before. Very few respected Brodein enough to survive it. Instead, she abandoned her anger and said, "The horses may drink, for their bodies work differently than ours. Anyone who drinks from the streams or lakes will grow sick and perhaps perish before we reach Teng."

"Dumbass," Boen grumbled at Ionascu and knocked him into the stream so that his horse could drink.

Laughter spread through the group at Ionascu's sputtering as he climbed back to shore. Smaller than Boen by nearly half, Ionascu knew better than to buck up in the Gaimosian's face. His eyes narrowed to dangerous slits as he plotted his revenge. He knew, or hoped, there'd come a time when Boen's guard was down. Even the smallest blade could kill.

Bahr grinned for no other reason than to release some tension but his thoughts never strayed far from the encounter with the Gnaal and that fact that they were being hunted by a creature more powerful than anything they'd come up against yet. The future grew dimmer.

ELEVEN

Choices

"Regardless of your feelings, we are left with the very real problem of being overwhelmed without achieving anywhere near our goals," Orlek said defiantly.

Ingrid's eyes flared with burning anger. "What you propose is abandoning this city! I can't leave all these people to Harnin's subjugation."

"I am proposing that we salvage what we can and attack on our terms, not his. Think about it, Ingrid. The plague killed almost a quarter of the population. Much of the fight has gone out of the survivors. Delranan is a shell of its former self."

Ingrid folded her slender arms across her chest defiantly. "We can change that, Orlek. You and I are the beginning of a new rebellion capable of erasing Harnin's stain from the history keepers. All I am asking for is a little time to implement my designs."

"To what ends? How many more need to die before we realize that we're not ready to fight this war?"

She paused, taken off guard by his comment. Death had become a constant companion for many of Delranan's people. "How many deaths would you reduce to meaningless sacrifice? I don't like the idea that a single person in the rebellion died in vain."

"Our choices are running out," Orlek said. He clenched his fists in frustration and began to circle the small room.

They'd taken Argis' body to an abandoned inn in what had been the center of downtown Chadra. Few people bothered to wander the burned-out husks after the plague hit. Not even Harnin's soldiers ventured to this ruined part of town, giving the pair near complete privacy. Ingrid positioned several squads of rebels in the surrounding buildings on the off chance Harnin did something. Stealing Argis was vital to her cause and Harnin knew it. He'd stop at nothing to reclaim the corpse and end the resurgent tide of rebellion.

Ingrid sat down, enjoying the feeling. Her legs were tired. Her body sore. She'd been going hard for the last week, ever since the raid to recover the body. More than once Jarrik and his goons swept through Chadra with less than maximum effort. Their zealous behavior combined with lackluster performance while on patrol led her to believe there was a rift between the remaining lords of Delranan. That meant opportunity and Orlek was standing in her way.

She hadn't come up through the rebellion ranks to usurp control from Inaella expecting to be stymied at every decision. The plague was damaging beyond measure, to both sides. Harnin was trapped in a corner. His hold on the kingdom tenuous at best. All it would take was the slightest breeze to change the fate of Delranan. She needed Orlek to see that. Or he'd need to be replaced as well. Winning a war was often as simple as having the right people in the right position. She wasn't afraid to make desperate changes when the situation called for it.

"Orlek, we need to strike now, while Harnin is still on his heels. You've seen how pitifully the patrols go about their work when they actually come down from the Keep," she insisted. "We can break them; perhaps even steal some away in the process. These aren't the regular Wolfsreik. They are part-time soldiers at best. We can win, Orlek, but we need to move quickly to secure our gains. I hate to think all I did was for nothing."

"No one would ever accuse you of such, but your idea is mad. I don't care if all he has is the reserves, they are still trained, professional soldiers. What fighters we have cannot win a stand-up fight. We'll be destroyed. Why can't you see that? The old council tried to fight head to head and was beaten every time. Only when Argis introduced his hit-and-run raids and ambushes were we moderately successful."

"The plague greatly reduced..."

Orlek shook his head. "The plague didn't do half as much damage to them as it did to us. Harnin locked his gates the moment he got word of infection. He sent most of his army off into the countryside before they could get infected, Ingrid. His losses are minimal. We need to regroup, draw his army out into the open and break them up into small units. It's the only way."

"What makes you so certain the population will fight with us? They have little reason to get involved with the rebellion that has largely been confined to Chadra. Peasants often tend to ignore the goings-on of city life."

She remembered being stationed in various villages and hamlets during her husband's career. While the villagers respected the presence of the Wolfsreik, they seldom showed appreciation for the drain on their economy the army produced. That atmosphere was burned into her mind, leaving her with grave misgivings as to their willingness to participate in a seemingly pointless struggle for power. Without them, taking the rebellion into the countryside was a pointless endeavor.

"The people have no will to fight," she added quickly before he could formulate more opposition. "They are content with their cows or crops. Our problems here simply don't concern them any more than Badron's war in Rogscroft."

"They also have no reason to support Harnin's madness. Many families have dealings with Chadra. Surely many more have lost loved ones. Word of the rebellion has spread to every corner of the kingdom by now. We will have the support we need to tear Harnin's army apart and expose him for the tyrant he is."

She knew nothing of Orlek's past though it didn't concern her. He had proven himself capable in the field and devoted to the cause. Her cause. Not Inaella's or the rest of the council. Men like that were important to the future. Ingrid recalled her last conversation with Inaella and how she vowed to burn Chadra to the ground. Recovering Argis' body changed her mind, if only slightly. There was still hope to be found within the burned-out homes and hovels. She just needed to find a way to inspire it.

"I can't move without more information. If we pick up and leave now we'll be exposed, ripe for the Wolfsreik to sweep in and destroy us without much effort," she said with finality. Her mind was made up, as was his. They were at odds.

Hurried footsteps quieted them. Ingrid drew her thin rapier while Orlek picked up his war bar. Close quarter combat was no place for a sword. He much preferred the weight of steel in his hands to crush a skull. Cold winds infiltrated the cracks in the walls, driving chill into the former bedroom. Small piles of snow drifted in the corners. The footsteps grew heavier. Aged boards creaked under the sudden weight. Incessant knocking pounded on the door.

"Ingrid! We need to leave now. Harnin's soldiers are coming straight for us!"

Responding to the urgency in the voice, Ingrid sheathed her sword and flung open the door to find a pair of her most trusted guards breathing heavily in the hallway. Their eyes were wild with fright. Both were breathing hard and had drawn swords.

"How did they find us?" she seethed. That there would be a traitor in her ranks infuriated her to great ends despite the acceptance that it was inevitable. People changed sides all the time when they thought they stood to benefit from it. Especially during the middle of winter when half of the city had burned to the ground and the other half was starving in the snow. She couldn't fault them for it but vowed to make the perpetrator suffer greatly before dying.

The taller guard shook his head. "We don't know. One of Malk's boys spotted an armored patrol marching down the main avenue. Jarrik leads them. They seem to know exactly where we are."

"We've been betrayed," Orlek offered needlessly.

Ingrid ignored him. "Have Lord Argis' body moved immediately. Take it to the safe house on the eastern edge of Chadra. We will meet you there shortly."

"Yes, Ingrid," the taller man said and bounded back down the hall without waiting for further instructions. The second guard remained to offer protection during their retreat.

Ingrid collected her bearskin cloak from the back of a chair and draped it around her slender shoulders. "How many are there?"

"Close to one hundred. There is no way we can fight them," the guard replied.

She cursed silently. A handful would be manageable and they could use the Wolfsreik weapons. Unfortunately the guard was correct; she couldn't tackle a full company with only a handful of under equipped, under prepared rebels. The risk was tantamount to suicide. "Have everyone scatter to their fallback positions. I don't want anyone getting involved unnecessarily. We'll have need of all our fighters before this runs its course."

The guard, reluctant to abandon the leader of the rebellion, nodded and hurried off. There was much to do if the rebellion was to survive.

The hooded figure entirely concealed at Jarrik's side moved with invigorated steps. This was a moment long awaited and only blood could satisfy the debt. Inaella strode through the remains of Chadra with shoulders level, back straight. A shadow of her former self, the plague all but ravaged her physically. She was weak. Most of her hair had fallen out and her eyes had bled so dry she couldn't stand to be in direct sunlight. Pocks marred her once flawless face, leaving her deformed. Instead of burrowing in and trying to find a place to hide from her pains, Inaella used the pain to build her confidence.

Going to see Harnin One Eye of her own volition was the first step in what she hoped to be the beginning of a new direction. The rebellion was fundamentally flawed to the point where she allowed it to decay. Argis' death served to further the degradation, but it was her own personal weakness, now excised from the plague, which led to the downfall and eventual usurping by Ingrid. Every time she closed her eyes she saw Ingrid's youthful face. Every time she closed her eyes she felt nothing but abject hatred for a woman that might have been a friend.

Naturally Harnin wanted to have her strung up and torn apart on the torture racks but she managed to persuade him otherwise. She offered gifts none of his commanders could. She gave him what remained of the rebellion. The plague stole many things from Inaella, but nothing so severe as the crimes Ingrid committed. For that she would dedicate the rest of her life to ensuring the blond suffered ignobly. Harnin, all too eager to end the rebellion and focus his efforts on preparing Delranan for Badron's return, accepted.

He added her to his council, reluctantly, and after much debate from his lords. She gave the one-eyed madman new life; hope he hadn't experienced in months. His only condition was in having Inaella prove her loyalty. She dispatched him with Jarrik and a full company of Wolfsreik with the task of rooting out the rebellion from the middle of Chadra. Failure constituted near immediate execution. She didn't let that bother her. Lord Death had already tried to claim her and failed. She still had purpose in this world. The fires of revenge clashed with hatred, keeping her warm on those cold winter nights.

"Surround the building! No one gets out," Jarrik bellowed and his soldiers deployed with the heightened precision the people of Delranan expected from the Wolfsreik. He turned to the hooded Inaella, "You had better be right about this."

"Our enemies are within," she replied confidently.

"If not, you die."

The wild look in his eyes left no room for doubt. Jarrik intended on killing her for the most minor reason. All he needed was the catalyst. Soldiers rushed past, torches in their hands. There were no calls for surrender. No urgency to have whoever occupied the ruined inn to escape while they could. No. Death was the only viable option for such dangerous enemies of the state.

Inaella watched the Wolfsreik with guarded interest. She bore no love for the army loyal to Harnin. They were as responsible for plunging her life into ruin as Ingrid's betrayal. Best case scenario involved both sides obliterating each other, leaving Delranan wide open for her to assume the mantle of leadership. Inaella harbored illusions of grandeur. She no longer viewed herself as a minor aristocrat struggling through daily life. The future of the kingdom was wide open. Why not a woman on the throne?

"We will all die, Lord Jarrik, I merely seek to have my enemies die before me," she replied tartly.

Something in her tone unsettled him for reasons he couldn't explain. She was a dangerous woman. Killing her now would isolate whatever nefarious plot she had and bring up his worth in Harnin's opinion. Desperate to escape the pack, or rather what remained of it, Jarrik needed to come up with a way to inflate his importance. Killing the new head of the rebellion and the former head in the same stroke would ensure his proper place in history. Ever the one to think of tomorrow, Jarrik stood on the precipice of greatness.

Torches were thrown into windows. Flames sprouted, timid at first. Jarrik ordered his soldiers in. Two soldiers kicked the doors open and stepped aside to let a full squad charge in. Swords drawn, crossbows loaded, the Wolfsreik began clearing the inn. The looks in their eyes told Inaella all she needed to know. There would be no survivors from this raid.

Ingrid rounded the corner to the back alley and came face to face with a lone soldier. Startled, he stared wide-eyed at her. Orlek snarled and leapt, driving his blade down between the neck and shoulder until the tip pierced his heart. Dark red blood squirted across Orlek's tunic as he snatched the soldier and eased the dying body to the ground before he fell. He dragged the body into the shadows and hurried Ingrid away. The dying soldier's legs continued to twitch for a few minutes longer.

"We're not going to make it," Ingrid whispered.

Orlek didn't have time for foolishness. "Not with that attitude. Now keep your lips together and run. We can escape but you must do it my way."

She obeyed, wordlessly following the fighter through the skeletal remains of Chadra. A stray dog barked. Crows cawed over the corpse of a cat. Ingrid could only hear her heart pounding in her ears. She was frightened yet exhilarated. She'd never felt so alive as right now. Ducking from Harnin's thugs with the future of the kingdom at stake. The sounds of armored soldiers rushing down adjacent alleys pushed her faster.

Orlek grabbed her by the shoulder and jerked her into a small alcove. Pressed against each other, she felt the heat from his body. The urgency of his breath. Ingrid started to question but his finger placed on her lips kept her quiet. Her eyes swept back towards the alley in time to see a pair of Wolfsreik march by. They'd clearly been given precise orders and now rushed to get into position to block the rear exits. Ingrid exhaled slowly once they left her sight.

"This is only getting more dangerous," Orlek whispered in her ear. His breath was hot, intimate. "We are bound to run into others."

"Our escape is finished," she added breathlessly.

He shook his head defiantly. "Not until I take my last breath. We will find a way out of here, alive."

She doubted that but admired his intensity. The rebellion needed good fighters like Orlek if they were going to wrest their kingdom back. Ingrid inhaled his scent just before he leaned out into the alley. Piles of trash lined the walls. A few corpses, long frozen in various poses of anguish, looked up guiltily. The plague had struck with such fury many were caught unaware and left to perish in the cold. Ingrid found it hard to swallow, but such was the way of things. All she could do was hope to survive long enough to make a difference.

"Come on, it's clear," he said and dragged her back down the alley.

They made it only a handful of meters before a gravelly voice bellowed, "Halt!"

Orlek shoved her. "Run! Get to the rally point."

Drawing his sword, Orlek turned to face his attacker. Three Wolfsreik soldiers formed a line across the alley. Their swords were drawn. Winds funneled into the alley blew their hair wildly. The pelts draping their shoulders were raw. The soldiers were angry and wanted retribution for matters even they weren't sure of. Orlek dropped into a low guard and waited.

The Wolfsreik sergeant gestured with his head, "I want that woman taken alive. Lord Jarrik needs a prisoner. Kill this one."

"You can try," Orlek taunted.

Enraged, the Wolfsreik attacked, two abreast. Within the confines of the alley they wouldn't be able to maximize their capabilities, giving him the temporary advantage. Steel clashed. Snow tumbled down from the rooftops, cascading onto the dueling soldiers. Orlek blocked, parried, and lashed out when he found an opening. The soldiers, while reservists, fought with the intensity of a lion. He was hard pressed to keep up. Blocking a wild blow aimed at decapitating him, Orlek stepped back and tried to catch his breath. Sweat dripped down into his eyes, stinging him.

"Rebel scum," the Wolfsreik sergeant snarled. "You'll be food for the rats soon."

Orlek grinned savagely. "That doesn't matter. Even if you kill me you won't win this war. We are stronger than you could possibly imagine."

Snarling, the sergeant said, "Enough talk. Now you die."

They charged, crashing into each other like two bulls. Both swung and hacked, desperately searching for a way past the other's defenses to end the duel quickly. Ingrid was the real prize. The sergeant renewed his assault, stepping back only long enough to let his counterpart attack.

Orlek was sorely outmatched. His death seemed an inevitable conclusion to a poorly thought-out plan. Not that it mattered. He was expendable. A minor player in a much greater game. Until recently he hadn't even been recognized by anyone in the rebellion. Ingrid's takeover changed that, made him into someone of greater importance. It wasn't enough. He was going to fall in an abandoned alley and be forgotten by history. Such was the way of hard men trapped in desperate times. He raised his sword to block a pair of quick overhand strikes. The force nearly drove him to his knees.

No one saw who fired the arrow or from where. The feathered bolt took the sergeant in his exposed throat, killing him instantly. The remaining Wolfsreik turned to stare, an impossible mistake. A second bolt took him at the base of his skull and penetrated downward to come out in the middle of his throat. He fell with a gurgling sound. Orlek looked up in time to see a handful of haggard rebels racing out of the shadows to claim him. Today wasn't his day to die after all.

TWELVE

Revenge

League after league rolled by in an endless trail. The army wound like a mighty armored snake almost a mile long. The pungent odor of hundreds of horses and soldiers that hadn't bathed in weeks permeated the air. Snow melted underfoot, transforming from pristine white to melancholic brown and gray sludge. For the soldiers marching alongside the horses and war machines it was just another day in the life. They were routinely exposed to harsh weather conditions, miserable chow, and a decided lack of sleep. Add the constant threat of ambush or the trauma of seeing friends die horribly and many weren't right in the head. The soldiers of the combined army were tired of war. Tired of watching horrors unfold around them. Tired of not having a warm home to go back to at the end of the campaign. War is many things, forgiving not among them.

"We're making good time," Piper Joach commented after drinking from his canteen.

General Vajna, sitting on a slightly smaller roan mare, shielded his eyes against the glare of the sun reflecting off the fields of undisturbed snow stretching out before them. "Aye. We should be at the city before the end of the week."

"Provided there is no delay," Piper added. The young commander took his work seriously, regardless of which side he fought for. He didn't like the idea of turning mercenary in the middle of a war but was honor bound to follow Rolnir down whatever path the general thought necessary for the survival of the Wolfsreik. "Have you noticed how curiously empty this part of the kingdom is?"

Vajna dismissed the apprehensions. "We practically destroyed the Goblin army in that last battle. They can't have that many troops left. I don't foresee much issue with our current course of action."

"Goblins are notoriously foul creatures, Vajna. Don't underestimate them. Grugnak had tens of thousands of warriors under his command. That force is what finally broke the siege and conquered the city. You'd do well to recognize their ferocity in battle. I've seen them in action. They are a capable opponent. Retaking the city will not be easy."

Vajna bristled at the mention of the sack of his home but kept his thoughts private. Joining forces with the Wolfsreik, his enemy, was difficult enough to accept, knowing they were responsible for killing thousands of his countrymen. He often wondered why King Aurec sent him to make contact. At first Vajna considered it a great insult. How could his liege denigrate him before his sworn enemies so casually? The question stole many sleepless hours. He didn't trust Rolnir or the smooth-faced Piper. Their execution of the battle of Grunmarrow loosened his attitudes, slightly, and opened the path for him to think clearly.

He looked at the slender Wolfsreik commander riding beside him. Dark hair and a handful of scars complimented Piper's demeanor. He wore a haunted look, as if he'd seen too much. Vajna didn't particularly care what Piper had seen or done before now. A month ago the two had been fervently trying to kill each other. War was fickle at times. Vajna had stopped trying to figure it out long ago. Better to just strap in for the ride and see where it ended.

"You forget we have the advantage," he finally said.

Piper eyed him quizzically. "How so?"

"Many of the soldiers in our army are from the city. They know the streets and buildings. Once we gain the walls we should be able to sweep through and take it back with little effort," he said proudly.

Piper felt immediate sorrow. "Vajna, I'm not sure what you've been told but Rogscroft is not what you remember. Grugnak and Badron have all but destroyed the city with their madness. You will not be pleased when next you look upon her."

Vajna opened and closed his mouth quickly. The possibility that Rogscroft was thoroughly destroyed always lurked in the back of his mind but he was loath to admit it, or even think on it. War demanded his focus on the present. Each action consumed his thought process, driving all else to the haze. Now Piper had dispelled his illusions. All his fantasies of a triumphant return crashed like broken glass upon stone. He tried hard not to let hatred take control but the urge was almost too hard to resist.

"Cities can be rebuilt," he replied. "No matter what violations the Goblins have committed King Aurec will see them set right."

"I pray you are correct, my friend," Piper said slowly.

They rode on, drawing ever closer to the ruin that had become Rogscroft city. Halfway through the day a lone rider came charging back to the column. His eyes bore a wild look. Sweat covered his face and hands. His horse was breathing hard, speckled with frothing sweat. Piper's guard rose and he ordered the vanguard into defensive positions. If there was any major sized force coming at them he knew they'd never deploy in time to stop them.

"Commander! The scouts are under attack!" the rider explained hurriedly. "We were ambushed by Goblins."

Vajna resisted the urge to draw his sword and attack. Too many details were still missing for that course of action.

"Where?" was all Piper said. He'd been involved in too many skirmishes and battles to let raw emotion overcome strategic thinking.

The rider took a deep breath, trying to calm down. "Less than a league ahead. We are sorely outnumbered."

"General, deploy the vanguard. I want us in combat order and ready to fight upon arrival," Piper ordered the senior Rogscroft officer. "Trooper, lead us to the scene."

The thunder of hooves echoed across the plains with the fury of the gods.

Mahn fired his last arrow and slung his bow across his back so he could draw his sword. Already at exhaustion, the older scout realized the use of close-quarter weapons would likely result in his demise. Dozens of Goblins already lay dead or wounded across the battlefield, as well as several soldiers of the combined army. He cursed his lack of foresight for allowing them to walk into the now ridiculously obvious ambush. More lives were lost in a fruitless cause.

He looked across the engagement area and was relieved to find Raste still alive. The youth still had much of the fire from the beginning of the war but was more evenly tempered. His hatred of first the Wolfsreik and then the Goblins kept him going when lesser men were forced to take a knee. Raste had killed more than anyone else Mahn knew during the long winter war, but at a cost he refused to admit. Each new death stole just a little more from what he was. Raste raked his sword across a Goblin's chest and spun to find a new foe before the body hit the ground.

"Raste! We need to find a way to retreat until the main body gets here," he called over the din of combat.

The Goblins attacked in force the moment after Mahn's scouts entered the light forest. Scores of the dark, barrel-bodied warriors burst from the tree cover with weapons bared. Three scouts fell before anyone recognized the threat. Mahn organized a hasty defense and stopped the tide before it swept them under. It was paltry at best. He knew it wouldn't be long before they were completely obliterated by the Goblins. Unless help arrived.

Raste barely had time to push his matted hair from his face before the next Goblin charged into him. Man and Goblin crashed to the ground. Raste's sword skittered across the unbroken snow, leaving only his hands. He hammered blows into the Goblin's face. The nose broke. Blood spattered. The Goblin warrior fought but was on his back and at a considerable disadvantage. Raste brought his knee up into his enemy's ribs. The second blow broke a rib. The Goblin raged.

Managing to get his forearm on the Goblin's throat, Raste pushed down with all his might. Saliva frothed, bubbling on the Goblin's lips. His gnarled fingers desperately tried to push Raste away. His arms and legs jerked and kicked. He slapped Raste's thigh repeatedly, each blow losing strength.

Raste rolled off the dead Goblin and vomited. He was a scout, trained to watch and observe. Close-quarter combat was still new to him, even after months of guerilla fighting and his stand on the city walls. What he lacked in experience he made up for in zeal. Every Goblin killed was one closer to liberation. One closer to a renewed Rogscroft. That didn't prevent his stomach from rebelling on the snow.

Mahn rushed to his side, clearly distressed that his friend and partner through many misadventures was seriously injured. Relief washed over him upon seeing the bile coating Raste's chin. The joy, he feared, was to be short lived. A horn sounded off in the depths of the trees. Deep and ominous, it could only mean one thing. Enemy reinforcements were on the way.

"You should have kept your lunch, Raste," Mahn chided gloomily. "It seems we're about to go to our graves."

"We can still fight," the younger scout replied hotly.

Mahn shook his head. More than half of his force already lay dead or wounded. The end was inevitable. He slid down from the saddle, determined to meet his end like a soldier of Rogscroft.

Piper spied the carnage and felt his anger boil over. He was tired of seeing wanton death for reasons no one understood. The Goblins were a stain on Malweir. As far as he was concerned the only way to excise them was to eradicate the entire race. Seeing so many surrounding a handful of Men cemented Piper's reaction.

"Swords!" he bellowed to the vanguard.

The world sang with the crisp sound of steel being freed from scabbards.

Piper didn't bother looking to ensure all was ready. He brought his sword forward and pointed towards the Goblins. "Speed of horse!"

The cavalry charged. Horses snickered. Men roared the battle cries of two kingdoms. Snow kicked up in clumps. Three hundred light horses converged into a tight wedge, Piper at the point. First blood belonged to him. Goblins turned, surprised by the sudden arrival of enemy cavalry. The one hundred Goblins were no match for a massed cavalry charge and they knew it. A few managed to gather their wits to fire arrows at the approaching riders. The bolts landed harmlessly in the snow.

Piper's force crashed into the Goblins like avenging angels. The air grew hot with escaping body heat. Blood colored the snow in random patterns. The body count rose. Only a few Goblins turned to flee. They were hunted down before getting very far. What had begun as a successful ambush ended in dismal failure. The Goblin attack was finished.

"Commander Joach, it's good to see you," Mahn said with a wry grin. He carried a begrudging respect for the senior officer. They'd never be friends, but as warriors, Mahn recognized professionalism. Piper Joach was a man he could follow into combat without any concerns for personal safety.

Piper removed his helmet. His hair was thick and clung to his head. His eyes were circled with heavy rings and struck through with thin red veins. He was exhausted but killing the Goblins helped invigorate him. Or perhaps it was saving so many lives that made him feel better about his situation. With each life saved the memories of guilt over that very first battle upon entering Rogscroft at the beginning of winter faded.

"I didn't want to arrive too early, Mahn. Being a glory hound doesn't suit me," Piper smiled in reply.

"You could have come a while ago and no one would have held it against you."

"What happened here?" Piper looked over the mass of twisted, broken bodies. *Will this ever end? Or are we destined to die in this gods forsaken wasteland?*

Mahn struggled to make sense of it before relaying what he knew. "We were moving in loose formation. The boys are good at what they do but we never spotted the Goblins. My best guess is they were hiding under the snow. They must have been tipped that we were coming. Caught us all by surprise and gave us a good thrashing before we managed to pull ourselves together and fight back."

"It's not surprising that they are expecting us," Piper replied. "They may be crude mockeries of life, but they aren't stupid. Contrary, they have a highly developed sense of battle awareness. It is impressive you managed to save so many of your command."

"If that's what you want to call it," Mahn said, his eyes lowered to the blood-stained snow.

Vajna climbed down from his horse and clasped the scout's arm. "You did well, Mahn. We know the enemy is awaiting us. They're not going to flee and give us back the keys to the kingdom without a fight. While your losses are grave, they are not without purpose. Remember their names, their faces. The time will come when we can avenge them all."

"Your general is correct," Piper added. "We have all lost soldiers in combat. It is no small matter but one every leader must endure. Don't let grief consume you as it did me. Nothing good can come of it."

Mahn shifted his gaze between them. Their words were logical and offered solace for the pain in his heart but he wasn't sure if he was capable of overcoming. He wasn't a proper soldier. "Thank you, gentlemen."

"What are your casualties and where is the rest of your command?" Piper pressed. The business of war was fluid and couldn't wait for one soldier to overcome personal obstacles.

"Thirteen dead, most of the rest are wounded," Mahn said absently. "The others are spread out in a line almost a league across in groups of twenty. I didn't want to get caught in this type of situation."

"Sound tactical planning. I could have used you long ago," Piper approved. "I'll have the surgeons look at your wounded. Details will bury the dead and a marker will be raised so that we remember this sight. It doesn't do for a soldier to die without anyone ever knowing."

"No sir, it doesn't," Mahn said. He offered a halfhearted salute and went to see to his surviving scouts.

From his knees in the snow, Raste looked on Piper Joach with newfound respect.

THIRTEEN

The March

"Word has just arrived of a severe ambush leagues ahead of the main body," Paneolus said, worried. His double chins quivered.

King Aurec winced, more from the annoying minister than from news from the front. He'd been fighting the Wolfsreik and then Goblins for nearly five months already with no end in sight. Losses were to be expected. He knew, as did every other soldier in the army, that they weren't going to win every battle. It was a lesson civilians like Paneolus would do well to learn.

"These things will happen, Minister," he said tersely. "Try as we might, there are going to be casualties."

"It was my understanding that our enemy was broken and Rogscroft was ours for the taking," the elder, fatter minister countered. "We never would have sanctioned marching on the city if Badron still had a sizeable force."

"I don't recall giving you a choice," Aurec growled.

Paneolus stiffened. His voice lowered threateningly. "You may wear the crown but your father did a poor job educating you in the ways of leadership. Stelskor didn't run the kingdom, Aurec. He was merely the figurehead for the decisions we made."

Flexing his fingers, Aurec squared on the minister. "What treachery is this? My father ruled Rogscroft and you served only at his discretion."

"Is that what you believe?" Paneolus laughed. "He did as he was told. Kings don't have power. He knew that truth and accepted it."

"Lies!" Aurec spat.

"No, but you wish they were. There is no kingdom in Malweir run solely by one person. Without the support of the council, who happen to be the wealthiest and most influential people in the kingdom, your father would have been an abysmal failure. Just as you will be unless you start listening to your betters."

Aurec felt like he'd been slapped in the face. He refused to believe the lies Paneolus spun about the ineffectiveness of his father. Stelskor was a good king who put the needs of his people ahead of his own. Hence his surrender to Badron and summary execution. Petty tyrants and despots ruled through fear, subversion. Not his father. Rogscroft enjoyed unparalleled periods of social justice, prosperity, and equality. No other kingdom in the north had been as progressive. Aurec took great pride in his father's accomplishments, hoping to follow in his footsteps.

Hearing Paneolus's accusations stung bitterly. Aurec struggled against the urge to plunge his blade through the minister's heart and burn the corpse. Discretion stayed his hand. He needed to know how many others were entrenched with Paneolus before acting, how many and how far they were prepared to go to ensure the future of Rogscroft went according to their plans. He was learning the hard way that he was in bed with snakes.

"What are you saying, Minister?" he said with clear warning.

Paneolus, emboldened by the apparent lack of confidence, pressed, "The crown you wear is through the whim of others. It would be a shame for you to lose it, or your head due to the lack of vision. These are troubled times, young Aurec. All is not what it once was. Badron has all but destroyed our way of life. A new order must rise from the ashes of the old. The wolves of winter have seen that the weak will perish before the end. Only strength can defeat what so many have already lost their lives to. Think of the future. Are you willing to boldly throw away the chances won by your sacrifices? Are you a better man than all your ancestors?"

Satisfied with his threat, the minister felt his power growing. He'd stood in the shadows for so long. Wasted decades of his life riding on the coattails of Stelskor. He managed to get petty bills signed but never anything substantial. Never anything that would have him remembered by future generations. Delranan's invasion gave him the window of opportunity he knew would never come. Now it was a matter of emplacing all his carefully constructed pieces and using them to full advantage.

While shrewd, Paneolus was no fool. He'd already waited a very long time. Aurec's youth and inexperience would work against the fledgling king, opening the way for Paneolus to enact the first steps in his plan for domination. He paused. Domination wasn't what he wanted. He wanted, needed, to be heard. To have a voice that registered with the people. He wanted to be adored by masses of leadership-starved people so that his name would be long remembered across the face of Malweir. Anything less was insulting.

He stared smugly at the open conflict twisting Aurec's face. That self-doubt opened new doors for Paneolus. Each moment Aurec spent dithering over the merits of what he'd just been told was a step closer to his eventual collapse. No one could successfully control an entire kingdom alone. Aurec had to realize this. The alternatives were as damning as they were restrictive. Worse, he didn't have enough military power to take the throne by force. Paneolus had thrown all his efforts into a singular gambit with every chance of failure.

Aurec opened and closed his mouth repeatedly before fixing his gaze squarely on Paneolus's puffed face. He studied the shorter, fatter person with newfound light. What he'd assumed was a loyal advisor to the king was no more than a twisted serpent begging to find light. Men like that were best discarded and removed from the histories. He briefly wondered how his father had been so blinded, if in truth he had been. Did Paneolus argue for Stelskor to stand and deliver his head to Badron's axe? There wasn't a place on Malweir the minister could hide if he did. Aurec would hunt him down to his last breath to find that measure of vengeance.

"Tell me, Minister, what would you have me do? Cede my position of rightful authority to a handful of politicians who've never handled a blade? Perhaps you would like to lead the assault into the city you so dearly wish to reclaim for your own?"

"Don't make threats you can't..."

"No, Paneolus. You're making the threats to the king of Rogscroft. Our kingdom might be shattered, our people nearly finished, but I will not bow my head to the likes of you. You're a worm that needs to be exposed for what you are. How many soldiers have followed your lead? How many enemy soldiers have you killed? Truthfully, what good are you?" Aurec demanded, his voice rising with passion. "My family built this kingdom through blood, sweat, and tears. They built it on the backs of proud men and women. They built it with their own calloused hands. Your hands are soft."

Blustered, the minister struggled to find a way past this unexpected reversal of momentum. "I serve the crown! Your father may have been king but it was through the wisdom and vision of myself and others like me that helped Rogscroft prosper. Don't be so blind as to believe he did it himself. But what would you know of these things? You, the wayward son, who so often chose to hide behind a sword and go gallivanting around the northern kingdoms like an ill-mannered whore. Perhaps you have forgotten that it was your illicit love affair with the princess of Delranan that started this whole mess?"

Aurec struck incredibly fast. His fist smashed into Paneolus's face with unchecked fury. Blood and saliva spurted from his mouth as a tooth broke free. He sputtered, throwing up his hands to ward off the next blow. Aurec struck again and again. Months of pent-up rage exploded through his knuckles. Reluctantly, he drew back and left the minister quivering in his own blood.

"You will **not** speak of her again in such fashion, *Minister*. Do I make myself clear?" he barked between heavy breaths.

Paneolus could barely hold his head up without tears building in his eyes. Unimaginable pain lanced across his face. He couldn't recall the last time he'd been punched. "More threats? I didn't think the king of Rogscroft would resort to violence so trivially."

"These are not sane times, as your words have so carefully shown me. Get on your feet, Paneolus, before I run my blade through your gut."

Slowly, deliberately, the battered minister rose, leaning on the field table for support. His legs trembled in anticipation of the next blow. His mind, already despondent, wandered off on shameless paths of regicide or worse. The hardened look in Aurec's eyes ended those shamefully. He wasn't a killer, but the newly crowned king was. Paneolus made his bid for power and came away wanting. There was but one thing left to do to reclaim any semblance of honor. "My lord, I made a grievous mistake. My life is yours to take."

His head bowed in shame. Paneolus refused to look Aurec in the eye.

For his part, King Aurec managed to contain his hostility. Instead of a power-mad snake, he only saw a weak, old man incapable of rising above his base emotions. "You are a sad figure, Paneolus. To think my father listened to the likes of you turns my stomach. I will not take your life, but let this moment serve as a reminder that your days of whispering in the king's ear are finished. The next time you speak to me I will slice your tongue from your mouth. Sergeant Thorsson!"

The grizzled sergeant burst into the command tent on cue. He wore a bemused look, as if he'd overheard the entire conversation and was merely waiting for the call. "Sire."

"Get this filth away from me," Aurec ordered. "I want him under escort at all times, even when he goes to piss.

He is hereby stripped of his titles, lands, and holdings. Upon return to Rogscroft and the reestablishment of the kingdom, he will be fortunate to serve as court jester."

Thorsson snatched Paneolus by the collar and jerked him towards the door. "This way, Minister. We've got a lovely spot picked out for you near the corrals. Perhaps mucking out the shit will clear your mind."

Saluting, he left Aurec to his demons.

Another day passed and with it another score of leagues. Aurec was forced to call an operational halt for the rear of the column to catch up. The army was getting strung out. Horses moved faster and further than the infantry. Each night the rear battalions trudged into camp later and later. Worn out, they weren't going to be able to fight once they arrived at the capital. Aurec's concerns compounded almost by the minute. Too many halts and they'd be forced to cut rations and waste too much time foraging. He couldn't see a way out and that caused many sleepless hours tossing in his cot. No king ever had an easy life.

"We're making good time," Rolnir said, taking a mighty drink from his canteen.

Aurec eyed the general suspiciously. His own ideations differed vastly. "How can you say that? We're falling behind schedule."

Rolnir grinned sheepishly. "You've never led an army this size in the field, have you?"

"I've been fighting since the first day you crossed the Murdes Mountains," Aurec replied tartly, still unsure where Rolnir was going.

"Young king, there are a great many mysteries in the world. The movement of a large body of soldiers one of them. We set a goodly pace at the beginning but it was never sustainable. Horses will come up lame. Infantry will get sick or injured. Supplies will run low and we'll just get plain exhausted. Don't let a few leagues unwalked dampen your spirits. We'll get to the city, but we need to be in fighting order to confront whatever Badron has in store when we do."

Aurec relaxed. Rolnir was an accomplished soldier and leader, far more experienced at leading troops in the field than Aurec. That didn't mean the young king felt secure in their partnership. He'd already been stabbed in the back by who he had thought was a trusted advisor and friend. Rolnir was the enemy not too long ago. What was there to keep him from switching sides again? Or worse, using this advance as a ploy to get Aurec in the open and destroy him once and for all?

Noticing the hesitation, Rolnir asked, "You're troubled by more than just this, aren't you?"

"Yes," he said. He struggled to find the right words. "None of this sits well with me, Rolnir. A few short weeks ago our two sides were desperately trying to kill one another. Now we're allies against your former king. You can see where my hesitation lies."

"You worry that I'll betray you and finish the job," Rolnir finished.

Aurec looked the general in the eye. "I am."

"The sign of a good leader. Never fully trust those you surround yourself with." He paused, choosing his next words carefully. "Badron had never given me reason to doubt where his intentions rested. He wasn't what I'd call a good king, but he was fair. Much of his despair arose after the death of his wife. She loved him dearly and it broke something inside when she died in childbirth, with your very own Maleela."

Aurec felt his stomach twist. He knew her mother had died in childbirth, a private memory best left unspoken. To hear it from the mouth of a relative stranger was almost insulting.

Rolnir continued before Aurec could interrupt. "He blames her for the death. Maleela was always a good child but suffering from the lack of love. Badron stumbled deeper into grief. Torment prevented him from making quality decisions. Combined with his jealousy for your father it was only a matter of time before the war started. Your mission to steal Maleela was the spark he needed. It was our duty to follow his orders. The invasion wasn't going to stop. Neither was he until your entire kingdom lay in ruins."

"Planning a winter war cut off from resupply and home by the Murdes Mountains doesn't make sense," Aurec said.

Rolnir shook his head. "No, it doesn't, but something darker was driving him. I don't know what. Many times I felt a dark presence surrounding him, lurking just out of sight. I'll be damned if I know what though. Then came the Goblins. How Badron knew to contact them or why is beyond me. Fighting alongside them didn't sit right with many of my boys. They're a filthy breed. Watching what they did to your city helped make up my mind. Combined with Badron's growing dementia it was only a matter of time before the leadership spoke of abandoning our king."

"I can't pay you," Aurec said lightly.

Rolnir barked deep laughter. "If that were the mitigating factor I'd never have turned against the crown. All my soldiers need is food, water, and a place to lay their heads. Our payment will come from winning this war and going home."

"I don't know what home is anymore," Aurec admitted. "This war has claimed more than I ever thought I had to give. I wish this were over."

"Soon. We've crushed most of the Goblin army and Badron barely has a thousand fighting men left. He'll fold and retreat back to Delranan." *Back to another war altogether. What have you done, Harnin? What happened the man I once called friend? Are all those reports accurate? When I get home will I find it just like Rogscroft?*

Aurec stretched, watching another column of haggard infantry trudge past. Their bodies were close to breaking but defiance flared in their eyes. They'd carry the fight to the heart of their kingdom and beyond, all at his behest. It was this moment Aurec realized just how abominable leading soldiers was. The strength and power of wielding an army was nothing compared to the inconsolable guilt he felt with every death.

"Who commanded the first battle?" he asked suddenly.

Rolnir eyed the young king queerly. "Piper Joach, why?"

"He was a formidable opponent."

"You gave him a run for his life. Many good soldiers were lost that day. He took the loss personally, you know. Piper is a proud man. He blames himself for what happened, even though it was a technical victory."

Aurec nodded gloomily. "And now he leads the advance."

"It's where he feels most comfortable. Getting him back in the proper frame of mind took a bit of doing, but he's one of the best at what he does. I wouldn't trust this army in anyone else's hands," Rolnir said.

"I need to speak with him before we reach the city," Aurec told him.

Rolnir said nothing as more soldiers marched past. His opinions of the young king just went up.

Meters turned to kilometers. Kilometers stretched into leagues. The combined army pushed closer to the objective. Men were tired. Horses exhausted. But the will to fight never left them. Former enemies formed tentative bonds. Silent animosity turned to timid laughs and finally all-out camaraderie. Even the stoic Pell warriors mingled with the lowland soldiers. The longer they spent on the road the closer they became. Bonds of fellowship sprung to life. Piper watched them all with newfound pride. He'd never thought such a thing possible.

"Sun's about to set. We need to find a bivouac," Vajna told him. The older general wore three days' worth of stubble and it irritated him to no end.

Piper offered a small grin. "Yes, General. I'll have the scouts begin."

The pair shared a laugh that would have been construed as grave insult only weeks earlier. Time in the saddle at the sharp end of the sword brought them closer together, until they liked working together. Piper and Vajna played off each other's skill and weaknesses effectively to form a cohesive command structure. Goblins and Badron loyalists ambushed them a handful more times since the first battle, each time with adjusted tactics. More and more the scouts were falling prey to traps, ambushes, and petty chicanery.

"How much longer until we reach the city?" Piper asked. It was the same question he'd asked every morning and every evening. The answer never satisfied.

"At this pace?" Vajna replied with an eyebrow peaked. "Who can say? These damned hidden traps are slowing our progress more than I expected. The scouts are forced to pick their way across terrain that should be easily passable."

"With mounting losses," Piper added. "We need a new strategy."

A great commotion erupted among the soldiers of the vanguard just behind them. Piper turned to find King Aurec's escort riding down a hastily formed avenue, making straight for him. He sighed. *What now?*

Vajna stiffened and snapped to attention, saluting with a clenched fist held tightly above his heart. Aurec slid daftly from the saddle and returned the gesture, welcoming the rigid formality of the military.

"The front is no place for you, sire," Vajna admonished. He'd already suffered the loss of one king. Losing another was unthinkable.

Aurec sighed. It was an old conversation had with everyone in the chain of command. No one believed there were times when a king needed to be seen leading from the front. Anything beyond the forward line of troops wasn't safe for anyone. "Relax, General. I came here for specific purpose and promise to return to the main body as soon as I'm finished." He turned to Piper and took a deep breath. "Commander Joach, it is my understanding that you commanded opposite me at the very first engagement."

Piper swallowed hard. *Where are you going with this*? "Yes, I had the honor of first combat."

"A lot of good soldiers on both sides fell that day," Aurec continued. The words, while difficult to say, were heartfelt. "You were a worthy opponent. I wanted you to know, before we reach the city, that I hold no ill will towards you. It is my honor to serve alongside you now as we begin the reclamation of Rogscroft. You are a good commander, Piper. And good commanders are a rarity in these troubled times."

Piper was speechless.

Thankfully, he didn't need to think long. A pair of riders came storming back from the front. Piper immediately frowned, thinking back to the initial Goblin ambush. He turned to give the order for the vanguard to mount up and get in battle order.

"Flames! The city is burning!"

Aurec and Vajna exchanged worried looks. The capital city was burning to the ground.

FOURTEEN

The Jungles of Brodein

The thunderstorm raged unchecked above them, though only a few drops of rain managed to win through the double canopy. What served as a cloak also trapped the heat in. Bahr and the others felt like they were melting under the sweltering humidity. Insects assaulted with impunity, injecting their special venoms through Rekka's mystery salve. Snakes and rodents of every shape and size moved through the underbrush. Larger mammals stalked the shadows and giant reptiles splashed in unseen pools. The jungle was harsh, unforgiving and exacting a terrible toll. Mercy was for the weak. Kindness a fool's gesture. Here only the strong made it through to the next day.

Ionascu ambled along on the back of the swayback mare given to them to haul the wagon. His legs had been beaten near useless by Harnin's goons, leaving him with a debilitating limp that would only slow the group down. Bahr gave him the choice of riding the mare or dying in the jungle. He scowled but climbed aboard. The broken man steadily devolved into delirium. His morbid songs turned outright offensive, bawdy and lewd. His scratchy voice echoed sharply through the jungle. Already he'd forced them to halt on numerous occasions as uncontrollable bouts of vomiting and diarrhea ravaged his already frail body, making him regret not heeding Rekka's earlier advice. Normally Bahr would have shut him up but they needed even a petty distraction to keep them from focusing on the constant pounding the jungle bore down on them.

They'd already gone nearly a week into the jungle and hadn't met a soul. Every night the Gnaal returned. A relentless predator always a measured step behind. It was hunting them, tracking the travel-weary band with defined purpose. Anienam worried more as the days went on. He lacked the strength to combat the monster despite centuries of magical lore and experience. The Mages were prepared for many things, but seldom were they called to battle demons of their own design. The best he could do was keep it at bay. But for how long, he didn't know.

Clothes were perpetually damp, clinging to the skin. It wouldn't be long before many of them began to suffer from immersion foot, jungle rot, or malaria. Anienam was an accomplished wizard but he lacked the medicinal skills necessary to keep them healthy. Perhaps Rekka had a few more tricks in her bag, though he doubted it. The jungle was an animal with a mind of its own. There was no viable solution to this dilemma or the compounding circumstances of them being hunted. Anienam simply didn't have the answers they were all looking at him to provide. He felt like a failure about to turn catastrophic.

"If this keeps up we're going to fall apart," Dorl griped under his breath. He'd given up trying to wipe the sweat from his brow, convinced it was going to saturate his flesh to the point where he'd become waterlogged.

Rekka reached out to gently squeeze his forearm. "You must learn the jungle. Make it your ally. Only then will you be at peace."

"Peace?" he asked quickly. "What kind of peace can there possibly be trapped in all the rain and swamps with who-knows-how-many monsters lurking out of sight?"

"There are no monsters here, only creatures you are unfamiliar with in the north. Brodein will continue to torment you until you either conform or perish. Those are the only options. My people learn from a very young age what works and what doesn't. Fighting the inevitable only makes the situation worse."

Rekka fell silent. Her focus was immediately drawn to a small copse of banyan trees. Her hand drifted to her sword as she tensed.

"What do you...what is it?" Dorl asked, his voice quickly dropping to a whisper.

She gestured with her chin. "In those trees. We are being watched."

"Shit. Nothol, go back and get Boen."

Nothol casually drew his blade and crept back. He didn't need to know the situation. His best friend's word was enough. Whatever Dorl and Rekka spied was enough to spook them. Nothol reached Boen in moments.

The Gaimosian noticed the bared steel and puffed his chest out. "What is it?"

"I don't know. Rekka seems spooked. They said to bring you," Nothol whispered.

Boen drew his sword and started walking. "Show me."

The pair wormed through the small trees and came up behind the sell sword. Dorl didn't bother looking but merely pointed into the trees. Boen squinted. His thick fingers flexed on the hilt of his sword. The time had come, another in an endless string, for battle. Boen relished the thought of exacting his brand of vengeance against whatever kept them up through the dark hours of the night. He readied to attack.

"Put your weapons down and you will live," called a stern, thick voice from the shadows.

Boen snarled. "Show yourself and I might. Keep skulking and I'll tear out your guts."

A handful of thick arrows slammed into the ground at his feet in reply. Boen tensed, ready to attack. Only Rekka managed to hold him back.

"No, do nothing."

"Are you mad? They'll kill us all if we just stand here," he raged back.

She shook her head fervently. "No they won't. Trust me."

"Who walks among the outlanders?" the same voice asked.

Rekka balked before slinking in front of the warriors. Her sword waivered slightly. "I am Rekka Jel. Chosen to defend the Guardian of ancient Trennaron and companion of the wizard Anienam Keiss."

"Rekka Jel has not been seen in many cycles," the voice returned. "You cannot be who you claim."

"I have no reason to lie. I am from the village of Teng," she replied defiantly. An odd memory tugged at the corners of her mind. She felt she recognized the voice but couldn't place it. Confused, Rekka stood her ground.

"Lower your weapons, imposter. I will look on you for myself and see whether you claim falsehoods," the voice demanded. "Should any of your companions move they will die where they stand."

"I don't take orders from jungle rats," Boen snapped. "Come in the open and face me like a man."

"Why would I want to do that? You are clearly more powerful and murderous than any I have in my party. Facing you would be suicide and I very much wish to live. Lower your weapon, outlander. The next arrow will find its way to your heart. Not even your immense size can stop the poison for very long."

Rekka gave the Gaimosian a knowing look. Despite his grievance at being told what to do, Boen slid his sword back into the scabbard and waited. Satisfied, she eased forward to stand between the two groups. She blinked twice, the partial combination of boredom and apprehension, and did her best to appear nonthreatening. Rekka hadn't been in the jungle for a very long time or seen any of the local tribesmen since being selected for her assignment, but she'd lost none of the edge required when dealing with them. Incomparable to the bitter northerners, the jungle tribes were hard in their own way. They followed the ways of nature, often letting the jungle dictate life or death. Rekka understood her confronters better than the peoples from the north.

"You have the looks of a tribeswoman, but we do not recognize you," her accuser said as he stepped into the light.

Rekka cocked her head in recognition. "I know you."

He was tall and lean, too lean to pose a viable threat to any perhaps except Ionascu. Years of harsh living left him muscled, sculpted like a statue in one of the grand cities. Jet black hair clung down to his shoulders. His cheeks were hollow, giving him a hungry look. Hawkish eyes the color of warm caramel glared at them under caterpillar thick eyebrows. His hands, while large for his medium frame, were calloused from a lifetime of hard labor. The leather loincloth hung down to his knees, matched by moccasins made from the same animal. Weaponless save for a long spear, he slammed the metal-capped butt in the soft ground and planted his feet shoulder width apart.

"Why have you come to the jungle? This is no place for your kind," he asked.

Rekka, head still cocked, answered slowly, "You are Cashi Dam. We are from the same tribe, though you seem to have forgotten. I am Rekka Jel."

"So you said," he snorted derisively. "But these are foul times. How can I take you at your word? Especially in the company of so many outlanders."

"You expect me to believe you have forgotten how you attempted to seduce me in the jungle one night?" she retorted.

Dorl shot her a dubious look. Just then Groge and the others burst into the small clearing. All the villagers rocked back at the sight, never imagining such a large creature.

"What's all this?" Bahr asked. Ironfoot stood at his side, axe barred and ready for a fight.

They marched the rest of the day, guided into the village of Teng by Cashi Dam and his band of hunters. Few words were spoken along the way, though Anienam immediately went forward to strike bonds of fellowship with the villagers. Dorl continued to hold his opinions, though he caught himself giving her angered looks. He had much to think on and none of it good.

Teng was one of those rare places that time seemed to forget. Thatch-roofed huts no larger than wagons dotted a series of small clearings. Bluish smoke from cook fires drifted up into the canopy. Jungle pigs, chickens, and an odd species of domesticated lizards wandered freely throughout the village. No one seemed to mind or notice. Small pens half filled with goats, sheep, and a small, horned deer-like animal were secured off on the far perimeter. The village stank of animal secretions and waste.

Women carried children on their backs, along with massive baskets of dirty clothes, rice, and vegetables. Young would-be warriors sparred with wooden rattans under the watchful gaze of seasoned warriors. Old ones sat around a small fire chewing a root found only in the deep jungle. They spoke in hushed tones with glazed eyes and trembling hands. Small children ran and played a rudimentary form of ball with their feet, laughing and giggling the entire way.

Bahr felt like he'd stepped into another world. Malweir, as he knew it, stopped the moment he entered Brodein and became something else upon entering Teng. Try as he might, he failed to reason how any society could exist in these almost prehistoric conditions in the modern world. They lacked all modern conveniences, though he couldn't figure out if that was bad or good. Too much often led to greed. He'd seen too many friends fall prey to trappings of their own creation. Did these jungle people do the same? He doubted it. There was nothing to covet, unless animal pelts held more value than gems or women.

Cashi Dam gestured for them to halt. "Wait here while I speak with our elders. Few are allowed to see Teng. Do not move from this spot."

Anienam answered for the group, not trusting the others to convey the proper decorum. The last thing he wanted was to get into a battle with Rekka's people so close to Trennaron. He'd spent countless hours putting together the perfect group of fighters and thinkers. Each had individual merit, strengthening the group in ways none knew. Any loss suffered needlessly would not only hamper their quest but send Malweir on a course of self-destruction.

"You have our word, Cashi Dam. We will not move."

Satisfied with the wizard's word, the warrior stalked off into the village.

"You take many liberties with our generosity," Boen accused. "I need no one to speak for me. I'm Gaimosian."

"That's exactly what worries me," Anienam fired back. "You need to step back and think with your mind instead of your sword. These are docile people unless you come threatening. Their spears and arrows are dipped with toxins I can't counter. We need them on our side if we're going to make it to Trennaron on time."

"Gaimosians do not forget insults, or injustices," Boen threatened.

The wizard sighed, knowing it was all macho positioning to save face. He'd never had time for such childish games. The end goal was much more serious than even Boen understood. Should they stumble or fall, the body count would rise higher than all the wars of the past combined. Malweir couldn't sustain such loses without total extinction of many races.

"What injustice comes from taking a moment to think?" he asked after a moment. "We are invaders as far as they're concerned. They met our threat with one of their own. No one was harmed, no grave insults delivered. Give me time to settle an accord. It worked in Venheim and Drimmen Delf. Why can't it work in Teng as well?"

Boen folded his massive arms across his barrel chest and grunted. Even he couldn't argue with cold logic. For all his bluster, he had no inclination toward killing these backward villagers. They weren't worth the effort. At least that's what he told himself.

Satisfied the immediate threat had passed, Anienam looked to the others. "Does anyone else have an issue with me settling this my way?"

Bored stares met his. They'd seen and heard it all too many times before. For most, this was just another pointless delay in a quest they didn't want to be part of. They'd lost weight, shed blood, and seen unimaginable nightmares unfold. Countless deaths of all types haunted many in the cold hours in the middle of the night. They were tired. Tired of loss. Tired of battles. Tired of being hunted and hounded by monstrosities that shouldn't exist. Reaching Trennaron and getting the Blud Hamr represented the end of their struggles, or so the consensus thought. Only Anienam knew the true depths of what they were going to endure before the end. And he was loath to tell more until necessary.

For now his focus was on the building tension between Dorl and Rekka.

Dorl Theed was many things. A compassionate, thinker was not among them. He fought for the highest bidder. Drank until the floor rushed up to slap him in the face. Slept with any woman willing to take his coin. He did it all without emotions, for they often served to get one in his profession killed before his time. He wasn't a bad person but didn't quite think he fell in the good category either. Dorl had been created by his environment. No one could fault him for that, not even the high and mighty wizard-son.

He took a seat on one of the charred wood stumps. His eyes never left Rekka. Conflicting thoughts played havoc with him. No matter how many times he thought he reached the appropriate conclusion to the dilemma in his mind a new wave of possibilities arose to taunt him. Life was simpler getting paid to fight. Dorl had seen many things in his young life. Experienced many unusual sensations, but love was the damnedest of them all.

He wanted to ask her about her relationship with Cashi. If there even was one. Normally it wouldn't have bothered him. He wasn't naïve enough to believe she'd never been with another man. After all, he'd slept with his share of women through the years. That's how life was. What she did before they met aboard the *Bane* was her business and held no bearing on their relationship. The ridiculousness of any jealousy was laughable. So why was he feeling it?

The answer wasn't as complicated as he wanted it to be. Of all the scenarios that could have played out it was Rekka bringing up their relationship that startled him. She'd talked so little of her life in Teng that he thought it wasn't much at all. Her life began and ended in Trennaron with some demented old mystic that should have passed on to the next world long ago. Clearly Dorl deluded himself. Rekka remembered much more of her village than she was willing to share. That unintentional deception gnawed at him. He found doubt where none should be.

"You should speak your mind, Dorl Theed," she whispered, taking a seat on the log beside him.

Dorl resisted the urge to shrug her away. "I don't know what to say."

"Yes you do."

He let out a slow, painful breath. "How important was he to you?"

She nodded, the gesture so minute he almost missed it. "He was to be my husband before I was accepted to go to Trennaron."

"Husband?" he blurted out.

"Do not let your imagination get the better of your common sense. The youth in Teng are betrothed before they can even speak. It is an old tradition." She felt silent, allowing him time to process what she'd said. Only when incomprehension lingered in his eyes did she add, "I did not love him, Dorl. Our incompatibility led to my being chosen to serve the Guardian."

Cashi returned before Dorl could respond. His face was stern. Conflicting emotions roiled dangerously in his dark eyes. "Come. The dream masters will speak with you."

They rose to follow before Cashi stopped them in place. "Only the wizard. The rest of you will stay here until it is deemed safe to have you in Teng."

Even Rekka seemed stunned as the warrior and wizard strode off, leaving behind a group of disgruntled companions.

FIFTEEN

Teng

Bahr paced the small area, hands clasped behind his back. His face was twisted in concern as he tried to figure a way out of their situation. Worse, the mistrust between the Anienam and the others was growing. As much as he wanted to intervene and smooth the matter away, Bahr knew he was next to powerless. He couldn't change opinions, especially if they were based on previous prejudices.

Flashbacks from his meeting with the Old Mother in Fedro distracted him. She provided pertinent information while sprinkling portents of destruction. He shared this with no one. Bahr's eyes drifted to Maleela. The soft, innocent girl he'd grown to love was gone, replaced with a hard, bitter shell of a woman who'd seen too much bloodshed over the course of a few months. His heart broke for her. She deserved better. A better father. A better family. A better life with the one she loved. Only he'd been hired to steal her away from that love under false pretenses. Yet another crime for Badron to answer to.

Armed guards watched them from afar. What appeared no more than casual interest didn't fool Bahr. They were being watched, scrutinized for any minor action that would give their captors an excuse to attack. His hopes of Rekka intervening were dashed by the cold reception she'd been given. Whatever had happened between Cashi and Rekka was bleeding over into his group. She seemed despondent to all conversation. *We all bear great weights. Hers must be twice as much.*

"We should do something," Boen said, passing him a half empty canteen. "Sitting like friendly prisoners doesn't go well with me."

"What would you have me do? We're outnumbered, all but lost, and in desperate need of resupply. Even if we managed to escape we'd be devoured by this jungle," Bahr retorted.

"If we kill enough of them we won't need to run. I'm no pirate but we can take this village over and push on. We're wasting valuable time."

"Is there ever a time when you don't think about fighting?" Bahr asked, harsher than he intended. Frustrations were clouding his judgment. He was tired. Normal thought processes, once clear and concise, were distorted, rendering him ineffective.

If Boen took offense he didn't show it. "I'm Gaimosian. I was born to fight. It is the curse of my people."

"You don't expect me to believe that your entire race was created for the sole purpose of combat," Bahr said, rolling his eyes. He threw up his hands and sat down.

Boen clenched his fist. "Gaimos was once the jewel of the west. Never was there a more beautiful kingdom. It is whispered we were not always warlike. My people grew wealthy off natural resources, gold, and gemstones. They crafted great weapons prized across Malweir. Kings sought out our craftsmen with great competition. It is said we rivaled the skill of the Dwarves."

"No one rivals a Dwarf when it comes to shaping steel," Ironfoot growled as he chewed on a dried piece of deer.

Boen waved him off. "It was inevitable that my people turned to the art of war. Why not? Crafting a weapon was one thing, but what was a sword compared to the razor-hardened edge of trained warrior? Nothing. Warfare became an art form. Great companies of mercenaries were hired by every kingdom. Gaimos grew in power. But what proved to be a boon also became a curse. Petty kings became jealous. They feared for their kingdoms while secretly coveting what the Gaimosians had built."

He paused to spit the anger filling his mouth. "A combined army of several kingdoms turned on Gaimos and razed it to the ground. Every city, town, and village was wiped from the face of the world without pause. What survived of the population was scattered to the four corners of Malweir. They vowed never to rebuild their home. Never to give in to the pettiness of organized civilization for it could only lead to evil. Thousands of years later we continue to fight, in small groups or individuals, but never as an army. The fear of total loss remains much too strong to ignore. So when you ask me if all I think of is fighting my answer is yes. I dream of the day when all the kingdoms responsible for robbing me of my heritage are laid low. Perhaps then Gaimos will rebuild and my people can have a place to call home."

"A grand dream but realistically no more than fantasy," Bahr replied. "How many thousands of years have passed since the fall Gaimos? Mankind has short memories except when it comes to dealing with those that caused grievous harm. Look at the Mages. It's been centuries and Anienam would be lynched today if he walked into the wrong kingdom."

Boen jabbed an angry finger at Bahr. "Mark my words, Gaimos will be rebuilt. There are thousands of us scattered across the world. Our time will come again, Sea Wolf."

"Sometimes even the basest of dreams is enough to keep us warm at night," Rekka said without looking up from the muddy ground. Her eyes were glossed over, locked in doubt.

Dorl, reluctantly, rose and went to sit beside her. He still carried wounds in his heart for reasons he wasn't ready to explain. That didn't stop him from realizing the foolishness of his actions. Whatever demons plagued his subconscious weren't to blame for Rekka's revelations upon being captured. He fondly thought back to their first proper meeting. She'd nearly taken his head off thinking he was the killer aboard the *Dragon's Bane*. It felt like years ago but in truth was a handful of months.

Most of his previous life was forgotten. The easygoing lifestyle meant little now that he had become enmeshed in a much greater world than any he could have imagined. Working petty jobs for a minor noble meant nothing compared to the world-changing severity of what he and the others set out to accomplish. He wrapped an arm around Rekka and pulled her close. She responded by resting her head on his shoulder and closing her eyes.

"Dreams are often insubstantial," Boen replied, his tone less severe. "I will always hold hope that Gaimos will rise again, but do not live my life by it. I am a Vengeance Knight. Battle is my life. I fight. I kill and I live. What more is there?"

Bahr ran a hand over his white hair. "Love. Family. Peace and the opportunity to live out your days without strife. All I ever wanted was a rocking chair and a porch to watch the last years of my life pass by. I've spent decades roaming the world. Pirating on occasion. Fighting when I needed to. Harnin stole it all from me."

"You see, Bahr. We are too alike to know anything else. Men like us weren't made to live ordinary lives," Boen admitted. "Our deeds are what historians will recall when the ashes settle."

Groge, much taller than them even while sitting cross-legged, blinked as he shifted focus between the two. Their world seemed so foreign. He'd never experienced violence on such grand levels. It disturbed him deeply, leaving a rot inside his soul. Killing was a plague his kind didn't endorse or participate in. It wasn't always so. Giants once were counted among the fiercest of races in Malweir. Foresight and the overwhelming burden of guilt drove them up to the highest mountaintops where they abandoned their weapons and began their pursuit of higher purpose. Groge was the product of centuries of pacifism.

Boen was an enigma. One he couldn't crack by watching him in action. Groge only reluctantly participated in the skirmishes they'd had since leaving Venheim. Survival was an instinct a lifetime of pacifism couldn't alter. Bahr, on the other hand, was a sad figure in desperate need of consoling. None in the group seemed to have the insight to offer what the sea captain needed.

Cashi marched back to them. His spear hung horizontally in a relaxed grip. The look on his face was a mixture of fury and regret. "The dream masters give you leave to enter Teng. But make no moves to betray their trust. My archers stand ready to take you down without notice."

Bahr rushed to speak before the others let their emotions interfere. "We will obey their orders, Cashi Dam. Where is Anienam Keiss?"

"He remains with the dream masters," Cashi replied gruffly. He clearly wasn't pleased with the decision to allow outlanders free reign in his village and took it as a personal affront to his honor. Yet even as he spoke he glared at Rekka. Bad memories filled his mind. She rapidly became the object of his hostility.

Bahr caught the look and moved to keep something from happening. "Will it be possible to resupply before leaving? We were in a shipwre…"

"All will be taken care of. You will have what you need and be gone before the next sunset. I will send one of my warriors to assist you." Cashi dismissed them without so much as a nod and stormed back into the village.

Rekka's eyes never left him, even after he disappeared around the corner of a hut.

Nothol set down a sack of rice and wiped the sweat from his face with an old rag. He fought off a yawn and went for another. He'd always liked hard work, using it to define his moral standards. Life had been good, better than a man like he deserved. Born to a middle class merchant family, Nothol quickly grasped mathematics and logistics. Working in the warehouse was fine but he felt empty at times. He needed more than what the mundane life of trading and factoring could deliver.

He secretly began exercising. Going so far as to hire a tutor in the arts of sword fighting and self-defense. Nothol's skill quickly grew to the point where he didn't need a tutor anymore. He began heading out to taverns and inns in search of odd jobs. The wait was short. A wealthy benefactor approached him with beguiling words and the promise of riches beyond his dreams. Young and inexperienced, Nothol eagerly accepted the job.

On the surface it sounded easy enough. Break into a warehouse and retrieve an item of great value that had been stolen. He wasn't working alone. Another sell sword met him outside the tavern. His employer introduced the roguish character as Dorl Theed. Nothol shook hands and began what would turn into a lasting friendship.

He smiled at the memory while trying to forget what had happened after. His employer didn't bother to tell him that he had to break into his father's warehouse and steal an item that rightfully belonged to Nothol's father. The resulting fire and pair of dead guards forced him to flee Chadra. Word traveled quickly and he was banished from his home. The world his father carefully constructed for him, heir to an empire, shattered around him. He was broke, homeless, and wanted by the law. Fortune hadn't smiled on him since. The only saving grace stemmed from his friendship with Dorl Theed. Making what he had to do next more difficult than he had hoped.

Waiting until Dorl arrived with his own sack of what looked like red potatoes, Nothol offered his rag and waited for his friend to catch his breath. "Have you ever imagined so much humidity?"

Dorl shook his head. "No. This almost makes me miss the winter. How can a land like this exist?"

"I don't know but it makes me want to know what else is out there that we haven't experienced yet," Nothol replied. Their passing along the fringes of the Jebel Desert offered rare glimpses into a sun-blasted, golden world completely opposite of the dense forests and snow-covered mountains in the north. Now the jungle continued to open his eyes in amazement. A sudden desire to continue traveling took life and began to mature.

"I've seen enough. I don't know about you but I want to go home, Nothol. This isn't what we signed up for," he said too quickly for Nothol's comfort.

Tired of the same discussion, he decided to get to the point. "Is everything all right between you and Rekka? You've been acting strange ever since we ran into Cashi."

"What do you think?" Dorl replied bitterly. "You're my best friend and all, but there are some things I need to work out on my own. I don't need anyone getting involved in this one."

Nothol frowned. "Stubbornness will bring you down, Dorl. This isn't the time to try and go it alone."

Dorl opened and closed his mouth. His initial reply died on his tongue. Instead, he managed to clear his head and think before speaking. "Nothol, I appreciate your friendship. You've helped me through a lot of dark situations. Saying this isn't easy for me, but I need to do this alone. You can't help."

The bigger sell sword spread his arms with a grin. "I had to offer. You're my best friend. If it hadn't been for your generosity I would have died in a jail cell. Just know that I have your back whenever you need it."

"Thank you." Dorl was humbled. Their normally unspoken bond of friendship had never been tested to the limits at which this quest was straining it. It felt good to know how much he could depend on the man responsible for his life on too many occasions.

"Anytime." Nothol snatched his rag back and went for another sack. There was still much work to be done and time was running out.

The villagers seemed insistent that they leave immediately following sunrise. Few, if any, in the group saw the need for such haste considering the duration of their quest thus far. Anienam droned about time escaping but it meant little to any of them. Whatever secrets he decided to keep were only harming the importance of their task. Men didn't expend full effort when their benefactor was reluctant to explain the details. Anienam was too blinded by his inner demons to notice. That distrust was in danger of spreading.

Skuld slid the fifty-pound sack from his slender shoulders with a loud grunt and stretched his back. He was wiry by all standards and poorly built for heavy manual labor. Much had changed since he stowed aboard Bahr's ship. He was stronger, tougher than before. His mind was sharper, as if confused by the conflicting urgings of Anienam and Boen's rejections. Contrary to all his bluster, Boen repeatedly told him that not everyone was made to be a warrior. Skuld initially took offense, only slowly realizing the truth as more lives ended before his eyes. But what the wizard promised made less sense. Skuld wasn't interested in magic and didn't think he wanted to follow in the crazy old wizard's footsteps. Being a wizard didn't have many benefits from what Skuld determined.

"You'll grow out of this stage soon enough," Ironfoot's rough voice called from behind. The stout Dwarf dropped a pair of sacks without so much as a grunt.

Skuld wanted to laugh but wasn't sure if the Dwarf captain was serious or not. "I've never had to work so hard in my life."

"Hard work builds strong character," the Dwarf answered. "If you'd been born in Drimmen Delf you would have been conditioning from a young age. Dwarves are naturally competitive, to the point of getting hurt all too often. You have smarts, but you lack strength. Don't worry yourself over it. Strength will come. Give it time."

"Do we have time?" the gangly youth asked.

Ironfoot rolled his thickly muscled shoulders. "Who can say? No one has properly explained just what this quest is all about."

"Why did you come with us?"

"One doesn't argue with the king of Drimmen Delf. Dwarves are loyal and obey without question. I am representing the Dwarven kingdoms. If the fragmented information your wizard said is correct this quest will help determine the fate of Malweir. It will not be said that Dwarves didn't do their part."

Skuld cocked his head. "You're not the least bit curious about what we're doing?"

"Dwarves aren't curious about much in the world of men. I will follow until the time is right to return to my mountain home, kill whoever needs to be killed, and take my place of honor in the halls of our heroes when this is ended. Life is simple, young Skuld. Don't seek to complicate it needlessly." Ironfoot paused. "Speaking of which, what do you see in that crazy old wizard? He's more trouble than he's worth."

"Anienam?" Skuld paused. He hadn't told anyone, though he suspected Bahr knew. "He thinks I have the ability to become a wizard."

Ironfoot guffawed loudly, making Skuld's face flush. "Magic is fading from this world, Skuld. Why do you think he's the last of his breed? The Mages had their run and messed it up. Whatever gods remain don't seem likely to give them a second chance. It's an age of steel and will these days. Gone are the days of magic users and good riddance I say. Anienam's a nice enough fellow, if quirky, but his sort only mucks things up for the common man. Don't fall for his guile. He's a wizard after all!"

This merely confused Skuld further. His mind felt muddled and, being overly impressionable, irrevocably lost. Warrior. Thief. Wizard. Orphan. What was he to become? Who was he? No answers were forthcoming. He was alone in the company of great warriors, royalty and wizardry. What did a boy like he have to contribute? He knew he should have stayed in Chadra and stuck with picking pockets. This wasn't the life he wanted.

Ironfoot saw the conflict in his eyes and slapped Skuld on the back. "Buck up, lad. Most youth seldom have an inkling of their true path. Yours will come to you, often when you least expect it."

"What am I supposed to do in the meanwhile? Boen wants me to be a warrior, or rather, he's adamant about talking me out of it. Anienam thinks I am his heir and Bahr thinks I should go home. I regret stowing away."

"Regrets are part of life. Every man has his share. It's how we deal with them that shapes our character," the Dwarf explained. "Don't be in such a rush to make things happen. Besides, we're probably all going to die on this quest anyway! Ha!"

Dismayed by the sudden burst of reality, Skuld watched Ironfoot amble back towards the supply hut. He wished he had parents. A normal life with a good home and the prospect of food each day. The hardships thrust upon him were overwhelming to the point he considered giving in. Malweir wouldn't miss one orphan boy. No one would. Skuld reluctantly went back to work, convinced it was no easy time to be young.

SIXTEEN

Bad Memories

Maleela, princess of Delranan and sole heir to the throne, sat on a small rock combing her auburn hair. Barely eighteen years old, she felt the crushing weight of the world bearing down on her slender shoulders. She liked to pretend she was a real princess, with handsome courtiers, a lavish room in a grand palace. The object of everyone's affection. Reality was much darker. Princess she might be, but one tainted with a family history of madness. It was her family that ripped the heart out of Delranan and ruined so many lives in Rogscroft. She despised her father for what he'd done.

The tears were all dried. What little she'd had to begin with were used early on. Her love for Aurec sustained her in the dark hours of the night when she wasn't sure she had the inner strength to continue. But she wasn't sure if he still lived. Badron had unleashed the wolves of winter under false pretense. Her love was the first thing to shatter. Fate conspired to keep her and Aurec apart. The quest to save the world--she scoffed at the idea that a handful of misfits were what Malweir needed--tore her away from the shackles of her life and sent her rushing to distant lands she'd barely read of. She hated feeling out of control but was powerless until they turned around for the return voyage.

Not that she'd ever had an easy life. Comfortable, to an extent, but seldom easy. With her mother dying in childbirth, Maleela was passed around between surrogate mothers and midwives until she was old enough to start taking care of herself. Her days were spent with the kitchen staff and servants instead of being pampered like her station deserved. She learned more secrets than she could keep, including her father's deep-rooted hatred for King Stelskor of Rogscroft. Some past slight propagated their feud. It was only a matter of time before Badron saw his opportunity and took it.

Badron blamed her for the untimely death, knowing the innocent child had nothing to do with any birth complications. That didn't stop him from manifesting his grief and sorrow into abject hatred for his only daughter. What should have brought them closer together only tore them apart. To her credit she never held it against him, at least not until recently. Maleela spent her childhood pining for her father's affections, getting only a cold brush-off instead. Indifference turned to anger, anger turned to disobedience and disobedience turned malevolent. She fully hated the man she had no choice but to call father.

Maleela tried clearing her mind. She closed her eyes and imagined Aurec's hardened face leaning close to kiss her cheek, whispering softly in her ear that everything was going to work out. She smiled but it was laden with sadness. Her heart ached, growing harder. The fairy tale she lived in was a prison far worse than any a poet might conjure with mere words. No matter how much she longed to be back in his arms she knew on a primal level that their relationship would never be the same. The feelings of pain that singular elicited took her to the brink of mental breakdown. She was strong but at the limits of her reserves mentally.

Nothing in her life made sense. Her only link to family was Bahr. Her reclusive uncle was hard beyond measure and unused to displaying any emotion, especially love. He'd given up his claim to the throne for whatever reasons and taken to a life on the open sea. Maleela viewed that as an act of cowardice, no matter how successful and renown he'd become. She wanted to cry on his shoulder, to feel the warmth of his love. Just to have him hold her tight like when Nothol pulled her from the river again would mean more than she could ever express.

Thoughts of her family dissatisfying to every degree, Maleela absently dug the tip of her dagger into the soft ground. Badron was hundreds of leagues away. Bahr wasn't a target and she had no way of knowing whether Aurec was dead or alive. Outlets for her anger ran low, leaving her with Ionascu. The crippled, demented old one brought bile to her lips. He was the representation of everything wrong with the world. What he thought was guile proved little more than a thinly disguised attempt at widening the rift between father and daughter. Not that the idea didn't have merit. She wanted nothing more than to be done with the entire sordid mess. Removing her father from power offered the most rewarding solution.

Maleela learned many things growing up. Treachery--what some would label politics--was an instinct she didn't think she had, at least not until Ionascu started hounding her. She found herself going back to visions of a throne occupied by the first queen in Delranan's history whenever her mind slipped. Between her father's distractions in Rogscroft and Harnin's purported debauchery ravaging Delranan, the path would be open for her to ascend to power. She already had the proper combination for a command staff and allies. All she needed was the military might to enforce her will.

She'd never taken a life and didn't think she ever wanted to get her hands bloodied. Having deaths committed on her command was another matter entirely. *Perhaps I could begin with Ionascu. He serves no purpose among us. Why does my uncle keep him alive*? The answers remained elusive, for she wasn't in the decision-making council. Ever since they followed the wizard into Rogscroft to steal her away from the one she loved, Maleela increasingly found herself on the outside. What secret plans did they have that they simply weren't telling her? The thought of being purposefully kept in the dark was maddening.

"You'll ruin your blade like that," Nothol's voice called from over her shoulder.

She reluctantly looked up. Any thoughts of murder or revenge fled, leaving her ashamed. "It's not really a good blade. Too old and weak to help much. Although it is good for filleting a fish."

"You should treat it properly. You'll never know when the time comes when you'll be forced to use it for real," he said.

Nothol took a seat on a path of moss across from her.

She did her best to keep frustration from showing. The last thing she needed was to be reminded of her uselessness in the group. "Nothol, when have you seen me wield a sword? My uncle ensures I'm never in harm's way. Maybe he's right for it, maybe not, but I have yet to get involved in any of the fighting."

"And you're complaining?" he asked innocently. "I'd give my right arm for the chance to be done with the violence. Don't get me wrong. I'm good at what I do but I want more from life. Every enemy I kill is one more piece of my soul that dies. Be thankful he protects you from the nightmares."

Stunned, she didn't know how to respond. Nothol was only a handful of years older but more experienced by far. To hear such blatant admission was shocking. She never imagined a man like that would regret his chosen lifestyle. "Why do you do it if it bothers you?"

He shrugged. "What else am I going to do? This is my life, Maleela. I'm good at what I do and I have just enough friends to keep me from getting into too much trouble. I earn enough to keep my belly full and a roof over my head. Well, most of the time. To be fair, this quest is getting on my last nerve. I really would like to go home, but I'll never tell Dorl that. I'd never hear the end of it!"

She giggled, imagining the falsified hostilities between them. It was that sort of bond, where one could do anything with little or no effect, that she needed to keep her balanced. A bond she sorely lacked. "I envy you, Nothol Coll."

He was genuinely taken aback. "Me? Why in all the gods would you envy me? I don't have a home. My father disowned me and I use a sword to get my point across. This isn't the sort of life you want to lead."

'We're not so different. My father has hated me from the moment I took my first breath. My family is either dead or insane and I would rather abandon all thoughts of going home than returning to that vile Keep." She took a stuttered breath. "I want the freedoms you enjoy."

He rubbed his freshly shaved chin. A bath in one of the freshwater pools and a shave were among the first things he did once they were given the liberties of going through Teng. He felt like a new man despite weeks of constant hardship. It's amazing what a little soap can do for morale.

"My life isn't freedom. I'm trapped in a world that will swallow me whole that one moment I stop paying attention," he said and paused. "Dorl's lucky. I think he's finally found love. Even if he is too hardheaded to see he's damaging it. He has something I never have and that makes him a rarity in our line of work."

"There has to be a better way, but for the life of me I don't know how. We're trapped in a vicious cycle. Only death awaits," Maleela said, head hung low.

"Don't let anyone convince you that you're not worth it, Maleela," Nothol told her with surety. "We'll pull through this and you'll find your way back to Aurec. Life has no choice but to get better."

"You really believe that?"

He nodded and gave her his most charming grin. "Of course, otherwise what's the point? I'm going to get some food. I never did like going to bed on an empty stomach. Leaves me feeling weird in the morning."

He walked off whistling, hands clasped behind his back. Nothol Coll was many things. He preferred to be a man that enjoyed life as it happened.

Night fell with the slow crawling of an army across endless plains in search of the un-findable. Life in the jungle took on a completely different feeling. Most of the villagers finished their chores and hurried within the safety of the village. Teng was nestled in the heart of the jungle where many large and terrible creatures roamed the dark. It was one of hundreds of similar villages scattered throughout the jungle.

Rekka felt out of place, as if her home was alien. She fondly recalled early childhood memories but lacked the context to make them meaningful. Teng didn't feel like home anymore. The people looked the same. The village was unchanged. She doubted anything had changed in a hundred years. Life was at its basest form deep in the jungle. Men and women hardened by the elements and taught from an early age that Brodein would swallow them the moment they weren't wary trudged about their lives in a meager existence.

The trappings of modern society didn't exist. People traded for what they needed rather than using coin to pay for it. There was an undeniable sense of peaceful coexistence between man and the jungle. Birds and small mammals ventured from the depths of trees to interact with the villagers. Snakes and spiders the size of dinner plates crawled along the ground, all but ignoring the people of Teng. Only the large predators remained hidden.

She'd only been gone for a little over a decade. Any connections once shared between herself and anyone else in the village were lost. Seeing Cashi Dam should have invoked certain emotions. They'd never loved each other, though she suspected Cashi had vastly different feelings than she did. He was a proud warrior, heir to the defense of Teng. Any woman would be proud to call him husband. His social status was bound to rise once the elder finally passed. Rekka wasn't impressed by the trappings of power.

She rebuked his advances in favor of training for her eventual apprenticeship to the citadel of Trennaron. Her life was meant for bigger, more important events than mere marriage to a village leader. Naturally Cashi didn't understand. How could any woman of Teng ignore his displays of strength? He grew angry after she turned her back and walked into the jungle. Rekka never had a real choice. She was meant to serve the Guardian just as he was meant to defend his village. The last she saw of Cashi Dam was with his fists clenched and face twisted in rage. She never expected to see him again.

Sitting at the edge of the jungle, the very same edge she had last seen him, Rekka replayed the events in her mind. Nothing had changed in all the years she'd been gone. Worse, her relationship with Dorl was unnecessarily strained by her reunion with Cashi. She didn't plan on meeting him again. Didn't plan on him still pining for her, but that was the cold reality of the situation. She saw it in his eyes. Cashi Dam still cared deeply for her. She closed her eyes and tried to flush the images away.

"The jungle is not safe at night, Rekka. You should know better than to sit here alone."

Rekka frowned. She desperately wanted, needed, to be alone to get her thoughts in order and find a way through the miasma of human emotion choking her. Cashi Dam's sudden arrival prevented any progress. "The jungle is not my enemy."

"Ah yes. You have spent many years traveling under the trees in the name of a higher calling," he replied. The derision in his voice was like a slap to the face.

"I do what I was called upon to do. Nothing more."

He shuffled closer. Each footstep the slightest whisper. "We all have duties. Your life is not so unique in that regard."

Rekka finally couldn't take any more and stood to face him. "Why have you come to me, Cashi? I am in no mood to use words carelessly."

"Is it not obvious?" he asked. That familiar look haunted his dark brown eyes.

"No. Speak plainly."

He fidgeted slightly, clearly nervous. Rekka's heart clutched. Her stomach twisted. She wasn't ready for this. Her eyes closed so that he wouldn't see the sorrow building in them.

"I love you, Rekka. The time has come for you to be my wife," he said. His words were strained, unsure. Cashi planted his spear in the ground and straightened his back in expectation of her reply.

Rekka despised her situation. She wasn't meant to fall in love. Part of being sent to Trennaron entailed limited human contact and no possibility of finding love. Cashi didn't understand. He couldn't. His place was here, with his people. Rekka willingly surrendered any semblance of a normal life in favor of serving a higher power. At least that's what she told herself. Truthfully, she ran away because she didn't love Cashi and was opposed to the entire arranged marriage tradition of her people. The antiquity of such actions wasn't necessary in today's world. Not even in Teng. She longed for the freedom of the open plains. The cold wind in her hair and the right to choose how to live her life. The confinements of an arranged marriage to a man she harbored no feelings for was a fate worse than death.

"We have been through this once before. In this very same spot. Must we return to the past without reason?" she said carefully. She might not have feelings for him but neither did she want to bruise his already fragile ego.

His face darkened. "Without reason? How can you say that? I have professed my love for you. Nothing has changed for me in all the time you've been gone. Your coming back to Teng is a blessing!"

Don't say it, Cashi. Please. If you value anything that either of us stands for, don't say it.

Cashi exhaled a deep breath. "I've longed for the day of your return. Never once did I stop loving you. I know I shouldn't say it, but you have been on my mind since the day you left. Can't you see? The gods want us to be together."

"Why can't you understand? We can never be together. The same gods you believe have guided our paths have other things in store for us both. Don't be so quick to misinterpret signs to justify your irrationality. Feelings must not be involved in this. It is the only way we can overcome the rift between us."

"I have waited years for you to return to me and this is how you repay loyalty?" he fumed. "Has your life at Trennaron been so void of humanity to leave you compassionless? I've turned down all others in the hopes of holding you in my arms for the rest of my life. I will not be denied again."

She paused. The thought of drawing her sword briefly entered her mind. Cashi was acting irrationally and she feared what he might do. Pride was the downfall many and he was ripe to take the first step off the cliff. Blinded to all but his personal need for a thing that simply didn't exist, he was potentially dangerous. The crazed look tainting his eyes told her she'd never draw her sword in time.

"Denied what? Our parents barely knew each other when they arranged our marriage. We were five! That is no life to live, Cashi. You and I both deserve better," she said cautiously. "Stop waiting for me and live your life. You have strength and will soon have the power and respect of the tribe. Any woman would be fortunate to have your hand. My life is already taken."

He tensed. Cold recognition flooded him, draining his strength. "It is another. You love one of the outlanders."

She opened her mouth but closed it just as fast.

"I've been a fool," he sneered. The warrior of Teng cast his spear down and stomped back and forth. "How could you abandon me for one of *them*? Do your own people mean so little to you?"

"This has nothing to do with our people. I have seen things inside Trennaron. Wondrous and terrible things at once. There is much to this world that you know nothing of. How can I go back to such simplicity after learning secrets of the world?"

If he heard, he chose not to acknowledge her. "Which one?"

"What?"

"Which one is it? I will call him to single combat. The victor will take your hand and your heart," he said. He was determined now. Her admission lit a fire in the depths of his soul.

Rekka pointed a slender finger at him as her eyes narrowed. "Enough! This hopeless romanticism has gone on for far too long. You don't love me, Cashi Dam. You love a thought. Nothing more. Are you so blind as to miss the truth right before your eyes? From this point on you will stay away from me and my companions."

"How dare you!" he all but shouted.

"You are a great warrior, but you are trapped in the shadows of a memory. I am not yours. I never was. Live your life. Become the leader our people deserve. This self-debasement accomplishes nothing. It is not healthy."

Rebuked, Cashi Dam retrieved his spear and fixed her with a withering glare. "This is not over, Rekka. Not by far."

He stormed back into Teng, venting curses in their ancient language. Thoughts of revenge twisted his mind. Rekka watched him go with mixed emotions. She didn't like the idea of ruining his illusions so bluntly but saw no other choice. Cashi Dam had grown headstrong and reckless since their youth. He was not the same. Nor was he what he should be. Lust had changed him into something she failed to recognize. He was entirely capable of flying off the handle and exacting his hostility on any one of them. She had to warn the others.

SEVENTEEN

Partings

Much to Bahr's surprise most villagers were up and about their chores well before dawn. He'd seldom seen such dedication, from any race. That train of thought brought him to his current companions. Never an odder group had he served with. A Dwarf, Giant, Gaimosian, wizard, and the woman from Teng. He couldn't imagine combining so many different cultures in one quest. Then there were the monsters and other foul creatures stalking them. Bahr felt another twenty years ripped from his life.

He'd never been much for believing in gods or magic. Life was life without much else to it. You were born and lived until you died. He didn't care so much what awaited after closing his eyes that final time. There wasn't a point in worrying about what he couldn't prevent, or control. Lord Death waited for them all. He'd discover the truth when it happened. Besides, there was too much to see in Malweir to focus on what came next. Answerless questions were a waste of time. The demands of the day all but drained him mentally. What little he had left was focused on keeping his friends alive.

Bahr was a realist though. He knew that just because he didn't have time for gods or other mythical beings didn't mean they weren't concerned about him. The dark gods had thrown everything they had at him so far, at least according to Anienam. He didn't know how much more he could withstand. The uneasy feeling of being hunted by the Gnaal lingered just beyond the edge of consciousness. He wasn't accustomed to being afraid of much but the very thought of the Gnaal sparked such fear it was all he could do to stay on his feet.

Sighing, he questioned why him. The Sea Wolf pulled his trousers up and headed back into the village proper. Even after six decades he still relished that first trip to the latrine. There were very few feelings like it. He caught the murmurs coming from his companions and a handful of warriors who hadn't stopped watching them since their arrival. Bahr had a mind to confront them to get the tension out of the way. Only the wisdom born from countless experiences prevented this. Boen may be itching for a fight but Bahr wanted to avoid as much conflict as possible. He didn't think he had enough left to carry them back to Delranan for the coming war with the dark gods. Wasting time and energy fighting tribal warriors made little sense in the grand scheme of things.

"They call this a wagon," Boen said and stared at the ramshackle cart barely capable of holding Skuld, much less hundreds of pounds of supplies. "I wouldn't let my mother ride this."

"I didn't know you had a mother," Nothol chided as he finished strapping down a barrel of fresh water.

Boen frowned. "Keep laughing. When this wreck breaks down and you have to carry the supplies we'll see who has the last laugh."

"I've been laughing since we left Delranan the second time," the sell sword replied glibly. "It's the only thing keeping me sane."

Snorting his understanding, Boen went off in search of something else to occupy his time. He'd been in the field and campaigns enough to know when to ignore the inconsequential. The wagon was not worth his time. Half of the floorboards were rotted through and the ropes serving as walls were just as bad. He doubted the wagon would last the rest of the day, much less the entire trip to Trennaron.

"How far do we have left to go?" Dorl asked to anyone willing to answer.

Anienam yawned and stretched. His bones creaked. His muscles screamed. He hated feeling old. "No more than a few days I should think."

"You think? Why aren't I reassured?"

Giving a cross look to the sell sword, the wizard explained, "The gods of light, in all their wisdom, saw a time when their dark brethren would attempt to return, despite their assurances that all sides would abandon Malweir. So they created Trennaron. It is a place of extreme power, tapped from the very soul of the world some say. I've never seen it personally. There are texts in the libraries of Ipn Shal suggesting the jungle *moves* around Trennaron, keeping it hidden from interlopers."

"Moves? As in picks up and changes positions?" Ironfoot asked skeptically. "Anienam, trees don't move in any direction except up."

"Or down," Nothol added halfheartedly.

"Yes, yes I know all that. You miss my point. The Jungles of Brodein are imbued with the magical runoff from Trennaron. There is magic in this place. That's why Rekka's dream masters can successfully see into the future. Otherwise they'd be shriveled old husks smoking lotus leaves and dancing naked in the dark. The jungle moves. Yes, it picks up and changes positions daily to confuse numbskulls like the two of you!"

Dorl gave Nothol a quick shrug and mischievous grin. "Guess we hit pretty close to the nerve to get him all riled up."

"Sounds like he didn't get enough sleep," Nothol added.

Anienam folded his spindly arms across his chest and sputtered.

"Relax, wizard. They're tugging your chain," Bahr said. "Although it was fairly amusing watching you lose your mind for a moment. We need a good laugh." He came close enough to whisper, "You don't really expect us to believe the trees just get up and walk around at night."

Indignant, Anienam merely said, "I know what I know."

Bahr playfully slapped him on the back. "How much is left to do before we can leave? The villagers seemed to want us gone in a hurry."

"A few more stacks of dry goods and we'll be ready," Ironfoot told him. "We did a good job last night. There's no rush."

"Not from our end at least." Bahr stared back at the group of warriors, clearly their watchdogs for the duration of their stay in Teng. "What do you suppose has got them so intent about us?"

He caught Dorl glancing towards Rekka and immediately understood. The weird dynamic between them suddenly grew more complicated with the reemergence of Cashi Dam. It was a complication Bahr neither had the time for nor the inclination to deal with. Part of the reason he'd never been married was to avoid situations exactly like this. Former love interests were bad news and carried the potential to tear the group apart. He didn't like the idea of leaving anyone behind, especially one of the group. *I can see the rush after all. I only hope Dorl doesn't do anything stupid to jeopardize our quest. Anienam says he needs us all. We can't afford even the smallest slipup.*

As if on cue, Cashi Dam stormed towards them, a host of young warriors eager to prove their worth against the outlanders. Their spears glittered with firelight. Rekka and the others rose and formed a loose semi-circle. Her hand was already on the hilt of her sword.

"Nobody do anything sudden," Bahr cautioned his people. "We don't want any accidents."

"Who speaks for you?" Cashi demanded with sudden formality Bahr hadn't expected.

"I do. What is the meaning of this?"

The tribal leader pointed accusingly at Rekka. "I have come for the one that claims Rekka Jel's love. If he is worthy he will defeat me in single combat."

Bahr looked back at Dorl. The sell sword was ready to attack. Turning back to Cashi, he said, "If he's unworthy?"

Cashi's grin was pure wickedness. "His corpse will be fed to the jungle."

A flash. Someone cried out. Weapons dropped. Blinded, Bahr stumbled back a step before running into Boen. Anienam strode forward, coming to stop between the groups. "There will be no duel this morning!"

His voice projected to every corner of the village. It was an old device the Mage orders employed during the war. He never imagined using it in Teng, amongst friends. Most of the villagers remained stunned. They clawed at their eyes. A few were on their knees with tears streaming. Anienam looked at his companions and saw fewer reactions. The direction of the blast had been focused on the villagers, though residual effects tormented the others as well.

"You are the proud warriors of Teng. Why do you debase yourselves for personal gratification when none is required? Have the people of Teng fallen so far from their lofty principles that they are unable to recognize valor, commitment, or integrity?"

"She abandoned commitment!" Cashi shouted. "None of this would be happening if she had fulfilled her duties."

"I am not cattle!" Rekka shouted back, unable to stand his torments any longer. "I tried to do this without suffering you embarrassment but you are intent on it. Very well. I never loved you, Cashi Dam. Our parents arranged our marriage when we were small children. It is your misguided sense of belief that prevents you from moving on. The world has changed since we were children. I am a grown Woman. A sword master and the defender of the Guardian of Trennaron. Who are you to reduce the meaning of my life to a mere concubine?"

Dorl smiled suddenly, as if a great weight had been cast from his heart. He realized that all the angst he'd been feeling was misdirected. Rekka was as solid as the day they'd met. He never had reason to doubt her. Ashamed, he moved to stand beside her. All the animosity was now reserved solely for Cashi Dam and his spoiled warriors.

"You were meant to be mine! The gods demand it!" Cashi protested. Each word was weaker than the first. Not even his lust was enough to keep him from understanding he was on the verge of becoming a laughingstock among his warriors. He'd lose all respect and fall to the bottom. All his dreams would go up in flames. It was time to tread carefully if he was going to salvage anything. Wheels turning, Cashi started forming a plan.

"Who can say what the will of the gods is?" Anienam asked them all. "We are just mortals. It is not for any of us to pretend to understand their ways. Are you so vain to pretend to know the will of the gods, Cashi Dam? Or are you still the one chosen to lead Teng into the future for the good of his people?"

"I am that man," he said slowly, pronouncing each syllable. "Very well. My warriors will not hinder your movement, but you are no longer welcome in Teng. Leave immediately. May the jungle swallow you all."

A few of the younger warriors balked, stunned by what they heard. No one ever wished ill of any traveler moving into the jungle. For Cashi to summon ill so blatantly upon their guests was unheard of. They looked over their shoulders, fearful the spirits of Brodein were already barreling towards them with death in their claws.

Bahr ignored the urge to spit at the young fool and simply said, "Finish loading up. This village isn't what we're looking for."

Cashi rose to the insult and stepped forward until Boen emerged and smiled. Pride was no match for the martial prowess of a Gaimosian and the jungle man knew it. Instead of retreating he stood his ground, hoping the display was enough to satisfy honor. The rest of Rekka's companions ignored him and went back to work. There was still much to do and little time left in which to do it. Most felt the sooner they were away the better things would get. All were willing to take their chances with the jungle rather than spend another moment in the suddenly hostile village of Teng. Only Rekka expressed sorrow. She bore no love for her home, but it saddened her to think she'd never be able to return.

The sun was just beginning to creep above the far horizon when the wagon groaned into motion. Horses sniggered. None of the riders spared a backwards glance. It had been a mistake coming here. One they were more than ready to put behind them. Only the jungle and Trennaron remained ahead. They were close to the Blud Hamr and completing their quest. The noose drew tighter.

EIGHTEEN

What Remains

Chadra was entirely unrecognizable. First the rebellion and then the plague saw to the permanent restructuring that left it all but a burned-out ruin. Those citizens fortunate enough to survive the plague fled to the countryside in the hopes of finding a place in nearby villages or, for those especially brave souls, deep in the south far away from civil war. Many froze to death along the way, for winter continued to worsen. The death toll was near catastrophic. It would be many years before the true reckoning of this winter was known, but Chadra and all Delranan would never be the same again.

Ingrid pulled the wool blanket tighter around her shoulders as they continued to ride. The arguments over staying in Chadra or moving to the countryside were rendered moot by Inaella's betrayal. Tufts of bright blond hair poked from under her hood. They were the only brightness in her world. Her first mistake was in thinking the plague had consumed the former leader of the rebellion council. She should have killed Inaella when she had the chance but a misplaced sense of honor prevented it. Ingrid didn't like killing. In fact, she hated the sight of blood. Her stomach turned every time. Going through the physical act of killing would shake her to the foundations of her belief system, leaving her a husk of what she could have been. She wasn't ready to make that leap, yet.

She briefly studied the endless sea of white drifts. Winters were normally harsh but this year proved much worse than any in recent memory. Abandoned homes were stripped of any usable wood. Families huddled under thick pines hoping for another dawn. Others simply gave up and went out into the wilderness to die. It pained Ingrid to see so much suffering, knowing she was part of the problem.

Coupled with her personal grief from so many losses, she turned inward and used it all to her advantage. She needed to feel rage to continue. Otherwise…

A trio of crows, black as midnight, burst from a small stand of white birch. Their calls mocked her. Ingrid looked back over her shoulder. They left Chadra two days ago and she hadn't been able to shake the feeling of being hunted. The Wolfsreik were relentless when given a task. Harnin drove them to extremes in his efforts to pacify the kingdom in his image. The crows served as a reminder.

"You need to relax," Orlek recommended.

"How can I? We barely escaped the city. Harnin will stop at nothing to find us."

He shook his head. "Harnin is blind, Ingrid. He hunts a shadow, nothing more. Even with Inaella's aid he can't catch up. The rebellion is effectively scattered now. There's no easy way for him to contain us. Not without killing off most of the population."

She reined in her horse. "Do you really think he'll go that far?"

"Once, no, but after everything we've seen? Harnin will burn Delranan to the ground so long as it suits his purpose. He's a vile creature." Orlek spat a wad of phlegm in disgust. "The gods have truly abandoned us to allow a man like that the freedom of doing what he wants."

Ingrid blinked to clear the cold-induced tears away. "Harnin does what his character demands. I don't know if blaming the gods helps anything. We know how he is. That should make it easier to combat him. We need to be the steel against his will."

"Save the speeches for the rank and file. I've been with you from the beginning and will continue to do so until the end. Just don't patronize me with grand speeches," he told her flatly. "I'm a soldier. Point me at the enemy and I know what to do. You're the brains behind the rebellion now. You can't afford to think small."

She didn't care for his tone but he had a point. Ingrid stole the leadership role from Inaella and success or defeat was squarely on her shoulders. She needed to force aside all thoughts of friendship, loss, or grief, and focus on being the leader the people needed. The rebellion was at a crossroads. Any movement in the wrong direction would damn their cause irrevocably. Ingrid felt the pressure mounting and wondered if she was strong enough to carry the burden.

They finally arrived at the small village of Fendi in the late afternoon of their third day of travel. Both Ingrid and Orlek were worn out. Their bodies ached from being in the saddle for so long. An impossible chill ran deep through their bones. Each had a few fingertips or toes with early symptoms of frostbite. Orlek had a large, raw spot on his right cheek from constantly being exposed to severe winds. Frost glistened in his hair. He'd endured worse over the course of his life, but nothing was as sweet as smelling freshly baked bread on the crisp winter air. His stomach grumbled in concurrence. Orlek slid to the ground and went to help Ingrid.

"We've made it. Hopefully others will have arrived," he said.

Ingrid scanned the village. All the thatch roofs had chimneys pouring rich, dark smoke. A good sign. The plague didn't appear to have made it this far west. She needed a new base of power. One Harnin wouldn't think to look, at least for the immediate future. Ingrid knew the rebellion was reeling, suffering defeat after defeat. There had to be a way for a quick victory. She just didn't know how. Nothing in her life prepared her for any of this. She didn't know much about tactics or warfare. She'd been a housewife up until the moment her husband died. More than ever she felt like a child playing with adults.

"Where are they?" she asked.

Not a soul could be seen.

Orlek, discouraged by the lack of reception, remained wary. His own past was private, for good reason.

He cringed to think what Ingrid would say if she learned he was a murderer. Some crimes were simply not forgiven. The rope marks burned into his neck were proof of that. He respected Ingrid, even with her lack of experience. Sometimes luck was worth more than real life experience. He looked around the village, seeing the same things she had noticed.

"It is cold outside. No sane person would be out in the elements," he speculated. His hand crept towards his sword. He couldn't trust anything to chance.

"There are few sane people left in Delranan," she countered. "We need to get inside. I don't want to be caught in the cold again when the sun goes down."

"Agreed. I believe the village inn is this way," Orlek said and nudged his horse forward.

They remained cautious even as they tied their horses up to the post outside the inn and went up the steps. Orlek led the way. Aged doors squealed open, threatening to fall from the hinges. Confidence uninspired, he pushed inside. Old clouds of smoke clung to the rafters. Most of the wood was yellowed, reminding him of jaundice. A thin coat of dust clung to the floor, marred only by the occasional boot print. Most of the tables hadn't been used in months. A half-burned fire stretched up the chimney. While safe from the elements, the common room felt anything but friendly. Three old timers sat at the chipped and scratched bar. A surly looking man with thinning hair and massive fists the size of slabs of beef stood behind the scratched counter. His right eye was missing and he either didn't care or was too poor to afford an eye patch. He stared hard at the newcomers.

"Close the door. I ain't paying to heat the outdoors," he ordered once they entered.

Orlek gently shut the door behind him and led Ingrid up to the bar. He doubted he'd be able to take the bigger man in a fair fight. Fortunately he was well-versed in fighting unfair. He took an empty stool and stared back.

"You got a problem, little man?" the bartender threatened.

Orlek shrugged. "I might if you don't do your job and pour me and my friend here a drink. It's damned cold outside and we've been out in the weather for three days."

"Sounds to me like you should keep on running. We don't like trouble around here."

"We didn't come bringing trouble," Orlek replied straightforwardly.

"Stranger, people always come with trouble. Just the way that it is these days." He turned to pour two wooden mugs of watered-down ale. "Where ya coming from?"

Ingrid passed Orlek a nervous glance, not unnoticed by the bartender. The soldier waved off her concerns, at least pretending he knew what he was doing. "South. Been a bad winter, what with the plague hitting us."

Those few patrons stiffened at the mention of plague and shifted away. Even the bartender balked. "We don't have none of that in Fendi and don't want none either. You need to finish your drinks and be heading on."

Orlek took the mug and gulped a hearty drink. "We're not going anywhere until we get some rest, food, and a warm room to sleep in. I'm tired of being on the road."

"How do we know you ain't carrying the disease?" the bartender pressed.

"Because they'd be dead already," a new voice answered.

A slender man with a bushy mustache stood at the bottom of the steps watching the scene unfold. The small handheld crossbow was barely visible from beneath his cloak. The bartender backed off, knowing danger when he saw it. The stranger, with eyes so odd they appeared almost red, walked straight up to Orlek.

"You took your sweet time in getting here," he said crisply.

Orlek rose and faced him. "You would have to if you had half the army looking for you."

The stranger extended his free hand. "Orlek. It's good to see you again."

"Harlan. Been a long time," Orlek said, returning the gesture.

Ingrid finally let out the breath she'd been holding and took a drink. The unanticipated tension was all too much for her already fragile nerves.

"Did you have any trouble finding the town?" Harlan asked, holstering his crossbow.

"Not really, but we did have to dodge more than a few patrols the closer we were to Chadra. Delranan's not safe anymore."

Harlan frowned. "Perhaps we should take this up to your rooms. I took the liberty of securing adjoining rooms for you on the second floor. Mister Farley here won't mind having two prestigious individuals spending a few days in his inn. Will you, Farley?"

The bartender scowled, but merely nodded. "No trouble at all, so long as the tab is paid."

"Don't fret about your purse. You'll be compensated handsomely," Harlan told him. "Have two plates of food brought up to my room with a pitcher of ale, the good stuff, not that swill you're serving behind the bar, and a pitcher of fresh water."

Farley didn't take kindly to being insulted but knew Harlan was more dangerous than he looked. The red-eyed man was easily capable of killing everyone in the common room without breaking a sweat. Some situations were best solved by keeping your mouth shut and doing what you were told. Farley did just that, cursing Harlan and his friends behind their back as they went upstairs.

Once inside the room, Harlan immediately went to look out the window. He purposefully chose rooms facing the eastern approach. He'd been playing the game long enough not to fall prey to being ambushed without every precaution being taken. Offering a chair for Ingrid, he took off his cloak and set the crossbow on the nearest table.

"You shouldn't have come in during the daylight. The One Eye has spies everywhere. I'm sure someone here is on his payroll, or looking to secure the safety of their family," he added. Harlan despised the One Eye almost as much as he did Badron. His reasons were his own and not a single living soul knew why. It was a secret he'd take the grave.

Orlek all but collapsed on the bed. "We didn't have much choice. That last storm almost did us in. You haven't been to Chadra in a while. The plague weakened everyone. People are starving. I barely had enough food to make it here."

"Is everything in place?" Ingrid interrupted. She was impatient to begin the next phase of the rebellion.

Harlan eyed her appraisingly. She had fire that translated to personal strength he could respect. Just what the rebellion needed if they were to win the struggle against Harnin. "Mostly. I have found enough people willing to carry on the fight. My people are scouring the countryside as we speak, moving from town to town in efforts to raise support and troop strength. Most of the outer towns hold no favor towards the crown. Badron's done a poor enough job garnering the support of the commoners. He's neglected most of these small towns. They don't care who's in control so long as they have a say in how the kingdom is run."

"Sounds like they're deluded to me," Orlek answered. "No king bothers with the peasants, at least not this far north."

"And it doesn't really matter, does it?" Harlan replied. "Harnin is running this kingdom into the ground one corpse at a time. We've got the upper hand even if he doesn't know it. Delranan is ready to explode. The previous rebellion leadership saw it but didn't know how to instigate it."

Orlek and Ingrid shared guarded looks. Reluctantly, Ingrid added, "It's worse than you think. Inaella survived the coup and the plague and has gone over to Harnin."

Harlan was taken back. "You mean she's now working against us?"

Ingrid nodded. The sting bit deep, fueling her desire to finally free her kingdom and be done with the whole sordid affair. Her eyelids fluttered closed. She hadn't realized just how tired she was until now. The pillow at the head of the bed, plump and soft, had never been so inviting.

Orlek saw the fatigue on her face and pushed on. "How many fighters can you raise in this part of the kingdom?"

"A few hundred I imagine," Harlan replied after some thought. "The winter makes it difficult to gather in large numbers."

"We'll need more than a few hundred. One Eye has thousands," Orlek replied, knowing just how grave the situation really was. Very few men, especially married ones, were willing to abandon their lives in deep winter to risk getting killed for no reason. Until a few weeks ago Orlek had been one of them.

"Which brings me to my second point. We are sorely outnumbered. The hundreds of volunteers we have willing to join in with us are peasants. Farmers mostly. They're untrained, ill-disciplined, and likely to kill their friends rather than the enemy. Harnin's soldiers are battle tested. They may be reserves, but they are Wolfsreik reserves. The best the rebellion had died during the plague or the great purges. We don't stand a chance with what remains."

Orlek ran a hand through his thinning hair. He didn't have the answers anyone sought. "There's always hope," he said defiantly. The words sounded empty even to his ears.

"Orlek, you should consider taking her and leaving to the south," Harlan advised. "Matters here will continue to devolve until the Delranan we knew is dead. Cut your losses and run while you still can."

The mercenary looked down on Ingrid, who'd fallen asleep. "She believes in us. What choice does that leave me?"

NINETEEN

Ruins

The combination of smoke and burnt flesh choked the air. A dark, miasmic cloud hung low over the city, reminding the combined army of a large death shroud. Trees stabbed up, void of all life. Their blackened trunks added death for miles. What forces Badron retained not only burned the city but the surrounding countryside. All water sources were poisoned, mostly with corpses. Supply warehouses were looted and burned to the ground. Any citizens still living, of which there were very few, dug deep underground to hide, silently praying they'd go unnoticed by the rampaging Goblins.

King Aurec insisted on being the first to ride into Rogscroft proper. He brushed off the cries and pleas from his top commanders. One monarch had already fallen. The fragile alliance couldn't bear to go through another. General Rolnir insisted a guard of five hundred if Aurec was to continue with his foolishness. Begrudgingly, he accepted. Banners and pennants waved in the dying breeze, the colors of two kingdoms as well as the shadow kingdom of the Pell Darga, whose swarthy warriors skimmed the shadows well ahead of the rest of the army. They had one purpose: kill any enemy left behind.

The last stretch of the road seemed to go on forever. Aurec was impatient to return to the castle. To right the wrongs committed by Badron and his army of defilers. His sword was already in his hand, even while knowing the enemy was long gone. Whatever he hoped to find buried in the rubble of the heart of his kingdom wasn't comparable to what awaited them.

Aurec reined in his horse and struggled not to vomit. Mounds of bodies lay piled along both sides of the road. Their grotesque angles, haunted faces, and putrid odors permeated the very ground. Hacked-off limbs and heads filled in the gaps. Badron, more likely Grugnak, ordered all the dead in Rogscroft to be left on the main avenues of approach as a welcoming home present for the fledgling king. Crows and vultures flocked by the hundreds to feast. Several soldiers in the guard turned their heads to empty their stomachs.

"How?" was all Aurec managed to say.

Venten, ever at his side, struggled to control his emotions. Many of the faces were of people he'd known over the course of his long life. Friends. Attendants. Shopkeepers and merchants. The soul of Rogscroft lay butchered like sheep. "Badron."

"Do you think...do you think my...father is in there?" Aurec stammered.

"Not even Badron would allow his favored enemy such a fate," Venten added. "King Stelskor will be in the castle."

"But all these people. What did they do to deserve such?" Aurec asked. His youth and lack of experience burdened him greatly. He needed to lash out. To retaliate, but against who? Without a target his aggression was pointless.

"We are at war. Armies of Goblins rampage across our lands. There will be more scenes like this from here to the Murdes Mountains. You must steel yourself against the atrocity. It is bound to worsen before the end."

Aurec squared off on his trusted advisor. "Your words are cold and callous, old friend. Did you counsel my father like this?"

"When he needed it," Venten replied solemnly. The pain of loss was still too much to bear. He viewed Stelskor's death as personal failure. "What are your orders?"

Aurec reluctantly set aside his personal issues to become king again. All his rage boiled down to impotence. He had no enemy to fight. No city to return to like the rescuing hero they deserved. His gaze lifted beyond the heaps of bodies to his beloved city. Once grand buildings of stone and wood were little better than rubble. Rogscroft was thoroughly destroyed. Not even the dead lived there any longer.

Untold desecrations filled the palace. Murals painted in human blood covered walls, arching up to the high ceilings. Bones, gnawed upon, lay scattered down the long halls. There was a terrible odor that no amount of cleaning would easily get rid of. Waste and offal from things Aurec wasn't willing to guess filled the shadowed corners. Lost was all the splendor Stelskor had tried to create. A gift to his people so that they might find strength when weakness threatened to subsume their will. Aurec stood in the middle of the throne room and struggled not to weep.

"Sire, patrols have finished sweeping the city. The enemy is gone."

Using his sleeve to wipe the tears filling his eyes, Aurec turned. "Thank you, Mahn. How many casualties?"

"Balko's horse tripped in the rubble and broke a leg. We had to put it down and he twisted his wrist pretty well," the old scout reported. "He'll be fine but can't use his sword until the wrist heals."

Better than any dead or wounded. Well, I've reclaimed my kingdom. Now what do I do? By all rights I shouldn't even be here. My father was the true monarch. I'm just a boy playing at being a man. This war has changed us all and I'm not sure for the better. Is it all a joke? Am I merely a pawn, a joke in some theological circle I'm not meant to understand? I wish you were here, Father. I need your wisdom. I'm not the man I should be. The longer this war lasts the more I can't help but think it was all my fault. I never should have gone to Delranan to take Maleela. Our love is the great curse between our kingdoms.

"Send the word to the main body. I want the Wolfsreik occupying the city by nightfall. Detail work crews to put the fires out, look for survivors, and begin constructing enough shelters for the civilians to get out of the cold." He paused. "Our city may be in ruin but we have an obligation to look beyond ourselves for the good of all. Make it happen, Mahn."

"Yes, sire," the scout replied and headed off on his task. He knew Rolnir hadn't left anything to chance and most of the Wolfsreik was already moving into position around the disaster of Rogscroft. Battle-hardened soldiers from all three armies saw it as their duty to restore order and faith to those few survivors still trapped in the city. Many of Aurec's forces were from the city proper and took it as personal insult. Those were the ones who worked the hardest. Mahn let Aurec alone for a while. The young king certainly had more to process than a mere scout. Even if that scout was nominated to the king's council.

A host of others passed him as he was leaving, bringing any personal moments for the king to an abrupt end. He grinned ruefully, suddenly grateful for being just a scout. Trading the freedom of the open road for the confinement of a throne wasn't wise. Mahn was made to roam the unexplored parts of the world, not wither away inside while life rode past.

"Mahn didn't feel like sitting through another meeting?" Vajna asked lightheartedly.

Aurec smiled, despite the solemnity of his surroundings. "He has a purpose to be about. Besides, he's earned the right to do what he does. How many others have put themselves on the line like that?"

Vajna could name plenty off the top of his head. The entire army had risked everything to meet with the Wolfsreik, Pell Darga, and attempt to reclaim a kingdom against hordes of Goblins soldiers. Boiling those actions down to a single man, regardless of who it was, diminished their deeds. Vajna believed that every soldier in the combined army deserved praise for his actions. He couldn't figure out how to tell that to his youthful king and still maintain his position.

"What's our next move?" Venten asked. He was eager to begin the cleansing process, to honor the late king.

Aurec sighed, still unsure which direction he wanted to move. Badron was loose somewhere in the kingdom, along with an unknown number of Goblins and men. There was no telling what damage they were capable of. "Badron has to be our first concern. As long as he remains at large he poses a threat to the stability of Rogscroft. We need to have units scouring the countryside for him. I would very much like to put Badron's head on the same pike he used on my father."

"He's fleeing back to Delranan in all likelihood," the elder man said. "There's no place for him to hide here. Every man, woman, and child will be looking for him."

"Badron's experienced enough not to move without knowing he could succeed. There must be some factor we're missing. I need Rolnir here," Aurec said.

"He's en route," Vajna replied. "Piper Joach is seeing to the disposition of the army but it's a mess. Every major industry and public work has been demolished. It will take weeks just to rebuild enough to keep the snow off our heads. Badron did a very thorough job in ruining the kingdom before he fled."

"If he fled at all," Aurec countered. "We must assume he is trying to get back to Delranan, as Venten suggested, but why? Reports are Harnin One Eye has claimed the throne for himself and turned the kingdom into a shallow effigy of what it once was. So what does he hope to accomplish by going home?"

"I don't see the point in worrying about that. Once he's gone, good riddance. Rogscroft is ours again and we have the solemn duty to rebuild it." Vajna, of them all, seemed tired of the war. He wanted to hang up his sword belt and retire already.

"Badron is my priority! He will pay for what he's done to our people, my family, and this kingdom!" Aurec shouted. The words echoed throughout the empty throne room.

Even Venten took a step back. No one had ever heard Aurec's rage before and the strength of conviction in his words shook their faith in what was morally right. The war changed many things. They were all vastly different from that first moment the Wolfsreik began the long march east. Death and suffering, once reduced to war gaming, were now so prevalent they had grown calloused to the sights of battle. Aurec was stronger, tougher, and meaner than a man his age should be. All thanks to Badron. Venten frowned, knowing there was only one inevitable conclusion to this sad state of affairs. One of them needed to die.

"Sire, General Rolnir is here," an aide announced from the entrance to the throne room.

Aurec waved him in, the angry scowl gradually fading as his mind calmed. He watched the Wolfsreik's commanding officer enter with the loping gait he now associated with the wolf soldiers. The fur cloak hugging him reminded Aurec of a wild animal, a barely restrained beast in search of fresh victims. The young king envied the general, though he'd never admit it. War came easy to one like Rolnir. Not so for Aurec. He wanted to be hard. To be the warrior king so many legends revolved around. Only he didn't have it in him. He was forced to rely on veterans like Rolnir and Vajna to execute his will on his enemies.

"The city is a disgrace," Rolnir said after stopping. He folded his arms across his wide chest and planted his feet shoulder width apart. The stance of a true warrior. "Badron and Grugnak have done everything they can to bog us down with recovery operations. It will be months, perhaps years before Rogscroft returns to any semblance of a habitable place."

"Time we can't afford to waste if we're to bring this war to a close," Aurec replied.

Rolnir's light red eyebrow rose sharply. "Is that your true intent?"

"Among other things."

Venten shifted his gaze from the king to the general. He'd been in the royal courts a long time and had seen many scenarios most people simply wouldn't believe, but this was beyond any of his reckoning. Aurec was determined to pursue this struggle to the ends of his people. The former general-turned advisor wanted nothing more than to retire to a secluded part of the world and be forgotten by history. He feared he wouldn't live to see the end of this war. So many friends had fallen over the course of the winter. Every time he turned around another empty chair sat at the table. Madness consumed those still living. Madness threatened to drag Aurec down and reduce him to his basest form. Venten needed to find a way to reverse the change, for the good of the king and his kingdom.

"Badron still has a card to play," he spoke up.

Aurec extended his hands. "What card? He's abandoned the city he once craved above all else. His army has sided with us and what remains of the Goblins are fleeing with him. Tell me, Venten, what card does he have left?"

"Maleela."

The singular answer made Aurec's heart skip. So focused on the prosecution of the war as he'd been he had all but forgotten her. No, not forgotten. Merely set aside to win. Any thoughts of her weakened his resolved. Left him hollow. With her by his side he felt like he could do no wrong. Perhaps if she remained with him he'd be able to find a clear path through this mess.

"You don't know for certain," was all he managed to say.

"No, but the possibility certainly exists. You must prepare yourself for every eventuality, Aurec. His hatred for her is well documented. What's to stop him from using her to get you to lay down your sword and surrender all we've won?" Venten pressed. He needed the boy to think clearly with his mind rather than with his sword.

Rolnir coughed gently, drawing all attention. "While I have no confirmed reports, rumor has it the princess escaped with her uncle and a small band of others, more than likely the same ones that rescued her in the first place and headed south. This information is unsupported and months old already. I haven't had much fresh information since snows closed the mountain passes."

"It's a risk we can't afford to take," Aurec said slowly.

Venten disagreed. "It's a risk that doesn't matter. We didn't seek out this war, but it came to our doorstep regardless. We struggled through many hardships to reach this point and you would abandon it all for the sake of one? Think with your mind, not your heart."

"One? She is so much more than just a number, Venten. You've served my family well for decades. Will you so blindly caution to throw away all I stand for? If Badron has her I will not risk her death for the sake of vain glory."

"Badron isn't the one you need to worry about," Rolnir suggested. "The last reports I received from Delranan said that Harnin has taken the kingdom for himself. Badron, so far as we know, is still in Rogscroft trying to find the fastest way home. That means the sea. He knows he can't cross the Murdes Mountains in deep winter. He'll make for the coast and secure passage west. Once he boards that ship, we lose all chance of stopping him. I advise sending strike units north with all dispatch to intercept and capture Badron."

Aurec looked at everyone in the room. His eyes bore the same steely hardness of flint in the morning sun. "Capture isn't good enough. I want Badron dead."

TWENTY

Shadow Games

The Goblin warrior raised his sword and attacked. His actions, deceptively spry for one of his weight and shape, were easily anticipated. Grugnak sidestepped the assault and lashed his own sword down. The razor-sharp edge ripped across the exposed warrior's back. Dark blood sprayed across the sullied snow drifts as the Goblin screamed. Not wasting momentum, the Goblin commander spun the rest of the way around and took his warrior's head.

Three others leapt in to attack before he had the satisfaction of watching the head drop and roll. Grugnak was hard pressed. It took every ounce of willpower to keep from being killed by his own warriors. They fought without honor, using tooth, claw, and sword in their efforts to bring him down. He lacked time to look but knew Badron and his handful of remaining loyal men were besieged similarly. Bodies already littered the ground. Some human, most Goblin.

The betrayal wasn't unprecedented. So many others had been cut down by their minions over time. What would have been an act of cowardice in civilized kingdoms was a way of life for the Goblins. Grugnak, however, had no intentions of letting his reign slip away so easily on a nameless field far from the security of the Deadlands. He hacked and tore into his warriors with unparalleled ruthlessness.

A fist knocked two teeth out. He spat them out with a mouthful of blood and saliva and drove his short dagger into the warrior's exposed armpit. The Goblin died horribly. Two others drove him to the ground. Fists rained down, breaking bones and bruising him deeply. He snarled and cursed. Darkness clogged his vision. His heart pounded in his ears, obscuring all other sounds. Grugnak felt Lord Death reach his long fingers out to curl around him. Not ready to die yet, the Goblin commander swung and cut the ankle of the nearest warrior. Blood spurted into his face as the smaller Goblin fell.

With one active opponent remaining, Grugnak was able to slide from beneath and get to his knees. The warrior was stunned, providing Grugnak the opening he needed to plunge his dagger into the other Goblin's belly. Guts and offal spilled as Grugnak disemboweled him. Disgusted, yet savagely satiated, the Goblin commander rose to his feet quickly and stalked towards the wounded Goblin desperately trying to crawl away.

"Thought you'd best me, scum?" Grugnak taunted before bringing his booted foot crushing down on the warrior's skull.

He looked for more targets but the traitors were either all dead or hiding away within the ranks to await another opportunity. Blood cooled on his armor and hands. His body ached from the severity of a beating he hadn't felt since obtaining adulthood. Disappointment grew as he noticed Badron and his men still standing, their own battle having ended. They'd come out alive, if not unscathed. Fate had other designs for the fallen king.

"Explain this," Badron demanded as he stormed up to Grugnak.

The Goblin contemplated taking the king's head. Killing him would give immediate satisfaction but little else. Without Badron's support Grugnak knew he'd be replaced and executed the moment the new Goblin army arrived. His inability to defeat Rogscroft and Delranan rendered him ineffective. No doubt Amar Kit'han already planned for his succession. Grugnak needed to find a way to make himself vital to the coming war.

He snarled. Spit and blood leaked from the corners of his mouth, down over the overextended lower jaw. "It is the season for betrayal."

"The Wolfsreik were subverted by that impetuous boy. Your Goblins are supposed to compensate their defection." The king of Delranan fumed but had little else. He wasn't strong enough to best the Goblin and they both knew it. Deception was necessary if he hoped to maintain their turbulent relationship, at least until the reinforcements arrived. "We must get to the coast in short order. Before the Dae'shan can counter my intentions."

"You seek to turn against them?" Grugnak asked.

Madness sparked in Badron's dark eyes. "I intend on reclaiming my kingdom and building a new army. The north is exposed, Grugnak. Wide open for an empire. I will become that emperor. Malweir needs a change."

"You speak strange thoughts. Fifty thousand Goblins march west to sweep the kingdoms of men under their boots. Your empire will be short-lived unless you obey the Dae'shan."

"I am no one's slave," Badron seethed. His fists clenched with rage.

All his life had been spent dedicated to others. He served his grandfather and father during their reigns. He served his people from the moment the diadem was placed upon his brow. He served his family, even after the death of his beloved wife. He served the Dae'shan, unwittingly, in their quest to open the gates to the dark gods' prison so that Malweir would once again belong to them. Badron was tired of being a servant. He was a king of men. The rule of the north belonged to him, not mythical gods or the foul-skinned Goblins.

"Can you trust your warriors to stay loyal long enough to reach Delranan?" he asked quickly. Badron was no fool. He harbored no illusions of the Goblins remaining at his side to the end. Grugnak's look spoke of a blade in the back the moment he thought it suited him best. Without the full support of the Wolfsreik, Badron lacked the allies he needed to put matters right. He needed a new army, fast.

"No promises. We have not killed all the traitors. War will see the strong survive. All others will be ground under our boots," Grugnak replied with surety.

Badron paused, choosing his next words carefully. Their already unstable alliance threatened to dissolve rapidly if both leaders continued with their headstrong attitudes. Both firmly believed man and Goblin didn't mix. Whatever trick of Fate changed the lost Dwarves into Goblins so long ago continued to bend and twist them into a miserable ruin of flesh. Their minds devolved into fragments of the past. Neither leader knew the truth of the past, though they were forced to endure the continuing echoes.

"You don't believe they will have need for you," Badron said. "Why should they? An entirely different Goblin army, five times the size of yours, is heading this way with a different chain of command, following new orders. Poor Grugnak, you've been replaced and don't even know it. Amar Kit'han used you and discarded you like so much refuse."

The Goblin pointed an accusing finger. "Mind your tongue! As long as I live I command the Goblin forces in the west."

"We shall see," Badron said quietly and stalked back to his horse.

There was still another day's travel before they'd reach the far northern shores. Another day of looking over their shoulders, fearing the sight of the Wolfsreik marching over the next rise. Rogscroft had become the most dangerous kingdom in the north, mostly attributed to Badron's actions. Despite all he'd accomplished here, it was no longer safe for the king of Delranan. The time had come to abandon his fading dreams.

This war was the culmination of his desire to humble King Stelskor. To break his mighty kingdom across the Wolfsreik's knee and leave Rogscroft a mangled corpse incapable of recovery. He'd done that and so much more. The havoc caused by the Goblin army was unparalleled in recent history. Stelskor's corpse was frozen, awaiting spring to begin rotting like the animal carcass it was. The major cities were reduced to mounds of rubble. A large portion of the population was dead or being slowly starved. Rogscroft would never recover, if not for one minor complication he hadn't been able to eliminate. Aurec and the traitorous Wolfsreik changed the entire dynamic.

Instead of razing the countryside, *his* army now aided in recovery and reconstruction efforts while fervently driving out all pockets of resistance. Goblins and loyal soldiers were murdered wherever they were found. Worse than his own army hunting him, Badron found the Pell Darga most contemptible. The dark-skinned mountain people struck like wraiths, leaving only corpses and bloodstains to mark their passing. Their short spears were found in the backs of dozens of his remaining forces. If the current attrition rate continued he'd have nothing left when he made it back to Delranan.

Left with two options, the king of Delranan considered turning on the troublesome Goblins now and forging ahead alone. He'd lose a great number of his own soldiers in the process, but the end justified the means. The unexpected freedom of solitude would allow him to accomplish his primary objective of reclaiming his kingdom from the One Eye. Grugnak's Goblins were in the way and easy targets. Wheels began to turn. The time was fast approaching when he could shed the excess weight of the Goblin army and look to the future.

Badron quickly mounted and ordered his soldiers to move out. There was still much ground to cover if he hoped to return to his kingdom and reclaim the stolen throne. Leagues rolled by as the beleaguered warriors fled north. Grugnak and his Goblins hung back, letting the men take the lead. They'd already been proven as the Pell's targets of choice. Goblins might be universally hated, but Badron had done the Pell wrong. Revenge was a trait in every race. An inescapable seduction of the mortal spirit. Badron's soldiers would die first, unless they turned on the Goblins. Grugnak laughed quietly. He was looking forward to the coming battle.

"He is breaking," Kodan Bak whispered. His acidic words drifted across the winds like a poisonous cloud. "You should have chosen another."

Amar Kit'han, floating inches above the frozen ground, merely shook his hooded head. "No. Badron is the catalyst the dark gods need. The gateway between realms is weakened with each new death. Badron's grief and hatred are pouring negative energies into the material separating our existence. Soon it will be enough to power the doorway."

"How many must die to begin the process?" Kodan asked. "We've been subverting Humanity for centuries, all for this singular event. Our enemies are many; allies thin."

"We don't need allies, Kodan Bak. We are the Dae'shan. Ours is a higher purpose. The time has finally come for us to abandon King Badron. Summon what minions we have. We must go to Arlevon Gale."

"Nothing is in order," the lesser Dae'shan countered. "The Gnaals have not returned from Brodein. Maleela has not been captured. Bahr and the wizard continue towards Trennaron unchecked. What success do you find in anything that has happened?"

Electricity formed a protective shield around Amar. His transparent body shimmered in haze. "Success, in this instance, is immeasurable. The tangible effects of so many deaths weaken the veil. The dark gods require sacrifice. The power from each soul taken has been harvested by the Olagath Stone since we came to the north. Once the stone reaches maximum capacity we shall strike a blow that will all but cripple the two kingdoms. The psychic scream will pierce the veil and bring forth our masters."

"Your confidence is…disturbing," Kodan admitted. His pale red eyes never left Amar's clenched fists. "Humans have stood in our way for countless generations. We've been beaten at every turn. What makes you think they will lose this time?"

"Because the humans are doing our work for us. The bulk of the Goblin nation marches on us. The might of the Dwarven Empire is fractured thanks to the subversion of an entire clan to the dark cause. Elves care nothing for the rule of Men."

"Yet the Aeldruin are allied with the Dwarves of Drimmen Delf," Kodan countered. "The addition of the Giants concerns me most. They have been sequestered on their mountaintops for so long they've rendered themselves irrelevant, yet one now heads towards the Blud Hamr. He can shatter the Olagath Stone and end our plans."

"The Giant will be stopped. They are not the warriors of old. Long has it been since one of their kind carried a weapon in battle. Have no concern for the one traveling with the wizard. The Gnaals will handle him, thus ending the wizard's desperate plan. Victory is all but assured."

Kodan Bak remained unconvinced. "You've spoken this before. Each time was met with failure. Your leadership has robbed us of any glory owed."

"Don't pursue this train of thought," Amar warned.

"Why not? The truth may sting but it sometimes needs to be said. What promise can you say that will ensure our victory?"

The leader of the Dae'shan recoiled, his rage turning into pure power unseen since the early days of Malweir. "You push the limits of acceptance, Kodan Bak. One day soon there will be a final reckoning."

"I long for it."

"Perhaps. For now we must return to Delranan. Arlevon Gale must be readied. The princess will be there shortly."

Amar folded into darkness and disappeared, leaving the lesser Dae'shan with an inflated sense of victory. The stars had finally aligned to see his rise. Amar Kit'han had led them down dark paths they never should have considered. His failures of leadership exposed grave weaknesses in their development. Kodan Bak wasn't as strong as Amar but there was still room for hope. After all, one other had gone before.

Artiss Gran, last of the true Dae'shan, marched across the crenellated battlements of Trennaron with only the impassive stone gargoyles for company. His eyes were locked in concern. The darkness at the edge of sight was consuming, smothering. He lacked the ability to see beyond the engineered conflict barreling towards him. After centuries of self-imposed exile in Trennaron, he felt events rushing to an end. The conclusion was still in doubt, though the enemy gained strength daily.

He'd spent hundreds of mortal lifetimes hidden away in the ancient halls. So much had happened yet he seldom had control over it. For a brief period the Mages would come to seek his counsel. They sought to learn the histories of the world, claiming curiosity for the greater good of all races. Artiss responded with vigor, even while knowing there was an inescapable dark undertone to several of the Mages. Their lust for knowledge inevitably led to the creation of the crystal of Tol Shere and the subsequent war.

Once, long ago, Artiss felt responsible for the near destruction of all life on Malweir. Then he realized it was never his fault. The dark gods forever sought to break their pact with the gods of light and return to the world to begin a reign of terror. Mankind was the easiest of all races to manipulate. Their fall came swiftly. He was powerless to stop them. Once the dark gods got their ideology in place it was only a matter of time before the world became ripe with chaos and greed. Time passed. Artiss Gran was forgotten by all but the most powerful. His fellow Dae'shan, now willing servants of darkness, left him to his solitary misery. He had become irrelevant. Until now.

"The final dawn is approaching," he said, patting the bleached stone neck of the nearest gargoyle. "After all this time I wish I had longer to prepare. Some events shouldn't happen."

Sorrow tingling through his bones, Artiss Gran headed back inside. His guests would be arriving shortly and he needed to unlock the wards on the Blud Hamr.

TWENTY-ONE

Attack in the Night

Bahr spent most of the day looking over his shoulder, unable to shake the feeling of being hunted by more than one creature. The Gnaal was lurking in the jungle, a monstrous presence ready to devour the world in seas of rot. Even with Anienam, the Gnaal remained a powerful motivator to reach Trennaron quickly. Bahr wasn't concerned about a demonic leftover from the Mage Wars. The threat was recognized and expected. What kept him looking back towards Teng was a jilted lover named Cashi Dam.

Youthful pride transformed into arrogance, rendering Cashi incapable of letting Rekka go. This was a fight Bahr related to, not that he had much experience with it. Love was fickle, certainly not in his plans for the future. That didn't stop any of the strange events since their entrance into the jungle from continuing. Bahr felt control slipping the longer they spent on the quest. Loath as he was to agree with Boen's singular way of thinking, Bahr needed a tangible enemy to fight. His sword ached to be used against foes needing cleansing, not scorned villagers or magical demons.

"You seem troubled," Boen told his friend, already guessing at the cause of his unspoken torment. "I still think you should have let me kill that upstart."

"There's been enough killing, Boen," he replied. Bahr almost laughed; even he found it hard to take seriously at this point.

Boen held no such reservations and barked his amusement. "I didn't think humor was your strong suit, Sea Wolf. This jungle sets me on edge. I wonder what a hearty fire would do to lighten things up some."

A great commotion erupted in the distance. The ground trembled. Trees swayed to an absent wind. Birds of every color burst into the sky to avoid the havoc rippling through the jungle. Horses whinnied. Dorl was thrown to the ground as branches crashed down around them. It stopped faster than it started.

Bahr steadied his horse and said, "I don't think the jungle appreciates your humor."

"Candor perhaps, but not humor," the Gaimosian replied. "All the more reason to be done with this place and on the road back north."

Bahr agreed for many reasons. The humidity didn't agree with him. The heat dried his skin, made him feel tired for no reason. He was a creature of the snow and ice, not verdant jungles filled with any number of poisonous plants or carnivorous animals. The very jungle wanted to kill them, as if it were a sentient entity capable of great malice.

"Mind your tongues! There is latent anger hiding beneath the surface," Anienam warned them all. "Words can be more powerful than you imagine."

Boen snorted. "Words don't kill. Only man can do that."

"Fool," the wizard spat. "There is more strength in spoken words than in your arm, Gaimosian. Words have started every war in history. Words will activate the machine required to breach the realms. Words can be channeled into our darkest thoughts, mimicking the nightmares we fervently try to hide deep inside. After your sword has rusted and your bones ground to dust there will still be words."

Boen passed off a nervous glare. He had no warmth in his heart for the wizard, though he did maintain a healthy respect for the relic. Sorcery held no place in modern Gaimosian life. Those surviving bloodlines seldom spoke of the time when their ancestors gathered at the place that would become Ipn Shal and form the rudimentary circle of Mages. Magic was anathema to everything the Gaimosians tried to accomplish. They relied on strength of muscle and steel. Cowards hid behind spells. For Anienam to lash out so brutally cut him to the bone. He was tired. Reluctantly, Boen forced himself to admit it was his *word* that kept him on the quest. *More damned words.*

The thought died on the tip of his tongue as a pair of thick banyan trees, ancient as the morning sun, exploded in a fury of slivers and flame. Dead birds and primates dropped from the branches. Smaller brush underneath the mighty stalks burst into flame. Thick, rich smoke curled up into the canopy. Twin monstrous figures loomed in the false darkness. Bahr felt the hatred pulse from their bodies and struggled to hold his food down.

"To arms! The enemy is upon us!" Anienam shouted and flexed his fingers. Whispering an ancient spell, the wizard cast his finger towards the larger figure. Blue-white energy flamed in a needle-like blast, striking the nearest Gnaal in the chest. The great beast roared in pain, relishing the feeling again after so many absent centuries.

The very air around them stunk of rot, disease. Their bodies were covered with boils and lesions, visible even through the miasmic darkness concealing the creatures. Created to destroy, the Gnaals were the definition of death itself. Whip-like tails thrashed behind them, sweeping smaller trees aside like fallen leaves in a storm. Their bodies were perpetually cloaked in darkness so foul the air around them died. They were hatred incarnate. An unthinkable deviousness that never should have existed.

Each one of the group found different shapes in the nightmare. Bahr was reminded of some great beast rising from the depths of the ocean while Boen steadied to fight one of the terrible lizards from the dawn of creation. Anienam saw them for what they were but lacked the strength of vision to view them unobscured. Only Rekka remained dispassionate about their foes. Trained in how to combat the dark arts, she relaxed her muscles and prepared for battle as plants and insects wilted and died around her. The rot slowly crept forward, washing over the jungle. Her heart bled at seeing the grievous wound being committed on her home.

The first Gnaal roared, a tortured song whispering of the breaking of the world. The second answered in kind. Their chorus twisted into a foul symphony that inspired deep-rooted fears in them all. Leathery wings flapped angrily. Their hate-filled eyes focused on Boen, marking the Gaimosian as the biggest threat. Even he trembled before their approach. Breaking off, the second Gnaal launched into the sky as the first charged into the adventurers.

Anienam brushed past Bahr to meet the onrushing Gnaals. Wave after wave of misery pulsated off their corrupt bodies. Ionascu fell to the ground, vomiting. Blood trickled from his ears. Maleela stood, frozen in shock. Skuld began crying and couldn't stop. The wizard used all his might to project his energy over the others but it wasn't enough. Two Gnaals bore so much residue anger it was all he could do to stay on his feet.

He lashed out again and was rewarded with a petrifying scream and the scent of burned flesh choking the air. Anienam's skin tightened with each burst of power. He felt his hair turning white. Countless years bled from the remainder of his life yet he continued fighting. It was all he had left. Anything less than his total effort would result in the death of those he'd sworn to protect. Malweir needed them all to survive the coming of the dark gods.

Boen overcame his initial paralyzing shock and bellowed an ancient war cry. His massive broadsword gleamed in the firelight, wicked and destructive. The Vengeance Knight charged at the enemy, knowing he lacked the strength required to kill them. His muscles strained against his will, threatening to revolt in the primal need to be set free. He was a caged animal remembering the scent of the fresh kill. Forgotten strength flowed to every end of his large body. The split second between when he attacked to making contact with the Gnaal whispered doom for them all.

Beast and man collided in raw fury. Flesh was cut. Their combined roars wailed a mournful song. Boen struck rapidly with three successive blows at the Gnaal's midsection. Without any definable body parts other than the head and arms, it was difficult to find any weaknesses. Boen continued to attack while the Gnaal reeled backwards without striking back. The Gaimosian got the idea that he was being toyed with and leapt back into a defensive crouch. The Gnaal attacked immediately.

Each footstep was like thunder. Leaves and burned embers popped up around the Gnaal. Elongated fangs sliced down from its upper lips. Boen witnessed the sheer intensity in his enemy's eyes the moment they collided. He braced himself for the impact but it wasn't enough. They crashed to the jungle floor and began raining blows on each other. Strong as he was, Boen knew it was only a matter of time before the Gnaal wore him down and killed him.

Lighting exploded in the Gnaal's face. Pieces of flesh, desiccated from a lifetime of disease, melted from its face. Boen rolled, vomiting as he came up on one knee. A black-shafted arrow plunged into the Gnaal's remaining eye. The great demon clutched at its ruined face, staggering back into the heavy trees still unaffected by the flames. Rekka Jel rushed forward to stand beside Boen, another arrow already notched.

The Gaimosian gathered a mouthful of spit and blew it into the nearby bushes. "My thanks."

Rekka offered a curt nod and remained vigilant. Gnaals were the consummate predators. Any minor victory she'd won was bound to be short-lived. They killed for sport, often reveling in a perverse form of pleasure derived from their pain. She'd fought them before, once, and barely lived to tell of it. Only her training under Artiss Gran saved her life.

"It will return soon," she whispered. Her almond eyes scanned the jungle ceaselessly. Her limited success came at Boen's expense. The Gnaal had been so focused on him it didn't notice her until too late. She wouldn't be so fortunate again.

Anienam's voice, much weaker than it had ever been, bleated, "All you, fall behind me! I can't protect you much longer."

"Wizard, we must be able to do something," Bahr insisted. Perspiration painted his face. His breath was still ragged from fear. "They must have a weakness."

Anienam nodded absently. "They do, but none any of you can exploit."

"What are we supposed to do?" Nothol asked as he half dragged Dorl behind the wizard. He kept staring up into the trees, hoping to find a glimpse of the second, uninjured Gnaal. The monster disappeared in the first moments of the fight and hadn't been seen since. Nothol had a sneaking suspicion it was busy circling around behind to attack.

"I will use the last of my remaining strength to cast a destruction spell. It should be enough to drive the Gnaals away for good, but you all must remain directly behind me and as close together as possible. Anyone caught outside of my radius will be incinerated."

"Wait, there is another way," Rekka said suddenly. Her lithe form slipped between the others to stand beside him and whispered in his hairy, right ear.

His eyes widened, clearly having the strength of her assistance unaccounted for. Once again he underestimated his companions. This time, instead of proving fatal, he took hope. He wasn't alone. Anienam turned to the others to begin issuing orders.

"Look out!" Ironfoot shouted and tackled Skuld to the ground.

A massive tree, ripped from the earth, was flung straight towards them, making them scatter before being immolated by the thousand pounds of wood. The tree raced towards them. Skuld closed his eyes and whimpered in the face of certain death. Death that never came. He felt the rush of wind. Felt a shadow fall across him. Leaves drifted down around him. The Dwarf looked up to see Groge catch the tree scant meters from him. He saved their lives, even as the massive tree took the Giant to the ground. Skuld cried like a helpless child.

For the second time in a week, Nothol Coll saved Maleela from certain death. His quick thinking took them both out of the tree's trajectory. They ran into the nearby trees and waited long enough to ensure another wasn't on the way. Nothol reluctantly let go of her hand long enough to draw his sword, having sheathed it before they fled, and turned back towards the clearing. That moment of distraction proved near-fatal.

A branch cracked the back of his skull, dropping him unconsciously to the ground. Maleela spun, short dagger in her hand, to see Ionascu confronting her. Madness filled his eyes. The heavy branch he used to club Nothol wavered dangerously in his hands. Saliva trickled from the corners of his mouth.

"Ionascu, what are…"

He pointed the club at her. "I gave you every chance! All you had to do was give in to your desires. None of this would be happening if you did. None of it!"

Fear gripped her. "You're mad. We need to find a way to stop the Gnaals and escape."

His laughter was a brittle scratching noise that tickled the back of his throat. "Don't you see? They're here for you! That's all they ever wanted. You must die, Princess."

Her eyes grew wide as he charged. Maleela braced herself, dagger pointed out in front. "Stay back! I don't want to hurt you," she pleaded.

He was already gone, lost in the quagmire of dementia. Months of pent-up frustrations finally took their toll as his mind snapped. The only thing he cared about was killing Maleela in the hopes of redemption by the Dae'shan. He swung wildly. She ducked, barely, and stabbed. The club whooshed as it went through where her head had been. Ionascu cackled and lunged. His weight took him off balance. He tripped and stumbled into Maleela. The impact drove both of them to the ground.

Maleela cried out, partly muffled by his being on top of her. She felt something wet spreading across her chest and immediately imagined the worst. Tears brimming, the young princess of Delranan finally managed to push her attacker away and crawl to safety. Ionascu rolled over until he lay flat on his back. Her dagger was lodged deep in his heart, killing him instantly. Maleela looked down at the blood covering her hands and blouse and wanted to cry. But instead of tears she felt only rage. Every childhood neglect and adult slight came flooding back in. She needed revenge for all the wrongs committed on her by her father and his people. Ionascu had once been a king's agent.

Maleela dropped to her knees and crawled to his corpse. Oddly, he seemed satisfied, as if all his demons had finally stopped tormenting him. She didn't care. He'd been nothing but deceptive and spiteful since leaving Chadra all those long winter nights ago. He represented everything wrong with the world: the physical manifestation of hatred, death, and rot. Ionascu may have come to terms internally, but the sight of him turned her stomach. She jerked the dagger free, hesitantly at first, and plunged it back down with all the hate she could muster. She stabbed again and again until blood coated her face and hands. His body jerked with each strike to the central nervous system.

Finally she collapsed. She wanted to cry. To burn away the pain with purifying tears, but there was none. Her tears were used up. She looked deep within herself and was horrified to find she liked killing him. It felt good to rid the world of one more villain. She wanted more. Maleela pulled herself up and, dagger in hand, turned to head back to the fight. She wasn't afraid anymore. The time had come for her to stand on her own two feet and become the princess her kingdom deserved.

Maleela looked up in time to see two large figures drop down on her. Concealed by the shadows of the double canopy while the battle raged, the Hags waited for their chance to strike. Unlike before, they had a solitary purpose.

Freina was to capture the princess and deliver her back to Amar Kit'han. With outstretched claws, the Hags attacked. Maleela's shout quickly turned into a scream as ragged claws dug deeply into her shoulders and jerked her skyward. Leaves drifted lazily down to where she'd just been.

TWENTY-TWO

Stolen

Her scream broke the sudden silence dominating the battleground. They looked around, desperate to find Maleela. Bahr grew frantic. He'd gone through so much to get her back and keep her safe he couldn't bear the thought of losing her now, this close to their goal. She was the only true family he had. And he couldn't protect her when she needed it. Failure gnawed at his already waning confidence. He drew a heavy sob before realizing it was unlike his character.

Anienam saw what was happening and shouted, "Snap out of it! It's the magic of the Gnaals! They are draining your confidence, leaving you open to their next assault!"

"Where is she?" the Sea Wolf called back. He slowly started to understand the delaying tactic used by the Gnaals. They wanted him to get distracted. To lose track of what was happening around him so that they could get to Maleela, his one weakness. Visions of finding her corpse torn apart in the jungle sickened his stomach.

They charged recklessly into the unknown, rescuing the princess being their solitary thought. Nothing else mattered so long as they recovered her from the Gnaals alive and unharmed. He headed back to where he left her without waiting for the others. He didn't get far. The second Gnaal dropped from the canopy and attacked.

Taken off guard, Anienam did his best to turn and confront the beast. His best years were behind him, and it was all he could do to fight back. His magic was weaker. The majority was spent on the first battle. He was on fumes, barely capable of withholding the Gnaal as it charged. Fortunately his friends were able to react in time. Battered, Boen led the way. His sword was raised above his head. His initial goal was to take a hand off. The rest he'd work out along the way. He never made it the Gnaal. The Gaimosian slipped on moisture-slick moss and went down.

The Gnaal roared. Poisons steamed from its flesh. Branches wilted. Leaves withered into shriveled brown husks. It saw Boen on the ground, trying to roll back up, and knew death was but a moment away. For the second time in as many minutes, Groge did the unexpected and blocked the attack. His crisis of conscience faded as the lives of his friends were in jeopardy. There'd be a time for reckoning with his god when he returned to Venheim, but for now they needed his immense strength and size.

Giant and Gnaal met, Groge towering over the beast by six feet. His massive fists hammered down on the beast, desperately trying to kill it. The Gnaal responded with claws and teeth. Groge was cut in a dozen places as he busied breaking ribs and bones. The sheer ferocity of the titanic struggle brought small trees down. Brodein had never seen such a battle and the witnesses prayed they never had to again.

"Go, all you! Get Maleela before it's too late!" Anienam shouted. He rolled his sleeves up and headed to aid Groge. Even a Giant's strength was limited.

Bahr grabbed Boen by the shoulder and propelled him along. Neither had the strength to fight a Gnaal and win. Dorl, Ironfoot, and Skuld joined them. Heart racing, Dorl didn't want to lose sight of them during the battle. They ran into the jungle as Rekka and Anienam aided Groge. Each had their own battles to fight.

Shadows crept in oppressively. Their vision was reduced to a handful of meters. Underbrush grew thicker the deeper they went. Bahr wished for torches but they lacked the time to get them from the packs. Unnatural silence secluded them from the rest of the jungle. Nothing stirred. All life had fled the moment the Gnaals arrived. Bahr began to feel claustrophobic. He needed the open sea again, not the coffin-like enclosure of Brodein's deepest heart. *How I'll ever find her in this nightmare is beyond me. I should have left the poor girl in Rogscroft. She doesn't deserve any of this.*

"Does anyone see her?" he asked. Desperation haunted his voice. He verged on pure panic. The sensation left him torn. Family was an alien notion he struggled to accept.

Ironfoot darted out in front of them. Reduced by his four-foot stature, the Dwarf had the best vision in the group. He could see in the dark, used to being underground for extended periods. He used that to their advantage, piercing the artificial gloom only to find nothing. He gripped his axe murderously. He'd read legends of other Dwarves that had fought Gnaals and bristled at the opportunity to do so himself. Ironfoot felt his talents were wasted stalking the jungle for a lone girl. Honor demanded he continue on. Find the girl and get back to the fight. Nothing else mattered.

After meters of not finding so much as a footprint he spied a scrap of light blue cloth. His mouth curled up in a savage grin. *Finally. A trail!* He bounded over a fallen log and clutched the cloth. He squinted into the gloom, tilting his head back to sniff the air. "It's hers. Torn from her tunic but I don't see her anywhere."

"There must be something else. Something you're missing," Bahr said.

"I'm a Dwarf. I don't miss anything," Ironfoot growled, uneasy with being questioned. "Whatever took her was no Gnaal. Look around. Nothing here has died. The monster would have killed every living thing it touched. This is damned peculiar."

"Over here! It's Nothol," Boen called deeply. He was crouching down beside the groggy sell sword as the others hurried over.

"What happened here?" Bahr demanded.

Nothol started to shake his head but quickly thought better of it. Great lances of pain shot through his skull when he tried to move. "I don't know. She was in front of me and then I got hit in the back of my head. Whatever did it was strong enough to knock me out. She was gone when I awoke."

"It was Ionascu," Dorl said slowly. His face lost much of its color. The sell sword stood over the dead man's body, pointing with his sword. "He must have snapped."

"The slimy bastard wasn't that strong," Nothol protested. "He couldn't have."

Dorl reached down to retrieve the heavy branch Ionascu had used as a club. "He didn't need to be strong to get you with this."

"Spread out. Search the immediate area. She might still be here," Bahr ordered. He couldn't bring himself to say the one inescapable conclusion they all thought. That she might be dead along with Ionascu. Bahr held onto hope as long as there was no body to prove otherwise.

Nothol was the first to return once the others fanned out to search the immediate area. The look on his face told Bahr all he needed to know. She was gone. But where? He owed it to himself not to give up, not after all they'd been through just to reach this point. Bahr redoubled his efforts. She had to be in the area. A fully grown woman couldn't disappear without a trace.

"Damnation. We need Rekka here. This is her jungle," Bahr said dejectedly.

Of them all, Nothol felt the pain of failure the most. He'd been with her last. He viewed her disappearance as his fault, a momentary lapse of awareness that led to her probable death. The idea of his inability to keep the ones he cared about safe mocked him. Grief stricken, the sell sword continued to look.

Groge swung with all his might. A mighty blow landing in the Gnaal's already mangled face. Dark blood exploded. Teeth dropped. Pulverized flesh clung wetly to the Giant's fist. Severely wounded, the Gnaal managed to rake its claws across Groge's stomach, drawing thick lines of bright, red blood. Anienam sent another blast of power, this one greatly diminished from his first, into the Gnaal's face to give Groge time to recover.

The old wizard sagged to his knees. His body was bordering on giving out. Darkness crept in around the corners of his vision. Rekka fired two quick arrows and reached down to help him. She understood they needed him if any were going to live long enough to return to Delranan. Groge dove back into the attack. The ancient fury lacing his blood flared. He felt strong. Powerful. He felt alive.

Two trees burst into flames directly behind them. Anienam's heart sank. The second Gnaal had returned. "We're doomed."

Rekka wiped the clinging strands of black hair from her face. "No. We will find a way. There must always be hope, wizard."

He wanted to laugh. What hope could there possibly be for this? The question faded on his tongue as a hail of arrows and spears riddled the second Gnaal. Anienam peered through the building haze and was rewarded by spying half a dozen warriors from Teng. They attacked the Gnaal with abandon. Despite never having seen a Gnaal, Cashi Dam led his warriors without hesitation.

Rekka's mouth fell open. Cashi and his warriors shouldn't have left Teng. Their bravery quickly turned into foolishness. The first died after getting too close to the surprised beast. A clawed hand reached out to crush the man's skull. The sound reminded Rekka of fresh fruit being pulverized. A warrior vomited. Another stabbed repeatedly into the Gnaal's exposed rib cage. The beast roared and wheeled on his attacker, backhanding him into the trees. He died as his back broke against the rough bark.

"Demon!" Cashi raged and leapt to attack. He'd come here to find Rekka and take her back. There was no denying the murderous intent in his heart. She embarrassed him in front of his warriors and no small amount of retribution was demanded. Rekka Jel needed to pay for her insolence. He wasn't a common villager.

Finding Rekka involved in a fight for her life was the last thing he expected to stumble across. The manner of creatures battling her stole the strength from his soul. Warmth fled his bones, giving him a cadaverous feel. His confidence shook when Ashru and Mehy died so quickly. They were both seasoned veterans, older and more experienced than he was. Their deaths would haunt Teng for many years. Cashi's sword struck the Gnaal's thigh and shattered into pieces on impact. He cursed and tried to jump back. The Gnaal was faster. Its tail slammed into Cashi, driving him to the ground.

Rekka, having recovered her bow, took aim and fired in the span of a single heartbeat. Her aim was true. The bolt struck the Gnaal in the left eye at the same time Anienam managed a weak bolt of power. Lacking any real punch, it was enough to keep the already distracted Gnaal from recovering in time to finish Cashi.

"Anienam, we must find a way to get them away from the Gnaal," she warned, leaving the threat unspoken. Death ruled this portion of the jungle. It was a matter of time before it claimed them all.

Back on his feet, the wizard coughed a wad of blood. "I don't have much left. Not enough to defeat both of them."

He looked across the ruined area to see Groge doing his best to rip the Gnaal apart. Foul, dark blood coated the Giant. An evil gleam blackened his eyes. Anienam recognized the blood rage. It wouldn't be long before young Groge became lost to his long suppressed instincts and transformed into a killing machine. It was one of the reasons the Giants abandoned life in the lowlands after the wars. Once lost to the rage, they were near unstoppable.

The second Gnaal ripped the arrow from its ruined eye and attacked the remaining villagers. The air sizzled as the whip-like tail nearly sliced the closest warrior in half at the waist. Moving with lightning speed, the Gnaal bit down on the shoulder of the next, devouring both head and arm. Alone, the surviving warrior edged back towards the trees. Any courage he once had fled down his leg as he emptied his bladder. The battle was over.

Both Gnaals stopped in mid strike. Their misshapen heads turned upwards, as if listening to an unknown song on the stale wind. Treetops rustled. A haunting echo reverberated deep into the foundations of the world. Both beasts launched up into the canopy, slashing through the trees as they abandoned the battle. Anienam watched, unable to comprehend what just happened.

"They had us," he whispered.

Rekka lacked answers. She expected a trap. Time running out, she hurried over to Cashi's side before the Gnaals returned. Kneeling, she ran her hands lightly over his broken body, looking to see if he was still breathing, checking for broken bones, and to see if he was bleeding. Sorrow filled her normally soft eyes. He groaned every time she managed to touch a broken bone. The richness of the blood slowly trickling from his mouth and ears suggested internal bleeding. Reluctantly, she was forced to admit he was already dead.

His eyes fluttered open, slowly focusing on her soft, round face. Broken teeth showed when he tried to smile. "Rekka."

"Do not speak, Cashi. You are gravely wounded," she said sympathetically.

A tear welled in his eye. "I am…dying. There is…much I need…to say."

She placed a fingertip on his lips. "Do not waste your words. I know the truth of many things, Cashi Dam. You are a great warrior. A good man. I wronged you and for that I am deeply sorry. You did not deserve my harsh treatment."

He closed his eyes. "No. I came…here…" A coughing fit racked his body. Fresh waves of pain made him scream. "To…punish you."

A last strangled breath escaped him and his body trembled briefly before life left. Rekka lowered her head and cried for the first time in many years.

Freina and Garelda, last surviving Harpies in the northern kingdoms, flew back toward Delranan. Their captured prey hung limply from their claws, swaying in the cooling air. Capturing Maleela proved less problematic than their earlier attempts but lacked any rewarding feeling. Their third sister, Brom, died of wounds sustained in their ill-advised attack in the village of Fedro. Her loss stung the Hags, further widening the rift between them and the Dae'shan. Freina decided this was the last act they were going to perform for their deathless masters. The Harpies had given up more than enough in a cause they didn't believe in.

It would still take many days to reach the frozen north. Days in which the Hags had ample opportunity to torture and abuse their victim for her previous crimes. Freina was a vindictive creature, blaming all others for the failing of her race. She dug her claws a little deeper and continued to fly. Delicious visions of misery urged her on. The princess of Delranan was going to suffer more than she had ever known before they reached Arlevon Gale.

TWENTY-THREE

Repercussions

They returned to the sight of the battle shortly after the Gnaals fled. Dejected from their loss, the weary adventurers struggled to find meaning in anything that had happened. Maleela was gone, lost to whatever foul fate the enemy decided upon. Many of the others were wounded. All were exhausted beyond good measure. Bahr had lost almost all hope before Dorl spied a single feather lying awkwardly in the brush. With nothing else to see, they hurried back to help the wizard, only to find the battle over. Each was relieved that they wouldn't have to fight again. Surviving the first time almost proved too difficult.

The Sea Wolf stopped at the edge of the ruination and struggled to contain his emotions. Where the jungle had been lush green and overpowering, now a burned wasteland remained. Countless dead animals and destroyed trees littered the area. He staggered under the weight of the unspoken pain exuded by the very jungle. Brodein had been wounded badly. Embers clung to many more trees, the flames slowly dying in the thick, damp canopy.

Nothol whistled low as he surveyed the damage. Not even the battle of Bode Hill seemed this intense. When his eyes fell on Rekka he reached out and slapped Dorl on the bicep. "Look."

Dorl Theed at first thought Rekka had been wounded. He rushed to her side, hoping against hope to keep her alive. He didn't see Cashi Dam's body until he already had her crying form cradled in his arms. His gaze instantly hardened before he noticed how the jungle warrior had died. Any anger he might have felt died embarrassingly. He held her tighter. "I'm sorry, Rekka."

She looked at him pleadingly. A look he misinterpreted for weakness. There was no way he could have known that she had steeled her heart against Cashi's death admission. She felt only anger at his ignorance. Cashi should have never left Teng. His desire to possess what didn't belong to him mocked everything she stood for. Rather than speaking the truth, Rekka held her tongue and gently laid her head on Dorl's shoulder. He'd already been through enough and she needed the respite.

"How did this happen?" Bahr asked after stopping beside the wizard. He looked the old wizard over for signs of injury. Anienam looked like death warmed over but Bahr couldn't find anything physically wrong. A good sign considering what he imagined lay ahead.

Anienam resisted the urge to collapse and go to sleep. "The Gnaals attacked as soon as your party left to find Maleela." He paused when he noticed the scrap of blue cloth and the feather clutched tightly in Bahr's hand. "We were at the breaking point when the warriors from Teng arrived. I doubt they came expecting a fight like this. All but one died in a matter of minutes. Rekka and I tried to save them, but the Gnaals were too powerful. We failed."

"The rest of us still draw breath. That's not failure to me," Bahr grunted back.

Anienam had no comment. His lack of foresight beyond the scope of the quest nearly cost them their lives, just as it claimed Cashi Dam and his warriors. He should have known better. Age didn't agree with him. His mind was growing weary, rusted from endless decades of struggle no one ever heard about. Not only had he failed them here, he nearly lost Groge to the blood rage. The Blud Hamr was another useless relic without the Giant to wield it. Trennaron was only days away. Anienam reaffirmed his faith in the righteous quest. They were so close.

Boen strolled up after they'd all returned and began gathering the horses and supplies. The wagon the villagers of Teng gave them was irreparably broken. He supposed a thousand-pound tree landing on it would crush just about anything. His own body felt like a reflection of the wagon.

Bruised and battered in more places than he knew he had, Boen hadn't had a beating like this in a very long time. He was beginning to rethink his career as a Vengeance Knight. Perhaps it was time to hang up the sword and find a home.

"Bahr, we can't linger," he said.

Bahr sighed. The Gaimosian was right, but he didn't need to voice it so soon. They all hurt and needed time to recover before forging ahead. The mental anguish over losing Maleela, perhaps for good, threatened to bring Bahr to tears. All he wanted was a moment's peace. Peace Boen's drive wouldn't allow.

"What am I supposed to do, Boen?" he asked, frustrated. "My niece has been taken. Gods only know what those Harpies will do to her, and you want me to push it to the back of my mind and carry on like nothing has happened?"

"What Harpies?" Anienam asked.

Boen explained what they'd found in the jungle while Bahr glowered at him. The wizard found himself nodding as Boen told the brief tale. His heart sank. After their battle in Fedro he figured them out of the equation. Granted, his knowledge of the ancient, dying race was limited, as was everyone else's, but he grimly concluded it was yet another mistake. Then it dawned on him.

"I very much doubt she was captured only to be killed," he said excitedly. Catching the menace in Bahr's eyes forced him to explain faster. "Think about it. The Gnaals left almost at the same moment Maleela was taken, or so I'm guessing. That means they all came with one purpose in mind. Distract us and steal the girl. The Dae'shan want her alive, though for what purpose I do not know."

"Dae'shan? I thought we left them far behind," Boen grunted.

"Technically we did, but they aren't bound by the same physical restraints we are. They can fold the air around them and go just about anywhere in Malweir. A neat little trick that has served their deviousness well over the years."

"Didn't you think this was important information to know earlier?" Bahr snapped. He was tired of being the only one to defend the wizard. More people had gotten killed because of his ineptitude. *How much longer before that corpse is me?*

Anienam shrugged. "Would it have mattered? None of us have the ability to counter it. I told you what you needed to know to keep you on task, Bahr. Anything else was merely useless data that wouldn't help us one bit. I've gotten us this far. Trust me to take us to the end."

"But you haven't, have you?" Bahr countered. "You've led us from one nightmare to another without pause. How many times have we nearly been killed since leaving Delranan? How many battles have we fought in the name of a thing most of us don't believe in? There are times when I think you are working against us."

He stalked off angrily.

Boen kept Anienam from following. "Leave him. He needs to work this out on his own. We've all been through a lot, him more so. That young girl is his only true family."

Try as he wanted, Anienam just couldn't relate to the concept.

"Wizard," Boen said and lowered his voice. "Who killed Ionascu? That girl didn't own an ounce of malice. Was it the Gnaals or Dae'shan?"

Anienam looked back to the jungle where Maleela disappeared. "I don't know and I'm not so sure that I want to find out either. Some deeds are best left in the dark."

Ironfoot finished tying the knot on the bandage over Skuld's arm wound and gave it a thorough once-over. Satisfied with his work, the Dwarf captain said, "Try to keep it dry and you'll be fine. It's not even a real wound, come to think on it. I remember this skirmish against raiders when I took a dagger between my ribs." He lifted his tunic and pointed to the knobbed scar running across his right side. "Right here, see? Hurt more than tickled but it drew enough blood to get me mad. I couldn't kill that man fast enough. See, they came out of…"

"Ironfoot," Skuld interrupted as respectfully as he could. The shock of being stopped mid-story left him with a dumbfounded look on his face. "I'm fine, really. Thank you."

The old Ironfoot, the one who was content working in the mines and fighting Goblins and Dark Dwarves, would have lashed out at the boy. Instead he chuckled. Being around Men must have made him soft. He lacked the brutal edge his people were renowned for. Rubbing his scar, Ironfoot lowered his tunic and went off. Perhaps the boy was right. There was a time and a place for stories. Preferably over a mug of dark ale.

Shrugging his indifference, Ironfoot ambled off to see who else needed help. He purposefully avoided the complications of Dorl and Rekka. There were just some problems he didn't want to get involved with. Besides, he had two wives of his own and it was a constant struggle to keep just one of them content. Let Dorl handle his own issues. Nothol seemed to be in just as much of a funk. Ironfoot suspected the sell sword felt responsible for the turn of events. It was a foolish notion. No one person was responsible for anything that had happened. Nothol Coll was just being selfish. The failure of their situation was the result of all their shortcomings.

Not wanting anything to do with Ionascu's corpse, Ironfoot marched on by without offering a second look. He hoped the broken worm-of-a-man died poorly. Such people didn't deserve honorable deaths. A Dwarf in that state would have taken his own life rather than continue to live in shame. Men had no such compunctions, however. Ionascu lived with venom in his heart and yellow on his back. The Dwarf more than once briefly considered planting his axe in the man's back. He'd be ridding them of a great cancer in the process. Much of the discourse among them stemmed from Ionascu. The Dwarf knew no one missed him, despite Anienam's insistence they each had a part to play. Frowning, he passed the dead Man and found himself standing before Groge.

The Giant sat by himself, weeping heavily. Ironfoot stopped short, suddenly unsure if he was ready, or capable, of handling the young Giant's issues. Not that there was much real choice. Boen and Bahr could handle themselves and he'd already made the rounds through the others. Ironfoot steeled himself for the worst. Groge it was.

"I didn't know Giants cried," he said lightheartedly.

Groge didn't look up but instead buried his face deeper in his hands. Ironfoot immediately had a bad feeling. He wasn't the most emotional Dwarf. His previous philosophy revolved around the proper use of an axe to solve problems. He looked the Giant over and concluded his axe wouldn't make a scratch. Best not to irritate the lad.

"Nothing can be that bad. You're a warrior now, lad. Time to start acting like it."

"I'm not a warrior. I've never committed a single act in anger," Groge said after wiping his eyes on the back of a sleeve. "Being in the lowlands is changing me, Ironfoot."

"Change is a natural part of life," the Dwarf replied. "Doesn't make any sense fighting it. Life moves on regardless of our desires. You got your hands bloody for the first time and lived to tell of it. That's a good thing."

"Is it?" Groge lifted his massive head to stare him in the eyes. "How can any being enjoy taking life? I feel less because of it. Generations of my people have hidden from this primal rage. I am the first to come close to succumbing. There is no honor, no pride left in me. I have failed my people."

Ironfoot was shocked. Confessions were often viewed as a sign of weakness. He didn't know the Giant well, but what he did know suggested a being of the highest honor. "Saving your friends lives isn't honorable? You beat back that Gnaal, keeping the wizard and the girl alive. Don't wallow in self-pity over fighting evil.

"I don't understand. You have great strength and a good heart. What disgrace have you placed on the Giants?" the Dwarf growled. He despised anyone feeling sorry for themselves. Even if that someone was close to twelve feet tall.

Groge exhaled a deep breath that smelled of rotten vegetables and chewed meat. "Long ago my people roamed the kingdoms of Malweir. We fought in the Mage Wars, killing many countless numbers of enemy soldiers. It was a terrible time. Those Giants lost to the killing frenzy attacked everything that got too close, including their own kind. Once the war ended, what remained of my people fled into the mountains with vows of peace. Peace at all costs. I broke that peace. I could feel the hate building in me, Ironfoot. It whispered to me, begging for release so that it could feed. I'm scared."

For once the Dwarf didn't know what to say. He tried to compare his own experiences with what the youthful Giant was going through but couldn't find any suitable. He was born to be a warrior. They fought mock battles in the training pits under watchful eyes. Everything in Dwarven culture spoke of martial prowess. To hear a being as large as Groge complain that he'd violated some ancient law governing self-control was ridiculous. A smaller individual would get a crisp slap on the back and a few choice harsh words to get his head back in the fight. Ironfoot simply didn't know how to handle a Giant.

"You're the only one that can get past this," he finally said. "Keep in mind that you did a good thing here and that time is running out to make your peace. My bones tell me there's a war coming. We're going to need you before too long."

The rest of the day passed quickly. They ate, tried to recover from their ordeal, and sat around in prolonged periods of awkward silence. Sleep, while desperately needed, was long in coming for all but Boen. The Gaimosian could sleep after anything. Dorl attributed it to his advanced age. Old people needed sleep more than the young. He felt childish with jealousy over such a simple thing, but Boen made the rest of them look bad. The sell sword stretched and dropped back onto his sleeping roll.

Instead of finding sleep he found himself looking at Rekka as she oiled and sharpened her sword. The pristine condition was gone, battered away against the leathery hide of the Gnaal. He doubted she'd ever be able to get it back into proper shape. While she busied herself in her work, Dorl noticed the olive-skinned jungle warrior steadily stripping his friends of their weapons, clothes, and belongings. The slender man painstakingly closed their eyes and did his best to clean the worst of their wounds. He was clearly in pain, having seen his friends die so violently. Worse was the knowledge that he alone had survived. Shame racked his battered body.

The lone survivor of the Teng warriors finished burying his comrades in their village custom. He stripped the bodies of everything but a loincloth, tied their hands and feet together, and gently took them all to the nearest body of water where he found a large banyan tree. Their bodies would forever be interned in a nameless part of the jungle, swallowed by other life forms so that all life might benefit. With a heavy heart he returned to the ruined campsite and collected what he could carry on his back.

He hefted his broken spear and looked Rekka squarely in the eyes with an accusatory gesture. "Their deaths are on your hands, Rekka Jel. Never return to Teng, for you will be hunted and executed for the murder of Cashi Dam and these warriors. You are a traitor. I name you outcast."

Rekka said nothing. She bowed her head in acknowledgment and returned to her sword. Dorl made to stand up and defend her but was stopped with a loving hand on his forearm. There were some battles he wasn't meant to fight.

TWENTY-FOUR

Trennaron

Endless miles of jungle dragged by at a grueling pace, punishing the invaders who dared to delve into the unseen heart of Brodein. The small band of adventurers pushed on without much regard for their surroundings. The singular purpose of reaching the mythical temple of Trennaron drove them when all else withered and died. Each of them lost weight. Their clothes began to rot and fall apart. The jungle intended to claim them much as it had countless others over the centuries. Not even the wizard was strong enough to stop it.

The days began to blend. Differences between night and day lost meaning. The canopy blocking out the sun and moon thickened the deeper they went. Only Ironfoot found comfort in the confining atmosphere. Much of the jungle reminded him of his caverns in Drimmen Delf. He took the point position for most of their trek while Anienam recovered his sorely depleted strength. Rekka knew what to expect when they finally arrived at Trennaron and she was being more tight-lipped than usual.

Grief and guilt haunted Bahr. Life as a sea captain was one fraught with peril, constantly exposing him to near winless situations. Failure was a strange companion he'd grown accustomed to being near. This sort of failure threatened to steal his will to continue. Strange that so little a thing could cause intense amounts of damage. He wasn't used to having a family, not from the day he abandoned his right to the throne and went in search of his own life. Having a meaningful relationship, even one still budding, ripped out of his hands on a whim bore great holes in the corners of his soul. Her abduction was his fault. Carelessness led them into the jungle. His lack of understanding of the situation worsened all their lives.

Yet they continued with him, not saying a word of the past. They followed his guidance with the unspoken knowledge that he was going to steer them in the right direction, get them to their destination and, hopefully, bring them home alive. It was a great weight threatening to become a burden. He was used to being a leader. Taking charge and being responsible for the lives of his crew went hand in hand with being captain. He enjoyed it. Relished the opportunity to watch his people develop and grow under his tutelage. This quest was changing his mind. He didn't want to be responsible for anyone. Bad things clung to them when he was.

Camp was established in the middle of a small stand of teak trees. Verdant moss blanketed the ground, providing a natural bed more comfortable than any they'd had since leaving Chadra so many months ago. Small talk broke the monotony, but there wasn't any real feeling to it. The sheer impossibility of what the Gnaals represented left them shaken in ways no one wanted to admit. Confidence waned at a time when it was needed to improve.

Bahr finished brushing his horse down and idly picked the coarse hair from the brush. The repetition soothed him and helped him forget the troubles hounding him. He looked out towards the camp, taking in each of them singularly. Dorl was bordering on becoming a jealous wreck. Rekka might as well be a statue. Nothol was oddly quiet, still blaming himself for losing sight of Maleela in the first place. Skuld stood on the edge. The boy was ready to break. Bahr hoped not. He rather liked the former stowaway. Boen was as implacable as ever. Groge hadn't spoken much since his combat with the Gnaal..

The only one that didn't seem bothered by what had happened was the Dwarf. Dour as he was taciturn, Ironfoot marched on without complaint. The stout Dwarf never tired. Never complained. He was a credit to his race and to warriors everywhere. Bahr wished he had more Dwarves along. He could conquer a kingdom with enough, despite their crude mannerisms and affinity for warm ale. Still, they were second best in a fight only to the Gaimosians. His initial reluctance to accept Ironfoot into the ranks faded after the battle with the river men. Ironfoot fought with a deadly combination of skill and ferocity. He was quite possibly their most valuable asset.

Bahr's gaze finally fell on the wizard. Anienam Keiss was a shadow of the cocky man waiting on Bahr's rain-swept doorstep. The swagger of self-righteousness was gone, lost somewhere between being buried under Chadra and the jungle. His overarching sense of purpose seemed diminished, as if he had lost his confidence. Bahr was ashamed to admit he took a measure of perverse enjoyment out of it, but he needed Anienam at full speed if they were going to succeed in getting the Blud Hamr and return safely to Delranan. Shoving the brush back into a saddlebag, Bahr headed over to the wizard. It was time they talked.

"I was wondering when you'd come around," Anienam said indignantly. They hadn't spoken since the outburst at the end of the battle.

Bahr felt his cheeks flush. It was a difficult thing for a grown man, swallowing his pride. "We should go somewhere. I don't want to disturb the others. They've been through enough. Let them rest while they can."

"Agreed." He held out his hand for Bahr to pull him to his feet and they walked back to the opposite side of the horses.

"I'm a man, Anienam. I make no excuses for my actions, nor do I expect anyone to do the same for me. This world is harsh and I need to be harsh along with it. That being said, I was…wrong to lash out at you. It wasn't your fault Maleela was taken. You didn't deserve my wrath." Bahr felt better with the admission, but still had a long way to go to get back to where they were at the beginning of the quest.

Anienam graciously accepted the admission. He knew it was as close to an apology as a man as proud as Bahr was going to give. It worked. "Captain Bahr, we have all been stressed greatly. This quest has taxed us all. I admit I've not been my best, nor have I given you all I have." He held up a hand to prevent Bahr from interrupting. "There is good reason for that. Much of what we are about to experience will test the limits of your faith and comprehension. We are dealing with forces beyond the scope of your imagination. I thought it best not to encumber the others with these details until absolutely necessary."

"While I question your decision-making capabilities, I won't deny the others have been through more than any of us imagined," Bahr gave in. "But you and I need to have a reckoning. The longer this journey lasts the more I find myself doubting you. We need complete trust if we're to continue. Anything less will take us past the edge of ruin."

"Agreed."

Bahr handed him a half-empty canteen. The hardest part of the conversation was passed, leaving the path forward ready for discussion. Compounding questions bothered him to great ends. He needed resolution before continuing, if only for his peace of mind. Trennaron wasn't far off according to Anienam's calculations. So close to the end of what had been a very long, grueling quest, Bahr needed to know as many variables as possible before they turned around and headed home.

"We should be there by tomorrow I think," Anienam said after swallowing. "Rekka's aid in this proves invaluable. Without her we'd never be allowed to find it."

Bahr appreciated everything the jungle woman had done for them, despite knowing less about her than he did the wizard. It seemed he'd made a bad habit of surrounding himself in mystery. "What makes her the key to all this?"

Anienam fixed him with a disbelieving glare. "You can't be serious. She's the sole reason we've made it this far. Trennaron is one of the oldest places of power in the world. Natural power, tapped directly from the world's core. Mystics and Mages swarmed there once upon a time to increase their lore. It has been guarded by the Dae'shan since the beginning of recorded time. Not the Dae'shan trying to kill us, but one who abandoned their wicked ways, choosing to remain loyal to the gods of light. A handful is chosen to defend the Guardian of Trennaron each generation. They come from all the jungle villages. Rekka is the chosen representative from Teng. It is an incomparable honor to serve."

"You're talking in circles," Bahr said.

"My point is the path to Trennaron will only be open to Rekka. We'd never find it by ourselves," the wizard finished.

Bahr nodded absently, folded his arms across his chest, and ambled back to the group. He had much to ponder before they arrived. More importantly, he thought of nothing else but keeping Rekka Jel alive.

With Rekka in the point position, the band of adventurers trudged deeper into the jungle. They didn't run into the Gnaals again, nor additional warriors from Teng. No one went this deep into the jungle without good reason, she explained. Bad things tended to happen when the predators all outweighed the prey. The going was slow thanks to the density of the undergrowth. Despite Anienam's reassurances that their pursuers were gone, Bahr couldn't help but feel like he was still being watched. Still, the journey continued.

Skuld's horse tripped over a half-buried root and broke its leg, forcing them to put the poor creature down. No one wanted to do it, but they couldn't risk the wounded animal bringing some of the more dangerous jungle cats or lizards down on them. Boen took care of it once the others moved out of sight. He didn't want the other horses getting spooked from the gore. He gave the horse a final, sorrowful pat on the neck before putting it out of its misery. Far from sentimental, Boen much preferred being around animals than people. It hurt him more to see the horse die than a friend.

They kept moving. Losing the wagon and a horse hampered their ability to move with speed. Skuld alternated walking and riding with Rekka. They were the two lightest of the group, putting less stress on her mount that way. Unnecessary supplies were dumped. The loss was regrettable but Rekka assured them they were close enough to Trennaron not to worry. That made them worry more. Nothing had gone right since Bahr agreed to Harnin's proposal to go into Rogscroft to rescue Maleela. They were desperate for a good break.

Another day came and went before the group discovered the abandoned looking one lane road in the middle of the jungle. Rekka's mood brightened instantly. Her sudden change in attitude proved infectious, spreading through the group almost instantaneously.

"We are close," she told them. "Follow this trail until sundown and we will arrive. No enemies will be near. Trennaron holds great powers and is warded by the most potent magic."

"Good. It's about time we were able to relax," Boen said, grinning.

Rekka turned her head sharply. "Relax? No. This is not the time to relax. Trennaron is protected, Gaimosian. The guardians will most assuredly try to prevent us from getting within the perimeter. We must be warier than ever before."

Boen frowned but kept his thoughts private. How would it sound to the others for him to admit he wanted to go home?

Clear of brush, the road hastened their movement. Bahr was glad to be done with the clinging jungle. He wanted to see the sun again. Feel the fresh kiss of warmth on his face one last time before entering the mythical castle. Birds of all colors became abundant the farther down the road they went. Their songs filled the air with majesty, the canopy providing a natural amphitheater of acoustics as the birds flit across the road.

The trees gradually pushed back until they formed a wide avenue capable of marching five horses abreast. Bahr spied the first golden rays of sunlight piercing through the veil of leaves, warming the plush grass. *How unlike home. I've never seen green so vibrant. This land is so foreign to me. Almost makes me wish I'd been born down here rather than the harsh north. Life has more of a chance for success this far south.*

Rekka, followed closely by Boen and Ironfoot, emerged from the concealment of the jungle into a massive clearing. The Gaimosian whistled shrilly. He'd traveled from one side of Malweir to the other but had never seen anything so impressive. The clearing formed a perfect circle, stretching for nearly a mile in every direction. Large birds flew by the arching treetops of the great banyans ringing the field. A herd of deer, brown with thick, white stripes running over their backs grazed without fear. Wildflowers blossomed in wide patches, transforming the clearing into a patchwork of colors. No clouds marred the sky, lending the world a sense of calm, peace. Boen almost felt at ease.

"This is an eyeful," he murmured, slowly sheathing his sword.

Rekka watched him. "You may yet have need of that. The protectors will know we are here already. It's best to stay on guard."

"From the deer?" he asked, choosing to disbelieve her cautiousness. "I've never seen a more serene place, Rekka."

"Have you learned nothing from your travels? Often the most innocent thing is the deadliest. But no, the deer will not bother us. I used to come out and feed them. The true protectors are atop the castle walls."

Boen frowned and urged his horse forward. If trouble was around he wanted to meet it first. Haze filled the center of the clearing, obscuring the structure carefully hidden within. Nothing Rekka said did Trennaron any justice, for it was protected against the common person. The only ones capable of seeing it were the ones it wanted. Boen refused to believe a building could decide who looked at it. His own superstitions were mocked back in the mountains when the ghosts of his forbearers had come to him with dire warnings. He failed to heed their advice. A lament he continued to feel the effects of. Begrudgingly, he decided to let Rekka resume her place at the head of the advance.

The mist gradually parted, as if sensing Rekka's return. They had their first views of ancient Trennaron. No words were capable of doing it justice. The walls stretched high into the sky and equally deep underground. Alabaster as bleached bones, the city-fortress bore a godly presence. No evil was permitted to enter, leaving Trennaron unsullied. There were no statues or monuments to vain glory. Nothing to supplant the inherent grandeur emplaced within the walls.

Spiked crenellations jutted like spears into the sky. Unlike other fortresses, Trennaron lacked murder holes or spy ports. There was nowhere for cauldrons of boiling pitch. No guard towers housing an infinite amount of weapon stores. The great, central dome was marred only by the oculus in the center. The ground around the base of the walls remained pure. There was no evidence of a moat or barracks. Trennaron wasn't built for warfare. Trennaron served a much higher purpose.

Golden faces were carved into the walls. Some smiled. Others stared back. A pair of cupped palms lined the main doorway, wordlessly offering protection for whoever was permitted to enter. The desire to commit violence dissipated quickly. Trennaron allowed no violations of its time immemorial rules. Legend whispered the gods of light constructed the castle as a focal point for wholesomeness. Virtue and righteousness were hallmarks of any who was allowed within. All else was cleansed from the soul. So long as a Guardian remained, Trennaron maintained its power. Malweir needed a place like this in such dark and troubling times.

Boen couldn't take his eyes from the magnificent structure. He imagined the Dwarf was having an internal fit, knowing his people would never be able to craft such a place. After all, how does one compete with the power of the gods?

He spied massive figures carved from the rock, spaced evenly across the tops of the walls. Their size gave birth to much speculation. None of his private theories seemed to have much value and he was forced to abandon thoughts towards them. For reasons the Gaimosian didn't know, he knew they were important.

He was about to ask Rekka what they were when one of them suddenly launched into the sky. That was followed closely by a score more.

"The protectors have awakened!" Rekka shouted.

TWENTY-FIVE

Ingrid's War

Half buried in the snow, Ingrid struggled to keep from shivering. Her teeth chattered to the sound of stones smashing together. Even with gloves on, her fingers turned bluish. Cold penetrated down into her bones. Her only comfort came from the knowledge that twenty others suffered the same. Brave people all, they'd given up the comparative comforts of their homes to assist Ingrid in turning the tide of the war back against Harnin. Most of the events in Chadra were hearsay this far out in the countryside, but every one of the people Harlan mustered were true patriots to Delranan. Their allegiances ran above crown and king.

They'd been waiting, half buried in the snow since before dawn to ambush the Wolfsreik supply train reported to be moving from one of the outlying bases back to what remained of Chadra. Ingrid's orders were specific and based on Harlan's scouts. Hopefully the intel panned out, otherwise the rebellion would be in need of a new command structure. All enemy personnel were to be eliminated while as much of the supplies as possible were confiscated. The people in the villages needed the supplies to sustain themselves until spring.

Orlek argued against her going. She insisted the only way to endear these new fighters to her cause was by leading from the front. Inaella's greatest failing as a leader was her refusal to be seen as an example for the rank and file to emulate. Ingrid was determined not to make the same mistakes. *That doesn't prevent me from making entirely different ones. I've never been a soldier, unlike Orlek or Harlan. This is all so new to me. All I can do is give my people the best they deserve and pray Harnin folds before we do.*

She knew there was no alternative. Death awaited every other avenue except success.

She looked over at the nearest snow covered body. Orlek. His eyes never tired as he scanned the road for signs of the enemy's approach. She envied his ability to always keep going in the face of adversity. Unanswered questions ran rampant through her mind as she toyed with trying to figure out what he'd been before the nightmare began. Everyone had a story to tell and, while most of them were plain and uninteresting, Orlek clearly had something he wanted hidden. Ingrid wanted to know what. Not that she needed to. Her life was a growing mass of complications, but the simple knowledge would go so far in soothing her aching psyche. At this point she needed every victory she could get, no matter how obscure.

A stiff wind blew snow in her face. The light powder was unsettling and got down her blouse. Ingrid shivered, wondering how it was possible she could get any colder than what she already was. Cold. Miserable and bordering on being dejected, Ingrid was ready to give in. She was starting to doubt the accuracy of Harlan's intelligence network. Placing both hands beneath her, Ingrid readied to pop up.

"Hsss," Orlek said quietly. "They're coming."

Ingrid felt trapped between powerful emotions. Her cheeks reddened from her foolishness in believing her people had failed her while her adrenaline began to pump with the prospect of meeting the enemy in the open field instead of the confines of the city. Until now she'd only battled in Chadra and a handful of the closer villages surrounding the capital. Fighting in the undisguised wilderness was an alien concept. She had trouble conceptualizing how her fighters would be able to successfully camouflage themselves while being in the open.

Orlek showed her. The open tundra comprising the vast majority of Delranan was lightly forested between stretches of seemingly endless leagues of open plains. There were perfect places for ambushes, most natural. This wasn't one of them. They had a clear view of the road stretching on, a dark streak in the middle of pristine snow. The drifts were piled so high Orlek managed to plant the strike force without any trace of being seen. He and Ingrid went into position last. Each dragged large pine boughs behind them to cover all the snowshoe tracks peppering the otherwise unspoiled snow.

Caltrops littered the road, threatening to become as much of a danger to her people as for the Wolfsreik horses. She preferred to take the horses alive. They didn't have much fodder but were in sore need of animals for quicker transport across the kingdom. Orlek argued against it. The horses were bred for war, even the draft horses. They'd prove more difficult than they were worth in the long run. Killing them might be the kindest mercy she could do. Despite the illusions of righteousness swirling in her dreams, Ingrid knew very few professional soldiers had switched sides.

"I don't see anything," she whispered back.

Orlek grinned, his brown-stained teeth in sharp contrast to the pure white of the snow. "Put your ear to the ground and listen. You can feel the vibrations of their footsteps. We have less than fifteen minutes."

Ingrid believed Orlek was suffering from frostbite of the mind. How could anyone hear vibrations in the ground and accurately judge distance and rate of travel? Regardless of how she truly felt, it was her responsibility to ensure her people were ready. Ingrid rose cautiously, her head and shoulders poking just above the frozen surface. Any fears she had faded. One by one she noticed the subtle shift of a pile of snow marking where one of her fighters was hidden. They were already preparing.

They'd rehearsed the drill to the point each knew their tasks as well as those of the person to their left or right. Orlek was a harsh task master who put his people to the test. He berated their mistakes while calmly praising outstanding performance. He brokered no failure. Anyone caught not doing their jobs was summarily dismissed and hidden away to prevent them from betraying the rebellion the way Inaella had.

"Relax," Orlek hissed. "They know their jobs."

She wanted to believe but this batch was unproven on the battlefield. They might easily break and run the moment pressure grew too intense. Each one understood death was more than likely, a fact she made no qualms of admitting. The failures of the past continued to plague her decisions towards the future. Orlek was forced to reel her in from time to time, a deed he strongly considered performing now. Ingrid was giddy to the point she threatened to give away their positions.

"We need these supplies," she said unnecessarily.

He let it go. Everyone calmed their nerves in their own way. Who was he to criticize hers? She was no great combat leader. Not even a mediocre one truth be told, but she pursued this rebellion with such passion, such fervor, he was swept up in the tide. Ingrid believed in a free Delranan. He wished more like her would spring forth. The rebellion needed bodies, strength in numbers, if they were going to outlast Harnin's five-thousand strong Wolfsreik. That still left them with the bulk of the ten-thousand strong main army returning whenever the war in Rogscroft ended. Orlek focused on his current enemy. He'd worry about the rest when the time came.

Minutes dragged by. She didn't think the supply convoy would ever arrive, but it did. And in much greater strength than she had anticipated. Orlek was used to being underestimated. His group of fighters was strategically emplaced along the western edge of the road, ready to ambush as soon as the horses stepped on the caltrops. A second, larger body, led by Harlan, was hidden in a stand of pines about a hundred meters away. They would remain hidden until the battle began and sweep in from the rear while the enemy was distracted. In theory the plan was sound. Orlek was about to find out just how sound.

Ingrid crinkled her nose at the stench of horse and riders who'd been in the field for too long. She didn't know how anyone could let their hygiene go for so long. The first riders came into view, followed closely by the wagons. Another thirty soldiers accompanied the supply train. Few of them were paying attention. They'd grown complacent since the victories in Chadra and over most of the rebellion, just like Orlek predicted. None of them expected to run into serious trouble this far out in the countryside. That would be their downfall.

Ingrid forced herself to remain still. It was one of the worst tortures she could imagine. She felt certain the scouts looked her in the eyes a dozen times while the convoy continued. Her heart quickened. Her mouth dried unnaturally. The sword at her side felt cumbersome. She wasn't a soldier. Pretending to be one now out of vain glory was foolish at best. Why wasn't the enemy attacking? She *knew* they'd seen her. What were they waiting for? The sickness of their cruelty pervaded her innermost confidence. She couldn't stand it any longer.

Orlek rose in a small avalanche of snow. His bow was strung and drawn. His eyes were sharp. Tensed muscles begged to be released. To exercise their anger in the song of flesh and steel. A horse kicked out and went down in a hail of grotesque screams. The second horse followed closely behind. Orlek fired. His aim was true. The shaft took the wagon master in the throat, pitching him off the side. The wagon teams immediately went out of control and bolted forward into the nightmarish mess of the caltrops even as the stricken scouts shouted and tried to warn them off. The rest of Orlek's fighters rose and fired one arrow each at the nearest targets.

Most struck a fresh body, though one or two managed to hit the same soldier. It didn't matter. The Wolfsreik were taken off guard. Orlek bellowed and his fighters charged while the enemy was still disoriented enough to lack cohesion. Ingrid was the last to rise, despite her jittery nerves and an unquenchable desire to strike first blood. Her timid roar disappeared in the growing chorus. She pointed her sword at the closest soldier, one of the fallen scouts. He was trapped beneath his horse; his leg crushed from the fall. Ingrid hesitated when she caught him staring back at her. The fright in his eyes was evident to a blind man.

"Do it," Orlek ordered with sternness that made her flinch.

Ingrid spent hours thinking of what it would take to turn the rebellion to her way of thinking, her vision for a stronger Delranan. How many imaginary soldiers had she killed over the course of the winter? How many times did she stand triumphantly over her vanquished enemies while her fighters cheered her name? Reality was much harsher than her dreams. Ingrid plunged her sword down into the fallen soldier. She vomited as the soft flesh tore and gave way to bone and the hidden organs within. The soldier gave a short cry while dark blood frothed on his lips. His eyes rolled back into his head in death. Tears filled Ingrid's eyes. She never saw Harlan's gallant charge from behind.

"Here, you need to drink this," Orlek said brusquely.

Ingrid, eyes burning from her tears, couldn't stand to look up into his face. She feared whatever judgments he had reserved for her. Shame heaped upon her slender shoulders. She'd been so eager to get into the fight that she never considered the cost it would take from her soul. Talking of battles and deeds of grandeur was well and fine, but the cold reality of watching a man she killed turn pale blue in a puddle of his own blood twisted her stomach. She wasn't cut out to be a field commander.

"Take it, Ingrid. You need warmth inside you," Orlek insisted. "There will be a time for self-loathing when this war is done."

She stared blankly at the snow.

Frowning, Orlek bunched his heavy cloak and sat beside her, forcing the flask into her trembling hands. "We're at war. Men die. There is no escaping that fact. The only way the enemy will die is if we kill them. You did what you had to do."

"I killed him," she protested.

He shook his head. "No. You killed an enemy asset. He was a soldier that would have run you through without second thought. Worse if you'd been taken alive. Men like that like to have fun with their captives before they kill them. Be thankful you struck first. The alternative would not have been to your liking."

"How do you do it?" she asked slowly. Each word inspired fresh pain.

He shrugged. "I don't think about it. You must harden your heart to do the kind of work I do. Killing isn't easy, especially for someone who's never done it. I'd like to tell you it gets easier with time, but it doesn't. Not if you let it get to you. The best way to do it is to put it from your mind immediately."

Orlek neglected to mention how the faces continue to haunt you night after night. He didn't figure she needed to worry about that right now. They'd just scored a major victory, even on such a small scale, and needed to capitalize on it before the enemy regained momentum. Other patrols were still out in the countryside. The faster the rebellion struck, the easier it would be to spread the enemy out. They desperately needed the Wolfsreik to disperse to strike harder and to greater effect. He couldn't do that with Ingrid wallowing in grief.

He fixed a stern, almost fatherly look at her. "Ingrid, there is no time for this. We are at a critical crossroads. Harnin will send all his might here once he learns of what we did. It's time to spread out and bring this kingdom to its knees. The people need you. I thought you purged the weakness from our ranks when we left Chadra and overthrew Inaella?"

Ingrid abandoned her misery and shot Orlek a foul glare. "You know why I did what I did, Orlek. Your hands are just as red as mine. The rebellion had grown stagnant. I did what needed to be done for the good of the kingdom."

"The kingdom or your own ego?" he asked.

"My ego has nothing to do with this! I am a patriot. Harnin One Eye has ruined our land, killed our people, and invited darkness into our hearts. He needs to be removed before we are all reduced to corpses frozen and forgotten in the harsh winter freeze."

Orlek cracked a tight grin and began to nod. "Good. That's the spark that drew me to you. Never lose it, not for an instant. We won't survive the war if you do."

"You make this all seem so reasonable, as if it's supposed to happen," she replied, already calming down. "I don't like killing, Orlek. I feel dirty."

He nodded again. "Killing's a dirty business. I'd like to say you get used to it but that would be a lie. My advice to you is to stay back in Fendi. You're in charge. Be in charge."

She took a deep breath to calm her nerves. Reluctantly, she drank from the flask. It burned all the way down into her stomach. Ingrid coughed as she felt the heat spread throughout her body. She sputtered, "Are you trying to kill me?"

He broke out with laughter. "This is Fendi's finest, Ingrid."

"More like cow piss," she scoffed before realizing the absurdity of what she'd said. A year ago she never would have been caught using vulgarity. Funny how much leading a war changed people.

She and Orlek shared a much needed laugh and he helped her to her feet. It was past time they returned to the quiet northern village. Without another word the rebels finished consolidating whatever they could use and headed back to Fendi. The trek was quick and uneventful. Thoughts already turned towards getting drunk in celebration, regardless of Orlek's caution. Their victory was minor with great threat of reprisal once word got back to Chadra Keep. Until then much needed to be done.

Secured in the relative safety of the inn's common room, Ingrid and Orlek eagerly awaited Harlan's return. The enigmatic man remained a mystery; one Ingrid wasn't comfortable with having in her life while so many enemies roamed the kingdom. They weren't safe until Harnin's entire regime was removed from power.

"He's late," she said between bites of rather gamey mutton. She'd never been a fan of lamb, but whoever was responsible for cooking the chewy meat on her plate thoroughly reinforced her feelings. Ingrid swore to starve before touching lamb again.

Orlek washed a bite of fat-laced meat down with dry red wine. "Relax, Ingrid. He'll be here."

"Unless he's dead," she countered hurriedly.

"Your optimism inspires me," he said and frowned. "Harlan will be here. Just have a little faith. We have other items to worry over."

"I know, but I can't help it. Especially after all we went through in Chadra. The supplies are being distributed throughout the village. Our share is being loaded and taken to one of the safe houses in the countryside, the old bear caves I believe. More people are pouring in. Keeping them armed and fed is proving to be a hassle." She paused, never imaging the trials of leadership could be so grueling. "We can only hope the other villages are meeting with equal success."

"The One Eye won't know what hit him if we can organize the kingdom before he wields the Wolfsreik. They're good soldiers, some of the best, but even they can't be everywhere at once. We still have a chance, Ingrid," Orlek told her. The confidence lacing his words left her inspired precisely when she needed it.

The door opened suddenly followed closely by Harlan and a swirl of snow. A fresh storm had blown in shortly after the rebels returned and was inundating Fendi with at least another foot. Orlek and Ingrid's plans were put on hold until the snows blew out. He stomped the slush from his boots and shook the snow from his hair.

"You look cold," Orlek remarked.

Harlan frowned sharply. "You go stand outside in this weather. I don't think winter is ever going to end."

"Look at the bright side, there's a good chance we'll all be dead before spring," Orlek said. "What news do you bring?"

Harlan took a moment to pull his bluish hands from his brown leather gloves and warm them over the fire. "Better than we expected. I was able to coordinate a series of attacks on their supply lines across a quarter of the kingdom. We raided three supply convoys and a mounted patrol. Not a bad way to start the war."

"The war has been going on for far too long already, Harlan," Ingrid reminded him. "What about casualties?"

"Minimal. Seven dead, thirteen wounded," Harlan answered. "The enemy suffered far worse and we managed to secure the majority of the supplies before they were damaged."

Ingrid was pleased, and more than a little surprised, with their initial successes, but the feeling was compounded with the knowledge that their base of operations was no longer secure. "Fendi is untenable. It's time to move."

"In this storm?" Harlan asked. "We'd lose more than we can afford. It's not worth the risk, Ingrid. At least wait until it blows over."

Orlek agreed. "Harlan's right. Moving in the storm isn't worth risking all we've won thus far. We still have time."

"Time is as much our enemy as the Wolfsreik, but perhaps there is merit in your approach. Our foes are as hampered by the storm as we are," Ingrid relented. "I want everyone ready to move the moment the last flake hits the ground. Harnin will be relentless in his pursuit. He knows, as do I, that we stand on the precipice. The success or failure of our next move could very well determine the course of this war."

TWENTY-SIX

Beleaguered

The decanter burst into thousands of tiny pieces as it crashed into the cold stone wall. One of the wolfhounds, patiently curled up under the aged table, snapped up and began barking. Torchlight flickered angrily across the walls. Centered in the rage, Harnin One Eye stood with clenched fists. His body trembled with unbridled anger.

"I entrusted you!" he seethed. "I gave you my confidence, despite my better judgments. You took my soldiers into the city and managed to get several of them killed. For what?"

Inaella stood her ground. "For the knowledge that the rebellion has been successfully driven into the countryside."

"Dispersed into smaller units capable of evading my army!" Harnin shouted back. "I had your precious rebellion dead within the city limits. Your ineptitude pushed them out where it will be next to impossible to get without burning the entire kingdom to the ground."

"You wanted your city back, One Eye. I gave it to you. You had Lord Argis executed from the tops of these walls, infuriating the general population and you dare accuse me of incompetence?" Inaella pointed an accusatory finger at him. "Your zealousness led us to this point. The rebellion was never confined to just Chadra. We were spread across Delranan in small cells waiting for the proper time when we could make a coordinated assault on every one of your power bases. Chadra was the control center for it all. You whine that I ruined your designs when in truth I gave you what you needed most: the total displacement of the rebellion command and control center. None of those cells can function in any other way but independently from now on. Accuse me all you wish, Lord Harnin, but you and I both know the inescapable truth of my actions."

Harnin paused. The desire to take her head surged through his blood. She'd quickly grown cancerous to all he stood for. Even when she'd been his enemy, Inaella was seldom this effective. The rebellion had never been more than poorly trained amateurs, even with Argis' training. This aristocrat woman, oh yes, he knew exactly who she'd been before all this, was part of everything wrong in Delranan. Yet he couldn't ignore the feeling that she had already done more for him than most of his lords combined. She was quickly becoming an indispensable asset. His anger subsided slowly.

"How do you propose to get at all the smaller cells?" he asked suddenly. Accusations no longer held sway in his discussion. He needed to step back and think clearly if he was going to have his kingdom secured before Badron and the Wolfsreik returned. *That's when the real fight begins.*

Inaella smoothed the front of her light brown dress and pursed her lips with thought. "Ingrid is a commoner. While she might have been married to an officer, she isn't one. She lacks the foresight to track the entire war. She'll take her time, moving cautiously while she tries to validate her tactics."

"You haven't answered my question."

She offered her best false smile. "Disperse the Wolfsreik into company-sized elements and scour every village, town, and city in Delranan. Take away their hiding places. Force them into the open where you can bring your full might to bear. You can crush the rebellion in one fell swoop and focus your attention on the coming war when the king returns."

She was careful not to include herself in the conversation. Harnin was notoriously unstable. Who knew what might upset him. It didn't take much imagination to envision him cleansing his own ranks, and what better place to start than with her? She needed to tread carefully to secure her rightful place in the new court of the kingdom.

Mention of Badron darkened whatever bright spot colored his mood. He lacked the manpower, logistics, and weapons to fight the main body of the army. His one advantage lay in the fact that the army had been at war for months and would be depleted almost enough to make the field even. None of that mattered unless he managed to get rid of the rebellion and consolidate his power base. Fresh winter storms hampered the construction of several small defensive positions being established along the roads leading from the Murdes Mountains to the east. Every likely avenue of approach was being covered with traps, ambushes, and revetments capable of holding up the enemy for weeks.

"You denounce this Ingrid in one sentence and praise her in the next," he said. "If I didn't know better I'd say you are not wholly on my side, Inaella."

The sound of her grinding teeth grated through the chamber. "She will die by my hand before this is done. I swear to you. There is no love in my heart for the rebellion. True, I gave them everything for the period I was on the council. She betrayed my trust and left me to die while her followers stole all I'd won. Kill all the others for yourself, but I will make Ingrid pay for her crimes."

Harnin wore a pleased look. "Good. Hatred is a cornerstone for people in our business. We grow stale without the driving force of hate. Dark days are coming to Delranan. Those caught without hate in their hearts will be driven to the ground and crushed beneath the rest. Embrace your hatred, Inaella. Use it to determine your actions and you will find yourself rising in my estimation. Perhaps one day you might even have a voice in my new kingdom."

He dismissed her with a simple wave. Insulted, Inaella held her tongue and stormed out. Her mind twisted with opposing thoughts as she wormed her way through Chadra Keep. Life had changed so dramatically over the past few months, she hardly recognized herself anymore. Her skin itched constantly from the scarring. Residual effects from the plague caused havoc in her body. She walked with a limp now and seldom went anywhere with her hood down. Inaella prided herself on being a realist, and realism demanded she accept she'd gone from the educated, aristocrat wife to a hideous being with a twisted soul. She was beyond the point of disgust. All her focus centered on revenge.

Every time she closed her eyes Ingrid's face mocked her. That effervescent smile framed by golden locks of hair. A faint measure of perfection meant to drive her down into the depths of despair. Hate was a new concept for her. Inaella spent much of her life in the lap of luxury, never having to struggle for anything. She'd been given all she asked for and more. Life as an heiress to a major factor with holdings in three kingdoms offered much. She attended the grandest balls and wore jewelry crafted by Dwarves. Inaella was the envy of society.

Those days were finished. The rebellion changed everything. Her home was burned when Harnin ousted everyone who'd benefited under Badron's reign. Her husband was killed for trying to defend his home and family. At the time she wasn't strong. She fled into the night rather than stand at her husband's side. She abandoned everything she owned, everything she was, for the false security of her own life. There was little doubt of her turning to the fledgling rebellion. Inaella poured all her anguish and self-loathing into turning the tide against Harnin. It was all for naught.

Ingrid robbed her of her revenge. Stole the opportunity to strike back into the enemy's heart in the name of her husband and for everyone who had lost in the early days of rebellion. Ingrid became the hero Inaella could never be. She became the face of the rebellion, a guiding force drawing others like moths to the flame. The rebellion had been a faceless entity until Ingrid's usurpation.

"You carry much grief with you."

She froze. Her hand immediately dropped to the dagger hidden in her robes while she searched the half shadows filling the hallway. "Show yourself."

"Not yet. The time is not right for you to see me. Take comfort in knowing that you are not alone. There are powerful forces moving behind the scenes in Delranan. Know that you are being looked after."

"I don't need looking after," she said defiantly. Her slender fingers clenched the dagger's hilt. "What woman needs a faceless voice whispering cunning encouragement while hiding in the night? I am my own woman. Save your petty assurances for those less fortunate."

Something rustled in the darkness. "Are you? How far you have fallen from grace, Inaella. The leaves have fallen from your tree, yet you still cling to the falsity of independence. What do you have left but the rot devouring you from the inside?"

Inaella felt the first inkling of gripping terror take root in the cold corners of her soul. *What is this foul voice whispering impossible promises? Am I going insane? Has my mind fractured to the point of seductive voices tempting me into further darkness?* Her skin prickled at the wispy sound of quiet laughter.

"Already your mind leads you down roads you wished did not exist. The world has not been kind to you. All you've known and loved has been taken, stolen like a child in the night. What allegiances remain for you? No home. No friends. No one to cling to when your bed grows cold from winter's kiss. This is not life."

"Your words are poison to me," she whispered. Tears welled in her eyes.

"Are they or are you so hollow you cannot stand to look back at the truth? There is passion inside you, Inaella. A great fire capable of washing this pathetic kingdom away with its cleansing tide. If only you were strong enough to reach out and take it."

"Be gone demon, I am no puppet." She forced the words, praying to the old gods for some sort of intervention lest she weakened and gave in to the dark temptations.

The voice hardened, as if angered by her accusation. "Demon! Why is it you mortals limit the depths of your imagination to demons and witchery? If you only knew the extent of the powers in this world you wouldn't blind yourselves to simplistic terms. I have walked the kingdoms of this world, crept across the halls of the gods, and seen the death of suns."

"Yet now you creep in the shadows," Inaella said. "Show me your face, demon."

"You mock what your meager mind doesn't allow you to understand. Be careful, little flower. I can kill you with a thought," the voice taunted.

She scoffed, all vestiges of fear erased by his inability to materialize before her. "I think you are a coward. Delranan doesn't need the likes of you, with your smooth words to make it better. We have existed for a long time and no manner of demon will change that! Now, be gone! I will broker no more indulgences from you."

The shadows strengthened. The hallway grew frigid. Her blood thinned. Plumes of breath steamed from her mouth and nostrils. Her eyes locked on his: bloodless red orbs filled with malice. She felt a part of her die in that moment. Crooked fingers stretched forth from the darkness, reaching for her heart.

"Do not tempt me with your casual stupidity again, *woman*, for the next time we meet I may not be so generous," the Dae'shan warned. "You live only at my whim. Still, I give you the opportunity to rise above all your base desires. Let me into your mind. Oh what wonders I can show you! Delranan deserves better than the twisted corpse sitting on its throne. You can take that position. All you need to do is reach out and take my hand."

Inaella collapsed to her knees. Her strength was false. She was found wanting. The temptation to do as he offered almost proved too much. She fought with all she had left, knowing it wouldn't be enough. Time slowed to a crawl. Fleeting glimpses of her sitting upon the throne, dressed in a bone-white gown with thralls lining the throne room filled her with hope and glory. All would kneel before her and pay homage. She would rule with fire, passion, and, above all, honor. Delranan would grow strong again under her stern tutelage.

She shook her head. It was just a dream. "I…can't."

The hand receded. The hate filled eyes dissolved back into the immaterial. "That is…disappointing. Think on your words, Inaella. I will return to you and present my offer one last time. You alone have the potential to change the course of history. Certain doom will fall if you decide to spurn my words."

He disappeared, leaving her hugging her knees between tear-filled sobs. Inaella lamented all her life had become. Not for the first time she considered running a blade across her wrists.

TWENTY-SEVEN

A Kingdom's Future

Aurec couldn't find sleep. He tried reclaiming his old chambers but the majority of the castle had been ransacked to the point of being condemned. All his old furniture was smashed and used for kindling. Life as he once knew it simply ceased to exist. Several soldiers and guards rummaged through the expansive castle and produced a small bed and night table for him. Attendants he'd told to stay in Grunmarrow until the winter war ended had clearly disobeyed him and unpacked his meager wagon and established a livable bedroom. That was all well and fine, but it wasn't *his* room. Aurec felt like a stranger in his home.

He thought fondly back to his nights in the castle with Maleela. She brightened the gloomiest night. Her charm and way that smile clung to her face long after she'd stopped laughing warmed him. Aurec wasn't especially sentimental but her absence left a great hole in his heart. The war continued, distracting him from finding his love. Or perhaps it was the other way. Maleela's loss prevented him from giving his total concentration to driving Badron and his Goblins out of Rogscroft. Pulled in opposing directions, Aurec struggled to find a balance that would see the successful completion of both tasks.

Sleep not forthcoming, the newly crowned king of Rogscroft pulled his tired body out of the hard bed and dressed in loose trousers and a wool tunic. Aurec went to the nightstand and dipped his hands in the cold water resting in an old metal bowl and rinsed his face. The briskness stole his breath, taking away his unending stream of nightmares in the process. Every time he closed his eyes he saw visions of Maleela being tormented by strange creatures. Fires raged around her. He watched as her will collapsed and she became something…less. Was it all a portent? Was Maleela even alive? His lack of certainty hounded his decisions.

Dressed and wide awake, Aurec donned his heavy robe and headed towards the kitchens. Cooks and supply personnel were busy around the clock fixing and serving food not only to the hungry soldiers but to what remained of the city's main population. Senior military officers initially protested, claiming supplies were already stretched too thin and feeding the general populace would weaken the army's ability to pursue Badron. Rolnir quashed that immediately. What better use of their supplies was there than to feed the beleaguered survivors of Rogscroft?

Aurec was able to remain out of the equation. All it took place before he was even apprised of the situation. Probably for the better, he mused. These were his people. He'd give them all they could eat if it meant they continued to live. That same day runners were sent back to Grunmarrow with instructions to bring everything and everyone. The reasoning was twofold. With the main army situated around Rogscroft proper, the rest of the countryside was exposed for attack should Badron have the numbers. Grunmarrow was no secret. If the king of Delranan wanted to strike a retaliatory blow it would be there. The civilian defenders would fall like harvest wheat and the army would lose valuable supplies and personnel. Aurec needed everyone in one centralized location to protect them.

Guards were scattered throughout the castle in pairs in the event the enemy left nasty surprises behind. Aurec rejected the idea until Venten and Rolnir jumped in to change his mind. Rogscroft had already lost one monarch. Losing a second in a matter of weeks would set the kingdom back irreparably. He took comfort from knowing soldiers stood on guard. Whatever treachery Badron had installed would be thwarted by the guards.

He nodded and spent a few moments idly chatting with the guards he passed en route to the kitchen. Most were barely older than he was. It felt strange knowing Rogscroft relied on these boys when so many veterans remained. He lamented it must have always been so. The old grow weak and either retire or are killed, leaving youth to streak to the front of the ranks to carry the colors. That a new generation could willingly step into its predecessors' shoes to fulfill the oaths to king and land struck a chord with Aurec.

The closer he got to the kitchens the more his stomach growled. He hadn't eaten since midday, much to his regret, and found he was starving. Bakers already had fresh loaves in the ovens, preparing for the morning rush. Aurec's stomach tightened in anticipation. He saw the faint orange glow radiating from the kitchens before turning the final corner. This had always been his favorite place in the castle. The warmth and combination of smells left him in constant anticipation of what the kitchen staff came up with next. He often snuck down here as a little boy to get cookies and treats when his father was busy. Aurec sighed with nostalgia. Life was so much simpler then. Now he had total authority to demand what he wanted. Perhaps the trade-off wasn't so bad after all.

He grinned from ear to ear upon entering the cavernous hall. Entire stags and hogs were being dressed and slow roasted with various spices and oils over roaring fires. A brew master, one Aurec didn't know they had, busied himself with a harsh winter ale in one of the corners. Soldiers liked to drink, for various reasons, so it made sense to have a supply on hand. Loaves of already baked breads, light and dark, were carefully stacked in one of the warming ovens. As much as he wanted to take one he resisted. The first batches always went to feed the civilians at the gates come dawn. He refused to steal from his own people. That didn't mean the head cook didn't have something special set aside for him.

"Your highness, you should be asleep, not down here with the rest of us," Master Eglyn said with a warming smile.

Aurec gave a customary wave. "A king has the discretion to do as he pleases, at least I thought I had until Venten and the others insisted otherwise. I never thought in all my life that the king was the most powerful person in the kingdom!"

"Your father often said the same," Eglyn agreed. "He couldn't get away from it all fast enough to come down here. Most times right after you."

Aurec felt his mouth open. "I never knew that. My father was always so proper I didn't stop to think of him as a regular man. I wish I would have known that. It might have helped bring us even closer together."

"He was a good man. A good king. You will be too," Eglyn said. "I've got your bread waiting. Right this way."

The king fell in alongside the portly cook. "Exactly how long have you been working in the kitchens, Master Eglyn?"

The master cook pretended to think before answering, "Oh, since before you were in diapers. Which, technically speaking, wasn't all too long ago."

Aurec frowned briefly. The monarch in him knew Eglyn should be put in his proper place, but the youthful king couldn't bring himself to alienate one of the men he'd known all his life. There were times when friendship and a warm personality to vent to meant more than the arrogance of kingship. "What keeps you down here?"

"That's easy. It stays warm. Winters are always miserable this far north. I'm too old to work out in the cold. Don't mind making bread and such so long as I get to stay warm and eat my fill of course. Baking is hard work, from sunrise to sundown. There's always something going on in the kitchens, young Aurec. Eh, Your Majesty."

"Aurec is fine, Eglyn, just as long as there's no one else around. I'd hate to think of the tongue lashing we'd both get if Venten heard you be so familiar!" he said and chuckled.

Eglyn nodded eagerly. "Very true. He's a miserly old fella, that one. A good man to have in a pinch but he's gotten hold of my hide more than a few times over the years."

"You and me both."

They shared another laugh as Eglyn reached into one of the warming ovens and handed Aurec the small loaf of dark bread with a small cup of fresh butter and mulled wine. He made to head off but Aurec stopped him and invited him to sit. Eglyn ignored the uncomfortable feeling he suddenly discovered and took a seat across the table from the king. Aurec tore the loaf in half and offered part to Eglyn.

"I never enjoyed eating alone, not even as a child," Aurec explained. "These days everyone wants my time, not my companionship. It'll do me good to have a normal conversation without the fuss of being king."

"Sounds to me like you could use it too," Eglyn said as he lathered a thick layer of the rich butter across his bread. "Suppose we all do from time to time. The boys down here laugh and carry on, even during the worst of times, but there's seldom any real talk. Guess they all want to leave their troubles behind too."

Aurec nodded as he chewed. "How long did it take to get the kitchens back up and running? The last time I saw this place it was filled with excrement and broken furniture."

"Vile creatures, those Goblins. I'd hate to see the way they treat their own caves." Eglyn's face darkened. "We spent the better part of three days just cleaning and repairing what was salvageable. Those Goblins did a fine job of turning my kitchens into an offal pit but they didn't count on my pride of ownership. Worked the lads nonstop, I did. Once it was properly cleaned and ready for visitors we began operations to feed the people. Begging your forgiveness, Aurec, but the people of Rogscroft always came first in my eyes. Soldiers can take care of themselves. It's the downtrodden ones that managed to live through the occupation I care about."

"You did the right thing. The people must always come first. My father taught me that when I was still sneaking down here for those delightful butter cookies you used to make."

"What exactly are you doing right now? Venten would have a heart attack if he knew you'd snuck out your chambers and come down here in the middle of the night. He's already an old man. I don't want to be the one responsible for sending him to the ground."

Aurec smiled. "I promise not to tell. How did your family fare during the war?"

Talking about it like it was already over sounded wrong, but Aurec knew, or at least was told, the best way forward was to act like the worst had already passed.

Eglyn took a drink of water from the canteen he constantly carried. "The wife and little ones made it to Grunmarrow before the city fell. Neither of my parents were that lucky, nor were hers. At least they were already getting on in their years. It's all I have to console us over their passing. Do me a favor, Your Majesty?"

How many others found themselves in similar or worse predicaments? It would take generations to rebuild. Aurec almost felt bad for whoever had the unenviable task of kingdom rebuilding once he died. Assuming Badron was finally brought to heel and the war ended.

Natural suspicions rose whenever anyone asked him that, but Aurec relented and listened. "What, old friend?"

"Find the bastards responsible for all this and put them to the test. It just ain't right for a man to get away with doing this to another."

They finished their snack in silence. Aurec had more than enough to think about. Sleep was never going to come.

"We've been through all this before," Venten argued. "Our position here isn't secure enough to carry the campaign back into the countryside. Refugees are pouring into the city daily, increasing demands on what meager supplies we have remaining. How many of them will freeze to death while waiting for new homes to be built? The castle can't support the additional numbers and our treasury is nonexistent. You ask the impossible."

"Badron escaping will put you in a worse position, Venten," Rolnir fired back. "My men are tired and ready to go home. They've seen enough war to last the rest of their lives but they all understand that this war will never end until Badron is captured or killed and made to answer for his crimes."

"To what end, General?" Vajna added. "We've been over this argument until each of us is so confused we're arguing for the opposing point of view. We're getting nowhere."

Aurec's yawn echoed around the modified council chamber, causing them all to stop bickering and look his way. What some took as blatant disrespect was an honest, heartfelt action from the decided lack of sleep. The king kept his embarrassment to a minimum while they sorted their feelings out.

"The king is right," Venten said quickly. "This bickering is pointless."

"Venten, I yawned because I am exhausted," Aurec said before matters could devolve more. "Though you have a valid point. We are at a crossroads, gentlemen. Badron must be dealt with, but this city needs to be rebuilt, for more than one reason. Rogscroft was a symbol and needs to become one again. The question isn't which is more important, but how can we accomplish both at the same time."

Silence answered him. All the advisors and senior commanders assembled in the small, octagonal room were seasoned veterans of their profession. They were also singular minded when it came to dealing with matters. Rogscroft was doomed until they managed to overcome their deficiencies and combine their expertise for the greater good of all concerned. Aurec didn't think they had that kind of time.

"Every day sees more of our citizens arrive with the hopes of us saving them," Aurec continued, hoping to prod one of them into conversation. "We are managing, if barely, to house and feed them. Those strong enough are being put to work in our reconstruction efforts. Frankly it isn't enough. We need tools, medicine, crops, and livestock. We need skilled workers capable of bringing this city out of the rubble. Shanty huts and poorly constructed shelters are well and fine for now, but unacceptable for the future. Gentlemen, we are short of every single thing necessary to rebuild and sustain even a small population. You are the smartest people in this kingdom. Scour the countryside for what we need. General Rolnir, I trust you've already enacted what we spoke of the other day?"

They turned as one to stare at the secret shared between king and general. Rolnir rose, grinning like a drunken fool. "Yes, Your Majesty, I have. Companies of cavalry are already pushing north and west to intercept Badron and the Goblin forces. I have permission from Cuul Ol to send men into the passes to scout a way back into Delranan. If Badron manages to return we will have no choice but to follow and take the war with us."

The last statement didn't sit well with him, for he suggested making war on his own kingdom against his own king. *How much more of a traitor could I possibly be? But the world needs to know of Badron's depravity. I only fear that when we return we'll find Delranan mired in as much desolation as Rogscroft. This war has gone on for far too long already. Even one more death is too many.*

"I assure you that if we must make war in Delranan it will be my utmost priority to ensure no civilians are needlessly killed nor their homes or farms destroyed in retribution of what happened here," Aurec reassured him.

"That does not make this easier," Rolnir said.

Aurec smiled. "Your prowess as a general is already well documented in Rogscroft. That being said it now falls on the rest of you to fix this kingdom. I don't promise an end to the dark times. There are no magical stores of crops waiting to appear when we need them the most. We must work for everything we have."

"I have teams sifting through the rubble in search of dry goods and perishables. The Goblins were thorough but not enough. Each day finds new stores," Venten admitted. "Other teams are taking away the rubble. What can be used is recycled and the rest burned in the hundreds of campfires around the city."

"Good. We may all die of starvation but at least we'll be warm," Aurec joked.

Nervous laughter sprang up around the room.

Vajna grunted his amusement. "You'll be presiding over an empire of bones, your Majesty."

"We are all responsible for not letting that happen," Aurec replied coolly. "What other business needs to be addressed this morning?"

He couldn't tell them how badly he wanted to go back to bed, despite his fears of seeing Maleela tortured or worse the moment he closed his eyes. His thoughts gradually took over, forcing their conversation to idle background noise.

She awoke to pain pulsing through her head. Her body felt abused, as if she'd been dropped from atop the water fall at Bryk Peak. How so much suffering could be stuffed into such a small frame eluded her rationale. Sparks peppered her vision when she opened her eyes. They eventually faded, leaving her with a fleeting sensation of blindness. Maleela tried to rise, at least to her knees, but the combination of pain and lack of muscle use left her immobile.

"Ah, good, she awakens," came a wisp of voice.

Another said, "She should be dead. The Hags were most unkind with their handling of her."

"Lord Death claims who he wants. The princess is destined for greater moments than the ignominy of a senseless death in a nameless place."

"This is a dangerous game," the second warned.

"It is the same we have played for thousands of years," answered the first.

Maleela tried to speak, her words nothing more than strangled croaks.

"You are dehydrated. Water and food will be made available to you. Do not worry. If we wanted you dead you never would have been brought back to Delranan."

Her heart stuttered. *Delranan! How in all the gods did I wind up back home? What manners of beasts does my father have in his employ?*

As if reading her mind, the first voice told her, "Your father is the least of your concerns, Princess. He is a puppet serving us, as you will be soon enough."

She felt the cold draft of their departure, leaving her once again alone in the dark. She tried to cry as all the dire possibilities dancing in her mind collided into one inescapable conclusion: she'd been brought home to suffer for her crimes against the throne. Her tears never came. They'd dried up long ago.

TWENTY-EIGHT

An Unlikely Ally

Boen tucked his sword close to his body and rolled forward to avoid being struck by the monstrous stone figure trying to decapitate him. Groge wasn't as fortunate. The Giant took the brunt of a blow and was propelled backwards. He landed with the force of a small quake and a loud huff exploding from his lungs. Having traveled from one coast of Malweir to the next, the Gaimosian had seen all manner of fighters, monsters and myths, but never anything as ferocious as what assailed him now. Not even Anienam's magic had any effect.

Rekka shouted something in those hazy moments right before the fight began but no one had heard, either that or they simply didn't listen. Only Boen and the Dwarf captain threw themselves whole heartedly into the fight. Ironfoot hacked away with his double-headed battle axe. Stone chips flew from the gargoyles with each swoop but the stone creatures continued to harass them. Nothol Coll tried firing an arrow only to watch it shatter on impact. The gargoyles were impervious to mortal weapons.

"Damn it, Anienam, do something!" Bahr shouted over the shrieking of stone wings.

The wizard wore a shell-shocked look as well as any hardened veteran. "Do what? They are made of stone. I've never encountered anything like this!"

Bahr growled. "Everything has a weakness. Find it so we can kill these things."

Anienam cursed under his breath but went back to trying to conjure an effective spell. He had quite forgotten about the fabled defenders of Trennaron and failed to recall any spell in all his lore able to defeat the gargoyles. Imbued with powerful magic far beyond the realm of the Mages, they were the perfect warriors.

Rekka slid in beside them. Her normally perfect black hair was disheveled. Her soft eyes bore a wild look. "Bahr you must order them all to put down their weapons immediately!"

"Are you mad? These things will kill us in a matter of heartbeats," he shot back.

She shook her head. "No. They are responding to the threat we pose. If we put down our weapons they will not attack."

He paused. She'd been locked away within the castle for years but that didn't mean she knew everything about Trennaron to keep them alive. On the other hand, her iron will and exuding sense of righteousness had a calming effect on him. He was able to think clearly. The gargoyles launched from the walls the moment Bahr and the others entered the massive clearing. They didn't attack until Boen drew his sword and rode to the forefront of the group. Until that point they seemed content with circling from a distance, as if watching to find any traces of hostility. Reluctantly, Bahr decided to trust Rekka.

"Are you sure?" He left the obvious unspoken. If she was wrong they were all going to die, quickly.

She nodded again. "Positive. Trust me, Captain."

Bahr stuffed his sword away and rose with his hands outstretched to the sky. He shouted, "Lower your weapons! Do it now while we still have a choice!"

The others were equally reluctant, but Bahr's tone eventually pushed through that stubborn refusal to abandon their only means of defense. Boen was the last to lower his sword. His great chest was heaving with exertion. Sheets of sweat made him appear glossy. His eyes bore that wild look he had when he abandoned civility to the whims of his killing frenzy. Inexplicably, the gargoyles ceased their assault and hovered menacingly well out of reach.

Bahr turned to Rekka. "That information would have been helpful before we entered the clearing. Are you trying to get us killed?"

"No, Bahr, but the protectors have a specific purpose and we are a band of warriors. It was inevitable that some form of conflict would arise upon our meeting. Boen and Ironfoot were preparing to attack the moment the gargoyles launched from their watch positions," she explained. "I was so overjoyed to return to Trennaron that I overlooked the situation. My apologies, Captain. It will not happen again."

"I hope not," was all he said.

Boen stalked towards him. Every minor characteristic cautioned anger. "What was that?"

Bahr stopped Rekka with his hand and stepped between them. "Calm down, Boen. We're not going to fight each other. Rekka made a mistake. No one got hurt. The only way we're going to succeed is by focusing on our next move."

"Mistakes get people killed," Boen growled.

"So does ignorance," Bahr fired back. "Something tells me this place has more than just those stone gargoyles protecting it. Am I correct, Rekka?"

She nodded. "There is magic at work all around us. The castle will know whether we are good or evil and take actions accordingly."

"What of the creature inside?" Bahr asked. "Will he help us?"

"Artiss Gran hasn't physically helped anyone in centuries. He is a mystery, even by our standards. I only saw him twice in all my time here," she answered.

Boen rolled his eyes. "What's the point? We came all this way for what? Exactly? I don't mind fighting, but there has to be a good reason. She's never seen the one person we've come to see. I may not be a genius, Bahr, but this smells bad."

"It doesn't matter now. We're here. Our only option is to push forward and see if this Artiss Gran has the answers we need," the Sea Wolf answered. "Rekka, will the gargoyles leave us alone if we mount up and continue?"

"As long as we do not take up arms again," she said.

"That's good enough for me," Bahr told her and climbed into his saddle. His eyes never left the circling figures high above. "Let's move out. It's getting dark and I don't fancy being caught out in the open again."

The others followed his lead and soon were on the path to Trennaron. The castle loomed closer with each step, growing taller and wider. No other structure on Malweir was so large nor majestic, nor were any castle gates so securely fastened. Bahr had the sinking suspicion Artiss Gran wasn't going to open them for anyone.

Anienam pulled alongside him and said, "That was quick thinking back there. You saved us, Bahr."

"I did what needed to be done," Bahr replied. "Can you tell me anything about what we're getting into?"

"Nothing I haven't already said," the wizard replied. "This is a strange place for me. I am still trying to learn the rules. We are going to have to rely on Rekka's insights to get us through this stretch of the journey."

"What about the Hamr? Will Gran give it freely?"

Anienam wished he had the answers. Their quest would pass smoothly if he could decipher the Dae'shan's plans. Time steadily slipped between his fingers like grains of sand and, even though he stood on the very doorstep of Trennaron, Anienam felt no closer to the solution than he had when he sought out Bahr in Chadra at the end of summer. Too many forces were working against him, making it difficult to keep up. The worst was the unnecessary capture of Maleela. Clearly the Dae'shan had designs for the princess, but what and why?

"I don't know. His position was created by the gods of light for the Dae'shan. It is impossible to say how he will react once we present our requests."

Bahr frowned. "I thought the Dae'shan were the bad guys? Why is one guarding a place of power?"

"They used to be neutral. Impartial Guardians of all power and lore throughout Malweir. Apathy set them against each other and finally led to their downfall to evil. Only one remained true to their purpose and he has hidden within these walls since that day. It is entirely possible he isn't aware of the situation in Delranan," Anienam explained.

Bahr struggled to keep up. Magic was anathema to a simplistic man like Bahr. He based his life choices off what he could see or learn. Invisible powers capable of crushing a man did nothing for him. The single fact he plucked from Anienam's words was that the Dae'shan either couldn't be killed or they had no interest in committing fratricide. That didn't bode well.

"Rekka, will Artiss Gran open the gates?" Anienam asked.

She cocked her head in thought, the sure answer of months ago no longer so concrete. "I do not see any reason why he shouldn't. He sent me to the north to warn you of the coming war. It stands to reason he knows as much as his former brothers, though I cannot say for sure. A being that powerful seldom takes anyone into his confidence."

Their answer came quicker than they expected. All the gargoyles suddenly tucked in their wings and swooped back to their eternal positions atop the walls. The massive gates groaned open when the group was still a hundred meters away. No guards poured out to meet them. Only a red-tailed hawk watched as they led the horses inside Trennaron. Its piercing glare followed their movement until the last person entered and the gates swung closed. The hawk screeched once before taking flight back to the jungle.

Dorl Theed looked over his shoulder to see the last glimpse of the outside world squeeze shut. A lump formed in his stomach. "Looks like we're in it now, eh Nothol?"

"Seems so. I wonder if this Gran fellow has any more tricks up his sleeve," he replied.

Dorl was too tired to care. He already figured on dying during this quest. What did it matter if it was here or back in Delranan? "Do you think we can trust him? I overheard Anienam talking about him being one of the Dae'shan."

"When did you make a habit of trusting anyone?" Nothol asked back. The notion clearly amused him.

"I don't, but we've run out of options."

Nothol stopped his horse and looked Dorl dead in the eyes. "You're not thinking of backing out again are you? We had a deal. Stick with this until we got paid and then wash our hands and move on to something better."

"A deal's a deal, Nothol. I've got your back for as long as you need me to. I just don't like how all control has been taken away from us and given to some shadow character we don't know if we can trust or not," Dorl said. His face darkened considerably. Many foul thoughts swirled in the back of his mind.

Nothol stayed silent. *My friend, we've never been in control, of any of this whole sordid mess. Our lives hang by the whim of wizards. And don't that just gnaw at your soul?*

Any further thoughts ended the moment a thin figure clothed in a stark white robe suddenly materialized in front of Bahr and Rekka. The jungle woman immediately dismounted and dropped to a knee with head bowed. The others looked from the new arrival back to each other in confusion.

"Welcome, friends. Trennaron is the last pure gift of the gods of light. To stand on these hallow grounds is as close to godliness as a mortal may come. Be at peace within these walls," the figure announced with disturbing authority. "Rise, Rekka Jel. You have served us well. All that was asked, you accomplished and more. You are a testament to your people."

Her cheeks flushed with remembered shame yet she obeyed. "Master, I have returned with Anienam, son of Dakeb, last scion of the order of Mages. He is accompanied by Bahr, brother of Badron and the rightful heir to the throne of Delranan."

The hooded figure looked over the group. "Where is the princess? I do not see her among them. Has she not come?"

Rekka swallowed. "Princess Maleela was stolen by enemy agents not two days ago in the jungle. I can only assume they are moving back to Delranan for some nefarious purpose."

The figure was silent for long, uncomfortable moments. "That is…unfortunate. She is a key to all this." He paused. "But where are my manners? You are exhausted from the arduous journey south. Food and beverages are already being made available for you, as well as hot baths and sleeping arrangements. Once you have finished we shall speak."

The robes fell apart like thousands of tiny snowflakes. Even Boen gasped. A door opened, silently urging the adventurers inside.

"What about our gear and the horses? We can't leave them here unattended," Bahr asked.

Rekka removed her saddled bag and slung it over a shoulder. "They will be seen to, probably better than ourselves. Trennaron has many attendants, Bahr. They are in good hands."

Dorl and Nothol exchanged wary looks before following suit. The door closed behind them without a sound.

"I haven't eaten that good since Drimmen Delf," Ironfoot said as he rubbed his widening stomach. His burp was so loud it rang from corner to corner. He chuckled. "Damned fine food. I feel like a king."

"You sound like a cow," Boen snickered. He tore a great chunk of beef off a rib bone and chewed greedily. Juices slid down his chin and into his beard.

Ironfoot barked a deep, rumbling laugh. "You're one to talk. I'd heard Trolls had better table manners than Gaimosians but never believed them until now."

Skuld's mouth fell open. So sure was he that a fight was brewing, he slid his chair out of the way. The last thing he needed was to be trampled by two angry individuals with something to prove. He took another mouthful of the dark, bitter ale and sighed. Nothing he'd eaten or drank in the last few months compared to the luxury pouring down his throat.

"Funny, but true mostly," Boen said and surprised them all. "Wizard, why didn't you tell us this place was like living in the lap of the gods? We might have been in more of a rush to get here!"

Laughter rippled through them until even Anienam smiled. Bathed and fed, they'd forgotten all the hardships and toils suffered on their quest and certainly abandoned thought of the next phase. Getting back to Delranan wasn't going to be easy at all. In fact, Anienam surmised it was going to be much harder than any of them imagined.

"Ah good, I see you have taken advantage of this lovely feast I ordered be prepared."

Banter faded and all heads turned to the hall entrance where a very old man with sad eyes stood watching. His wrinkled hands were clasped in front of his waist. Once pristine robes were stained, faded through time and use. His beard was long but thin. What hair remained circled a growing bald spot. Dark brown pinpricks peppered his skin.

Rekka rose and bowed again. "Master."

"There is no need to stand on formality for me, Rekka. I am an old man, far older than even Master Keiss. A time will come when my title will be used but it is not this day. Tonight, we are all equals. Or so I hope. Truthfully, it's been so long since we had visitors I'm not sure I know how to properly entertain anymore. My name is Artiss Gran, and I am the last steward of Trennaron. Welcome."

"The honor is ours, Master Gran," Anienam answered smoothly. "Long have I desired to look upon the wonder that is Trennaron. No story or legend in any of the races of Malweir gives this glorious castle justice."

"Trennaron is the last home of the gods. Much of what resides within these walls goes beyond mortal comprehension," Artiss explained. His tone was like a father showing off his favorite child. "I wish times were more civilized. That way I'd be able to give you a proper tour.

Unfortunately my…brothers have seen fit to make their final bid for control of Malweir. It is a tragedy that these last days have fallen on you all, but an unavoidable one. If not you it would fall to others. While you do not know me, I know much about each of you. Long have I watched your lives, your trials and tribulations. It does my heart good to know the fate of the world rests in such capable hands."

"I think I lost my appetite," Dorl whispered to Nothol and set his food down.

Anienam rose to stand beside the Dae'shan. It was then he noticed that Artiss Gran hovered several inches off the ground. "Time is escaping us, Artiss. We need the Blud Hamr to stop the other Dae'shan from bringing the dark gods back to Malweir. Will you help us?"

Artiss Gran smiled sadly. The lines on his face twisted into odd patterns. "Your quest is well known to me for I am the one responsible for sending Rekka Jel to you with a warning. The Blud Hamr is here. It is a powerful weapon capable of destroying the dimensional portal." He paused. "I would speak with you, son of Dakeb, and Captain Bahr if you please. The rest of you I implore to take advantage of the plush beds and freedom from pursuit. If you are curious, I'm sure Rekka can show you some of the finer points in Trennaron."

"We've come a long way and survived many battles. None of us like the idea of being left out now," Boen said almost instantly. "There's enough mistrust between us already. You threaten more needlessly. All our lives are on the line and I personally don't take kindly to not knowing all the facts."

Any negative reaction from Artiss failed to appear. The elder Dae'shan spread his hands in what was meant as a warming gesture. "I make no efforts to conceal any information from any of you, but what I have to say concerns matters for these two alone. It is their past that I must discuss. Any knowledge I can glean from their confessions will help me formulate the best way to deal with my brothers. By all means, if you feel slighted, I invite you to attend this conference. Though, I doubt a brief history of Bahr's childhood will hold much interest for anyone."

Satisfied he wasn't being lied to, Boen nodded curtly and took his seat. There was still plenty of food left and his appetite was waiting. None of the others spoke up, giving Artiss leave to conduct his interviews.

TWENTY-NINE

A Dark Past Revealed

"I had this room built to accommodate guests. As an immortal I lack the base human needs. I haven't eaten, slept, or used the privy in a very long time. One of the perks of my position I suppose," Artiss said after his guests took seats in comfortable, cushioned chairs set in front of a roaring fireplace.

Expensive wood paneling gave the room a homey feel, complete with an ornately detailed rug covering much of the marble floor. Rare books filled the shelves running the length of one wall and equally rare liquors on the other. Anienam had never seen the grand library of Ipn Shal the way it was meant to be, before the war, but he imagined this was its equal. Generations of people were born and died without ever stepping foot into a room of this quality.

Bahr resisted the temptation to snuggle back into the high back chair and drift off. Fond memories of sitting in his favorite room at his estate outside of Chadra left him torn between emotions. Thoughts of his old life returned suddenly, mocking his current station. Sailing the oceans and seas of Malweir was liberating but ultimately hollow. He had friends, wealth, and enough of a reputation to keep him well taken care of past his death, but the lack of family left him broken on the inside. He didn't know which direction to take his life, leaving him floundering in uncharted waters. It was a sad fact he'd been unwilling to admit to anyone, especially himself, since fleeing the burning ruins of his estate several months ago. The pain grew daily, making his life more unbearable the further from home he traveled.

"Captain Bahr, there is a question that I must know the answer to before we proceed further. Your answer will help me base my next decision," Artiss told him without wasting time. Only he knew how much was left to accomplish before they could return to Delranan and attempt to stop Badron, the Dae'shan, and the dark gods.

Bahr shifted uncomfortably. He didn't enjoy exploring his past, especially to complete strangers claiming to know more than was possible. Then again, he'd never been confronted with any immortal creature before. Artiss Gran puzzled him to great ends. Bahr found it difficult to place trust in anyone he hadn't known for years. The cast of characters assembled around him earned it through their actions. He'd only known Boen for longer than a few years.

"Why do I get the feeling this is going to be uncomfortable?" he asked sharply.

Artiss replied quickly. "Because it will be. The past is seldom easy for us to speak of. I should know. My own past is filled with acts of dismal failure. The pain of being cast from the Dae'shan continues to haunt me. If I have learned anything through the centuries it is life is not kind, nor does it care for our individual whims. We are born and cast to the winds. The inert cruelty of it comes with death, only I cannot die, not in the conventional sense."

"Before we discuss my troubled past I want to know what led to your breaking with the rest of the Dae'shan. Don't take it personally but I'm finding it hard to accept from one of the beings that has been actively trying to kill us halfway across Malweir. What reassurance can you give me that you are indeed what you say you are?" Bahr demanded. He'd been played for the fool long enough. Time had come to take matters into his own hands.

"Your reluctance is expected, naturally. I sometimes find it difficult to accept and I've been mired in this life for a very long time," Artiss agreed. "Why should you trust me? Honestly, you probably shouldn't. I've been exiled, branded a traitor. The gods, should they ever return, will more than likely reduce me to cinders for my failures. I have abandoned all I once knew and, though I maintain the sanctity of Trennaron, I do so with an empty heart. Some, like the Gaimosian, would brand me coward, others far worse. Why should you trust me? I am the only being in the entire world capable of helping you stop the dark gods from returning."

Tension filled the ornately decorated chamber. Anienam decided to get involved before Bahr ruined all his carefully developed plans. "I don't believe Bahr meant you insult, Artiss. We have come far, losing some of our own in the process and finding ourselves lost in the middle of too many impossible scenarios."

"Don't put words in my mouth, wizard," Bahr threatened. "I want to know what he brings to this game that makes me place my hard-earned trust. His words are brutal, honest, and spoken from the heart. That's good enough for me. Very well, Artiss, let's get on with this."

Artiss concealed his relief and passed Anienam a knowing look suggesting he should have trusted the Dae'shan from the beginning. "Thank you, Captain. My question is simple enough in design but more complex to answer. Why did you abandon your claim to the throne of Delranan?"

Bahr froze. Of every possible scenario going through his mind, this wasn't even considered. He'd walked away from his family so long ago he almost didn't remember the reasons. Certain pains needed to be smothered. His strength only spread so far. When he finally found the words, they came out slowly and uncertainly. "There was nothing for me in Delranan. My father was a bitter man. He ruled fair enough but showed little love to either my brother or me. I never felt wanted. His desire for absolute control left a sour taste in my mouth. I wanted nothing to do with politics or crowns."

"But there is more," Artiss pressed.

He nodded. "Indeed. I knew I couldn't escape the responsibility that falls on every firstborn son. I was born to become a king, yet I lacked the conviction to want to be one. All I could think of was the damage it caused in our family. My brother's jealousy only compounded my torment. Badron coveted my legacy. He always seemed filled with odd hatred for me, as if he knew he should have been born first. It led to many fights and no few broken bones." He grinned ruefully as almost forgotten memories came flooding back.

"It's amazing how different two brothers can be. We're only a few years apart in age. A lifetime in attitude. Badron always craved power. He was the sort of child who burned the wings off insects when no one was watching. It didn't take long before his evil streak came out. Not to say he didn't try. Badron was a very bright boy with more capability than I possessed. He quickly learned the ways of the crown while studying to become something more than merely a second son. I imagine he would have been shuffled off to the Wolfsreik if I bothered to stay and take the crown. The world might even be a better place if he had but I wasn't going to sit through the abuses any longer than necessary."

Bahr paused to drink deeply from the crystal mug of ice cold water. Nestled in the middle of a sweltering jungle, there shouldn't be any sort of ice or cold of anything. Magic, he surmised, and let it stay at that.

"My greatest mistake, at least in my eyes, was in telling Badron I wasn't going to take the crown when we were in our early teens. He took that information and used it to his advantage at every possible junction. I believe he poisoned my father's mind. Soured him against me. I was treated like an outcast. My father was already a hard man. Every action after that only made it more difficult for me to leave my chambers. Badron drove in the nails harder until I couldn't wait to flee Chadra Keep. No one chased me the night I did. I'm sure my mother wept but I never went back to see her before she died.

"I never bothered seeing my father either. They were dead and in the ground before I returned from my travels. Somewhere along the way I discovered the folly of my ways. Leaving Delranan to Badron's greedy hands was a grave mistake. He tried to rule justly at first, but his lust for power drove him down a dark path the rest of the kingdom gradually began to follow. Harnin One Eye became his chief disciple.

That combination proved to be my homeland's eventual downfall."

"Matters are worse beyond your reckoning," Artiss added. "But please continue. We will discuss more when you are finished."

Bahr gave the Dae'shan a queer look but fell back into his story. "The longer I stayed away the more I realized I never should have left. I should be wearing the crown and ruling Delranan in the best fashion possible. The people deserved better, but I had been too weak to accept anything other than my own selfishness. I never bothered looking beyond my personal borders. It's funny. I hadn't thought about this in many years, so long I'd almost forgotten it all. Coming home proved easier than I imagined. Badron tried to oppose me but I had commissioned the *Dragon's Bane* and was building a large estate on the outskirts of town. My powerbase was growing in direct opposition to his. Our rivalry would eventually come to a head.

"Badron came with a company of his private guard. He sought to oust me from Delranan for good and seize my holdings. What he didn't expect was close to a hundred bawdy sailors who were coming off a week-long drunk and entirely loyal to me. Many good men died that day. Some were friends, others not. Badron finally broke off hostilities and called a truce. He and I went inside and hashed out very stringent terms. As long as I didn't interfere with his rule of the kingdom he'd leave me alone. It was a fair enough deal. He got the hassles of crown and state while I built my own empire on the seas. Our deal lasted right up until the moment my niece was stolen from Chadra Keep in the middle of the night."

He sat back and exhaled. No one living had ever heard that story and the telling took a heavy toll. He felt deflated. His mind rambled without discernible direction. Bordering on the brink of being lost, Bahr couldn't help but dwell on the decision to abandon his home. *What have I done? Has my selfishness ruined an entire kingdom?*

Artiss fixed him with a soft, knowing look. "Your doubts are necessary and well-founded. This war will claim many souls before the end. Take comfort in the knowledge that even had you remained in Delranan the Dae'shan would have found another corrupt soul. Your kingdom would still suffer, for reasons you have yet to fathom. The last nexus in Malweir lies in a long forgotten set of ruins called Arlevon Gale."

"The Gale? It's hardly more than a pile of ground stone," Bahr said. "What power could possibly lie in such a place?"

"The gods of light were cunning in their punishment. They knew their dark brethren could only attempt a return once every thousand years and in only one of three places. Heroes have risen through the ages and now only one nexus remains. Delranan is the final battleground. If the Dae'shan win it will mean the end of the world as we know it." Artiss hovered over to the fireplace and stared down into the cackling flames. "One final place. One final meeting of old friends. I was forbidden from taking part in the previous battles. A handful of Boen's ancestors banded together not long after the fall Gaimos. They destroyed the nexus at great cost but started something greater. Mankind learned they possessed magic. It all came from Gaimos. The self-proclaimed Vengeance Knights were the founders of the order of Mages."

He turned and smiled at Anienam. "That's right, Anienam. Your ancestors were Boen's. When the smoke clears we find it's not a very large world after all. The second battle occurred a thousand years ago in the land of Gren. Your own father led a small band of heroes into that dark land and stopped the Silver Mage from recreating the crystal of Tol Shere and opening the nexus. They nearly didn't. The dark gods were almost entering our world when a young boy stabbed the fabled Star Silver sword into the nexus, ruining it forever and losing his life in the process. A shame really, but all great victories must come through sacrifice. I wish it weren't so, but not even my immense wealth of knowledge and power is capable of changing destiny."

It was Anienam's turn to reel through shock. He knew much of his father's history but not everything. Some pains had been too open for Dakeb to divulge his darkest secrets. Clearly the mission to kill Sidian in Gren was too much for him to burden others, including his own adopted son, with. Whatever knowledge Dakeb had of the dark gods and the nexus died with him. It was a wound Anienam regretted more given their current situation. He often wondered why Dakeb had chosen him. He was naturally talented but not overtly strong with magic. There was only one possible conclusion. One he dreaded asking but knew he must.

"Artiss, am I Gaimosian?" His words were strained, broken.

Artiss Gran said, "Yes. That's the reason Dakeb chose you. You have near unlimited potential residing inside you. He knew, as do I, that you can unlock strength not seen since the sundering between the gods. You are the chosen one that will take the war to its inevitable conclusion."

"Not quite what you were expecting when you got here was it?" Bahr chided, finally feeling superior to the normally smug wizard. While he took personal enjoyment over seeing Anienam squirm with coming to terms over what he didn't know, he knew their task just got immeasurably more difficult.

"It's been a long time since I was last caught off guard," Anienam admitted. "What other delightful bits of lost information do you have for us, Artiss?"

"Not yet. All will be revealed in its proper time. There are some truths you aren't prepared to receive." The Dae'shan went back to the fire. "The power of the dark gods transcends everything on this planet. They have always existed. Unlike fairy tales told by loving mothers, the dark gods have always been evil. It is a sad fact that good cannot exist without evil to balance it. Life, you see, is all about balance. Without it we would crumble and fade. The gods of light understood this. That's why they left Malweir after their errant cousins were banished. One faction cannot and should not have total control over all life."

"You mean to travel with us and fight at our side?" Bahr asked. Loath as he was to seek counsel from another wizard, he was forced to admit they needed every advantage they could get their hands on. He liked the strength and diversity of quality in their little group but with each strength came a weakness.

Groge was unquestionably their greatest asset but he seemed mired in a downward spiral of self-hate after fighting in the jungle. Boen was capable of flying off the handle at the drop of a sword. Dorl was so smitten with Rekka his inattentiveness threatened to get one of them killed. The list went on. His own misery felt the worst. All his thoughts centered on getting Maleela back. Nothing else really mattered.

Artiss offered a sympathetic look while shaking his head. "I cannot leave Trennaron. Any attempt to leave would open the gates for evil. I am the chosen Guardian of this wondrous place. For me to leave is almost instant death. I am so old that I would crumble away to dust if I left now."

"I thought you were immortal."

"Not even the gods are immortal," Artiss replied. He grinned at the shock on Bahr's face. "Yes, even gods die. All it takes is for us to stop believing."

"If it's that easy why are the dark gods still lurking in the background?"

Artiss nodded his approval. *This man is sharper than I imagined. Perhaps there is hope for the world after all. If only his brother had been able to look beyond the borders of his greed and seen the kingdom needed him more than they needed a war we might not be in this sad state of affairs.*

"You are correct, Bahr, but it is not that simple. The dark gods are largely irrelevant to a great portion of Malweir's population. Whispered names no longer important. Those few of us who remember are mocked for petty indulgences of the past. Very few people are willing to look back to see where they are going. Banishment reduced the influence of the dark gods but didn't kill them. People didn't stop believing, they just forgot. The differences are subtle, imperceptible to the untrained eye, but very large in the grand scheme of how the universe works. So long as they remain forgotten they have power."

"And the Dae'shan seek to capitalize that power. Why?" Bahr asked after reasoning the inevitable conclusion.

"When you've lived for millennia there is a decided dearth of new things to do," Artiss replied flatly. He turned back to Anienam. "The Mages were a whim. A minor plaything the Dae'shan used to study the races, searching out their weakness and strength. I'm sorry to say but your adopted father was merely a pawn in this great game. The crystal of Tol Shere was their idea. My brothers corrupted your kind and brought about the singular most destructive war in the history of the world."

"That was over a thousand years ago, what more could they hope to achieve in the same scenario?" Anienam asked. His insult went unspoken. The Mages were responsible for a great many sins carried out on the world. Knowing the Dae'shan used them like children's toys did little to assuage the guilt of association.

"I find myself suddenly lacking the desire to carry on. What's the point? It all seems like an inescapable cycle we are doomed to repeat. Perhaps letting the dark gods win will change it up," Anienam said in defeat.

Bahr couldn't believe his ears. The one constant during their quest had been the enigmatic wizard. He always saw the positive when the others could see only darkness. Anienam Keiss wasn't well thought of among the others, nor was he despised the way Ionascu had been. They quickly learned he wasn't going to give a straight answer while constantly guiding them in the right direction. He'd gotten them to Trennaron only to abandon his own ideals.

Bahr didn't like the thought of his greatest magical asset giving up. "I think you need to get some rest. I've never heard you speak like this, Anienam."

"Bahr is right. You of all people need to retain your faith," Artiss seconded quickly.

Anienam grinned sheepishly. "Why? You said it yourself there is little point to this grand cosmic game. I'm beginning to think all the gods would best be left to die in the cold imprisonment of the night skies. We don't need them meddling in our lives."

"The gods of light share your point of view," Artiss said.

Both men looked up sharply. Bahr replied first. "Explain that. If the gods of light aren't going to interfere, what chance of victory is there?"

"The gods of light spent millions of years watching life develop on Malweir. What started as the smallest organisms grew into what we are now. They studied everything as it developed, content in their accumulation of knowledge. Only when the dark gods took interest in ruining all they'd accomplished did the gods of light become active. Their wars raged down through the centuries until they were finally able to gain the upper hand and banish their errant brothers. With the dark gods effectively cut off from Malweir, the gods of light decided it was time to abandon this world. It was time for men to rule."

"We haven't done that great of a job," Bahr said.

"No, but what can be done has been. The races of Malweir have all surpassed the expectations of the gods. I think they'd be proud of all our accomplishments," Artiss said fondly. He noticed the confusion twisting Anienam's face. "You are troubled?"

"Deeply," Anienam admitted after taking some time to straighten out his thoughts. "There is a central theme to all this, Artiss. Brothers. Why brothers? The gods. You and the Dae'shan. Bahr and Badron. What makes brothers so important?"

"I was wondering when one of you was going to string it all together. The brotherhood issue is a metaphor for the dichotomy between good and evil. Always two sides to each argument. Neither can function without the other to counterbalance it. Each time good or evil gains the upper hand the other faction mysteriously comes back to disrupt the flow of power. It has been this way since the dawn of creation. Balance is the key to all life, no matter how large or small. Without it we would all crumble to dust and fade away from the heat of our own fires."

Bahr yawned and stretched legs. His face was shadowed with thought. "None of what you said bodes well for us, Artiss. You offer aid but say you can't leave Trennaron. What chance do a handful of mortals have against all that's lined against us?"

"Chance is often a matter of whim. When there is a will there is the inert possibility of success," Artiss replied. "Don't be so quick to abandon your inner strength, Bahr. You have been given all the tools necessary to combat the rising tide of evil. All but one."

"The Hamr."

Artiss nodded. "Yes. The Blud Hamr. I shall take you to it in the morning. My attendants will see you to your rooms. Your journey has been long and arduous. Take comfort in these walls. No evil will befall you here. Eat and rest. You have come far but the journey back will take more of a toll than you can possibly imagine. Good night."

Bahr and Anienam rose and headed back towards the dining hall with much to think on and heavily troubled hearts. The look into their pasts would haunt them for many nights to come.

THIRTY

Blud Hamr

The view from the top of Trennaron's walls was her favorite in all Malweir. Rekka tilted her head back and enjoyed the cool predawn breeze tickling her neck. This time of day left her feeling calm. A moment when she was able to push aside all the darkness and focus on her core being. Her inner turmoil bled away with the song of a hundred species of jungle birds. She smiled, genuinely for the first time since realizing the strength of her love for Dorl. Such tender moments were irreplaceable and came only once in a lifetime.

"I surmised you'd be up here," Artiss called from behind. "You always did enjoy watching the sunrise."

Rekka turned and bowed, slightly embarrassed she failed to notice his approach.

The surprise in her eyes lightened his mood. She claimed they'd only seen each other a handful of times when in fact he had watched her from the moment she first arrived. Artiss Gran was the master of Trennaron. All that happened within the walls were known to him. They may not have interacted physically, but he knew all there was to know about her, more than she did.

Rekka had no knowledge of this. She often suspected he watched but had no evidence. Sworn to defend the last loyal Dae'shan and the secrets of Trennaron, Rekka meant to give her life should it become necessary. Whatever Artiss Gran did was his own business. She performed her duties to the best of her abilities without concern for what the master of the castle did. Such honor demanded strict adherence.

"Relax, Rekka Jel. I didn't come here to criticize you," he said softly. "It is a marvelous view, is it not?"

"The finest I've seen in all my travels," Rekka agreed.

Artiss smiled in a fatherly way. "Much majesty remains in Malweir if only we know where to seek it. I trust you've taken adequate opportunity to observe our heroes?"

She nodded. "Yes. They are an interesting bunch."

"I'd like your report now," he told her. The fact she'd been sent to not only bring these specific individuals back to Trennaron but to spy on them as well wasn't lost on her. Rekka knew her task and performed it with flawlessness.

"Their diversity gives them great strength though they remain hindered by personal demons and moments of intense insecurity. Their dynamic has great potential for success if only they can overcome their individual differences. Bahr is the strongest. His fire burns brighter than any of the rest. What he lacks is purpose. Until now he's merely gone along with the quest, keeping his personal beliefs private. Losing Maleela hurt him. It spurned him into action against our enemies. I don't know if it will be enough to keep him steady through the end."

"His niece is perhaps one of the most important pieces in this puzzle," Artiss said. "Should she turn against the light we will lose Malweir."

"We do not know where she was taken," Rekka told him.

"More than likely to Arlevon Gale. The Dae'shan will seek to turn her against us, thus permanently severing the family link and uniting father and daughter in dark cause. Bahr must be watched and kept on purpose. What of the others?"

"Boen is a wild factor. He has the strength necessary to survive the final battle but the propensity to fly off on a vengeful tangent. Bahr keeps him in check, but I don't know for how much longer. This quest is taking him back to his primal instincts. He could jeopardize our successes. The sell swords are steady, capable men we can rely on."

"Is your relationship with Dorl Theed going to prove problematic?" he interrupted.

Rekka swallowed quickly. "No, Master."

"Good. This is one of those times when we all must look beyond our base desires and put the needs of the world ahead of our own. Forgive my interruption, please continue."

"The boy Skuld confuses me. He has the potential to become a Mage but the heart of a warrior. Thankfully he's lost the edge Boen inspired in the beginning of the quest. I'm not sure what he will be. Captain Ironfoot borders on bestial. He is a pure warrior who brings the unique knowledge and point of view of the Dwarves. Groge is the least reliable. He is the only one capable of wielding the Blud Hamr but has no will whatsoever of engaging in combat. He wallows in grief after defending us from the Gnaals."

"Perhaps he is right to do so," Artiss added. "The Giants long ago abandoned violence. Some claim their race has improved for it, others deem them lesser for their convictions. Regardless, only Groge can wield the hammer. He must be made to understand his importance. The Olagath Stone can only be broken by the Blud Hamr. Convince him, Rekka. We need him to overcome his limitations for the greater good."

She nodded. "That brings me to the wizard, Anienam Keiss."

He held up a hand to stop her. "We don't need to discuss him. I already know his fate and it is not one I choose to share. Anienam will do his part for the good of all races. Of that I have no doubts."

Rekka accepted the comment for what it was though she began to question his motivations. Artiss Gran was all-knowing, or so she'd always assumed. His many secrets translated into all their lives. She normally had no qualms with this. Riddles were part of the way of life in Trennaron and she'd been forced to grow accustomed to it to stay ahead of her commands. That didn't alleviate her rising concerns over what was going to happen to the wizard. Rekka admitted she was rather fond of the eccentric old man. The thought of ill befalling him worried her gravely.

Artiss waved dismissively. "What is your assessment of the group? Are they strong enough to succeed?"

Rekka opened her mouth and closed it just as fast. Until now she'd kept the thought in the back of her mind. Time and emotions blended to the point she'd become invested in their success or failure. She was just as much a part of the group as Bahr or Skuld. Detaching her personal feelings left her disjointed. "They have great strength that can be used to their advantage when times become dire."

"But?" he asked with raised brows.

"For each strength there is a corresponding weakness. Unity of purpose can only take them so far before they fracture and break. There are moments when the group fails, like the moment Maleela was captured."

"Her loss hurts gravely but there is little to be done for it now. We must focus on preventing her from being turned to evil's purpose," Artiss said and sighed.

"Her distraction could prove fatal. Bahr is governed by emotions. He will not stop until she is back at his side. It is an interesting dynamic for two people who seldom met and did not know each other," Rekka added. The promise of family struck deep emotional chords, especially after her recent ordeal with the warriors of Teng.

Artiss watched her memories play across her troubled face but held his tongue. She needed to work through her misgivings to find the total peace required to perform her task. Rekka was an immeasurable asset he was fortunate to have emplaced. If only Bahr and the others managed to keep their petty differences to a minimum, they might have a chance. He studied his pupil. She had strength, courage, and the right amount of conviction, but was embroiled in turmoil. Her mind wasn't in the right place. Too many conflicting thoughts pushed through logic corridors to collide with unchangeable moments in time. Running into Cashi Dam proved more challenging than he had envisioned.

"And you, my dear? Where is your mind right now?" Artiss asked, catching her off guard.

"I don't understand your question," she replied.

"The events with villagers from Teng must weigh on your soul. Are you troubled by them? Does it disturb you to be banished from ever returning home?" He pressed, deliberately, to accurately gauge her poise. She had no way of knowing, but she was the glue keeping this quest together.

"My heart has grown cold over the issue, Master. Teng will always be my home, whether I accept my banishment or not. Cashi Dam's ignorance was regrettable but ultimately unavoidable. Whatever emotion he carried was not love and that led to his death. I will stay the course. Malweir must be saved from the dark gods."

Her reply was swift, the words flowing rapidly without any trace of emotion. Far from ruthless, Rekka understood the necessity of being harsh in harsh times. Any associations with her home, severed as they were, wouldn't interfere with her task. She'd been chosen to serve Trennaron and the Guardian for a specific purpose. Anything less than complete effort meant doom for a great many people.

"A very political answer. One that belies the hard layers around your heart. Good. Keep your defenses up. I rely on you more than you know, Rekka Jel. You are a good pupil, one of my best." He paused to enjoy the first rays of golden sunlight slicing through the banks of dark clouds on the eastern horizon. "Where are the others?"

"They await in the dining hall. Do you want me to fetch them?"

"No. I will be down shortly. The time has come for them to see the object that has taken them from their wintery homes. I must prepare the Blud Hamr vault."

Rekka stalked off while Artiss watched the sunrise a moment longer. His heart felt heavier than normal as he contemplated what opening that vault meant for the world. Reluctantly, the Dae'shan folded his robes in on himself and disappeared.

Conversation faded and eventually died when Rekka entered the dining hall. A dozen empty benches each capable of seating twenty adults surrounded the handful of heroes. Half-empty plates of green apples, jellied ham, light and dark breads, cheeses, and boiled eggs filled their table. Goblets of ale and water interspersed the food. The air had the faintest hint of pipe tobacco smoke, reminding her of times better spent.

"There's still enough food to feed a company of soldiers fresh off campaign," Bahr offered upon seeing her.

Rekka smiled warmly. "Thank you but I have already eaten. I rose much earlier to practice my drills."

"Why does that sound ominous?" Boen asked.

"Perhaps it is, though I don't mean it to be so. Master Gran has requested you all to join him down in the vaults. He is opening the Blud Hamr."

Her words cut into them like knives. All the long weeks and months of the quest had boiled down into a singular moment; one they never felt was going to arrive. They'd fought and bled across a large portion of the world to get here. Friends were lost. New enemies made. It was all in the past now. The great clock of their adventure finally wound down, leaving them at the edge of gaining what they so desperately sought. Bahr rose first, followed closely by Anienam.

"Let's get on with it. I'm dying to see if this trinket lives up to the reputation Anienam crafted around it," the Sea Wolf said.

Several of the torches on wall sconces flickered from unfelt winds. Trennaron itself seemed to grow quieter as if it knew the significance of what was occurring. Rekka waited for the others to finish eating and wipe their mouths. She'd never admit it, but she wanted to behold this once ancient weapon as well. The implications the Blud Hamr brought forth were varied. She might be set free from her tenure at Trennaron once the dark gods were ultimately defeated. Artiss Gran would choose another, giving her the freedom to pursue Dorl Theed and possibly marry. The thought left her warm as she led the way down long, unused corridors.

Trennaron was a winding maze of implacable passages. Marble of every shade and color filled the halls, dwarfing the grandeur of any other palace. Arched ceilings made the castle look much larger than it was, which wasn't saying much considering just how big Trennaron was. Immaculate statues of Men, Dwarves, Elves, and races they couldn't name lined several of the halls. Heroes of old, Rekka explained. She pointed out the statues of Delin Kerny and Fennic Attleford, the two boys responsible for killing the Silver Mage and ending the last attempt to bring the dark gods back. There was the statue of Kavan the Gaimosian. His deeds were legendary as he was the first to destroy a nexus. Celegon the Elf stood with keen eyes and the mighty Star Silver sword, Phaelor, in hand. Ironfoot gazed upon the immense statue of Norgen the Dwarf, a legend from a thousand years ago. Beside him stood Grelic the Giant of Thrae. All these heroes had contributed to preventing the dark gods' return. There seemed little doubt that fresh pedestals would be erected for whoever was fortunate enough to survive this fight.

Rekka led them to a grand, winding staircase that plunged deep into the bowels of the world. Hesitant at first, they only followed when Boen shamed them into it. Gaimosians seldom felt fear of any kind. He certainly wasn't about to show any in the heart of the castle of the gods of light. Rekka explained some of Trennaron's history, what little she could, as they went down. Built as a reservoir of knowledge, the castle stored the wealth of the gods on Malweir. There were no caverns of gold or jewels. No priceless stones or gems. Knowledge was power and Trennaron boasted the largest, most complete compendium of history in the world. Every minute fact was recorded and stored by a host of scribes all but chained to their desks and ink pots.

There were few questions as flight after flight of stairs went past. Many of them found the trip exhausting while imaging how difficult the return trip was going to be. Not even months on the trail conditioned them enough to keep their knees from burning or their breathing labored. Dorl was certain they were going down to the center of the world. Only Ironfoot bore no qualms. Dwarves were a stout race used to pushing deep underground.

At last they halted on the final landing where many struggled to catch their breath. Anienam, Bahr, and Boen all secretly cursed getting old. Their bodies were sore, haggard representations of what they'd once been. Time was an ever cruel trickster intent on beating them down until only dust and bones remained. When they finally managed to regain a small measure of self-control they looked in amazement at their surroundings. Grand, cavernous halls spread out in each cardinal direction. Each was large enough to fit an army and filled with hundreds of torches and hanging braziers. The walls were smooth, the dirt the color of a burning sun. The floors compacted to the point where not a speck of dust was visible. Surprisingly, there was great warmth. The caverns were brightly lit and almost enjoyable to be in.

Ironfoot whistled low. "In all my years I never imagined taking in such sights. This must rival even the tombs under the Twin Spires of Ragnash."

"Surpass is more appropriate, Ironfoot," Anienam corrected. "There is no equivalent in all Malweir to what we are witnessing, except perhaps the dragon roosts far to the west. Rekka, how far underground are we?"

"A half of a mile," she replied. "Master Gran is waiting. The vault is down the southern corridor."

They shuffled down more than a mile of corridor to come to a massive, vaulted door made of a strange metal none of them had ever seen. Wooden crossbeams formed a large cross similar to what the Giants of Venheim used in their worship to their one god. Anienam puzzled over the similarities of faith, certain the emblem was symbolic of religion. Each culture worshipped their own gods with specific rules and rituals. Finding evidence of contrary religious beliefs in the temple of the gods of light puzzled him to great ends. The vault door groaned open before he could ask the obvious questions distracting him.

Artiss Gran floated out towards them, arms folded within his pristine white robes. "My friends, what you are about to witness is a sight none have seen since the foundations of this great castle. I warn you to stay on the path. I will not be held responsible for you should you fail to follow this one instruction."

"What could be so dangerous?" Dorl asked sharply.

Artiss blinked twice. "Trennaron holds many powers; some for good, others not. Heed my advice, Master Theed. Now, if there are no other simplistic questions, please follow me."

He turned and went inside, followed closely by Rekka and then the others. Nothol reached out and slapped Dorl hard on the shoulder and gave a deep scowl. Dorl shrugged and kept walking. Intense heat washed over him the moment his boot stepped into the chamber. Sweat drenched his face and chest in moments. His eyes stung. His hair dripped wetness. Dorl raised an arm in a futile attempt at blocking the heat and looked ahead. What he saw dropped his jaw. The majesty of the corridors was immediately dwarfed by the intensity of what sat ahead.

A diamond-shaped structure stabbed towards the ceiling. The walls were made of glass, perfect and reflecting the heat of the flames surrounding the octagon-shaped stairwells leading up to the diamond. Dorl had grown up with legends of the underworld yet none of them were close to the hell of what he saw. The ground was blackened. The air smelled of brimstone. Dorl had the urge to vomit.

Artiss stopped them just inside the vault. "Behold! The resting place of the fabled Blud Hamr. This tool was crafted with singular purpose. Only you, Groge, can wield it. It is your responsibility to use the hammer to destroy the

Olagath Stone, thus severing the link between dimensions and trapping the dark gods forever. Are you willing to accept this task?"

All eyes turned to the Giant. While he was more than humble as a traveling companion, his reluctance to engage in combat proved disturbing, leaving each with doubts as to whether he was going to fulfill his part of the quest. Groge took a deep, calming breath. He hadn't thought about this moment. It seemed so far away, even as they drew nearer to Trennaron. Now, confronted with his basest beliefs and the knowledge only he could wield the hammer, he found all doubts gradually flee. Groge stepped forward with Gaimosian confidence.

"I do," he said sternly.

The unspoken tension separating the group dissolved. The time had finally arrived for the realization of the weight of what they were attempting to do to strike. Gouts of flame easily the size of small houses burst skyward, throwing molten rock and quickly fading flames up in torrents. Artiss Gran felt great relief. Even his foresight couldn't predict whether Groge was going to accept the challenge or not.

"A wise decision," the Dae'shan replied. "All you know this, once you step foot into the vault you will forever be cast down a path that will ultimately end in direct conflict with the Dae'shan and possibly the dark gods themselves. There will be no turning back."

"We understand," Bahr answered for them after pausing to stare into each of their eyes. Any personal doubts were forgotten after seeing the wary confidence looking back at him.

Boen grunted and folded his thick arms across his chest after moving to stand beside Bahr. "I've been waiting for this for months. Let's get on with it."

Nothol seconded the sentiment. "Now's as good a time as any. Besides, we'll at least get to go home."

"Under the pretense that you might perish," Artiss explained. He needed each to declare their intentions freely. Otherwise the quest was doomed to fail.

"We're not getting any younger," Bahr said.

"Very well. Follow me and do watch your step. Malweir needs you all."

The Dae'shan glided across the long-forgotten floor. Small trails of dust kicked up in his wake. One by one the others fell in line behind him, careful to take the exact route as Artiss. They'd only walked a few meters before arriving at the base of the first set of steps. A moment earlier it appeared far away. The ground shook frightfully, as if it knew what was about to take place. The walls closed in only to dart away. Rocks and dust fell from the cavernous ceiling. Flames exploded in dynamic displays of force. More than once the group halted as they felt sure the very ground was about to crack under their feet. Only Artiss's confidence kept them moving.

The stairs were made of alabaster, their pale white glow in stark contrast to the hues of red and brown surrounding them. Artiss Gran ascended the stairs with utter surety. A faint thumping could be heard over the roar of flames: subtle, reminiscent of a heartbeat. Bahr passed Anienam a sidelong glance but the wizard ignored him. This was neither the time nor place to cast the shroud of doubt.

They gained the level surrounding the diamond chamber housing the hammer. Slick, the floor was smooth glass. Nearly lost within the reflections of flame were thousands of faces, ghosts of souls long condemned to eternal darkness. They cried wordlessly. They implored for release. Bahr felt sickened. Of all the strange sights he'd witnessed this was by far the most unsettling. He'd never bothered to put much thought into what happened after death. A man in his profession merely assumed there was only darkness and he'd return to the earth from where he came. The faces haunting the vault turned his stomach. Were they trapped or summoned by powers he failed to understand?

"Pay no heed to the faces," Artiss warned. "They will pull you down and make you one of their ranks if you peer too closely."

"What are they?" Boen asked. The Gaimosian felt on edge. His thoughts instantly went back to the confrontation with the ghosts of his ancestors in the Borgin Pass at the beginning of their quest.

"Fools mostly. They once served the powers of darkness. Each was captured and brought back to serve. Whatever corruption was in their hearts at their time of death binds them to Trennaron. They are now guardians for each of the vaults in the sublevels." Artiss kept moving towards the small doorway at the center of the diamond. "The gods of light are both wise and vindictive towards those who abuse them. So long as you avoid temptation and keep moving these ghosts will not harm you."

Dorl told Nothol from the corner of his mouth, "That doesn't sound very reassuring."

"What does? This place shouldn't exist. I feel haunted just stepping foot here."

"There are many places in the world that *shouldn't* exist, yet they do and it will do us all well to remain wary until the final battle is finished." Artiss scolded softly. "Groge, be mindful and watch your head. The hammer may have been specifically designed for Giants to wield, but the vault most assuredly was not."

He slipped inside the diamond, leaving the others in the doorway.

"After you, wizard," Bahr said, picking up on the initial reluctance of the group. *If anything bad is going to happen, this is the time. Better Anienam take the brunt of an attack than the rest of us.*

Anienam followed without hesitation, ever eager to gain new insight and knowledge he might be able to use to further his cause. Deep inside he knew that rebuilding the order of Mages was borderline impossible, but he refused to strop striving for a return to the glory days. Ipn Shal would rise from the ashes again, hopefully with better results than the previous version. Whatever he managed to glean from Artiss Gran and Trennaron only furthered his cause, provided they were able to stop the dark gods from returning.

Momentary darkness blinded him. He stumbled from the depravation before his vision returned. Eyes wide open, Anienam gazed up at the pointed ceiling. Reflections of sparkling light dazzled the chamber. He'd seen many incredible, implausible sights over the course of his lifetime but nothing comparable to the vault of the Blud Hamr. Power resonated from the planet's core, vibrating the ground subtly.

The short tunnel behind suddenly filled with Bahr and the others, all eager to catch a glimpse of the fabled weapon necessary to win the war. All expectations were dwarfed by the majesty of the hammer. Suspended through invisible nets of power, the Blud Hamr hung in the air, gently rotating. Old, leather straps were wrapped around the handle. Strange emblems were carved on the exposed black wood handle. Runes no living being on Malweir could remember. The massive head was roughly the size of a small boulder yet shaped and crafted into a block with sharp edges. Gems were crafted within the stone, lending a magical appearance unseen in any weapon since. Crisscrossing straps secured the stone to the handle, though Anienam suspected it was more than simple straps. A weapon of this stature was imbibed with more magic than a wizard of his caliber was capable of.

Artiss Gran halted beneath the hammer and turned. "Behold! The Blud Hamr. Only with this weapon can the Olagath Stone be destroyed. You all are the first living souls to witness this sight in fifty thousand years. Take in the majesty. Let the power fill your weary hearts, give you strength, and open your minds. Purge your souls of impurity and venom. Only through total dedication to light, to justice, will you be able to succeed in your appointed task."

"It's a sight, that's for sure, but now that I see it I don't know if I have the proper strength to follow through," Groge replied.

His mind raced back to their earlier conversation concerning the Olagath Stone. It was an artifact previously unmentioned by Anienam. Almost as old as the Blud Hamr, the Stone contained the misery of souls; forever suffering until the moment of release. If Amar Kit'han managed to fill the stone he and the other Dae'shan would be able to open the pathway between dimensions and bring forth the dark gods. The Stone needed to be destroyed to seal the rift. Getting the Olagath Stone away from the Dae'shan in time was another matter altogether.

"Each soul has different degrees of strength. You will find yours before the end, Groge of Venheim," Artiss reassured him. "The time has come for you to claim your birthright. Step forward and take the hammer."

Reluctance stiffened his twelve foot frame. Talking about doing it was one thing, reaching out to take it another matter altogether. None of his dreams adequately prepared him for the weight of what he *had* to do. He thought back to Joden's teachings. The elder forge master was considered one of the wisest of their kind yet even he had no advice on what the young apprentice was going to encounter.

The young Giant gathered what courage remained and stepped up beside Artiss. He closed his eyes, whispering prayers to his god for strength. His hand rose in slow motion. Thick fingers curled around the hammer. Warmth spread through his body. Massive thunderclaps assaulted his eardrums. Spots of colors blossomed and collided before his eyes. The world went white.

THIRTY-ONE

The War Goes West

"Report, Sergeant."

A crisp salute followed. "Sir, we followed a large body of tracks right up to the town's border. There's no doubt it was Badron and the Goblins." Anger flashed behind his eyes. Speaking the words were nearly as bad as discovering the truth.

Piper idly scratched at the stubble irritating his jaw. He'd been hoping to catch his former king out in the open. "Is there a chance he hasn't fled back to Delranan?"

"Doubtful but I'll have the lads sneak in at dusk. We can move faster under cover of darkness. I didn't notice any masts in the harbor though," he added in afterthought.

That says it all. Our prey has escaped the trap. Rolnir won't take this well, nor will young Aurec. It looks as if the war is going to continue on into spring. "I want every house, building, and tavern thoroughly searched. Detain anyone who protests but ensure Rogscroft soldiers are the ones doing it. We don't want to incite another rebellion. Cavalry will canvas the surrounding forests in the event Badron's holed up waiting for a ship to come in. If he's still in country I want him found and captured before dawn." *This war has gone on long enough. We're all strung out and ready to go home. Only, we can't go home until Badron is removed. Then we have Harnin One Eye to deal with. Either way, we've got a hard road ahead.*

"Yes, Commander," the sergeant said and saluted again and rode back towards his waiting troops.

Piper frowned deeply. The furrow creased his exposed forehead. Helmet strapped to his horse, Piper Joach enjoyed the momentary feel of the cold wind in his hair. He'd been in the field for far too long and, despite being borderline exhausted, wanted to end the campaign in Rogscroft personally. After all, he'd been in command of the first skirmish. It was only fitting he brought it all to a close. General Rolnir agreed with his point of view, thus sending a large contingent of soldiers north in a seemingly futile attempt at cutting off Badron's escape route.

The port town of Dredl hadn't suffered many effects of the war. It was a major seaport, for Rogscroft, and had a steady stream of supplies coming in throughout the course of the winter. Rudimentary defenses were established along the perimeter. Piper approved of the townsfolk wanting to protect their homes but their defenses were more than inadequate to keep out a force larger than a squad. Badron and his Goblins would have rolled through Dredl like a harsh winter storm. *Only there's no sign of a struggle. No wreckage or debris. Not even a corpse in the snow. Where have you gone, Badron?*

"Lieutenant Klevk, dispatch a team of runners back to General Rolnir. Inform him and the king that we have reached Dredl and there is no sign of our enemy." He paused, knowing he should wait until the scouts returned with positive confirmation before sending a report back to headquarters. Misinformation might easily prove more damning to their cause. Still, Rolnir and Aurec needed up-to-date information to facilitate the execution of the next phase of the war. Piper felt trapped between the proverbial rock and hard place but was left with little real choice. The king needed to know.

Badron despised the salt spray coating his beard and cloak. He failed to see what his errant brother found appealing about the sea. It was too cold, too turbulent to accomplish much of anything. He didn't recall the last time his stomach felt so rebellious. Three times since dawn he emptied his guts into the roiling sea. Harsh winds slashed through his clothing, digging deep to the bone. Nothing but dark water splashed and rolled for as far as his eyes could see. The boat would roll and sink if a bad storm came south, killing all aboard without a trace. Badron had grown to hate everything about the water in a very short period.

Six other boats trailed behind, stretched out for a third of a league. Each carried remnants of his once powerful army, now reduced to mere hundreds of half-starved survivors eager to get home or get revenge in equal amounts. None of them knew the truth of what awaited, the carnage and depravation Harnin committed in the name of his personal brand of justice. Many had lost families, loved ones. Their lands razed to the ground or taken by the crown in a greedy attempt at consolidating power. Delranan was no longer the kingdom they remembered. It had become much, much worse.

Whispered promises by the Dae'shan did little to assuage Badron's grief. He only wanted what was best for his legacy when first undertaking the endeavor in Rogscroft. Necessity made him harsh but he never wished for harm to befall his mighty kingdom. The desire to conquer Stelskor drove him forward while exposing a terrible flaw: Harnin One Eye. His former right hand had grown decadent, if all reports from Amar Kit'han were to be believed and transformed Delranan into a fragment of itself. *The One Eye has much to answer for. I'll crush the life from his throat with my bare hands.*

Badron harbored no illusions as to the state of his kingdom. If his own actions in Rogscroft were any indication, Delranan surely suffered worse, especially if the Dae'shan were involved. The king couldn't prove it, but his instincts screamed Amar Kit'han and the other were playing both sides off each other. To what purpose he couldn't figure out. There was an undeniable air of evil about the mysterious, hooded beings, though what their true intent in the north was went beyond his rationale.

Knowing would solve a great many issues but Badron detested being in their presence. His skin crawled each time the Dae'shan opened his mouth. How much hatred and venom could a single being contain before becoming consumed with his own fires? Badron briefly considered enlisting Grugnak and the Goblins to help take down the Dae'shan but the swarthy cave dwellers seemed intent on serving their dark masters. Frustrated, the deposed king of Delranan could do nothing more than stare off into the ocean and wish.

His thoughts turned to his daughter. Maleela was the unwanted child. The killer of his wife, her mother. Inadvertent as it might have been, she ruined all his plans for life. He knew, without wanting to admit it, that he'd never have acted on his urges of conquest. Rogscroft would still be standing and Stelskor would still be an unspoken rival trapped on the far side of an imposing mountain range filled with the hostile Pell Darga. No harm would have befallen the north. He had no way of knowing the depths of events unfolding around him.

Amar Kit'han never told him of the Dwarf rebellion the Dae'shan had incited. Or how an entire clan of Dwarves had fallen to the darkness. He didn't know far along the quest to reclaim the Blud Hamr was, or if any of the heroes still drew breath. Fifty thousand battle-hungry Goblins were coming to change the face of the north for all times. The kingdoms of men would fail and darkness would sweep across the world. All it required was a spark. A spark Badron had unwittingly lit when he ordered the Wolfsreik to march on Rogscroft.

He never regretted that decision. Stelskor had been a constant thorn in his side for decades, more so than his own brother. The two might have begun as friends but their friendly rivalry turned into jealousy, at least on Badron's part. He wanted access to the central kingdoms of Malweir. The trade benefits would enhance his coffers and increase his standing among the ruling class. Rolnir's betrayal robbed all that. The former king of Delranan was forced to slink away from his conquests and back into his own kingdom without getting caught. He'd been hunted all the way out of the capitol city to the coast and would assuredly be hunted from the moment he arrived in Delranan unless they found port somewhere along the coast that wasn't being guarded.

The possibility was narrow. Much of the coast was filled with barren crags incapable of landing anything larger than a fishing vessel. Forests of thick pines blanketed the land for leagues inland, providing more than adequate protection against prying eyes. It would also conceal any spies, making the crossing dangerous. Badron wasn't concerned with danger. It was the one constant that had been in his life since he attained adulthood and took the crown from his father. He relished the opportunity to engage in deceit as well as the occasional battle. The sad reality was he wasn't prepared for either. He'd run his gambit but fell short. Now armies from three kingdoms were actively hunting him. Reaching Chadra Keep was going to prove more problematic than anything he had done up to this point.

"We'll make landfall by tomorrow night if this storm blows out instead of in," the captain mentioned idly.

His black hair was thinning and matted to his head. His beard had fragments of bone and worse burrowed all the way down to his chest. His eyes were hard and never stopped watching Badron. Thoughts of robbing the monarch and dumping his corpse into the frigid northern waters entertained him from the moment he agreed to contract. A king like Badron wasn't worth much in ransom so the captain would have to make do with robbing whatever he could take and be done with it.

No fool, Badron knew exactly the sort of man he'd hired and fully expected to be confronted before making landfall. He grinned tightly. The captain didn't know the Dae'shan was lurking below decks, clinging to the shadows and gathering information. He didn't think Amar Kit'han was finished with him yet but couldn't trust to complacency. Badron already had plans of his own. The moment the captain made his move, it would be his final on Malweir. Grugnak and a small contingent of Goblins were prepared to take over the ship, leaving just enough crew alive to pilot them ashore.

Badron nodded absently, his mind exploring the different possibilities ahead. "Have you a place large enough and secretive enough to put us in?"

"Aye. The coast is rocky but there are small bays and draws capable of landing our boarding craft. I'll get you back on dry ground no problem, so long as you pay what you promised," he added with latent threat.

Typical. Thieves always think of their purses before their necks. "You'll be paid in full for your services, Captain. All you have to do is get us there without being spotted."

He dismissed Badron with a flip of his hair. "Shouldn't be too hard. Delranan doesn't have a navy, nothing worth worrying about that is."

A problem I am going to have to remedy when I regain the throne. Men like you are the scum on the bottom of my boots. "We've never had great need for one. Who needs to worry over pirates or raiders when I have a ten-thousand strong army at my fingers?"

The captain laughed. "Had. Last I heard those Wolf soldiers had gone over to the enemy and left you high and dry with this pack of gray skins. Seems a damned shame for a king to lose everything and get left with the scraps."

"Circumstances don't stay the same for very long," Badron replied tartly. "The day is fast approaching when all the north shall fear my name again."

Hiding his concern, the captain played off Badron as being arrogant. "Words don't win kingdoms. Your enemies are lining up to have a go at your throat. Delranan is a dark place these days. Lots of evil deeds and folk moving about. What with the plague I'm surprised there's anything left worth owning."

"What plague?" Instant concern sparked his attention.

"You hadn't heard?"

Badron shook his head. "Tell me."

"A few weeks back there was a terrible plague that swept through the kingdom. I heard it began in Chadra and pushed outward. Hundreds died in the first few days. Thousands more in the following weeks. Between that and the rebellion I'm guessing a large portion of the population is lost."

Badron felt true pain in his heart, though he refused to show it. He'd given Delranan his life only to see it all fall to ruin. He listened as the captain explained all that had occurred since the war in Rogscroft began. It seemed almost too surreal despite everything he'd done and been through. He truly was the ruler of an empire of bones. Images of fields of sun-bleached skeletons haunted him as the captain talked. He didn't know what to do. How to make it all better. Life had spiraled out of his control.

He still had the ability to change it all. To reclaim the stolen glory in the name of his family's honor. Delranan would be great again. He'd raise another army, more powerful than the first. Any who'd oppose him would be swept away like flotsam on the tides. A new dawn was approaching, one in which the house of Badron would awaken and find itself strong. Killing Harnin was but the first step.

Badron walked away while the captain was in midsentence. Waves crashed against the hull as the ship drove closer to Delranan and the new front of the war.

Grugnak spied the conversation from his bolt hole just under the quarterdeck. Too much sunlight and the natural revulsion exhibited by the crew all but confined the Goblins below decks. Being back in the gloom comforted many, Grugnak included. He'd been away from the Deadlands for too long. Walking amongst men in the open chafed at his instincts. Goblins belonged in darkness. It was the purpose of their existence. Any opportunity he found to return to the darkness was a welcome respite.

Badron's words echoed in his mind. The Dae'shan never bothered explaining their purpose or reasoning. Grugnak didn't care. He'd been given the opportunity to travel unhindered into a kingdom of men to plunder and kill as much as possible without reprisal. It had been grand for a time, until the wolf soldiers turned on their king and persecuted the Goblins. Now they were both hunted. Badron lost his army while Grugnak's was all but destroyed. There wasn't enough time left in his life to extract the necessary amount of revenge. Still, the Goblin commander had a special dagger reserved for Badron the moment he was no longer necessary. Silently, patiently, the Goblin listened, watched, and waited.

THIRTY-TWO

Ingrid

"Another seventy-three fighters came in during the day," Orlek announced gleefully before downing a mouthful of almost brackish ale. "That brings our fighting strength close to two thousand just in this quadrant of the kingdom."

"Two thousand won't be enough once Harnin marshals his full force and marches on us," Ingrid replied almost too quickly.

Two days had passed since the successful string of ambushes on Wolfsreik supply trains. Two days in which she'd gotten nearly no sleep. Fears of being discovered or worse, betrayed, prevented her from thinking clearly. She saw enemies lurking behind every building and in every shadow. It had happened before. She harbored no illusions that it wouldn't again. Treachery had become the currency of the realm.

Ingrid bore her share of the blame. Abandoning Inaella at her greatest moment of need had been a sound tactical decision but poor from the humanitarian point of view. True, she fully expected the former leader of the rebellion to succumb to the plague and pose no further threat, but finding Inaella in the employ of Harnin One Eye was almost too much to bear. Ingrid couldn't help but believe she'd created more of a problem than solution.

Harlan frowned from his seat beside the fireplace. Boots propped on the back of a rickety chair, he was kicked back, trying to regain some of the warmth stolen from a long day's ride across Delranan. His thoughts centered on warm ale, semi-edible food, and the middle daughter of the local crofter. Everything else prevented him from enjoying the night. "You should look at the positive rather than the negative. Our rebellion is growing. You've successfully taken it out of Chadra and into the countryside. There is no way Harnin can crush it without committing much more than he has available to the field."

"Harlan's right. You need to relax," Orlek seconded. "This new phase of the rebellion is just starting. You might not realize it but there are a lot of people depending on you to keep them alive until winter breaks."

"I never wanted that responsibility," she protested.

In truth she didn't. Ingrid was content with her daily life, leaving the politics of the moment to those who knew better. Those people didn't and the kingdom plunged into complete chaos. Anarchy spread like a wildfire until nothing of the old Delranan remained. It fell to people like her to pick up the pieces and try to make a better life. Life that wasn't coming as long as Harnin was on the throne. Becoming a hero didn't interest her. She was a simple woman trapped in turbulent times.

Orlek set his drink down and leaned forward to look her in the eyes. "Ingrid, good people don't get the choices the rest of the world do. They either stand up for what's right or they get trampled underfoot while evil rolls over them. What hero in any story every wanted to be one?"

"Hard times make heroes," Harlan practically echoed. "Like it or not you have people looking to you, just like you wanted when you saved the rebellion from Inaella's lead. Mothers, children, the old and the sick are all looking at you to save them. It's too late to turn back. Leave the past where it belongs. I say if you can't change it don't bother worrying over it."

She hung her head. Difficult decisions seemed to be flying at her faster than she could deal with them. "What must I do?"

"Honestly? Do what your heart tells you. It will lead you to the only possible conclusion more times than not," Harlan said with a smile in his voice. He reached into his faded jacket pocket and produced a short stem pipe already packed. The strike of the match sizzled through the common room they'd adopted as their base of operations during their stay in Fendi. Soon the smell of earthy tobacco drifted across the room.

Ingrid frowned. "You make it all sound so gallant, so graceful. Too many people have died fighting this rebellion. Few of them were on my shoulders until I assumed command. All that follow from this point forward will be mine to bear as well. When have you ever been held accountable for so precious a gift?"

Harlan's light-hearted demeanor soured. He turned towards the cackling fire and said no more. Some pains were still too close to speak of.

Orlek ran a hand through his hair and slammed his palm on the counter. "Damn it, Ingrid, what is this? You took control of a dying group and have produced numerous victories. You almost singlehandedly turned this war around and gave our people, your people, hope again. Now you want to take it away for the simple reason that you can't handle it? That's childish."

"How dare y…"

"I dare because you're giving me no choice! This is your war now, Ingrid, not Inaella's. We will either win or lose by your decisions. Now stop acting like a spoiled child and be the leader you were always meant to be."

Her cheeks reddened but she kept her mouth shut. There were times when a proper dress down was appropriate. This was clearly one of them. She replayed all she'd said and done in her mind and, in retrospect, concluded that her actions since killing her first man two days ago had been excessively selfish. Orlek and Harlan were both right. She was a leader now whether she liked it or not.

Ingrid's first action was to deploy her forces to achieve maximum effect. Harnin wasn't going to be content with staying around the capitol. Any logistical problems could be resolved by breaking the forces up into small units with enough supplies to sustain a prolonged effort in the field. Getting them to where they needed to be to cause maximum havoc was another issue altogether.

The rebellion sorely lacked wagons and horses, even after their successes raiding the supply trains. They needed more of each if they were going to cover large areas of ground in a timely, effective manner. Time was a luxury she didn't have. Word had come in just that morning that Harnin was moving out into the countryside. It wouldn't take long before they realized what had happened to their supplies and would come looking for the responsible party in force. That left her with one inescapable conclusion.

"We must prepare to leave Fendi," she said unexpectedly, reversing her previous thoughts.

"So soon?" Harlan asked. His gloom seemed temporary, having already faded. "This is still a secured location."

Golden hair danced around her face as she shook her head. "Not for much longer. Harnin will be heading this way much sooner than we'd like to believe. Word should reach Chadra Keep in the next few days of their losses and it won't take a genius to realize our general location. He has enough forces to circle this entire portion of the kingdom and tighten it around us. Unless we escape to the next fallback position before he can act we'll be trapped."

"The implications suggest a measure of error," Harlan said. "We spread our initial attacks out in a wide enough pattern to keep him guessing. The only way he'd know for certain which part of the kingdom to look would be if we had a spy in our ranks."

"Which we must assume we do," Ingrid countered firmly. "Many of us were loyal to the crown and the Wolfsreik at one point *after* the war began. Harnin will have loyalists emplaced within our camp just as we do in his. Or at least had until Lord Argis was discovered."

Argis' loss hurt more than any of the current leaders were willing to admit. He'd provided key tactical advantages to fighting the Wolfsreik while bolstering support for the rebellion. The executed lord was the singular greatest asset Ingrid could have ever hoped for, and Inaella had squandered him to the point where Harnin took his head on the Keep's walls in front of the populace. *Yet another reason to despise that man. I vow to take his head the same way he took Argis'.*

"I don't see how anyone this far out could be loyal to the crown," Orlek told her. "Most of these villagers never had deeply set loyalties to Badron. They paid their taxes and did their part for crown and kingdom but much preferred being left alone, forgotten by the king. This is a simple life out here."

"Simple or not I wouldn't put it past anyone to accept his offer for the right price," Ingrid answered.

Harlan exhaled a thick plume of bluish smoke. "How do you propose we discover the truth? No one in their right mind is going to admit being a spy in the middle of a war. That's instant execution."

"We leave it alone for now. Break the fighters up into small groups with missions so far apart they couldn't possibly exchange information. Tell on the group leaders what their tasks are and where they need to go and make each believe theirs is the primary objective. Any spy will be forced to work three times as hard to get word back to Chadra Keep."

"While giving us time to learn their identities and remove them," Orlek finished. Where Ingrid and Harlan, to an extent, were reluctant when it came to killing, he bore no such hesitation. He'd killed more than his share and intended to keep doing so until the war ended. Only then would he find peace. He hoped.

"Exactly," Ingrid confirmed. "I want you two to pick twenty men and women. Good, strong candidates or heads of family if there is enough. Each one will be responsible for a specific area of Delranan and have one hundred fighters at their command. Our first order of business is the disruption of their supply lines. Once they are harried to the point of keeping their precious supplies at home we can focus on taking out their smaller outposts and bases. Most of Harnin's efforts are concentrated to the east. He fears Badron's return and rightfully so. The deposed king had ten thousand soldiers at his disposal, paling Harnin's forces by more than two to one, combat losses notwithstanding."

"Come on, Harlan, old friend. She wants us to go back into the cold," Orlek said glibly.

Harlan pretended to frown and emptied his pipe. "A cruel mistress she is, Orlek. Soon she'll have us shoveling snow to make a proper ambush sight before too long."

Ingrid rolled her eyes and waved them out the door. They had much to do before she would be comfortable enough to sleep again. Her greatest fears were breathing down her neck. Harnin and his army were coming to get her. Led by an overly vindictive Inaella, he would stop at nothing in catching and killing them all. Ingrid couldn't let that happen. The time had come to take the fight back to the One Eye.

Harnin ripped his dagger from the chest of scout and kicked the body to the ground before he died. Thin ropes of crimson blood splashed down around the poor man. The second scout meekly bowed his head, hoping to avoid the same fate. The lord of Delranan eyed the trembling soldier harshly. His dagger waivered. Blood dripped slowly from the exposed blade.

"You dare bring me news of this sort?" he raged.

"My lord, our captain thought it wise to dispatch us with the news immediately. Our losses were severe." The scout's words came quickly and lacked confidence.

Harnin lifted his dagger. "Stop speaking. I have grown tired of the gross incompetence surrounding me. Go back to your captain with orders to continue operations. I want the rebels found and executed. Leave me before I decide to mount your head on a pike."

Saluting, the scout bowed and hurried off before Harnin changed his mind. Skaning and Jarrik exchanged nervous looks while deciding what to say. Harnin's mood continued to devolve into borderline madness. Reason slipped through his fingers the longer the war drug on. Compounding matters was the inevitable return of the main army. The only way Harnin would be able to deal with Badron and the Wolfsreik effectively was through crushing the rebellion and putting the rebels in chains on the front lines. They'd die horribly but they might take enough of the Wolfsreik with them to make a difference in the outcome of the war.

Already on the fringes, Jarrik decided he had nothing to lose. "That could have been handled better, Harnin. Killing our own people doesn't endear you to them and we need every available body to fight the war in the east."

"Don't assume that I need your counsel, Jarrik. You have failed me too many times already. It's not much of a stretch to imagine you with Argis' face," Harnin seethed. "I may need every loyal citizen but I do not need the fractious actions you seem so fond of."

"I am merely bringing forth a different point of view, Harnin. The war isn't going well for us. The plague should have all but ended our problems but Ingrid was able to escape with Argis' body. Inaella has been helpful but not highly effective."

Throwing the dagger into the already battered oak table, Harnin stalked back to his throne with a dire look haunting his face. "Perhaps I need to send the two of you west. That way if the enemy does overrun us I won't have to worry about either of you fouling my plans in the future."

Skaning finally spoke up. He'd sat in the background for too long. Lords were changing so rapidly he felt sure it was time to ascend to a higher position. As one of the last remaining old lords, he had just as much authority and knowledge of how Delranan worked as any of them. "Lord Harnin, sending Jarrik would certainly show our seriousness at eradicating the problem but will also leave us vulnerable on the eastern front. We will have need of quality commanders when Badron does decide to return."

"Very well, I accept your offer. Take command of the troops in the east, Skaning. Our enemies will be coming soon, at winter's end in the least."

"Who will command here in Chadra?" Skaning asked in protest. Harnin's command threw him off guard, leaving the bigger Man exposed.

Harnin fixed his eye on both captains. His intent was clear. There was to be no discussion on this matter. No chance to change his mind. "I will. This city belongs to me, what little remains of it. If it is to fall it will do so with me standing atop these very walls. I want both of you to leave before the end of the week. Neither Ingrid nor Badron will be so generous with their timelines. Take the fight back to the enemy and drive them into the open. Jarrik, you will have three thousand troops at your disposal. Find the rebels and crush them. Do not fail me again, Jarrik. I had no qualms with taking the head of one friend. A second will bother me less."

Jarrik could only nod and march away. There'd come a time and place to try and end Harnin's treachery, but it wasn't here. Chadra Keep was ripe with insecurities, hampering any efforts to overthrow Harnin. He had no other choice but to accept his assignment. Furious, Jarrik stormed through the wooden halls to find Inaella. The sooner they left this city of the dead the better.

Inaella jumped at the sudden knocking on her door. She'd been confined to quarters, for lack of a better term, since her last confrontation with Harnin. The One Eye continued to blame her for all his woes, including the loss of Argis' corpse and Ingrid. She'd been refused numerous audiences and put under guard. Her only grace came from not being confronted by the mysterious shadow figure from the hallway again. The knocking intensified, propelling her out of her chair to answer it. Jarrik was the last person she expected to see when she cracked the heavy wooden frame.

"Open the door, Inaella," he said with a frown. "It seems we are to work together once again."

"What do you mean?" She failed to keep the surprise from her voice. Inaella never expected to see the outdoors again, at least not until the executioner came to take her head.

He crossed his arms over his chest. "Harnin has deemed it necessary for us to travel northwest in an effort to hunt down and destroy the rebellion."

Inaella hesitated. She'd come to view her captors with great disdain, fearing them to be lesser men than she had imagined during the height of her power. Harnin was a petty tyrant playing at something greater. Jarrik and the others were mere sycophants in comparison. The sudden change of heart offered the barest glimmer of hope but left her wondering how long before she felt the cold kiss of steel plunging into her back.

"I thought I had fallen out of favor," she replied tersely. "Harnin is as callous as he is shallow. Why not kill me now and be done with it? I cannot stand this absent torture any longer!"

"Torture? You know nothing. The sickness of Harnin goes far beyond mere torture. He is influenced by dark powers. They drive him mad while the kingdom suffers. Still, he is in command and his orders stand. Gather your belongings. We leave in the morning."

The door slammed shut, leaving Inaella trapped in her solitude with a new set of nightmares keeping her company. It seemed each new dilemma offered only death. The pock-marked plague survivor was coming increasingly close to welcoming it. Delranan had become a horrible land.

THIRTY-THREE

The Trap is Set

Aurec crumbled the paper in his hands and cast it into the fire. One arm on the mantle, he gently lowered his head and closed his eyes. Tears threatened to spring forth and it was all he could do not to let them. Rolnir and the others wouldn't understand his exposed weakness, not after all they'd been through over the course of the winter. Instead the young king closed his eyes and tried to focus on the positive. Rogscroft was free of the Delrananian invaders. The kingdom belonged to the rightful rulers. The war, which had claimed so many lives and brought ruin to all corners of his kingdom, had finally come to an end. Not the end he envisioned when accepting Rolnir's alliance, but an end nonetheless.

There was no point in delaying the inevitable conversation with his closest advisors. They all knew what the message said, even if they hadn't read it. Aurec's reaction told them more than they needed to know. Badron had escaped. He'd managed, some-how, to elude a sizeable cavalry force and Cuul Ol's Pell Darga hunters and found passage out of Rogscroft with the remnants of his loyalist forces. The end Aurec so desperately desired crumbled through his fingers. He took a few deep breaths to clear his mind and calm his nerves before turning back to those assembled.

"Badron's gone. Piper and his force arrived in Dredl too late."

Venten felt his heart clutch deep within his chest. "Perhaps they avoided Dredl in favor of a smaller port. We all knew they were en route to the town. Badron was no fool."

"No, Venten. He's gone. A second set of scouts returned with a detailed report. Several key townsfolk corroborated the facts. He commandeered a small fleet of pirates, for lack of better terms, to take him back to Delranan."

Rolnir bore the brunt of the news with unusual passion. His loyalty to Badron died the moment the Goblins enacted their campaign of atrocities. He wanted the capture of his former king more than any one of those gathered, except for Aurec, whose personal hurt went deeper than most, and was willing to risk all on the endeavor. Piper's reports were disheartening. There'd be no easy way of stopping Badron once he returned to Delranan. Worse, the Wolfsreik wouldn't be able to return until the snows in the mountain passes melted enough to permit passage. Wheels already started turning. He'd make his people dig through the passes if necessary. Anything to get to Badron before the king managed to worm his way back into Chadra Keep.

"We're left at a severe disadvantage," he said dryly. "There's no conceivable way for us to get the bulk of the army back into Delranan before Badron has time to enact the next phase of his plan."

"A plan we don't know," General Vajna suggested. "He wants to reclaim his kingdom but that doesn't mean he won't find a way to reconcile with Harnin. Those two seem cut from the same cloth. I don't trust either as far as I can spit."

"Nor should you. Badron and Harnin were once very close, but there was always a strange undercurrent between them," Rolnir explained. "They each had visions of Delranan's future quite opposite from each other. Harnin won't be so quick to relinquish what he's taken and Badron lacks the military power to do it."

"Unless the soldiers in Delranan go back to the king," Aurec suggested. "Surely they'll feel obligated to follow king over advisor."

"Possibly," Rolnir said slowly, "but unlikely. The soldiers of the reserves have been under Harnin's command for many months. They'll enjoy the freedoms he offers and won't sell themselves cheaply just because Badron returns."

"This would all be a damned bit easier if we had a way of knowing what was happening there. The Murdes Mountains are an imposing natural barrier working against us," Venten said and slammed a fist into his palm. "We're effectively blind to all goings-on beyond our own borders."

"I agree, and that needs to change," Aurec answered. "Perhaps our Pell friends can offer assistance. They'd be able to sneak down into the lowlands and discover what we need so we can plan accordingly."

"Cuul Ol and his people have been great assets in the prosecution of the war, Your Majesty, but they never promised to do more than liberate the kingdom. We might be asking too much," the older advisor replied.

"I don't see a choice, Venten. Our options are exceedingly limited. Best case scenario is to move the army to the base of the mountains and wait for the thaw. Time is decidedly against us since this winter had been worse than any in recent memory. We can cut down on response time by pre-staging the army at each of the three major passes. Doing so will not only cut down on movement times but give us greater opportunity to deploy our forces once they reach the far side of the mountains." Aurec stopped to look at the map hastily plastered to the near wall.

Much of the castle renovations were proceeding well enough despite the inordinate amount of filth and sheer havoc Badron caused. The cleaning would take months. Time for Aurec to execute his campaign in the west.

Rolnir rose and went to the map. He wished he had as much detailed intelligence when planning the invasion of Rogscroft. Perhaps the war would have ended sooner and the Goblins wouldn't have arrived. "Sounds plausible. These passes are large enough to funnel five abreast. We could have the bulk of our combat strength in Delranan by the end of the first day. Dawn of the second at the latest. Supply trains and follow-on forces can continue to trickle down while the main body establishes a front and prepares to move towards Chadra."

"Provided Harnin isn't expecting us," Vajna added. "It seems to me that the man will be expecting your return and the only way to move an army as large as the Wolfsreik is through the Murdes Mountains."

"Sergeant Major Thorsson, what do you think?" Aurec asked the freshly minted senior enlisted advisor to the new army.

Thorsson couldn't help feeling uncomfortable given the situation. He'd been a line soldier for so long with few aspirations. Being thrust into the spotlight left him feeling inadequate on levels he didn't know he had. Saving Aurec had been a thoughtless act, one any soldier in his position would have done. He never anticipated that singular deed would place him at the pinnacle of the enlisted ranks.

"We should expect Harnin, with depleted forces, to come at us the same way we went after you, General, when the Wolfsreik first invaded," Thorsson said flatly. "No disrespect intended, but they'll be the guerillas this time."

"None taken, Sergeant Major. You provide sound advice but we have one major advantage Harnin isn't counting on," Rolnir said thoughtfully. "The Wolfsreik has already encountered a guerilla campaign and has learned how to adapt tactics to successfully counter it. We also have the additional benefit of your armies to further hamper Harnin's forces. Remember, his soldiers are the reserves. They didn't train full time, nor did they muster when we did. We all share the same uniform but our levels of training are vastly different. Once I can establish a cavalry line with infantry support I don't foresee any problems with rolling through whatever defense they've established."

Aurec moved closer to study the map. He'd been to Delranan several times but normally under the cover of darkness. His liaisons with Maleela were forbidden by both fathers, forcing the pair to sneak their way through life. What little he knew of the Delranan terrain was hampered by these facts. He needed Rolnir more than ever.

"Rolnir, can you find areas large enough to bivouac fifteen thousand soldiers, horses, supplies, and wagons?" he asked.

The redheaded general's eyebrow peaked. "Fifteen? What about the other five?"

"I need to keep something back in reserve in the event the unexpected happens. Can you retake Delranan with fifteen thousand?"

He half shook his head. "More than likely. We'll be faced with supply issues from the beginning. We have the advantage of numbers but Harnin's had time to establish quality defenses. Fighting on our own kingdom is a level playing field. The only unknown is whether he's turned the populace in his favor or not."

"Civilians on the battlefield get in the way more than not," Vajna said. Rogscroft had its own problems with that issue in the initial stages of the invasion. Hundreds of civilians wanting to do their part for their kingdom were killed through their own ignorance. Farmers didn't make good fighters.

"True but enough of them with rudimentary training can hamper an army to the point of failure," Rolnir countered. "We can't take the chance. Our combined forces must be prepared to encounter all scenarios."

Aurec disliked the idea of fighting civilians. Or with them for that matter. He'd witnessed firsthand how families were torn apart needlessly. Meaning to do good, they broke and ran when the enemy pressed too hard. They lacked cohesion born from endless hours of training on the parade fields. Fighting them proved more problematic for a myriad of reasons. Each one killed was someone's father, son, or brother. Sometimes even mothers and daughters. Soldiers were trained to combat other soldiers, not civilians.

"We need to take every precaution not to kill the civilians. Disarm and capture them but not kill. We're not going there to make war on Delranan itself. All I want is for

Badron to pay for his crimes. Killing the general population won't speed that effort."

Rolnir rubbed his tired eyes. They burned from overuse and he'd had a constant headache for the last three days. "You want Badron. I want Harnin. The only way to save Delranan is by removing both. Your Majesty, this is not going to be easy. Many of my soldiers will have deep-felt issues about attacking their homeland. Even if they don't voice it, that concern will linger in their minds with every engagement, in every village we move through. Remember that armies survive by foraging off the land. Ours will be no different. The only problem is we'll be taking from the very people we've come to protect."

Aurec suppressed the urge to laugh. "I think it's safe to assume we have more than just rampant foraging to worry about. Soldiers cut loose can do more harm than good while on campaign. While I don't think we need to worry about rape or murder, the possibility is there. They've been at war for a long time. Getting out of that frame of mind will be beyond difficult, especially once they see what has happened to their homes."

"There's nothing that can be done to cushion that particular shock, Aurec," Rolnir said. "Our best bet is to push through the temporary pain and accomplish what we're setting out to do. There will be time to pick up the pieces when it's finished."

"Speaking of which," Venten interrupted hesitantly, "What exactly are our objectives? Obviously the capture of Badron and Harnin, but what else? Delranan is a large kingdom, roughly twice the size of Rogscroft. How far do we need to advance to consider the campaign successful?"

Aurec looked to Rolnir. They were allies but each had differences of opinion concerning the Delranan campaign. Grave injustices needed to be answered for, not only here in Rogscroft but back in Rolnir's own kingdom. Aurec would be happy with the complete removal of all vestiges of Harnin's leadership though he suspected Rolnir wanted a great deal more.

"Our goals should be the same as they were here in Rogscroft. Chadra needs to be reclaimed. All Harnin's loyal forces rounded up and detained long enough to prove their loyalty. None of Badron's former lords can be allowed to escape. They are just as much to blame for the downfall our great kingdom as Harnin. Nothing less than the complete and total change of regime is acceptable."

Rolnir's words were harsh, lacking empathy while filling the council chamber with hatred. So much had changed over the past weeks he was no longer certain who he was. The one constant was how much he despised what his king had done to his kingdom, his home. Finding the proper words proved more difficult than he wanted. He frowned. Wars change men, for the worse more so than the better. He felt twisted inside. A shallow fragment of what he had once aspired to be. Conditions of self-misery aside, Rolnir knew he could easily become lost in the doldrums of his uncertainty.

Aurec laid a supporting hand on his shoulder. "There you have it, Venten. We have a tall order to accomplish on an ill-defined timeline. General Rolnir, how soon before we can have the army mobilized?"

"Once the order is given I can have units heading for bivouac sites in the foothills by tomorrow evening," he replied after quick mental calculations. "Moving piecemeal will keep the roads open and any unnecessary strain on the local economies."

"It will also give us the opportunity to continue establishing positive control here in the city. The army needs to move out but the majority of combat forces are involved in restoration operations. With the massive influx of refugees into the city we're already hard pressed to provide shelter and food," Venten added.

As much as he didn't like the idea, Aurec knew there was no choice. "The refugees are going to have to earn their keep. Draft every able body to the work details but do it nicely. Rogscroft belongs to us all. Remind them of that and we should get as close to full cooperation as can be expected. Hungry people are willing to do more for less."

"The treasury was depleted, even before Badron emptied the coffers," Venten said quickly. "The war stretched us to our fiscal limits. We won't be able to pay them."

"Payment will come in the form of food and shelter," Aurec said just as fast. "Give a soldier incentive and he'll work twice as hard." He smiled fondly at the memory of his father saying the exact thing several times after Aurec's uninformed arguments about state. "Our people are nothing if not resilient. They'll work and, while more than a few will no doubt gripe and complain, the vast majority will do their share and more to ensure this city is rebuilt. Having claim on a new home or shop won't hurt their motivations either."

A quiet chuckle rippled through them. Aurec continued, "Right now we're looking at approximately one tenth of the city capable of housing people. Winter is coming to an end, thankfully, and I fully expect more refugees coming in. We must be prepared to handle them. Venten, I am entrusting the kingdom to you in my absence. Find out who did what in their previous lives. Bakers, butcher, farmers, crofters. Everyone had their place in life and we're going to need each and every one of them to continue restoration efforts."

"Your Majesty, you don't mean to leave me behind when you begin the invasion?" Venten protested. He'd been alongside Aurec since the raid to rescue Maleela and his father, Stelskor, long before that. The very thought of being separated in the direst of times left him winded.

"I don't see much of a choice," Aurec said softly. "We've come a long way in a matter of days but there is so much needing to be done I'd be surprised if we can accomplish it in my lifetime. I don't suspect we'll return before summer, next winter at the latest. Thankfully there's no need to leave an occupation force as we're now allies in restoring justice to the north. I can think of no one finer to leave the future of our kingdom to. Venten, you know more about running a kingdom than I ever will. Rogscroft needs your experience now."

Humbled, Venten bowed his head and held out his hands. "How can I possibly refuse? Rest assured, young Aurec, I'll do my best to keep recovery on pace. You don't need to worry."

"I didn't think so," Aurec replied happily. Venten's determination often dwarfed his own. There was never any doubt of him acquiescing. Rogscroft needed a true statesman, not an upstart boy who'd be thrown the kingdom amid one of the worst wars in history. "Are there any other concerns?"

"Supplies," Vajna said. "We've been fairly well-off since combining our forces but maintaining adequate supply levels for the journey over the mountains and a prolonged campaign in Delranan will be problematic at best. Combine that with the fact we're coming out of a particularly severe winter and I've no doubts we'll see mild cases of starvation in some instances. The good news is water will be in abundance."

"At least we won't die of thirst," Aurec said and half laughed. "Find a way to keep us fed. I don't care how. I need Cuul Ol and his clan leaders. They must have stores available or know of a way for us to obtain more."

"That shouldn't be too difficult," Rolnir said. "Plenty of our supply lines were raided during the crossing. I'm assuming the Pell have more than enough stocked up to see us through to spring."

Aurec snickered. What little he'd managed to learn from the Pell Darga certainly didn't refute Rolnir's claims. "Very well. Gentlemen, the time to take the war into Delranan has come. Generals Rolnir and Vajna, you have your orders. Get the army moving and ready to cross the mountains the moment the weather allows. Venten, good luck to you. Dealing with civilians is far worse than angry soldiers not being paid."

"What of me, your Majesty?" Thorsson asked dourly. He bore a wary look, as if dreading what came next.

Aurec turned to the grizzled veteran. "You, Sergeant Major, will be at my side the entire way. Someone here needs to slap me back into my place when I get out of hand."

Thorsson nodded. "I can do that."

Satisfied they'd planned as well as possible for their limited intelligence, Aurec gave each a final look before saluting them. His stomach threatened to pull up out of his mouth. Defending Rogscroft was one thing, invading another kingdom completely different. History looked unfavorably on invaders, but he wasn't going to Delranan in the hopes of attaining glory or riches. Aurec meant to liberate a people from tyranny. He hoped his father would be proud.

THIRTY-FOUR

Heroes Chosen

Bahr couldn't take his eyes off Groge or the Blud Hamr. He'd been remarkably unimpressed with the weapon when first setting eyes on it. The only difference he was able to discern was that it was larger, much larger, than a normal war hammer. He wasn't even sure it was crafted for war, to be fair. It seemed too delicate, as if it would shatter on impact. His hastily formed opinions dissolved the moment the Giant took hold. Untamed power all but drove them all to their knees.

Thin, blue lines of electricity danced across the surface. The blinding white light skewed the normal colors, turning the world into shades of colors Bahr had never known. There few times when he'd felt as insignificant as in the moment the hammer's power flared. A proud man, Bahr went through life focused on the now. He'd witnessed mystery and mayhem in equal shares but never a moment so pristine as now.

He eyed the Giant with newfound approval. The youthful Groge stood straighter, sterner. His boyish façade melted away, exposing a gritty, untested warrior. Bahr wondered if Groge's stance on nonviolence melted with it. In a way he hoped not. There was too much violence in the world. Too many foul souls trying to break down justice and order. More good people were needed, even if they came in the form of a Giant from Venheim, a land many had either forgotten or simply didn't believe existed.

"Groge of Venheim, you have been accepted by the Blud Hamr as if only fitting since it was your very clan that crafted it." Artiss's explanation was loud enough so each of them could hear without straining. "It was your very first ancestor who was commissioned by the gods of light in anticipation of future events. They knew the treachery of their dark brethren ran deep and such tools would be required before the end. You are the legacy of their forethought."

Groge bowed his head without taking his eyes off the hammer. He felt stronger, somehow wiser, as if the hammer imbued him with unknown fragments of historical fact. "I…never knew," was all he managed to say.

Artiss drifted closer. "Nor should you have. How can anyone go through life knowing that they have been preordained to participate in a battle to decide the fate of an entire world? Do not begrudge the gods of light for their discretion. It was that foresight that enabled you to develop into the Giant you are now. All you. Gods can be cruel or kind in equal part. Their kindness left all you to grow and learn at your own pace.

"While I will not presume to know their true purpose, the gods of light manipulated genetics and time to bring you all together at specific points in your lives. You are the best and bravest of all the races. Victory or defeat rests squarely in your hands. Will you stand and rise above all your predecessors or fall in abject failure while Malweir burns around you? I do not have the answers though I wish I had. This war is unlike any other that has been fought since recorded history began. Thousands of years long and costing millions of lives, the final battle between the gods is about to occur. You are the chosen heroes, arrayed against an undeniable cast of utter evil."

Boen stretched his lower jaw. "You make it sound dark."

"Isn't it? Boen, of vanquished Gaimos, you fight an impossible battle. How many others came before you and fell? The numbers of your own kin would astound you. I make no promises of your survival. This battle will claim several of you, win or lose," Artiss explained grimly. His face hardened, as if he knew a secret he remained unwilling to divulge. A secret, which if it escaped his lips, could easily damn their quest long before the heroes reached the ruins of Arlevon Gale.

The Gaimosian lifted a heavy hand to stop Artiss from lecturing further. "All I need to know is who to attack, ancient one. I've been a warrior for a long time. Warfare makes sense. Keep your magic and mystic nonsense."

Any offense Artiss took went unknown. The last true Dae'shan merely blinked twice and turned to Bahr. "Captain Bahr, brother of Badron. You have hidden in the shadows for far too long, ignoring your birthright. The time has come for you to claim what is yours. Delranan has fallen into squalor, decay. The people bleed every day. They need strength and honor restored if there is to be any hope of victory. You can no longer hide from responsibility. Are you willing to become more than the sum of all your predecessors?"

Bahr felt like he'd been slapped in the face. Memories of being scolded by his father distracted him. Times weren't so simple anymore. He felt nervous, as if being forced into an uncompromising situation that never should have been. In truth he knew it was always there, lurking in the unseen distance like a long lost relative. Years bled off his life as he lived in constant denial. Life was so much easier avoiding all the worry and trouble. He had the freedom of the open seas but, in retrospect, came to realize that freedom was a restrictive prison keeping him from achieving anything in life more than a mere sea captain. The sudden realization that most of his life was little more than abstract failure haunted him.

He looked up at the hovering Dae'shan and swallowed his nerves. "I am, though it is not a task I look forward to."

"Difficult decisions seldom are," Artiss replied sagely. "We are all the children of our own created environments, Bahr. Personal demons plague each of us. The ones awaiting in Delranan happen to be yours. I cannot change the past, nor see into the future. What fate you may meet, what fate any of you may meet, once you return to the northern kingdoms, is beyond my scope of knowledge."

"That isn't very reassuring," Dorl blurted before Nothol could stop him.

Artiss turned to the sell sword and fixed him with a withering glare. "Dorl Theed, ever you have suffered from self-doubt and an undeniable lack of conviction. What you possess in skill and wisdom is lost behind an endless wall fear. Lord Death will come quickly if you do not find a way to give yourself fully to the mission. Wars are won through will. There are certainly times when it becomes necessary for each of us to question whether the direction we choose is correct, but you have gone far beyond that point. All decisions but one have been taken from you. Either commit fully to this quest or abandon all you have struggled to obtain over the course of your short life. The choice is, naturally, yours, but choose wisely. In unity there is strength of purpose. You cannot achieve such on your own."

Dorl opened his mouth and closed it quickly as if knowing the answer didn't need to be said immediately. The combination of shame and regret left his shoulders sagged, his head bowed enough for each to notice. He understood Artiss's reasoning, though he mildly disagreed with being chastised in front of his friends. Not as proud as Boen or experienced as Bahr, Dorl stumbled through life in the best manner he knew. He'd never been confronted with a life-altering choice like the one before him. Making it wasn't going to be easy.

"Take heart. You have fine friends. Nothol Coll couldn't be a finer friend to have at your side. He has ensured your life on many occasions and will for many years to come. Cherish that friendship for not everyone has it. You've been doubly blessed. Rekka Jel is one of the finest I have ever known. Selfless and competent, she is the epitome of professionalism, loyalty, and courage." Artiss paused to smile warmly at her. "Rekka, I realize we've only interacted a handful of times during your tenure but my words are heartfelt. It has been an honor having you in Trennaron."

His words left her suddenly uncomfortable. "I don't understand."

"I release you from your service. Go with my goodwill and blessings. The dangers you face ahead are far more perilous than you can possibly imagine. These fine people will need you, as does Master Theed if I'm not mistaken." Artiss turned before she had the opportunity to argue. He was the master of Trennaron. No living soul on Malweir had claim over his authority.

Rekka bowed meekly as mixed emotions ran through her. She'd accepted the position with the full understanding that it was for the duration of her lifespan. Cashi Dam's misguided love drove her willingly into Artiss Gran's arms, liberating her from the smallness of her previous world. She became so much more than what simple village life offered. She mattered. Now she didn't. Artiss Gran released her from her obligations while silently condemning her to whatever fate the gods had in store for the others. The mixed poison was difficult to swallow, despite the knowledge she'd be at Dorl's side through the end. She took her place there now, leaving Artiss free to move on to the next.

The Dwarf captain bristled under the scrutiny, planting his feet shoulder width apart and folding his thickly corded arms across his barrel chest.

"Ironfoot, rare has it been for one of the Drimmen Delf Dwarves to grace these halls yet your kind have been among the staunchest supporters of righteousness in the world. You are a fine warrior. One unparalleled across many cultures. The time is quickly approaching when your martial prowess will be tested. You will bend. Whether you break or not depends not only on yourself but these individuals around you. Do not give in to fear for it is the mind killer. Others will look to you for their safety, even knowing you may not be able to provide it. The wars you've fought in the past helped defined the Dwarf you've become but they pale in comparison to the nightmares coming to you. Be firm. Be a Dwarf and the sun will shine on your steel again."

Ironfoot twisted his lower jaw from right to left and spit a wad of phlegm at his feet. He was a Dwarf of Drimmen Delf. What more needed to be said? Silently criticizing the Dae'shan, Ironfoot waited for him to finish going through the group. His mind was already on to packing out and deciding which weapons would best suit his needs in the next phase of the quest. Logistical issues notwithstanding, Ironfoot had plenty to worry over before considering his return to his home.

"Perhaps young Skuld will be able to finally decide on his course in life," Artiss transitioned without delay. "You have the foundations of a strong man capable of a great many achievements. Life is an open book in your hands if only you can remove the cobwebs clogging your mind. You've been given many avenues of development to pursue. Warrior, wizard, thief. Only one of them is the right choice. All others paths lead to violent demise. Fear not, young man. I see greatness in your future."

"Thank you," was all Skuld managed to say before shyness got the better of him.

Artiss nodded just as politely. His gaze finally settled on the wizard where he spent many long moments locked in private deliberations. Anienam Keiss was perhaps the singular most key element to the entire equation. He'd been privileged to be the last in a long line of powerful, influential figures but didn't truly understand what that meant. He was a protector. A guardian of the wealth of knowledge passed down through the ages. The last in line. Artiss briefly wondered what was going to happen to the wealth of Ipn Shal when the last Mage finally passed. Part of Malweir would die as well.

"Anienam, you and I might have grown to become friends if the situation was different, but times such as these seldom give us the opportunity to choose our course. You carry the heaviest burden of us all, myself included. I empathize with your pain. Doubt is in your mind as well. You worry over every minor decision. Fret over what might have been. Always wondering if you made the correct choice. These are the burdens of knowledge and leadership. Your father was once a great Mage. He advised kings and queens while defending Malweir from the evil of the crystal of Tol Shere and Sidian the Silver Mage. You worry whether you have the same ability. I can think of no better person to lead this group into Arlevon Gale."

"All you, this war is coming quickly to an end," Artiss announced. "Whether you like the thought or not, you are all key personnel to bringing that end about. Succeed or fail, your actions will affect the lives of every living soul on Malweir. I applaud each of you for willingly, though I realize that term may be slightly skewed, stepping forward to defend life. Without your contributions I fear darkness would have already won. There is still time enough to reach Arlevon Gale and stop my errant brethren from succeeding. The dark gods cannot return to Malweir until the appointed hour in which the passage between dimensions is aligned. Groge must use the Blud Hamr to destroy the Olagath Stone at the moment the nexus opens. Only then will you stop the dark gods and end this conflict that has consumed the world for tens of thousands of years."

Silence replaced the sound of his voice. Stern echoes reverberated through the cavern. Flames licked up in great gouts, reflecting on the diamond structure. Artiss Gran floated in the center of the chamber remembering an earlier age when he'd undergone a similar task with Amar Kit'han and the others. That time ended poorly for all races, though few suffered as much indignity as Artiss. His shame permeated the generations, leaving nothing but a husk of his former self. Bordering on the edge of becoming lost in memory, Artiss finally nodded.

"Unless any of you have objections, I believe it is time to reconvene in the dining hall. Traveling back to Delranan is going to be tricky at best and will require all my strength. In fact, I'm not entirely sure I remember the proper incantations. Never mind. We can figure it out. There is still time."

Bahr looked at Anienam but was met with a mild head shake. This wasn't the place to confront the singularly most powerful being on Malweir. Each of them was tired from the exhausting trek through Trennaron and down into the bowels of the world. The climb back already proved daunting. The last thing any of them needed now was additional conflict. Bahr and Anienam might not see eye to eye but they were willing to set any differences aside until the proper moment.

Imbued with newfound purpose, the group stood taller, straighter. Their heads were high on unrealized glory. Artiss escorted them out of the diamond and back down to ground level where he turned them back over to Rekka. He disappeared after excusing himself, leaving them feeling more than a little uncomfortable. They'd already seen Gnaals and Dae'shan disappear in the same fashion. Having an ally capable of doing the same wasn't comforting. Soon stomachs started growling, distracting them to the point where they were eager to return to the surface. Rekka took them back to the never ending stairwell and Trennaron proper.

Questions filled them all. They'd already seen and done more over the past few months since leaving the dungeons of Chadra Keep, more than anyone had the right to ask. Worse was in store. Thoughts of the coming struggle barreling towards them left many apprehensive. Wars were terrible events where civilians often paid the ultimate price. This theological-based warfare was new to all them, leaving each with grave misgivings and natural mistrust in a great many things. One unspoken question burned brightly in each of their minds. With time steadily running out, how were they going to reach Delranan in time? Only Artiss Gran knew the answer and he wasn't in a sharing mood.

After one final night of peace and the relative security Trennaron offered, the adventurers would return to the quest. Odds leveled, if only slightly, but the enemy still held most of the control as well as the initiative. Bahr still felt much of the frustrations alleviated by obtaining the hammer. He could finally envision an end to a quest that had taken months and an emotional toll far beyond the limits of imagination. So close to the end, he couldn't help but wonder how many of his friends were going to live and how many were already dead but didn't know it. He pushed all thoughts of the quest aside and began the long climb back to the surface. The quest, as well as any life or death decisions, could wait until the dawn.

THIRTY-FIVE

Unexpected Guests

Thord, king of the mighty Dwarf kingdom of Drimmen Delf, sat upon his throne with his head cradled in a meaty palm. His head ached from an overindulgence of mead the night prior. His clans were in the middle of a weeklong celebration dedicated to their victory over the dark Dwarves at the battle of Bode Hill. Casualties were high, on both sides, but would have been higher if not for the daring nighttime raid led by Ironfoot and Bahr to destroy the enemy's cannons. Gunpowder weapons were relatively new inventions solely contained within the Dwarf world. A fact Thord was grateful for. Malweir wasn't prepared for the sheer levels of destruction cannons and rifles could produce.

The smell of old beer and cold meat permeated the room, bringing him to verge of vomiting more times in the last few hours than in his entire life. His belly was full, closer to bloated, from continuous ingestion of food and drink. Pipe smoke clung to the ceilings in foot thick clouds. Passed out Dwarves lay slumped on the floor and draped across tables. Servers ran lines carrying empty mugs and plates and bringing fresh ones in, reminding Thord of ants returning to their nest. Normally he wouldn't have condoned such perceived debauchery but this was cause for special celebration. Their enemy and direct rival was crushed. It would take generations to rebuild to the point where the dark Dwarves threatened Drimmen Delf again.

Thord concentrated to open his eyes. Red-laced and heavy from the lack of sleep, he heard the heavy march of hobnailed boots marching towards him before he managed to focus on the young Dwarf dressed in war armor. Thord groaned inwardly. The major fighting was over but there were still small firefights and occasional contact between Bode Hill and the Fern River. Armed patrols swept the battlefield for booby traps and hidden pockets of resistance. Snipers and small packages of explosives rigged to trees were reaping enough damage to make most military commanders nervous, almost fearful of a counter assault.

The Dwarf halted at the base of the throne under the stares of several Dwarves sober enough to realize what was happening. Many straightened at his approach, eager to hear his reports. Some matters not even mead could dull. The scout slammed a gloved fist to his breast plate and bowed his head.

"Report," Thord grumbled. He tried, unsuccessfully, to accurately read the scout's face. The inability to do so bothered him more than the Dwarf Lord was willing to admit.

"Sire, I've come with grave news to the east."

Eyes narrowed dangerously, Thord leaned forward. "Go on, out with it. What news?"

"An army of Goblins is marching west. They will cross the Fern River in a matter of days."

Dozens more lifted their heads. The false security of peace through hard-earned victory on the battlefield shattered around them, but Dwarves and Goblins were ancient enemies and well versed in each other's tactics.

Thord's throat felt dry suddenly. The very air he breathed tasted stale. "How large is this army and where did the information come from?"

"It has been estimated in close to fifty thousand, sire," the scout said breathlessly. "Faeldrin of the Elves came to our command post on Bode Hill bearing these tidings. This news was brought by a force of Minotaurs."

Gasps rippled through those close enough to hear. Larger and more aggressive than any other race in Malweir, save the Giants, the bulls hadn't been seen or heard from in centuries. They were among an increasingly growing list of races verging on extinction as man steadily became the predominant species. Thord didn't care one way or the other. No one bothered much with the Dwarves and those foolish enough to do so were dealt with accordingly.

"Where are these creatures now?" he asked sternly. The thought of an enemy army far surpassing his own in strength dispirited him, if but slightly. His natural penchant for war surged to life despite the knowledge that his ranks were greatly reduced after their civil war with the dark clans. He simply couldn't afford to fight a new war against so large a force. Not without being willing to sustain unacceptable losses.

"Still days away from the river crossings," the scout answered quickly so as not to rouse his king's ire. "The Elf lord has returned to Drimmen Delf with an envoy from the Minotaur kingdom. They await you in the reception hall."

Thord rose without thought and followed the scout to the outer gates on the eastern slopes of the Kergland Spine. Any effects from mead and a decided lack of sleep retreated to the darkened corners of his mind as he focused intently on his first encounter with one of the fabled, and partially forgotten, Minotaurs of the kingdom of Malg. He wasn't disappointed. The giant bull warrior towered over him, easily doubling Thord's four-foot-five-inch frame. Thickly corded muscles tensed beneath boiled leather armor. His war bar was slung over a shoulder. Pointed horns curled towards the center of his forehead, lending him a menacing façade.

He bowed as gracefully as only a bull could. "King Thord, my lord Krek sends word of a great Goblin force moving towards you. He also sends his regards. The army of Malg will arrive within the next ten nights."

Reeling from the unexpected, Thord could only scratch his jaw. He'd never expected to see one of the bulls, much less an entire army coming to his aid. So intent on the Minotaur, he scarcely noticed the slender Elf standing beside him.

"Lord Thord, Faeldrin sends his compliments as well and wishes to inform you that he has already dispatched riders west to Rogscroft and Delranan," the Elf said hastily. Born under the open sky, Elves despised languishing under the hostile mountains. He was eager to be back with his kin.

The Dwarf king spat angrily before slamming a fist into the reddish rock. "Damnation. We can't fight an army that large. Not now."

"Faeldrin and Krek wish you to know that you do not stand alone," the Elf, Euorn, replied. "Aid is coming but the Kergland Spine is not the battleground."

"Then where?"

Euorn gave Thord a deadpan look. "Delranan. All the ills of our time will fall upon the northern kingdom. You must prepare your army to march."

Normally darkness was the rebellion's closest ally, but with limited cloud cover and a half moon hanging in the midnight sky, this night was anything but. Ingrid pulled her double-thick cloak tighter around her shoulders, desperately trying to prevent the wind from cutting down between her neck and blouse. Not even her long, curled blond hair was adequate protection against nature's fury. She glanced over to Orlek and decided, for the hundredth time this night, that she didn't like him.

They'd ridden out of Fendi shortly before dusk and had only gone about three leagues. This far out in the wilderness the snow was deep, undisturbed by anything larger than a passing deer. Orlek promised to lead their small band to shelter before too long, at least before dawn. Ingrid doubted he'd be able to keep that promise. The wilds of Delranan were no place for the weak of heart, or for those who weren't familiar with the ravines, open plains, and thick forests. Plenty of skeletons lay buried beneath the snows, not all them animal.

"How much further, Orlek? I can't feel my fingertips," she complained.

Normally he would have scolded her for showing weakness in front of the soldiers, but the hour was late and he could barely feel his own fingers. They needed to stop soon or risk losing more people to frostbite. He didn't relish the thought of burying another body needlessly. "I've sent scouts forward to at least find a nice copse of firs. It shouldn't be long now."

He snickered at the false bravado in his tone. Even he didn't believe it. The truth was he was filled with just as much uncertainty as she was, but he'd never admit it. The only thing he really knew was they were circling south back towards Chadra. Under normal circumstances he would have dismissed the notion as foolhardy. The longer the rebellion dragged on took heavy tolls on both sides. Exhaustion, combined with the fear of Badron's return from the east, left Harnin's forces exposed. They made more mistakes than usual and would never expect Ingrid to double back to the ruins of the capitol. Even so, Orlek was apprehensive. He didn't like being exposed either.

"Why do I feel like I've heard you say that already?" she asked smarmily.

Because you have. I never asked to be thrown into this situation but you're deadest and determined to drive this war in your direction. So long as you stand so shall I. There are times when I hate having morals. "Try thinking of something else. The cold makes us act oddly."

"Oddly?" Ingrid almost snapped. "I can't feel half of my body and the other half doesn't like me. I can only imagine how the others must feel."

"Ingrid, we've all suffered harsh winters. This is nothing new," he said dismissively. Soldiers complained. Why should she be any different? As long as they complained he knew there was hope. It was when the silence took hold he needed to worry.

She frowned. "Winters we all spent huddled beside a warm fire with food and drink aplenty. Half of our fighters are too young, too inexperienced to know anything but a soft life. We need to find shelter soon or many will either perish or leave in the night." *And we need every able body we can get if we can expect to defeat Harnin. Winning this war isn't going to be easy but I know we can do it. All we need is a little good fortune and enough able bodies to push the Wolfsreik to point of realizing their losses aren't justified.*

Orlek disliked hearing it but the truth often stung. She needed to know he was doing his best to lead them to shelter but nothing was guaranteed in war. Any village they encounter might easily house an enemy garrison, ending their rebellion before Ingrid had the opportunity to enact her grand vision. Harlan was heading north with the majority of the rebels. The war was going to be won, or lost, in the north, not this deep in the southern part of the kingdom.

"Ingrid, I've got concerns," he admitted in confidence. Even in the middle of the night, when words traveled far and loud, his voice was a bare whisper.

She reined in her horse and waited. White breath plumed from her mouth and nose. She struggled to keep from shivering, bordering on condemning the attempt as futile. Orlek mirrored her, for the most part. His cheeks seemed hollow. He'd lost more than a few pounds over the course of the winter. Gray hairs sprouted in his stubble and across his head. Permanent lines marred his eyes, stretching out like cracks in dry mud. She hadn't realized it until now, but Orlek was suffering far more than she.

She was suddenly angered. The stubbornness of some continued to surprise her. All he had to do was tell her and she'd be more willing to see his point of view. How was she supposed to make decisions without being fully informed? "Orlek, there's a stand of trees up ahead. Send a few men forward to scout it out and we'll set up camp. I think we can get away with risking a few small fires so long as we build screens to keep the flames from being seen from a distance."

"Coffee and some hot soup wouldn't be bad either," he said reluctantly, hoping it came off as jovial.

She flashed him her best grin, one reserved only for those special people in her life. "Now you're pushing it."

They rode the rest of the way in silence. Each harbored personal thoughts on how best to continue. Those thoughts merged far down the road. Harnin One Eye was a stain on the history of their once great kingdom that needed to be cleansed from the record keepers. Ingrid and Orlek both hoped to be able to succeed in that goal without losing too many fighters, or each other. Throughout the rest of the night Ingrid sent brief, fond looks at Orlek without him knowing. He was an incredible asset and was on the verge of becoming a better friend. She'd be lying if she didn't acknowledge the feelings growing in her heart. She only hoped they lived long enough to find out whether those feelings were strong enough to lead somewhere. Ingrid's eyes slowly drifted close without her noticing Orlek's gentle stare from across the fire.

EPILOGUE

Two long days and nights. That's how long it took for the Hags to deliver their captive to the Dae'shan. Two long days and nights of claws gripping, wind biting, and no food. Her muscles burned. Body ached. She felt incredible pain that had previously been unimaginable. Maleela drifted in and out of coherence as the Harpies tirelessly sped north to what she had to assume was Delranan. Hope died. Once her father got his hands on her she'd endure a fate worse than death. Or so she supposed. Little did she know the Harpies' true intent.

Unconsciousness mercifully claimed her, taking her down strange, twisted paths. The murder of Ionascu played out over and again. Disgusted with her actions, Maleela suffered through intense waves of guilt. She'd never wished to harm anyone before that point and still defended that he had forced her hand. She tried rationalizing the moment through denial and intent. Anything to ease the wounding in her psyche. Murder was murder, however, and no amount of self-justification mattered when it came to the blood permanently staining her hands. Worse, the more she focused on the way his face twisted with pain as her blade sank into his withered flesh, the way blood frothed and bubbled on the lips of the vile Man, the more she enjoyed it. Ionascu had been a worm of a Man who, in her opinion, served no purpose. He'd committed acts of treason as well as grave crimes against Maleela and the others. Death seemed appropriate.

She finally awoke. No longer dangling in the sky, the princess of Delranan lay on a cold, hay-covered floor. The darkness surrounding her was nearly pure and she panicked. Her foot lashed out, kicking over a small bucket filled with brackish water. She heard tiny claws scrambling out of the way. Rot and decay assaulted her senses and it was all she could do not to throw up. Her stomach growled, tightening from hunger.

"Poor Maleela," a voice snarled from the dark.

Maleela cringed, immediately recognizing the bitter, acidic tone of Ionascu. The fact that he was already dead by her hands meant little in her current delusional state. Anger and fear washed together. Her fists clenched. "Go away!" she shouted.

Laughter mocked her. "I'll never leave you, Princess. You took my life. That's a debt I am going to relish repaying. A life for a life."

"Leave me alone," she said weakly. "I want to be left alone."

"But you are alone. You've been alone from the moment you drew your first breath. Twenty years of suffering and neglect have made you into the hollow shell you are today. Unloved. Unwanted by her own father. What are you but a mockery of life? The gods should have seen fit to let you die with your mother."

Maleela changed suddenly. Weakness left her, replaced by intense rage. She hadn't asked for the hardships in her life. Nor did she wish to grow up without a mother. It wasn't her fault her mother died during childbirth. Wasn't her fault but she shouldered the blame from the beginning. She felt hate. She hated her father. Her dead brother. She hated Aurec for not being there when she needed him the most. Hated Bahr for abandoning all bonds of family out of cowardice. And she hated Ionascu for the intensity of despair he inspired deep within.

"Speak no more, worm! I killed you once and I'm glad of it. Speak again and I will plunge my knife into the memory of your very soul!"

The laughter faded, leaving her alone in the nightmarish darkness once again. Maleela collapsed into unconsciousness and knew nothing else.

"All too easy," Amar Kit'han hissed. "Her mind is more pliable than I anticipated."

Kodan Bak, ever lurking at his side with murderous intent, wasn't convinced. "The purity of her soul will be difficult to break. She will not be so easy to turn."

"I don't need to break her, just bend her enough so she breaks herself. Chaos taints this family, Kodan Bak. Father and daughter aren't so different. She will break and take his place at our side. The time is nearly upon us."

Badron had been a useful puppet, as was Harnin, but they were never intended for anything other than mass confusion and the spread of chaos. Tasks which they performed admirably. Badron's ill-directed war against neighboring Rogscroft plunged both kingdoms into inescapable war. Harnin's subversion had been a pleasant side effect that further stole attention from the Dae'shan's true efforts. Arlevon Gale needed to be prepared to receive the dark gods. No one thought to look to the abandoned ruins south of Chadra as both kingdoms tore themselves apart.

Each new death and act of torment released psychic energy filled with anguish that was drawn into the Olagath Stone. Once levels reached the appropriate amount the Dae'shan would be ready to unleash that raw power and open the nexus between dimensions. Amar Kit'han could feel the end of his centuries-long quest drawing ever closer. Lifetimes of failure, near misses, and regret were ending. The time of darkness was fast approaching and he would be crowned a king once the dark gods returned to lay claim to the world. It was all so very near.

END

BOOK V OF THE NORTHERN CRUSADE
THE
MADNESS
OF GODS AND
KINGS
CHRISTIAN WARREN FREED

A PREVIEW OF
THE

MADNESS OF
GODS AND KINGS:

Book V of the Northern Crusade

ONE

Ingrid

Black smoke mingled with dust as the handful of horses sprinkled through the battling infantrymen thundered across the tiny farmstead. A pair of dappled geldings already lay dead in the snow covered fields, their riders having bled out shortly after. Spent arrows and broken spear hafts jut up at random, turning the fallow potato field into a macabre scene. The old barn, rickety and half broken down, was blazing away. Flames licked high into the late winter sky as the sounds of cold steel clashing sang its grizzly song across the tundra.

An arrow whistled past Ingrid's head, too close for her liking. The reluctant warrior knew she had nothing to prove by being caught in the middle of another battle but she'd vowed, not only to herself but to the others in the rebellion, not to stagnate like the previous council. Perhaps if they'd had more nerve to be seen on the front with their people the rebellion wouldn't have almost been destroyed by Harnin One Eye's forces. Her earlier crisis of faith abated after many long nights of deliberation with her shadows and Orlek and Harlan. Their insights had thus far proven invaluable in keeping as many of her fighters alive as possible while Harnin continually spread his own Wolfsreik reserve forces thin across the breadth of Delranan in a vain attempt at stopping her. Ingrid felt momentum rebuilding with each passing dawn.

None of that would matter if she got herself killed out on this lonely farm. She accompanied a platoon sized element out from their mobile bivouac site thirty leagues northwest of the capitol city with the intent on seizing the farm to lay an ambush. The vast majority of the rebellion was peasants and farmers, not like the trained professionals they were facing. She knew they could go toe to toe in a pitched fight, leaving little alternative but to strike through guerilla tactics. A thick network of spies and local informants stretched from the far western coast to the base of the Murdes Mountains in the east. Every movement Harnin made was observed and reported back to the central command structure of the rebellion. Sometimes that meant delays of days, bordering on weeks. Delays Ingrid was forced to tolerate as she struggled to keep one move ahead of the One Eye tyrant occupying the throne.

They'd arrived at the farm in the predawn hours only to find a Wolfsreik supply train reinforced with heavy infantry already camped out. Both the farmer and his elderly wife had been killed long before Ingrid arrived, under suspicion of treason. The lieutenant in command found the couple's winter stockpile and wrongfully assumed it was for the rebellion. Ingrid spied their bodies hanging from the barren branches of an old oak tree just in front of the farmhouse.

Faced with the tough choices of fleeing back to their camp without making contact or fighting an essentially losing battle, Ingrid reformulated the plans and struck just as fast as she could get her people into position. They fired the barn with flaming arrows as other archers targets the wagon horses. Wagons couldn't move without horses. The Wolfsreik was either going to have to abandon their supplies or, after fighting a long battle, carry them on their backs. Neither prospect suited the wolf soldiers.

Ingrid gave their lieutenant credit for how quickly he roused his soldiers and formed a defense. She'd barely had time to send her meager cavalry, more akin to light raiders, around behind the farm while her archers continued an occasionally punishing barrage. A handful of wounded meant little in the enemy's capabilities however. The Wolfsreik locked their heavy shields in a wall and effectively reduced any aerial assault to mere nuisance.

Any initiative the rebels once held dissolved like so much spring snow as Harnin's soldiers organized and defended. They made no move to go on the assault, content to wait for Ingrid to counter and make the next move. Any notion of a stalemate ended abruptly when Ingrid sent her cavalry in from the rear and infantry from the front under cover of archers. The battle remained stagnant for the first few minutes before the enemy lines cracked. Ingrid sent the largest men first. Their combined weight bowed the enemy line, distracting them enough for her cavalry to strike from behind. The Wolfsreik square broke and it quickly became a melee.

Hand to hand combat was fierce. Men, and an occasional woman, fell dead or wounded. Their rich blood painted the melting snow. Ever the opportunists, Ingrid's rebels snatched up the better quality weapons from fallen Wolfsreik and surged ahead with renewed confidence. Ingrid was able to stay behind, barely, as her forces steadily overwhelmed the surviving enemy. She didn't offer quarter. Neither would they. This type of war didn't allow for prisoners. Each side bore that burden into battle every time. It was a sad fact that countrymen killed countrymen with ruthless abandon in the name of causes they didn't truly understand.

Ingrid didn't pretend to understand them. An officer's wife, she'd been around the army for as long as she could remember. Many of the men fighting her now seemed familiar, invoking fond memories turned painful by the war at the very least. She often wondered if any were once friends. Thinking of killing former friends didn't sit well. None of her previous emotions meant anything in the ongoing struggle for the soul of Delranan. She fought just as harsh as her enemy and expected the same from them.

She looked up, trying to find the archer that had come within a breath of killing her, spotting him just in time to catch Orlek plunge his short blade down between the neck and shoulder. The archer died with a grimace locked on his bearded face. Orlek's scowl prevented Ingrid from smiling. His displeasure with having her on the battlefield was well known to everyone in the command cell.

The archer's death signified the end of the real fighting. Ingrid's rebels hunted down the surviving Wolfsreik, mercifully ending the wounded's suffering with a quick swipe across the throat. She couldn't watch. Death was her boon companion but she viewed their relationship in a foul atmosphere. Even after nearly a full winter she still couldn't stomach watching a man die, much less killing one herself. *All the more reason to return to the village and lead from behind the scenes. Getting yourself killed will only make matters worse for everyone. The rebellion's been through so much I don't think they could stand going through another restructuring.* She saw that sentiment echoed in Orlek's dark eyes as he stalked across the distance separating them.

"What do you think you're doing?" he fumed.

She held up her hands in protest while letting him vent. There wasn't much point in trying to stop him, not when his emotions were amped up. He was a man after all. *It doesn't help that we have feelings for each other.* She sighed. Romantic entanglements never worked out in these sorts of situations. One of them was bound to end up face down in a field, leaving the other a broken husk of a survivor. She almost prayed it was her dead in the fields, that way she wouldn't have to bear the heartache of seeing a second man she loved killed.

He paused momentarily after noticing her reluctance to engage. "Don't give me that silent treatment, Ingrid! I'm serious. War isn't a game. Men die, horribly. You're the leader of…."

"Of the rebellion. I know this, Orlek but that doesn't negate my responsibilities in being a leader. These men and women need to see me out doing what leaders are supposed to do. We've had this argument a hundred times since fleeing Chadra. Inaella and the others were more politician than leader. How can I inspire anyone when they never see my face?" she fired back.

Ingrid placed her hands on her hips, daring him to give her further fuel for her to attack with. She had just as much passion for Delranan as her rebellion and would argue like a badger until her opponent saw her point of view.

"Ingrid, we're slowly turning the tide back against Harnin," he said, much of the earlier conviction bled from his voice. "But we can't maintain momentum if you get killed by a stray arrow."

"Only that wasn't a stray and you know it. He meant to kill me. I'm a recognizable figure now. Harnin has my description plastered in every village he has the tiniest grip on. I'm a target now, Orlek. Hiding me away won't change that," she told him. "He'll stop at nothing to get at me and cut the head off the rebellion for good."

Orlek's shoulders sagged. "We should have made sure Inaella was dead before leaving."

"She's only a small part of the problem."

He barked a bitter laugh. "Women scorned are seldom small parts. I have a feeling she's one of the main driving forces in Harnin's new offensive."

"Of course she is," Ingrid replied. There'd been rumors of a pock marked dark haired woman at the front of Harnin's formations as the campaign waged across the western part of the kingdom. Until Ingrid had confirmation there was little point in pursuing them. She wanted Inaella dead more than any other save perhaps Harnin himself. Once, she pitied Inaella. The woman had lost everything and been stricken with the plague. Whatever remained was a shallow representation of the woman she'd been. Hatred fueled her thoughts, hatred for Ingrid. There was a reckoning coming and Ingrid could only hope something foul happened before it arrived.

"Inaella knows all your secrets. She'll stop at nothing to see you hanging from the gibbets over Chadra Keep," Orlek needlessly said.

Ingrid finally allowed some of her ire to calm. Living with Inaella's wrath was a burden only she could bear. Anyone else caught in the path would either be swept aside or driven under. Their fire threatened to consume the northern kingdom all lost amidst the growing conflagration between good and bad. No one in Delranan knew anything about the coming storm between the gods and their minions here on Malweir.

Flashing a soft smile, Ingrid pushed a lock of blond curls from her face. "I can't let her stop our progress. She's only one woman and lacks any knowledge of where we've come since leaving the city. Her information is outdated. Harnin will see her for that and, from what I can guess, will have her strung up or sent to one of the labor camps in the east for wasting him time."

The camps were equally rumor. Ones she tended to believe. Even before the rebellion fractured and abandoned the major cities Ingrid had heard mention of Harnin's troops fortifying the east against the eventual return of King Badron and his much larger, more professional army. No doubt Harnin felt trapped between two raging conflagrations. Dealing with the rebellion in a swift, efficient manner was his best option, especially with the ten thousand strong Wolfsreik returning from campaign in Rogscroft. Ingrid still had a chance, albeit a slight one with a closing window of opportunity.

"All I'm asking is that you bear with me until we can force this ordeal to a conclusion," she told him with all sincerity. "We can break Harnin. Leave him ineffective and bloodied when Badron returns."

"Where does that leave us though? We've all heard dark things about the king. How can we trust him to treat us or the kingdom any better? For all we know he'll come after us the moment he's done crushing Harnin." Orlek frowned. Deep creases lined his weather beaten forehead. A soldier, he'd chosen to keep his past hidden from Ingrid. There were some things she just didn't need to worry about. "Right now we need to focus on mopping this mess up. We can't afford to let any of Harnin's men escape."

She felt the weight dragging her heart down get heavier. Killing was never easy, nor should it be. It took a different kind of man to take a life. Those rare few finding perverse pleasure in the deed left stains on all humanity. Ingrid ordered men killed because she had to. Because there was no other viable solution to ending the rebellion in Delranan without letting Harnin win. Too much had happened already. Too many depravities. Too few people standing up for what was right. The imbalance of social justice spurred her decisions. Her conscience would have to wait to be dealt with once the fighting ended.

"Order the cavalry to hunt down the survivors. As much as I'd like to take prisoners we can't afford the manpower necessary to guard them," she instructed.

Orlek sheathed his short sword. "The men know what to do. I'll see to it. I suggest you get inside the farmhouse and try to get warm. It's a long ride back to camp and we need you with all your fingers and toes, if you take my meaning."

She forced a smile. Frostbite was a very real concern plaguing the rebels as they struggled through the deep snows previously untouched by anything larger than a bull moose. "Leave me a few to take care of the farmer and his wife. They didn't deserve to die, especially not at the hands of the same army sworn to defend them."

"Of course," was all Orlek said. The rebellion had seen its share of civilian casualties. A sad fact of war was that more civilians wound up getting killed than soldiers. This farming couple was merely the latest in a long line of victims.

Ingrid watched him walk away with mild interest. She couldn't help but wonder if they'd ever find the path back to normalcy or would Delranan suffer under the cloud of madness until the great fire went out of the world? Unwanted answers assailed her as she stalked inside with heavy heart.

BIO

Christian W. Freed was born in Buffalo, N.Y. more years ago than he would like to remember. After spending more than 20 years in the active-duty US Army he has turned his talents to writing. Since retiring, he has gone on to publish over 25 military fantasy and science fiction novels, as well as his memoirs from his time in Iraq and Afghanistan, a children's book, and a pair of how to books focused on indie authors and the decision making process for writing a book and what happens after it is published.

His first published book (Hammers in the Wind) has been the #1 free book on Kindle 4 times and he holds a fancy certificate from the L Ron Hubbard Writers of the Future Contest. Ok, so it was for 4th place in one quarter, but it's still recognition from the largest fiction writing contest in the world. And no, he's not a scientologist.

Passionate about history, he combines his knowledge of the past with modern military tactics to create an engaging, quasi-realistic world for the readers. He graduated from Campbell University with a degree in history and a Masters of Arts degree in Digital Communications from the University of North Carolina at Chapel Hill.

He currently lives outside of Raleigh, N.C. and devotes his time to writing, his family, and their two Bernese Mountain Dogs. If you drive by you might just find him on the porch with a cigar in one hand and a pen in the other. You can find out more about his work by following him on social media: